D1625052

NOIR

ALSO BY CHRISTOPHER MOORE

SECONDHAND SOULS

THE SERPENT OF VENICE

SACRÉ BLEU

BITE ME

FOOL

YOU SUCK

A DIRTY JOB

THE STUPIDEST ANGEL

FLUKE: OR, I KNOW WHY THE WINGED WHALE SINGS

LAMB: THE GOSPEL ACCORDING TO BIFF, CHRIST'S CHILDHOOD PAL

THE LUST LIZARD OF MELANCHOLY COVE

ISLAND OF THE SEQUINED LOVE NUN

BLOODSUCKING FIENDS

COYOTE BLUE

PRACTICAL DEMONKEEPING

NOIR

A NOVEL

CHRISTOPHER MOORE

WILLIAM MORROW
An Imprint of HarperCollinsPublishers

This is a work of fiction. Names, characters, places, and incidents are products of the author's imagination or are used fictitiously and are not to be construed as real. Any resemblance to actual events, locales, organizations, or persons, living or dead, is entirely coincidental.

NOIR. Copyright © 2018 by Christopher Moore. All rights reserved. Printed in the United States of America. No part of this book may be used or reproduced in any manner whatsoever without written permission except in the case of brief quotations embodied in critical articles and reviews. For information, address HarperCollins Publishers, 195 Broadway, New York, NY 10007.

HarperCollins books may be purchased for educational, business, or sales promotional use. For information, please email the Special Markets Department at SPsales@harpercollins.com.

FIRST EDITION

DESIGNED BY WILLIAM RUOTO

Library of Congress Cataloging-in-Publication Data
Names: Moore, Christopher, 1957– author.
Title: Noir : a novel / Christopher Moore.
Description: Hardcover edition. | New York, NY : William Morrow, [2018]
Identifiers: LCCN 2017022082| ISBN 9780062433978 (hardcover) | ISBN 9780062433992 (trade pb) | ISBN 9780062791443 (large print) | ISBN 9780062434005 (ebook)
Classification: LCC PS3563.O594 N65 2018 | DDC 813/.54—dc23 LC record available at https://lccn.loc.gov/2017022082

ISBN 978-0-06-243397-8 (Hardcover)
ISBN 978-0-06-285815-3 (B&N Exclusive Edition)
ISBN 978-0-06-285830-6 (B&N Exclusive Signed Edition)
ISBN 978-0-06-287209-8 (B&N FD Edition)
ISBN 978-0-06-285831-3 (BAM Signed Edition)
ISBN 978-0-06-285832-0 (Indigo Signed Edition)

18 19 20 21 22 LSC 10 9 8 7 6 5 4 3 2 1

THIS BOOK IS FOR JEFF MONG,
MY FRIEND.

AUTHOR'S NOTE

This story is set in 1947 America. The language and attitudes of the narrators and characters regarding race, culture, and gender are contemporary to that time and may be disturbing to some. Characters and events are fictional.

NOIR

PROLOGUE

I did not scream when I came in the back door of Sal's Saloon, where I work, to find Sal himself lying there on the floor of the stockroom, the color of blue ruin, fluids leaking from his various holes and puddling on the ground, including a little spot of blood by his head. Now, I am the younger brother of an older brother who often measured the worth of a guy by his ability to not scream under pressure, and insisted, in fact, that if any screamlike sounds ever reached Ma and/or Pa, this younger brother, me, would receive a pasting such as I had never known, including severe and painful Indian burns to the bone—a threat my older brother, Judges, may he rest in peace, backed up with great enthusiasm through most of my boyhood.

So, first I closed the back door, made sure it was solidly latched, then I glanced through the doorway into the front of the bar, which was still dark, and only *then* did I scream. Not the scream of a startled little girl, mind you, but a manly scream: the scream of a fellow who has caught his enormous dong in a revolving door while charging in to save a baby that was on fire or something.

So when I was finished screaming, I looked around and spotted the big wooden crate in the middle of the stockroom with big black letters stenciled upon it reading *DANGER! LIVE REPTILE!*

The crate was open, some kind of straw that had been in it scattered around, and then I saw the torn envelope and the letter lying by Sal's dead hand. It was from Bokker, the South African merchant marine, to me, and I realized what the crate had held.

I gave Sal's stiff a quick once-over, and yeah, there were two puncture wounds on his neck, swollen like boils, marks of smaller teeth in a crescent shape below that.

Full-blown electric jitters ran up my spine and I froze, holding the letter like I just got a telegram informing me I had just been violently croaked. Stop. I didn't know, exactly, what a black mamba looked like, but from what the South African had told me, they were large and dark and very fast, so I was pretty sure there was not one between me and the two feet to the back door, but there definitely might have been one still in the saloon somewhere.

I should have called someone. I needed to call someone. Not the police, I thought, since they might be looking for me regarding kidnapping one of their own, and also, since Sal took the big nap by way of a snake I bought and paid for, and as I had miles of motive, there might be some suspicion. So, no. I could have called my folks, I supposed, even though I hadn't called them since I left Boise. "Oh, hi, Ma, I know you haven't heard from me in years, but I got a little problem—" Nah.

So I thought, hey, the phone is all the way inside the saloon, on the wall behind the bar—*the bar*—where a giant, deadly snake could be napping, and then I thought, *perhaps a pay phone*. Perhaps, I thought, I should go see my business partner, Eddie Moo Shoes, and discuss the dilemma in which I found myself, and while at it, inform him that he *was* my business partner in a venture that seemed to have gone somewhat pear-shaped.

I took a deep breath and held it while I dug into Sal's pocket for his keys, found them, then stepped politely over him and out the back door, scooting his leg away a little as I went, so it would be easier to get back in. Once outside in the alley, I locked the door, and sighed as if I'd stepped safely off a minefield. But when I turned around there were two tall, thin guys in black suits, hats, and sunglasses, standing there behind me—and I mean *right there*. It's like they'd been waiting for me. They were trying to act unflappable, but they were flapped more than somewhat by my second manly scream of the day.

There are times in a guy's life when he finds himself floating facedown in a sea of troubles, and as hope bubbles away, he thinks, *How the hell did I get here?*

I mean, I didn't know then what the two mugs in black suits knew, which was that across the vastness of space, we were being studied by intellects far superior to man's, by beings that regarded us with envious eyes and, slowly and surely, were drawing their plans to come to our world and motorboat the bazooms of our dames.

Yeah, a dame, that's how it starts . . .

SAMMY AND THE CHEESE

S he had the kind of legs that kept her butt from resting on her shoes—a size-eight dame in a size-six dress and every mug in the joint was rooting for the two sizes to make a break for it as they watched her wiggle in the door and shimmy onto a barstool with her back to the door. I raised an eyebrow at the South African merchant marine who'd been spinning out tales of his weird cargo at the other end of the bar while I polished a shot glass.

"That there's a tasty bit of trouble," said the sailor.

"Yep," I said, snapping my bar towel and draping it over my arm as fancy as you please. "You know what they say, though, Cap'n, full speed ahead and damn the torpedoes." So I moved down the bar toward the dame, beaming a smile like a lighthouse full of charm, but trying to keep my limp on the Q.T. to discourage curiosity.

"I don't think that's what they were talking about, Sammy boy," said the sailor, "but steam on." Which is the kind of cheering a guy will give you when figuring it's no skin off his nose if you get shot down.

"What can I get you, Toots?" I said to the dame. She was a blonde, the dirty kind, and her hair was pinned up on her head so it kind of shot up dark, then fountained out yellow every which way in curls at the top—which made her look a little surprised. Her lips reminded me of a valentine, shiny red and plump, but a little lopsided, like maybe she'd taken a shot to the kisser in an earlier round, or the valentine heart had acute angina. Crooked but inviting.

Then the dame fidgeted on the barstool, as if to get a better fit on her bottom, causing a gasp to go through the room that momentarily cleared the smoke, as if a truck-size dragon had sucked it out through the back door. It's not that a lone dame never came into Sal's; it's just that one never came in this early, while it was still light out and the haze of hooch hadn't settled on everyone to smooth over a doll's rougher edges. (Light being the natural enemy of the bar broad.)

"The name's not Toots," said the blonde. "And give me something cheap, that goes down easy."

There then commenced a lot of coughing as all the guys in the joint were suddenly paying attention to draining drinks, lighting cigarettes, adjusting the angles of their hats and whatnot, as if the dame's remark had not just floated like a welcome sign over a room full of hustlers, gamblers, day drunks, stevedores, sailors, ne'er-do-wells, and neighborhood wiseguys, each and every one a hound at heart. So I looked over the shotgun bar, trying to catch every eye as I was reaching down, as if I was going for my walking stick—which is my version of the indoor baseball bat most bartenders keep, and even though my cane was ten feet out of reach, they got the message. I am not a big guy, and I am known to have a slow boil, but I have quick hands and I put in an hour on a heavy bag every day—a habit I picked up due to my inability to know when to keep my trap shut, so it is known that I can handle myself. Most of those mugs had seen more than one guy poured into the gutter out front after thinking my sunny disposition and bum foot made me a pushover, so they kept it polite. Then again, I also controlled the flow of booze. Coulda been that.

"What do I call you, then, miss?" I asked the blonde, locking my baby blues on her cow browns, careful not to ogle her wares, as dames often do not care for that, even when it is evident that they have spent no little time and effort preparing their wares for ogling.

"It's missus," she said.

"Will the mister be joining you, then?"

"Not unless you want to wait while I go home and grab the folded flag they gave me instead of sending him back to me." She didn't look away when she said it, or smile. She didn't look down to hide her grief or pretend she was pushing back a tear, just looked at me dead-on, a tough cookie.

First I thought she might be busting my chops for calling her Toots, but whether she was or wasn't, I was thinking the best way to dodge the hit was to act like I just took a shot to the body.

"Aw, jeeze, ma'am, I'm sorry. The war?" Had to be the war. She couldn't have been more than twenty-three or -four, just a few years younger than me, I guessed.

She nodded, then started fussing with the latch on her pocketbook.

"Put that away, it's on the house," I said. "Let's start over. I'm Sammy," I said, offering my hand to shake.

She took it. "Sammy? That's a kid's name."

"Yeah, well, the neighborhood is run by a bunch of old Italian guys who think anyone under sixty is a kid, so it's on them."

Then she laughed, and I felt like I just hit a home run. "Hi, Sammy," she said. "I'm Stilton."

"Pardon? Mrs. Stilton?"

"First name Stilton. Like the cheese."

"Like what cheese?"

"Stilton? You've never heard of it? It's an English cheese."

"Okay," I said, relatively sure this daffy broad was making up cheeses.

So she pulled her hand back and fidgeted on the stool again, like she was building up steam, and all the mugs in the place stopped talking to watch. I just stood there, lifting one eyebrow like I do.

"My father was a soldier in the Great War. American. My mother is English—war bride. They had their first real date after the war in the village of Stilton. So, a few years later, when I was born, that's what Pop named me. Stilton. I was supposed to be a boy."

"Well, they totally screwed the pooch on that one," I said, and I gave her a quick once-over, out of respect for her nonboyness. "If you don't mind me sayin'." Suddenly I wished I was wearing a hat so I could tip it, but then I realized that she and I were probably the only people in all of San Francisco not currently wearing hats. It was like we were naked together. So I grabbed a fedora off a mug two stools down and in a smooth motion put it on and gave it a tip. "Ma'am!" I said with a bow.

So she laughed again and said, "How about you fix me an old-fashioned before you get in any deeper, smart guy?"

"Anything for you, Toots," I said. So I flipped the hat back to the hatless mook down the bar, thanked him, then stepped to the well and started putting together her drink.

"Don't call me Toots."

"C'mon, it's better than 'the Cheese.'"

"But 'the Cheese' is my name."

"So it is," I said, setting the drink down in front of her and giving it a swizzle with the straw. "To the Cheese. Cheers."

Then I wanted to ask her what brought her into my saloon,

where she was from, and did she live around the neighborhood, but there's a fine line between being curious and being a creep, so I left her with the drink and made my way back down the bar, refilling drinks and pulling empties until I got back to the South African merchant marine.

"Looks like you charmed her, all right," said the sailor. "What's she doing here, by herself, in the middle of the afternoon? Hooker?"

"Don't think so. Widow. Lost her old man in the war."

"Damn shame. Lot of those about. Thought I was going to leave my wife a widow a hundred times during the war. Worked a Liberty ship running supplies across the Atlantic for most of it. I still get nightmares about German U-boats—" The sailor stopped himself in the middle of the tale and shot a glance at my cane, leaning on the back bar by the register. "But I guess I was luckier than most."

So after feeling top of the world over making the blonde laugh, I felt like a four-star phony all of a sudden, which happens like that, but I shook it off and gave the sailor a punch in the shoulder, letting him off the hook. "Doesn't sound that lucky," I said, "considering your cargo."

"Like Noah's bloody ark," he said. "That's what it is. You haven't sailed until you've sailed through a storm with a seasick elephant on board. Had a stall built for him in the hold. Poor bloke that has to muck it out will be at it for days. We offloaded the animal in San Diego last week, but the stink still lingers."

"Any tigers?" I asked.

"Just African animals. Tigers are from Asia."

"I knew that," I said. I probably should have known that. "Never seen a tiger."

"The big cats don't bother me much. They're in iron cages and you can see what you got, stay away from them. Push a bit of meat into the cage every few days with a long stick. A *very* long stick. It's the bloody snakes that give me the jitters. Next week our sister ship is bringing in a cargo of every deadly bloody viper on the Dark Continent, going to a lab at Stanford. Snakes don't need to eat, so they're just in wooden crates. You can't even see them. But if one of them was to get loose, you'd never know until it bit you."

"Like a U-boat?"

"Exactly. There'll be a dozen black mambas on board. Those buggers grow ten, fifteen feet long. Saw one of them go after a bloke once when I was a kid. Mambas don't run away like a proper snake. They stand up and charge after you—faster than you can run. Poor bastard was dead in minutes. Foaming at the mouth and twitching in the dirt."

"Sounds rough," I said. "That settles it. I am never, ever going to Africa."

"It's not all bad. You should come over to the dock in Oakland in the morning and see the rest of the menagerie before we off-load. I'll give you the grand tour. Ever seen an aardvark? Goofy bloody creatures. Will try to burrow through the steel hull. We got two aardvarks."

"Aardvarks are delicious," said Eddie Shu, because that's the kind of thing he says, trying to shock people, because it is a well-known fact that Chinese guys eat some crazy shit. Eddie is a thin Chinese guy wearing a very shiny suit and black-and-white wingtips. His hair was curled up and lacquered back to look like Frank Sinatra's. I didn't see him come in because I was trying to keep an eye on the blonde, so I figure he snuck in the back door, which no one is supposed to do, but Eddie is a friend, so what are you gonna do?

"Pay no attention to this mope," I said to the sailor. "He lies like an Oriental rug."

"Fine," said Eddie. "But as the Buddha says, 'A man who has not tasted five-spice aardvark has never tasted joy.'"

"Uh-huh," I said. "The Buddha says that, huh?"

"Far as you know."

"Eddie Moo Shoes, this is Captain . . ." And here I paused to let the sailor fill in the details.

"Bokker," said the South African. "Not a captain, though. First mate on the *Beltane,* freighter out of Cape Town."

So Moo Shoes and the mate exchanged nods, and I said, "Eddie works at Club Shanghai down the street."

"Who's the tomato?" Eddie asked, tossing his fake-Sinatra forelock toward the blonde. I found I was somewhat defensive that he called her a tomato, despite the fact that she was that plus some.

"Just came in," I said. "Name's Stilton."

"Stilton?"

"Like the cheese," I explained.

Eddie looked at me, then at the sailor, then at me. "The cheese?"

"That's what she said."

"Have you seen her naked?" asked Moo Shoes.

Now, in the meantime I had been watching various patrons circle and dive on the blonde, and each of them limping away, trailing smoke, shot down with a regretful but coquettish smile. And meanwhile, she kept looking up at me, like she was saying, "Are you gonna let this go on?" Felt like that's what she was saying, anyway. Maybe every guy in the place felt that way. This Stilton broad had something . . .

"Oh yeah," I said, answering Moo Shoes. "She *walked in* naked, but I had to ask her to put on some clothes so as not to distress the upstanding citizens who frequent this fine establishment on their way back and forth to Mass."

"I'd like to see her naked," said Moo Shoes. "You know, make sure she's good enough for you."

"Not for you, then?" the sailor asked Moo.

And Moo Shoes nearly went weepy on us, hung his head until his Sinatra forelock drooped on the sad. "Lois Fong," he said.

"Dancer at the club," I explained.

"That dame wouldn't so much as punch me in the throat if it made me cough up gold coins."

"It's a Chinatown thing," I explained further. "They have customs and whatnot."

"We are a mysterious and ancient people," Eddie said to the sailor.

"But you *have* seen her naked," I said, clapping Moo on the shoulder, a ray of fucking sunshine on his dark despair.

"On the job," Eddie said. "So has everyone else at the club. Don't think that makes it any easier."

Then I noticed that the blonde's drink was low and it was time I paid her a visit, so I held up a finger to mark the place in Moo Shoes's sulk. "Be right back."

"Another old-fashioned, cupcake?" I said with a grin, daring her to get sore at me.

"My name's not—" And she caught herself. "You buying, wiseass?"

"Me? There's a dozen guys in here already offered to buy you a drink."

"Maybe I was waiting for a better offer," she said—rolled her eyes, batted her eyelashes, then sighed wistfully—well, fake wistfully—which made me laugh.

"You know it doesn't cost me anything if *I* buy you a drink, like it would one of these mooks."

"Which means you won't think I owe you anything in return, like one of these mooks, right?"

"No, no, no," I said. "Perish the thought." Then I leaned in, hoping to perpetrate a little conspiracy. "Although I have told my friend Eddie back there that I have seen you naked, so if he comes over, cover my bet, would you?"

"I have a birthmark on my right hip." She winked.

"That's the spirit!"

"Shaped like Winston Churchill."

"That must be a sight to behold," I said.

"How about that drink, Gunga Din?"

I like a dame who knows her Kipling, or any poetry, for that matter, as I am a sensitive and poetic soul. My dear ma was an English teacher, and from the time I squeaked out my first word she steeped me deeply in metaphor, simile, symbolism, alcoholism, and all the various iambs of the poetic tradition, all of which have served me greatly over the years in pouring drinks, welding ships, bird-dogging broads, and waxing poetical on both this and that.

So I was about to say the same about the Kipling to the Cheese, when the door flew open behind her and in walked Sally Gab, aka Sal Gabelli, my boss, followed closely by an air force general with so many campaign medals on his uniform that it looked like someone was losing a game of mah-jongg on his chest.

The bar was called Sal's, after the aforementioned Sal, although there is no sign that says so, and over the years the joint has been known as Flossie's, Danny's, The Good Time, Grant Avenue Saloon, The Motherlode, Barbary Belle's, and a half-dozen other monikers going back to 1853, when the place first opened on the same spot. I am told that the long oak bar and beveled-mirror back bar came around the Horn on a clipper ship with sailors who dreamed of striking gold in the California hills. Currently the sign read only *Saloon,* Sal being too cheap or too smart to put his name over the door. Sal was well known in the neighborhood, but also well known to be such a douche bag that no one would have been surprised to see a long red rubber hose and nozzle trailing out his pant leg. The joint might have survived the great quake of 1906, but Sal knew that having his name on it just might be enough to bring it down.

"General," said Sal, a rangy fifty-year-old who was in perpetual need of a shave, wore suspenders and an ill-fitting suit, and held a cigar in his jaw at all times, "this is Sammy Two-Toes, my guy with his ear to the ground in the neighborhood. He'll be able to help you out with your little problem."

I cringed a little at the nickname, which only Sal used, and I gave the general the once-over. He was a tall fellow, pushing sixty, with a pencil-thin mustache. When he took his hat off, he revealed a jailhouse window of dark strands of hair combed over a bald pate. "Sammy," he said, as if he wished he had a rank rather than a name to call me by. It would be a low rank, I guessed from his tone, and he just nodded, not offering his hand to shake, as I was clearly beneath his consideration.

"Two-Toes knows all the hustlers in town, don't you, Sammy?" said Sal, who suddenly realized he was talking over the shoulder of a dame and stepped back from Stilton to give her a gander. "Hey, sweetheart—"

"Hold that drink, Sammy," Stilton said, standing up and putting her finger in Sal's face to shut him up, a red-lacquered nail a half inch from poking him in the eye. "I gotta scram."

Before I could say anything or make a move, she kept her one finger in Sal's mug while she threaded her other hand through the strap of her pocketbook and held it up to put the halt on me, which I did. "I'll see *you* later, handsome," she said, and in a single move she dropped both arms, pirouetted, and slid out the door while her skirt was still twirling, leaving me, Sal, and the general not a little dumbfounded, and me feeling like luck took a powder on me. Lost, is what I'm saying.

"Extraordinary," said the general, still looking at the spot Stilton just vacated. "Now that's exactly the type of young woman—"

"The gimp is your guy, then," said Sal, cutting him off.

Just then Eddie Moo Shoes came sliding behind the general along with a couple of other guys. The evening crowd tended to clear out when Sal was around, as many found him revolting, going back to the war, when he gouged military guys for the privilege of buying watered-down hooch past off-limits hours.

"Catch you after work for a bite," Moo Shoes said.

"Sure," I said. "Meet you at the club."

Eddie waved and was gone. Sal said, "I told you no fucking Japs."

"He's Chinese," I said.

"Same difference," said Sal.

Now, Sal knew his place was only a block out of Chinatown, and that the Chinese were in San Francisco long before the Italians, and that his Italian fisherman ancestors had been selling fish to Moo Shoes's Chinese forefathers for five generations, but he chose to ignore that in favor of showing his patriotism to the general with indiscriminate discrimination. But the douche bag is my boss, and he gave me a job after the war, when jobs were not easy to come by, and under somewhat *phonus bolognus* circumstances that I would rather not have revealed to the general public and law enforcement in particular, so I let it pass.

"What can I get you, General?" I said, looking past Sal.

"Scotch, neat. Single malt if you have it." He looked around the joint and assessed it as the kind of place that wouldn't have a single malt. Most bars these days don't. The Scots had to suspend distilling it during the war and it's not a quick process, but I remembered seeing something . . .

"I'll see what I can find."

As I rummaged around under the bar, Sal said, "General Remy's just in town for a few days, meeting with some mucky-mucks, but he's coming back next week."

"I'm hoping to make some arrangements for some—some—social company upon my return." For a military guy, the general seemed a little uncomfortable being in a bar. Maybe it was just Sal's bar, and how those two ended up together was a mystery to me as well.

Sal said, "The general is commander of a base back east."

"Oh really?" I said, my head still down with the spiders and the dust, looking for Scotch. "Where is that?"

"Roswell, New Mexico," said the general.

"There it is." I popped up from under the bar with a dusty bottle of Glenfiddich. "Never heard of it."

"No reason you would," said the general. "Nothing ever happens there."

"Right," I said, uncorking the bottle. "Double?"

"Please," said the general.

So I poured, thinking not at all about New Mexico, but about the Cheese, and how she walked out without my getting her number, or even finding out if she lived in the neighborhood, and wondering if she'd just jitterbugged out into the great beyond, never to be seen again. But then I thought, No, she stood up, and stood up to Sal on my behalf. And even though I didn't know where she came from, where she went to, or how to find her, it felt like I was going to see her again, and when I did, something was going to happen—something big and strange and hopeful, and there wasn't a goddamn thing I could do about it.

2

TALL HOUSE OF HAPPY SNAKE AND NOODLE

T he fog lay spread across the city like a drowned whore—
damp, cold, smelling of salt and diesel—a sea-sodden street-
walker who'd just bonked a tugboat . . .

"Fog's a little slutty tonight," said the cabbie, leaning against
his hack at the curb outside Sal's.

A foghorn moaned out on the bay.

Sammy flipped his coat collar up until it met the brim of his
hat. "A little tart," he agreed.

"Take you somewhere?"

"Nah, I'm just heading down a few blocks." Sammy pointed
across Broadway, which was the border between North Beach,
the Italian neighborhood, and Chinatown. "Thanks."

The cabbie tipped his leather cap. "Cookie's later?"

"Maybe," Sammy said. He made his way across the deserted
boulevard. The streetlights floated above in their vaporous auras
like lost spirits, never reaching the pavement. The shops on Grant
Avenue—groceries, souvenir stands, restaurants, butchers—were

dark except for the odd stripe of neon cutting the night here and there: CLOSED; MASSAGE; a COCA-COLA sign; a happy glowing dragon holding a bowl of chop suey.

It was only seven blocks from Sal's to Club Shanghai, where Eddie worked, not even half a mile, but after three blocks the damp and cold made Sammy's foot ache and he'd wished he'd taken the cabbie up on his offer. *June gloom* in the city, or as Mark Twain had put it, "Summer in Frisco makes a guy want to snatch a flounder up by the lapels and slap the damp off of him." (One of Twain's lesser-known quotes.)

As he paced his path out with his walking stick, Sammy thought about the Stilton dame, *the Cheese*. Something about her. Not that she wasn't easy on the eyes, she was, although not a knockout—but kind of sweet-looking, the type of broad you could take home to Mom then ravage in the spare room under urgent whispers while Mom harrumphed her disapproval to Dad about just what manner of floozie would allow herself to be named after a stinky English cheese. In short, he liked her, and by getting up and putting the chill on Sal and General Remy when she did, she'd showed him a kindness, although a sneaky and crooked kindness, which he also liked. He wanted to see her again and he was a little sad he didn't know how to make that happen other than by showing up for work and hoping she came in.

When he stepped into the deep carpet and red velvet elegance of Club Shanghai, Sammy saw Eddie Moo Shoes standing at the host's station next to a younger guy in a tux who was working the book. It was two thirty in the morning, and while the band was on break, a Glenn Miller record was playing. Smoke and the sound of conversation were streaming out of the club's big main room.

"Hey, Sammy," Eddie called. "You met Lou?"

"Low," the kid corrected.

"He's learning," Eddie said with a grin. None of the employees at Club Shanghai used his Chinese name, the entire theme of the club being Asian players in Anglo roles, which had kept Shanghai and a half-dozen other clubs of its type going strong through much of the Depression and all of the war.

Sammy was shaking the kid's hand when Lois Fong tiptoed up in a gold pair of pinup Mary Janes and a sequined gold sheath of an evening gown unzipped to the small of her back. "Be a doll, Eddie, would you?" she said, presenting the creamy V of her back for his ministry. Eddie worked the zipper halfheartedly, like he was closing the casket on an erotic dream, then patted her on the bottom to signal the deed was done.

"There you go, kiddo," Eddie said.

Lois pouted at him over her shoulder. "Not all the way, sweets. A girl's gotta show a little sample."

Now Eddie pouted as he pulled the zipper back down a couple of inches.

"Thanks, pal," she said. She kissed the air by his cheek and ran a fingernail under his chin as she scampered off toward the lounge.

Sammy cleared his throat. "Hey, Eddie, if you want to stay and take care of business we can catch a bite another time."

"Nah." Eddie pulled some keys from his pocket and threw them on the host's stand. "She says I cramp her style when she's working the lounge. Let me get my coat. What's it like out there?"

"Chilly," Sammy said.

"Yeah, in here, too," said Eddie.

They walked side by side up Grant Avenue until Eddie took a sharp right into an alley.

"Shortcut?" Sammy asked. Normally they went to Cookie's Coffee, a diner in the Tenderloin, one of the few places open all night, but Eddie was headed in the wrong direction.

"New place," said Moo Shoes. He dodged between trash cans and abandoned crates and Sammy did his best to follow, navigating in the haze by trying to stay on the dim shine of wet bricks, like trying to follow a stream of black oil through a maze of shadows. The smell of fish and rotting onions clung like cobwebs, letting go for a brief few seconds when they stepped out into Kearny Street, before Eddie dove down another alley.

"Moo, are you taking me someplace to murder me? Because I'd prefer to be croaked someplace a little less dank."

"Relax, we're here." Eddie pointed down the alley to a small curl of orange neon that flickered OPEN, buzzing like a dying bee, next to a battered red metal door. "You said you wanted to learn about Chinese culture."

"You keep it in this dump?" Sammy looked at the doorway. It led into a brick building jammed between two other buildings, the entire structure no more than eight feet wide, but going up the same four full stories as the buildings flanking it—as if someone had seen a very narrow alley and thought, Now that's a place I'd like to stack some bricks, a place where they can't possibly fall over.

Eddie pulled the door open, releasing a rush of yellow light, steam, tobacco smoke, and a cloud of vapor that Sammy would identify later as the odor of dusty old guy. He didn't know how he knew that, but that's what it put him in mind of. Inside he could see a long counter running all the way to the back of the building, ending at what looked like a dumbwaiter hatch. Along the counter sat a row of perhaps thirty very old Chinese guys, dressed in everything from traditional silk jackets to yellow fisherman's macs, but most in dark Western wool suits. They were either hunched over steaming bowls of soup or smoking pipes and cigarettes—most of them so wrinkled and desiccated they could have been constructed entirely of scrotal skin. A younger guy in an apron was making his way up and down the service side of the counter carrying a big steaming pot and a ladle. A dozen of the old guys looked to the door.

"*Gwai lo,*" one of them muttered.

"*Gwai lo,*" the rest mumbled down the line, then turned their attention back to their soup.

"What's that?" Sammy whispered.

"Nothing. Follow me." Eddie took a step into a very narrow stairwell to his left. He listened for a second before ascending the stairs. Four steps up, turn, four steps, turn, four steps, turn. It was like climbing a staircase in a phone booth. They emerged into another long narrow hallway with another counter inhabited by more old Chinese guys, although this bunch seemed somewhat younger than the nut-sack crew below. Sammy was the only Anglo in the joint, but he was used to being the outsider, so he just followed Eddie's lead.

"*Gwai lo,*" several of the old guys mumbled, before going back to their conversation or their soup.

"What? What?" said Sammy.

"There's two empty stools," Eddie said, shimmying behind the diners.

When they were seated in the middle of the counter—so tight their shoulders were touching along their neighbors' shoulders on either side—another guy in an apron came by with his steaming pot and ladle and said something in Cantonese to Moo Shoes.

"You want jook or noodles?" Eddie asked.

"I want a cheeseburger," Sammy said.

Eddie said something to the apron guy, who tossed a couple of empty bowls, chopsticks, and spoons in front of them, then skulked away, muttering.

"We're having noodles," Eddie said.

Sammy looked around at various old guys' soups. "The fuck is jook?"

"It's rice porridge. Very hearty. This place is a jook house. Been here since we built the railroad. Guy's working, runs in here, slurps some jook—maximum food, minimum time."

"And we're here instead of Cookie's because?"

"Culture?" Moo Shoes ventured.

"Yeah, no," Sammy said.

"My grandmother said that jook warms the heart."

"Which is why we're having noodles . . ."

"Fine," Eddie said. "I want to go back to the club when Lois gets off at four and I'm hungry and this is the only place open in Chinatown this time of night."

"You coulda just waited for her."

"I woulda loved to, but the ponies are encouraged to hang out with patrons in the lounge between and after shows. She thinks I'm going to get in the way of her finding some rich *gwai lo* sugar daddy."

"Wait, what's *gwai lo*? That's what all these guys said when we came in."

"Uh, it means 'new friend.' "

"I don't think so," said Sammy.

The old guy next to Sammy leaned over and said, "'White devil.'"

"No," said Eddie. "Don't listen to him, he doesn't even speak English."

"Can mean 'ghost person,'" said the old guy on the other side of Moo.

Sammy looked from one geezer to the other. "Hey, screw you guys! I am *not* a white devil!"

"Calm down," said Moo Shoes. "It's just an expression. No one thinks you're actually a white devil."

"White devil very touchy," said the old guy next to Sammy.

Sammy turned to the geezer and balled his fist under his chin. The old guy grinned, maybe six teeth total. Sammy laughed and patted the old guy's shoulder. "Yeah, a little too touchy, pops."

To Eddie he said, "So you're going to go back to the club just in time to see her leave with some white devil?"

"I hope not. I just want to be there—you know, throw the dice. Maybe my number comes up one of these nights. I got it bad for her, Sammy. I guess maybe I'm just a sap." Moo hung his head, fixing his eyes on the beat-up wooden counter as noodles were ladled into their bowls.

Sammy doctored his noodles with soy sauce and some chili paste, then blew on them to give himself time to think. In this nighttime world where everyone was on some kind of hustle, looking for some kind of angle, a guy seldom let his guard down, so when a pal opened up like Eddie just had, when a guy showed he needs sympathy, put his half-broken heart out there for another guy to see, he needed to be handled gently, very much like a fragile little baby bird what has fallen out of the nest . . .

"Moo Shoes, you're a goddamn idiot!"

"What?" said Moo. "No. Maybe. Why?"

"That doll has more angles than she's got curves, and you know it. If a guy is going to wreck his life on a dame, it should at least be a surprise. Putting the chill on you is the biggest favor Lois has ever done you."

Then Moo Shoes launched into a soliloquy on the beauty, charm, and perfect astrological alignment (Monkey/Rat) of Lois Fong, and how he, a third son of a launderer, wasn't worthy of the attention of such a creature. Out of respect, Sammy tuned him out and concentrated on his noodles, which were quite tasty indeed. He watched the jook guy take orders and collect empty bowls, then shamble down the narrow aisle to the end of the counter, where he deposited them in the dumbwaiter. He closed the hatch and pulled a cord, which must have rung a bell somewhere. A few minutes later, the dumbwaiter returned with another steaming pot and a stack of clean bowls.

"This broth is tops," said Sammy. "Chicken?"

"You haven't even been listening."

"I have. You are longing for Lois Fong, who thinks you are shit on a stick, hold the stick. Right?"

"No. Lois likes me. She says I make her laugh."

"Well, I'm no dame, but you *are* a snazzy dresser, and you are not completely horrible to pass an hour with, so it seems to me that Lois does not realize what she is missing. You are a diamond in the rough, Moo."

"I got no car, no house, and I share an apartment with four other guys."

"And you are often more than somewhat short of folding money, as well."

"My people like to gamble," explained Moo. "Luck is a big thing in Chinese culture."

"I am paying for the noodles, I take it?"

"How about this broth? Huh?" Moo Shoes slurped some broth from a big porcelain spoon.

"Delicious, huh? Huh?"

Sammy looked up from chasing some noodles around his bowl with a chopstick. "Lois put the bite on you for your tips tonight?"

"Borrowed. She has expenses. I'll pay you back Friday." The old guy next to Eddie tapped him on the shoulder. "You, too," Eddie said. Then to Sammy: "I started a craps game here last Monday, thinking that my venerated elders are new to the game, but gambling is gambling, and they are Chinese, so they will be happy to part with some of their cash as part of the price of learning."

"Didn't go well?"

Eddie leaned in to Sammy and whispered, "These old fuckers are fast learners. Look, I have cash, but I can't let these guys know it." Eddie picked up his own chopsticks and showed Sammy the grip. "You need to use both chopsticks. Here, like this. I thought I showed you. See, you just move the one."

Sammy mimicked Eddie's move and managed to strangle a couple of innocent noodles. When the counter guy came by again, Sammy paid him for the soup.

Eddie said, "What was the deal with the brass with Sally Gab tonight?"

"Runs an air base in New Mexico. I don't know where Sal found him, but he thinks I can find him some broads for a camp-out he's having next week with the Bohemians."

"So why does Sal not just go to Mabel's on Post Street and arrange for some girls to be delivered? I am guessing that it is not the first time she does business with the Bohemian Club."

"That's just the thing, the general does not want professionals. He wants normal dames, what you might meet at the butcher shop or on a train, in cotton dresses and smelling of Ivory soap, so that the Bohemians can feel that it is their charm and not their money that causes the girls to surrender their knickers."

"Even though the normal girls will be paid to come to the campout?"

"That is what I gather. The general feels that bringing normal Bettys who go moony over the old, rich, and powerful Bohemian guys will put him in a most favorable light with their club."

"Which he is not one of?" Moo Shoes shoveled a tangle of noodles over the edge of his bowl into his mouth with a slurp.

"I gather that this is the whole reason he concocts this caper. It seems that despite the many ranks and medals and airmen under his command, the general is regarded by the Bohemians as strictly a guest, but once he provides them with a gaggle of dolls to dote upon them and be impressed and perform further nasties of their own free will, he will be in."

Eddie let some noodles slide back into his bowl as he looked up to see if Sammy was yanking his chain. "He tells you this?"

"No, this part I piece together while cleverly spying from my position two feet away across the bar, a place where, evidently, I am completely invisible unless they need something from me."

"Douche bags."

"That would be my assessment, yes," said Sammy.

"That's the stupidest goddamn thing I've ever heard."

"Also correct, and that's saying something, considering the Lois Fong variable."

"And Sal comes to you for this service because . . . ?"

"I am extraordinarily charming."

"If a guy goes through life as Sal Gabelli, sure, I can see how he'd think that."

"And I am loaded with street smarts . . ."

"And as someone eating noodles you are paying for, I would have to agree there as well."

"And I know many citizens, many of them dames."

"All of them Sal also knows, but who wouldn't take a leak on him if he was dying of thirst."

"True," Sammy said.

"And you are going to accomplish this roundup of normal Bettys in calico and pigtails and whatnot—"

"Judy Garland in *The Wizard of Oz* was mentioned," Sammy said.

"You are going to round up these *Dorothys,* how?"

"I am going to go to Mabel's on Post Street with a generous stack of the general's doubloons and arrange to have a few of her most Dorothy-like girls scrubbed up and pigtailed and asked to refrain from swearing or disrobing until the Bohemians are well in the bag, which I am told is early in their campout."

"That might work."

"It will for Mabel and the girls, and I will keep my august position behind the bar." *As well as keep Sal from rolling on me to the cops and sending me to prison for an extended stay,* Sammy thought.

"You know, Janet Chang at the club can sing the shit out of 'Over the Rainbow.'"

"I'm not clear yet if Sal is going to be there, Moo, and we know how he feels about persons of the ornamental persuasion, but if he's not there, and she wants to spend a weekend oiling old rich guys, I think we can find a spot for her on the bus."

"A whole busload of whores . . ." Eddie looked up toward the smoke-stained ceiling like he was receiving a vision from the patron saint of nookie.

"And Toto, too," said Sammy.

"And for this you will be paid in the amount of . . . ?"

"I told you. I get to keep my job," said Sammy. *And out of prison.* He really should tell Moo.

"And for this Sally Gab and his tin soldier chased away that luscious doll at the end of the bar?"

"The Cheese," Sammy provided.

"Exactly," said Eddie Moo Shoes. "Not only are you pimping for free, you are upside down by one delicious Cheese at the hands of that dago fuck. This is a bad deal, Sammy."

"When I think of all the guys down on Third Street eating Salvation Army soup, I think keeping my job is not such a bad deal. And besides, I think I will see the beauteous Cheese again."

"You got her phone?"

"Not in full."

"You got *some* of her phone?"

"Nah, but she says she will see me later."

"Oh, well, you should have said. A *see you later* is as sure a bet as the sun rising in the east. I would give six-to-five on a *see you later*."

"No one cares for your sarcasm, Moo Shoes."

"Look," said Eddie, tossing his head toward the dumbwaiter at the far end of the counter. "You got to see this."

A buzz moved through the room, excited exclamations in Cantonese that sounded to Sammy like someone throwing a drawer full of silverware down the stairs. As the dumbwaiter hatch opened, it revealed a glass box perhaps two feet wide and three feet high, and in it squirmed dozens of very active snakes, all struggling to get above the three or four inches of liquid at the bottom of the aquarium.

Eddie said something to the old guy next to him in Cantonese and the old guy rattled something back that sounded like someone assaulting a broken banjo. The old guy's eyes lit up and he started digging in his pants pockets in a manner most frantic.

The guy in the apron wrestled the box of snakes out of the dumbwaiter and onto the counter, then went back for another huge pot of noodles. Another apron guy came up the steps and joined the first guy and scooped steaming noodles and broth into a bowl.

"You guys are going to eat those snakes, aren't you?" Sammy whispered to Moo.

"Just watch."

The old guys had all pulled bills out and were waving them in the air at the noodle guy like guys calling out bets at a craps game. The guy with the glass box opened the hinged lid and the snakes all struck at his hand, missed, then slid back down into the liquid. He took a very long ladle with a bowl that held maybe a jigger, reached into the tank, scooped some of the amber liquid from the bottom, then poured it over the noodles the other guy was holding. The noodle guy then ran down the counter to the farthest guy and delivered the bowl to an ecstatic old man, then snatched the twenty-dollar bill out of the old guy's hand.

"Snake piss," Eddie said, all but giggling.

Sammy watched the process again as a bowl of noodles and whiz went by.

"Twenty bucks?" Sammy said. "A double sawbuck for a scoop of snake piss? Don't these guys know there's a war on?"

"There's not a war on anymore," said Eddie, reveling in Sammy's dismay.

"Yeah, but I don't have another saying and this is the daffiest thing of all the daffy things you have pulled on me."

The old guy next to Sammy tapped him on the shoulder and said something in Cantonese, while pointing at his crotch.

"He says it will give you the dick of death," Eddie translated.

The old guy grinned, stood, pushed his crotch against Sammy's shoulder, and twanged something in Cantonese again.

"He says it gives you a shaft of steel," Eddie translated. The old guy bumped against Sammy's arm. "He says, *feel it.*"

"I don't want to feel it," Sammy said. "Sit down, pops, before I am forced to loosen your last tooth. Eddie, tell him to get his wang off of me."

Eddie did and the old guy did, just as his noodles and snake piss arrived, which the old guy dug into.

Sammy looked at Eddie. "So that works?"

"Feel for yourself."

Sammy started to stand and Eddie pushed him back down. "Relax, old Chinese guys will eat and drink all kinds of weird stuff to get a boner. The stranger and more deadly the better. Those snakes are sea snakes, the most deadly in the world, so they give the best boners, but I've seen them with coral snakes, rattlesnakes, a cobra once. The more deadly, the better stiffy."

"But they're paying twenty bucks apiece to slurp piss?"

"Twenty bucks a scoop. Some really old guys get two or three scoops. It's not all that bad. They feed the snakes nothing but beer for a couple of weeks to purify them before they bring them in here."

"How do they get the snakes to drink the beer?" Sammy asked.

Moo Shoes shrugged. "Free pretzels?" Big grin.

"Moo Shoes, you are both a mook and a jamoke. You, sir, are a jamook."

Sammy did a quick count of the guys at the long counter. There were around forty, and all of them except him and Eddie were waving twenties or slurping snake whiz. "So there's a counter like this on every floor?"

"Yeah," said Moo. "All the cooking and dishwashing is done in the basement."

"And it's like this every night? With the snakes and everything?"

"Not always. Only when they can get the snakes. They don't live a long time in that glass box. But yeah, when they have them, all four floors are full from midnight on."

Sammy did some quick calculating, scratched his chin, then stood up. "I gotta go, Moo."

"Ah, shucks, Sammy, I didn't mean to chase you off. You know I love sharing Chinese culture with you, just to see you get the *gwai lo* heebie-jeebies."

"Nah, it's not that. I want to get home and catch twenty or so winks. I'm going to head over to the docks in Oakland in the morning. I need to see a guy."

"In the morning? In the A.M.? Really?" They were nighttime guys.

"Yeah, I can do it. I've done it before. I think I got an angle on something."

"Okay, Sammy. Thanks for the noodles. You want me to put the word out to find the Cheese dame?"

"Sure, but keep it on the sly. I don't want to scare her off."

The old guy next to Sammy grabbed his crotch and said something in Cantonese.

"He says you can give it a squeeze before you go," Eddie translated.

"Tell him thanks, but I'm good," Sammy said. "Eddie, can I have a word, outside?"

"Sure," said Moo Shoes. He followed Sammy down the stairs and out into the alley.

"I need to borrow a hundred bucks," Sammy said.

"I just told you, I'm broke."

"Yeah, and I backed you up, because you were saying it for the benefit of those old guys, but I got an angle on something, and I need to borrow a hundred bucks. This works out, you're in for half."

Eddie looked over his shoulder, then all around the alley, before pulling a money clip out of his pants pocket. "This leaves me with ten bucks to last the rest of my life. What if Lois wants to go out later?"

Sammy took the money and pocketed it. He said, "Moo, a guy can't throw a stick in Chinatown without hitting a young doll with potential, and odds are that she will pick up the stick and make a delicious soup from it, so as a pal, let me advise you to leave Lois Fong to the white devils, and go for one of them."

"First, most Chinese dolls' families won't let them have anything to do with someone like me who works in a nightclub, and second, you don't know what it is to have it bad for a dame, but you will, then we'll talk."

"Fine," Sammy said. "Thanks for the loan. I got to go see a guy about a snake."

3

THE KID

Around noon the kid clocks me with a pillow and I come awake to a room that is unpleasantly bright, even with all the shades pulled. Anyways, I am sleeping the sleep of the mostly innocent when the kid jumps on the bed astraddle me and starts pummeling away on my melon with a sack of feathers like he's trying to beat out a fire, while shouting thusly:

"Get up, ya mug *(whack!)* ya mook *(whack!)* ya lazy bum *(whack!)* ya gold-bricker. On your feet, loser—"

And here I snatch the pillow from his hand and wind up as if to pillow him well into next week, when I remember that he is only a kid, and a smallish one at that, and it is on me as the man here to teach him, which would be better accomplished if I stitch him up in a potato sack and stash him in the cellar for a day or two until he calms down, but then I catch a glance at the clock on my orange-crate nightstand, which reads a little after noon (and I have been out to the docks in Oakland and back already this morning).

"Kid," I say, "it is only noon, and not the agreed-upon time of after three, and furthermore, why are you not in school, and finally, and do not think this item is less important because I bring it up last, but why in the hell are you standing on my bed with your dirty shoes?"

And the kid jumps off the bed and runs over to the heavy bag, which hangs in the hexagonal alcove of my small apartment, and starts pounding on the bag as he says, "I took my shoes off before I jumped up there."

And I look, and indeed, the kid wears no shoes, but has two socks so dirty as they might be knitted from mud, and from the front of each protrudes a once-pink but now filth-burnished naked toe. In fact, the kid, from his toes to the top of his newsboy cap, is covered in a fine patina of street grime, as one might find on an unfortunate urchin in a Dickens novel. He could be nine or he could be twelve years of age—I do not know and I do not ask—but he is small and has the aspect of a very sour-faced little Jimmy Cagney. In short, he is a horrible little kid.

"And it's summer, dummy," says the kid, "so there's no school. But I have a message for you, so you can just pay me a bonus, and don't try to hold out on me, because my uncle Beemis is a union man and he will knock the tar out of a mug for not paying an honest fella's wages, and I want to go to the pictures. There's a new one down to the Alhambra, with Bogey and that skinny doll from *To Have and Have Not,* and it's supposed to be shot right here on Telegraph Hill, so pay up or I won't tell you the message."

First, I don't know why the kid thinks I have tasked him with taking messages. He lives with his ma in my building, a Victorian with six apartments (a couple of blocks from Sal's), and he is always sitting on the stoop or loitering about the halls, while his ma is upstairs entertaining his various uncles. The kid's dad was killed in the war, and although I have never seen his ma, she seems to keep busy looking after various uncles. If she is not a professional it is a safe bet that she is a very hardworking amateur. For all I know, the kid might have offed dear ma and stashed her body in the icebox months ago, but that is unlikely, as the kid is entirely too small to accomplish the hydraulics of such a move, even if he is well stocked with enthusiasm and bad intentions.

Anyway, one morning, two years or so ago, I stumble in around 7 A.M., having indulged perhaps more than recommended in the consumption of spirits and the construction of merriment, when I encounter the kid on the stairs as he is heading out for school. So I says to him, "Look, kid, my alarm clock is on the bum, and I feel that I may be sleeping more than somewhat soundly today, as I am very tired. I need to make it to work at four this afternoon, so I'll give you two bits if you come up and wake me up when you get off from school, and do not leave until I am on my feet."

Actually, my alarm clock is not on the bum, but I have been known to fling said clocks crashing to alarm-clock Valhalla upon a certain morning after I have indulged in spirits, and since I am new on the job at Sal's, and it is soon after the war ends and jobs are in quite short supply, I need to make my punch-in time.

Well, the kid takes this as a permanent assignment, and from that day unto this, hits me up for two bits a day for waking me up, as well as taking messages, screening visitors, coaching me on the heavy bag, and casting aspersions on the occasional lady friend who joins me for a sleepover, saying "tramp" and "floozie" to them as they leave in the morning, when they are at their most vulnerable. So, even though the kid is horrible, he is almost an orphan, what with his pop deceased and his mother practicing her athletic pursuits, and I do not have the heart to tell him that the two bits for waking me up is a onetime thing that he has misinterpreted. I don't remember ever giving the kid a key, but evidently I did, and he refuses to give it back. Ever.

"C'mon," says the kid, whacking the heavy bag with his dirty little dukes. "What are you, some kind of cream puff? Give me twenty good minutes on this thing, and don't spare the gas."

"What's the message, runt?"

"Why, I'll bet my uncle Davey could take you out in the first round, ya macaroon."

"A macaroon is a cookie, kid."

"No it ain't. You're a dirty liar."

"What's the message, and who's it from?"

"It's from that Nip cocksucker with the black-and-white shoes."

"Don't talk like that."

"What? *Nip* is just Nip for 'Jap.'"

"I meant the other thing. And he's Chinese, not Japanese. What's the message?"

"He said to tell you like this: 'The Cheese is a biscuit-slinger at the five-and-dime on Polk.' What is that, some kind of Nip code? Why, my old man would have just popped that Jap cocksucker right on the spot, if he wasn't dead."

"Yeah, I'm sure he would," I says, not really paying attention anymore. Why would Eddie drop by to tell me such a thing in the middle of the day? I am surprised, in fact, that he is even awake at such an hour, but why couldn't it wait? Maybe he feels bad about dragging me into that joint where I am invited to sip snake whiz and touch an old Chinaman's dong, so he wants to make amends. What Moo doesn't know is that no amends are required, as I already have an angle on the snake whiz place which will make us a small fortune. Maybe.

"I'm telling you, that guy is a Jap spy," says the kid. "He couldn't even say 'squirrel.' That's how they spotted spies in the war, if they can't say 'squirrel,' you blast 'em."

"That's Germans that can't say 'squirrel.'"

"Yeah, well, he wouldn't say it, no matter how much I threatened him. What's that tell you?"

"That you're a pest?"

"Yeah, what do you know, ya bum? Sleeping till noon."

"I'm supposed to be sleeping until three, and I do not appreciate you giving my pals the third degree."

Then the kid gives the heavy bag one last whack and pads over to my bedside with his hand out. "Pay up. Two bits for the message and two bits for the wake-up."

"You'll get nothing and you'll like it," I says. "Did you make coffee?"

"No. Pay up."

So I sit up in bed, reach down, and grab his little run-down shoes from the floor. "Take these and get out."

And the kid snatches the shoes from me and heads out.

"Fine, you welsher. You know, if I'da known you were going to welsh on my wages I wouldn't have woken you up. I ain't even going to tell you what I heard on the radio."

"Don't use my radio," I tell him.

"Fine, I ain't even going to tell you that a guy saw a flying saucer up by Mount Rainy in Washington."

"Mount Rainier," I tell him.

"No it ain't," says the kid. "You don't know. You weren't even listening. Probably Martians."

"There's no such thing as Martians, kid."

"Yeah there is. They're coming to take our dames. You're a stinkin' liar."

"Fine," I says. "Go away."

"Fine," says the kid, hand on the doorknob. "I'm gonna go see that Bogey movie, and I ain't gonna tell you a stinkin' thing about it. You can just suffer, ya Nip sympathizer."

"Go," I says.

"I'm going," he says. "You can just sleep in and eat a pile of fish heads when you wake up."

"Fine!" says I.

"Fine!" says the kid, stepping into the hall. "And you're out of milk."

I keep some milk and cornflakes and bread and butter and stuff in the apartment in case the kid gets hungry.

"Fine!" I says.

"Fine!" says the kid. And he slams the door.

I still have a few hours to sleep, and I can probably wake up to the alarm clock, so I have a quick whiz and return to bed with a towel to drape over my eyes against the unkind light of day. When I set the alarm clock I tell it, "Sorry, pal, but this afternoon you may die for that little fucker's sins."

So I'm forty minutes walking to work because I go a mile out of my way to walk past the five-and-dime on Polk Street, which is not along the route of my normal, three-block sojourn to Sal's. I just walk by, and I can see there's a dame working the lunch counter, but she is not by any stretch the Cheese, as she is red of hair and more than somewhat plain. Just the same I walk the whole block without giving in to my limp, and I hold my walking stick like I'm a guy in a hurry, carrying an umbrella on a sunny day, or perhaps a deer slayer padding through the forest with his bow in hand.

Do I stop in and ask after Stilton to the red-haired dame? I do not.

Do I leave word that Sammy from Sal's stops by and please tell Stilton best wishes? I do not.

I just walk by, and as I go, I am thinking that I am a first-rate sap. What am I, nine years old?

I ask, because I know this feeling. See, when I am nine, little more than a child myself, I fall in deepest, darkest love with a little doll called Molly Warner, who is in my third-grade class and has a most fetching brown bob hairdo, as well as a facility with long division, which I find, at the time, borders on the mystical. I am smitten to the deep end of my soul, and I express my love, first by writing the aforementioned doll's name on little pieces of paper and eating them during class, and later, when I find out where she lives, by walking past her house four to five times a day with my brow knitted in concentration, maybe anger, as I have convinced myself that I am at my most dashing when my brow is knitted in a Douglas Fairbanks manner. (The knitted brow being my fallback position on dashing after several days of concentrated pencil-thin-mustache growing ends in despair.)

Anyway, at the time, we live about a mile outside of Boise, down a little cul-de-sac off Marston Road, and Molly lives in a big white house halfway into town on the same road, so I have to do quite some walking to pass by her house repeatedly, and the only place my mother allows me to go, unless she sends me to the store for this or that, is the library. So, in hopes of being spotted by Molly Warner, I construct emergencies of a literary nature, that can only be solved by a new book, which very much delights my mother, the English teacher, who is quite busy taking care of my father, two brothers, and one sister, all while teaching English and preparing for the Great Depression, which is nigh upon us.

Well, on none of my many, many walks do I ever spot the magical Molly, but I am sure that from behind closed curtains she sees me and my brow, as tightly knitted as a store-bought sweater, and I am more than somewhat convinced that she has spurned me and broken my heart, although I have not worked up the nerve to even talk to her. But in the meantime I have read through all the cowboy, pirate, and jungle boy novels the library has to offer in my reading level, and have, in fact, progressed to reading all the novels of Mr. Mark Twain, Mr. Jack London, Mr. Edgar Rice Burroughs, and beyond, until by the time my heart is sorely broken I am able to comment upon Dostoevsky's *Crime and Punishment* while shooting marbles and catching frogs, which enriches those activities not at all.

Anyway, third grade passes into fourth and I have developed into a brilliant and melancholy little guy, and while I am still slow to screw up my courage to approach Molly, I am sure the next day will always be the day I will say something, and she will fall into my arms, and we will go off to live in the jungle together in a tree house with just the apes and the elephants and maybe the occasional leopard, which I will kill with a knife to impress her. But one day, in the summer, as I am making an extra trip to the library, I see a moving van outside her house, and before I am able to say anything, she is gone. Moved away. Forever. One more day and I would have said something. The next time I saw her, I am certain, I would have. I am still certain.

Which is exactly how I now feel as I walk past the five-and-dime and don't so much as pause to look at the key chains, let alone ask after Stilton. And then I realize why Eddie Moo Shoes sends me this message. He thinks that Stilton is my Lois Fong, and although there is little reason, beyond her being easy on the eyes and exhibiting no little moxie, for me to have designs on the Cheese, I am hooked, caught, doomed—in short, he thinks I am a sap just like him. And I am.

But the next time I see her, if I see her, I will not let her get away. The next time for sure. Or perhaps I will join the seminary. After the Molly Warner catastrophe I contemplated becoming a monk and even wrote to a seminary in Chicago to ask them to take me to live a quiet life of spiritual despair, but I never heard from them, the bums.

"Dog pizza," said Sal, first thing when I walked in. He was wearing a black apron, a bow tie, and a white shirt with garters on the sleeves, looking like the type of bartender who gets shot in westerns.

Sal's is the kind of joint where when you open the door in the afternoon everyone looks up like rats caught in a spotlight eating the brains of a friend dead in a trap. No one is happy to be caught in a bar at four in the afternoon. Even the old alkies who migrate through the neighborhood in the morning to meet a shot already set up for them when Sal opens are a little ashamed; they growl at the light like Frankenstein at fire. Sal wiped down the bar with a tattered rag like he was mopping up blood from a fresh ax murder, listless, like he knew he was just stirring the gore on the surface. I cleaned up when he left.

"Dog pizza?" I said. It sounded like something Moo Shoes might bring up trying to throw me a curve. *Yeah, my people have been eating dog pizza for a thousand years. It makes your willie wag like a puppy's tail. Try a slice.* Fucking Moo Shoes.

"Have I mentioned that my people are from Napoli?" asked Sal.

"You might have." *Only about eight thousand fucking times.*

"Well," said Sal, "it is a well-known fact that pizza is invented in Naples, as well as pasta—"

"And the douche bag," I said.

"Really? I never hear that," said Sal.

"Yeah," said I, spinning up the engines. "In fact, when Leonardo da Vinci is in Naples he does the first early drawings of the douche bag. Naples is to douche bags what Kitty Hawk is to airplanes."

"Yeah, well, I did not know that, but from now on I will add

40

it to my story. Anyway, perhaps you have noticed that since the war, with all the guys coming home and getting married and trying to raise families, and with all the apartments in the city filled with citizens who come here to work in munitions factories and shipyards, new houses with yards are being built out in the Sunset District for these new families, so suddenly there is a preponderance of pets in the city."

"A *preponderance?*"

"Yeah, it means a shitload. Anyways, when I am at the store picking up coffee for me and the old lady, I notice that a guy can not only buy several kinds of dog and cat food, but also pet snacks, like doggie donuts and kitty crullers."

"You don't say?" I said.

"And then I am thinking, maybe if a guy can get an angle on that market, there is a sizable fortune to be made. So first I think, I am an expert in procuring and distributing certain beverages, so I think that perhaps a line of dog and cat spirits might work."

"But no?" I guessed. Sal made the money to buy the bar during Prohibition, procuring and distributing certain beverages for very high profit due to their illegal nature, and since repeal he'd been searching for a new angle on that business. During the war he did quite well for himself by watering drinks and selling servicemen liquor at very steep markup during off-limits and curfew hours, but since the Japs surrendered, business declined more than somewhat.

"It turns out that dogs and cats do not care for liquor at all, but prefer licking their own balls to even the best bourbon."

"You do this experiment yourself?" I asked. I was checking my back bar and my kegs before I started my shift. As usual, Sal had restocked nothing at all.

"There are some dogs who sometimes frequent the trash barrels out back, and I put a saucer down with some prime Kentucky goof juice to draw them in. But they stay away at some distance, variously scratching and licking their private parts with great enthusiasm. So I am thinking, perhaps they need to have a taste first, then they will take to drinking, so to draw them in, I grab a piece of pizza left over from my lunch, which I pick up at Napolitano's down the street. And soon they are all gathered around, quite interested, as I tear off pieces of pizza and toss some to each mutt in turn, but even when I shove one's nose into the bourbon, the mutt is not interested. Then it comes to me, what I am missing the point of, even if it is right there in my face . . ." Here he paused for dramatic effect.

And I, as has often been the case, did not shut up, as would have been prudent. "You tasted dog balls to see why they were so delicious?"

Sal scowled at me as he said, "No, smart-ass, I realize that what I need to do is make pizzas just for dogs. Little ones. Put them in boxes, and sell them to all the new families with their new dogs all over the new suburbs."

"Well, it sounds as if you have found your angle, boss," I said. "Dog pizza in a box. Can't miss."

"I was thinking Sal's Dog Pizza," said Sal. "But it doesn't have a ring like Doggie Donuts or Kitty Crullers."

"I could work on the name for you," I offered. Now I just wanted Sal to get out of the saloon so my afternoon regulars would come in. I could see a few had peeked in only to take a walk when they saw Sal still around. "I wrote a lot of poems when I was a kid."

"Nah, I'll figure it," said Sal. "I need you to work on that other thing for the general."

"About that," I said. "I am not sure how, exactly, to go about such a task of finding a whole gaggle of young, single dames who will want to keep the company of rich old guys up in the redwoods."

"Well, you will offer them plenty of cheddar, is how," said Sal. "The general assures me this is no problem."

"But why does he not just hire professionals?"

"Because muckety-mucks such as belong to the Bohemian Club wish to be appreciated for their charm and dignity and whatnot, and do not wish to feel that they have to stoop to paying for some tail. And furthermore, the general, who has worked himself up from being a grunt airman in the Army Air Corps to commanding a base somewhere in the middle of New Mexico, wishes to become a Bohemian, which he can only do if they invite him, and despite his rank and his medals, they do not, so he wants the Bohemians to owe him a favor."

"I see," I said, which I saw last night after overhearing them. Although I do not see why a guy who has worked his way up to being a general cares about being in a club that does not want him, unless that is the reason itself. The Bohemians were a fixture in San Francisco for quite a long time, and there was no little mystery about what went on at their camp up in the redwoods a couple of hours north of the city, but rumor was that very powerful guys from all walks of life gathered there to come up with some very influential capers having to do with running the world, such as the Manhattan Project and the New Deal and whatnot. It seemed that they had as members most of the last dozen or so presidents, as well as captains of industry and the odd artist or writer, which they kept around so their name wasn't completely phony. But why guys with that kind of weight cannot procure their own female company, I cannot figure. "How does this task fall to you?" I asked.

"It falls in my lap by sheer luck," said Sal. "Last night, Tony Cannelloni, who is a legacy member, invites me into the city branch of the club on Taylor Street. In the twenties I get liquor for the club, so I am well regarded by one and all. So we are in there, smoking cigars, and it is all very leather wingback chairs and dark wood paneling and whatnot, and in comes the general with another member, a guy who I think is a lawyer called Alton Stoddard the Third, who drops the general in our laps for safekeeping while he goes off to the can or something. Soon we get to chatting, and when Tony Cannelloni goes over to say hi to some other mook, the general reveals that he is only a guest, but he has been invited to the big to-do up at the camp next week, and he very much wants to be a full Bohemian, but he can't find an angle. So we talk about this and that, and he realizes that I am no little connected in the San Francisco community, so he appeals to my expertise. 'I need to bring something to the club they cannot otherwise procure,' he says. And this leads to that and up comes the plan to bring the regular Bettys, and he hires me to do the dirty work, which I accept with vigor, as I need a fresh pull with the Bohemians, as they can be a very large source of filthy lucre for those of us in the entertainment business."

"And so you turn this task over to me, why?" I asked.

"Because you are connected on the street," said Sal.

"But I am only here for a couple of years, while you—"

"I am married a long time and am no longer conversant in the world of single dames," said Sal.

By which he meant, no one liked him, and except for Tony Cannelloni, Ronny Biscotti, and a few other Knights of Columbus not nicknamed after desserts, no one in the city would so much as slap Sal to get a bug off their hand, let alone do him a favor, as he had used up much goodwill in the pursuit of profit.

"I don't know, Sal," I said. "I do not think that I am your guy—"

"No, you're my guy, Two-Toes," said Sal. "Because I am not a war hero like you."

And here something between anger and ice ran up my spine, for only Sal and very few others knew that I was no war hero, and he used the "Two-Toes" moniker to make this crystal to me.

"But, Sal," I said, "why do we not just—"

"Do not for a second think that you can just get some girls from Madame Mabel's on Post and dress them up like Bettys from next door, because the general is no sap." (Sal always said "*Madame* Mabel" with her title, like she was a doctor or senator or had received an advanced degree in Salami Concealment from a respected College of Floozie Management.) "Make this happen, Sammy, or a little bird may tell the cops a story about a guy he knows who is going by an assumed name, a guy who clocked a cop and walked while being transported to a work detail for multiple drunk-and-disorderlies. Am I clear, *Two-Toes?*"

In my defense, that was the last D&D I received. I'd lost my ID and I never gave them my real name, so while I may indeed have accidentally knocked out a cop and walked away from a work crew, they never knew who they were looking for. Of course there are fingerprints and a John Doe mug shot on file down at the county somewhere, but the guy in that picture is various shades of bruised and bleeding, due to three displeased, recently discharged Marines who I suggested had especially close relationships with their mothers. That picture probably doesn't even look like me. Anyway, Sal set me up with a new name, an ID, and a job, where he pays me less than the going rate because I owe him. When I took the deal I never knew how much and how long I'd owe him.

"Clear," I said to Sal. "I will figure it out, boss." I just needed him to go—get out of there—in case Stilton came in while he was going on about the war-hero thing. Even if I was building nothing into something, pulling another Molly Warner made-up romance, even if I never saw her again, I didn't want to see her right then, with the war-hero thing in the air.

Then the front door opened behind me and a shadow of weaselly caution fell over Sal's face. Over my shoulder I saw Pookie O'Hara filling the doorway, 260 pounds of crooked cop in a rumpled suit that looked like it had had enough food wiped on it that if you boiled it for soup a poor family could eat for a week on it.

"Hey, Officer," I threw to Pookie, but he just growled and made a show out of moving a barstool back far enough to get his big belly up to the bar. Normally he would remind me that he's a detective inspector, and not a mere "officer," but he was about to strong-arm a free drink, and since Eddie Moo Shoes once accidentally mentioned that I keep a glass behind the bar in which I have rubbed a dead rat, just for special occasions, which is entirely untrue but highly effective at assuring civility in certain citizens, Pookie let it go. I could tell this steamed his clams no little, which is exactly what I was going for. I didn't want Pookie camping at my bar, and that veined pink potato of a nose showed he did more than a little bar camping.

Now Sal was in no mood to stay. Something was going on with Pookie. "Give my best to the missus," I said, giving Sal the out that he was looking for, and it worked.

"I sure will, kid," he said. "And she's expecting me. I gotta go." Then, under his breath, "Not a word to anyone about that other thing, right?"

"Right," I said with a wink. "Dog pizza." Clearly whatever angle he was playing with the general and the Bohemians, he did not want Pookie O'Hara to be a party to it.

He avoided looking at the big cop and headed out through the back. Pookie tried to call him back. Before I had a chance to ask the cop his poison, the front door opened again and sunlight blasted a smoky arc through the saloon, causing patrons to grab their hats for protection. When the door squeaked shut again and the light abated, the Cheese was sliding onto the stool at the end of the bar like a weary angel.

4

DINNER IN NORTH BEACH

I could let Sammy tell you this part of the tale, but let's face it, when it comes to the Cheese, Sammy's got all the perspective of a bucketful of dark. I been telling the parts Sammy doesn't. Don't worry about who I am, I know things. My people know things.

She was wearing a little red hat with one of those net veils that reached to the tip of her nose, to be mysterious or to keep the flies out of her eyes, but certainly not for modesty or there would have been netting at her bustline, where her bosoms were rising out of her sundress like the waxing twin moons of Barsoom. So the Cheese slid up to the bar just around the bend from Pookie O'Hara, who ogled her wares with no discretion whatsoever, as if working as a vice cop somehow gave him license to view all dames as merchandise—or perhaps he was just a lowbrow mug who wouldn't know how to treat a member of the gentler sex if she smacked him upside the head with a sack full of vaginas. Sammy was thinking the latter, and he made a great effort not to ogle her himself. Out of respect.

"Hey, handsome," she said to Sammy. "Can I get a bourbon and ginger ale?"

"One of those for me, too, rocks, hold the ginger," said Pookie. He leaned in to Stilton. "Little early for a dame to be in a place like this on her own, ain't it, Toots?"

"I'm not on my own. I'm here visiting my boyfriend, Johnny."

"Sammy," Sammy said. He set the drinks down in front of them. Gave hers a swizzle, wished he really had a dead rat glass for him.

"Sammy," repeated the Cheese. A wink to Sammy over a dainty sip of her drink.

Sammy didn't want to, but he guessed he had to introduce them. "Officer O'Hara, this is Mrs.—"

"Toons," said the Cheese. "Punani Toons." She offered her fingertips, for a shake or a kiss, Sammy couldn't be sure. "Charmed, I'm sure."

"Punani?" asked the big cop.

"Father was Hawaiian. Pet name he had for my mother. No idea what it means. A type of orchid, I think."

Pookie choked on his drink. Sammy turned to the back bar and pretended to do inventory to hide his grin.

"Hey Tiffin," said Pookie, "what was Sal's hurry getting out of here?"

"Tiffin?" said the Cheese. "I thought you were Italian."

"Long story, pumpkin," said Sammy. "Not in front of the nice policeman."

"I feel like I don't even know you anymore," said the Cheese, putting on a pout.

"Hey," said Pookie, "I don't like a guy makes for the exits as soon as I come in. It ain't polite."

"Sal got a call from the missus right before you come in," Sammy said to the cop. "Dames, what are you gonna do?"

"You sure he isn't trying to put some action together tax-free?" asked Pookie, pushing his hat back on his head. "He knows he's got to always pay his taxes, don't he?"

Sammy couldn't even fathom how Pookie already knew that Sal was thinking about getting into the business of recruiting dames for entertainment purposes. It was well known that Pookie O'Hara exacted a tail tax for any and all transactions in the north end of the city. "I pour drinks, Officer. I know how Sal wants me to pour drinks. He wants me to pour yours for free. That's what I know."

"Kid, I ain't paid for a drink in this town in twenty years. That's just due, not a favor."

"That's what I know," Sammy said. A shrug.

"Well, I got some contacts down to the Bohemians, and they think that Sal might be arranging something for them."

Of course Pookie had contacts at the Bohemian Club. Sammy had heard the story at Cookie's Coffee. Before the war O'Hara had walked a beat in the Tenderloin. It was a big deal because he walked the beat alone, with a nightstick in hand—he'd been an institution, of sorts. The Bohemian Club's city digs were at Taylor and Post Streets, right in the heart of the Tenderloin. No way he hadn't had dealings with them.

The cop downed his cocktail like it was a shot. Ice jumped in the glass when it hit the bar. He reached into his pocket and flipped a silver dollar on the counter. "That's for you, kid. And don't put it in the till. I drink for free but that don't mean you don't get paid."

A dollar was a damn good tip on one drink and Sammy was skeptical. Pookie O'Hara's reputation preceded him and it was all stick, no carrot.

"Tell the gentleman thanks," said Stilton.

Pookie tipped his hat to Stilton, nodded to Sammy. "You let me know how Sal keeps up with his taxes, then," he said.

So there it was. Pookie thought he had just bought Sammy for a buck. They watched Pookie drag himself off the seat with a groan. He was ambling toward the door when it opened and in a split second the sunlight was eclipsed by a black fellow about twenty-three feet tall and half again as wide, wearing a tux and tails.

Now, Pookie was quite unused to encountering someone larger than himself, and it was well known that before the war, he made it his personal mission to keep the north end of the city free from people of the colored persuasion by administering many threats and beatings, so he pulled up, and, somewhat nonplussed, said, "Hey, buck, I think you're in the wrong place. They don't serve coloreds here."

Sammy froze behind the bar. The Cheese's eyes were darting back and forth from the door to Sammy like she was watching a ping-pong match.

"Well, that's okay," said the big man in the tux, gentle as a lullaby, " 'cause I ain't colored."

Sammy slowly backed over to where his cane was leaning, then stopped himself. "He's doing some work for me, Inspector," he said.

"Yeah?" asked Pookie.

"Yeah," said Sammy.

Stilton nodded slowly at the flatfoot, as serious as Saint Joan lightin' a cigar, to confirm the tale.

This gave Pookie an out, which he needed, unless he wanted to pull his gat and start blasting, because he no longer carried the nightstick that shored up his reputation when he walked the Tenderloin prewar, and the small pocket sap he carried now wouldn't get him far with the giant in the tux.

"Well, you watch yourself, boy," he said to the big man, then did an awkward sideways shuffle to get through the door.

When the door eased closed and the saloon returned to smoky twilight, the big man was sitting at the bar in Pookie's vacated seat, just around the corner from Stilton. Everyone in the joint was looking at him.

"At ease," Sammy called to the day drunks, and they went about their business. Then to the big man, "Hey, Lone."

"Hey, Sammy," said the big man, his voice a bass-fiddle drawl sounding out of a mine shaft.

"What can I get you?"

"Just a Co-cola," said the big man. "I'm 'bout to start my shift."

Sammy caught Stilton nodding at the big man, then at her glass, then throwing up an eyebrow as if to say, *Introduce me, you blockhead.*

Too late.

To the big man the Cheese said, "You work around here?"

Lone looked a bit startled at the question, but smiled. "I work the door down to the Moonlight on Broadway. They a jazz club."

"I know it," said Stilton, dazzling a smile that would have put a figure skater or a racehorse receiving roses to shame.

"Lone," said Sammy, "this is Stilton. Stilton, this is Lone Jones."

"Charmed, Lone," said Stilton, offering her hand. Lone looked panicked for a second, then took the tips of her fingers and gave them a gentle shake.

"Lonius," said Lone. "Short for Thelonius."

"I thought *Theo* was short for Thelonius."

"No, ma'am. Not for me it ain't. Mama calt me Lonius 'cause wouldn't nobody play with me when I was little."

"Lone's mother lives with him here in the city," Sammy said.

"We rents us a little place over to the Fillmore. Mama put up them calico curtains she like, grow some flowers in boxes in the window. Cute as a bug's ear. We lived over to Hunters Point till Sammy got me the job over to the Moonlight. But it's just temporary until I get in the Secret Service—"

"Hey, hey, hey," said Sammy, like he was reining in a runaway horse. "*Secret,* Lone. *Secret!*"

"Oh yeah," said Lone. "I forgot. Sorry, ma'am. I ain't supposed to talk 'bout it."

"Well, just the same, a pleasure meeting you," said the Cheese. Then to Sammy, who was fidgeting in place because he wanted to check on his customers, but didn't want to leave Stilton there with Lone, she said, "You'll be here until two?"

Sammy nodded, his stomach flopping, his heart on a roller coaster.

"I'll see *you* later, then," she said, a slow and sultry wink on the *you.* With a smile at Lone she waved toodles to the two and was out the door with a swish of her skirt.

You could get a full meal and a glass of red wine for a buck and a quarter at any of the family-style Italian restaurants in North Beach, but the Cheese liked Vanessi's on Broadway because there was a counter by the open kitchen where the cooks looked out for her when she was on her own. She was one of the restaurant tribe, even if she'd only been dealing breakfasts off her arm at the five-and-dime for eighteen months. Of course she had to put up with the cooks getting fresh, but they kept it pretty tame, what with actual families eating at tables nearby.

A couple of guys, business types, sat down at the counter, but before they could slide down to pitch woo at her, Vinnie, a ham-fisted ox of a cook, plopped down a water glass full of Chianti in front of Stilton as he cast a threatening glance at the business guys and said, "Here you go, sis."

He might as well have set down a glass of diphtheria for the

way the two mugs were suddenly trying to pay attention to anything, anywhere else, but Stilton's end of the counter.

"Thanks, Vin," said the Cheese.

"New hat?" asked Myrtle as she scissor-stepped her way into
the seat next to Stilton. She was a rangy redhead with lots of
legs and quite a little gawkiness. She still wore her pink waitress
uniform from the five-and-dime, the apron rolled up and stashed
in her purse. She had put on her face and primped her hair up a
little, pinning it back with a tortoiseshell comb she'd picked up
in Chinatown, so she wasn't the same plain Jane that Sammy had
seen through the window that afternoon.

"Well, don't you make a girl feel like a dishrag fresh from
mopping sweat off a hobo?" said Myrtle, giving the Cheese a
once-over.

"Don't be silly, you look nice," said Stilton. "Ran late?"

"Yeah, didn't have time to go home and change. Had a couple
of campers at the counter. Drinkin' coffee and smoking. Regulars,
so I couldn't throw 'em out. I swear, sometimes I miss the war, the
shortages, the blackouts . . ." She sighed wistfully.

"Wading in that milky river of sailors flowing up and down
Broadway in their bell-bottoms," Stilton said, teasing.

"Those were the days." Another sigh. Myrtle, suddenly con-
scious that the two business guys at the other end of the counter
were listening, said, "Not that I'm a floozie or nothing, because
I'm not."

"'Course not," said Stilton.

"She is, though," Myrtle said to the business guys, who
laughed.

"Am not!" said the Cheese.

Vinnie set a glass of Chianti down in front of Myrtle. "These
bums bothering you, doll?"

"Nah," said Myrtle. "They were just doing what Tilly hoped they would when she packed herself into that dress."

"Yeah, I didn't notice," said Vinnie. He headed back around the stainless counter to the line and pointed to the business guys, then to his eye, then back to them again, to let them know he was watching them. They made a fuss about putting on their hats and taking their business elsewhere.

"Well, there you go," said Myrtle. "Chased off another pair of perfectly good guys."

"Those guys?" said Stilton. "Those guys are both married and looking for a reason not to go home to their wives. You could see it in their eyes. Both of 'em old enough to be your dad, anyway."

"Easy for you to say," said Myrtle, gesturing from Stilton's cleavage to her smart red hat. "Why, if I had your figure I'd marry the richest guy in San Fran. And I'd drive around in a convertible Cadillac. With the top down, even when it was cold, just so I could show off my furs. And I'd smoke my cigarette in a long black holder so my lipstick didn't get messed up. I'd flip ashes on everybody as I went by. And I'd curse in French when I got stuck behind a cable car."

"In French?" said Stilton.

"Yeah. Cursing in French is classier. It ain't even like cursing. More like poetry."

"You was my old lady, you'd be fartin' through silk," said Vinnie, coming around the line again. "What can I bring you dolls?"

"Lasagna," said Stilton.

"Same," said Myrtle.

"Them's gonna take a few more minutes. We got to heat them in the oven."

"Yeah," said Myrtle. "Maybe we'll have another glass of wine or two."

"*One* comes with the meal," said Vinnie.

"Fartin' through silk, huh?" asked Myrtle, a drawn-on eyebrow raising sly-like.

Vinnie shrugged, causing rolls of fat to bunch up on his neck like a stack of sausages below his chef's toque, then grabbed the bottle from under the counter and filled both of their glasses. He was married to one of the daughters of the owners, had five kids, and the only thing he ever got out of flirting was a basketful of empty Chianti bottles, but hey, he was Italian, and there were expectations.

"So?" said Myrtle, dragging out the *so* to invite a story. "The new guy?"

"He'll do," said Stilton. "He's nice. Funny."

"He's cute, and you never had one come by work before, so he's got that going for him, but a bartender? There's no future in that, kid." Myrtle had seen Sammy when he came by the five-and-dime earlier. So had the Cheese, but she'd bolted into the back and hidden, shy as a schoolgirl, before he'd seen her.

"Yeah, well, I've had a future. I don't need a guy to take me away from everything. I don't need a guy at all. He'll do, for now. Probably."

Myrtle cringed a little and took a sip of her wine. When she wasn't crackin' wise or slingin' plates, Stilton carried a little sack of sorrow with her that could knock the sparkle out of her wide Lucille Ball eyes and the shine off her surprised hair. "Look, Tilly," said Myrtle, "what I said about the war. I know it was harder for you. I didn't mean—"

"Forget about it," Stilton said, and she was about to say how Sammy would do because he seemed a little broken, and that's how she liked them, but then, being as there is no small town so small as a neighborhood in a big city, Sal Gabelli slipped onto the stool next to Myrtle.

"Evening, ladies," said Sal. "Hope I'm not bothering you." He wore his overcoat over his white shirt and bow tie from the bar.

Myrtle wrinkled her nose, thought she smelled vinegar on him, but it was probably just stale booze.

"Hey," said Sal, pointing at the Cheese, "didn't I—"

"Nope. Wasn't me. I'm new."

"Don't mind her, mister," said Myrtle. "She's got one of those faces."

"Right, right," said Sal. "You ladies waiting for your husbands to get off work?"

"Here on our own," said Myrtle. "Just a couple of used-to-be Rosies trying to get by in the big city." She meant "Rosie the Riveters," as both she and Stilton had worked the shipyards during the war.

Sal threw a nod to one of the cooks, who caught his eye and recognized him. "Well, maybe I could help you with that," said Sal. "I might have an opportunity for you gals to make a little folding cabbage, if you're interested."

"We ain't floozies. Tilly, do I have a *floozie* sign pasted on my back? Sure, her, I can understand the mistake, but I'm wearing my waitress uniform, for Christ's sake."

"Nah, nah, nothing like that," said Sal. "This is completely legit, aboveboard, girl-next-door stuff. I just thought you might be able to pocket a little cheddar, if your husbands don't mind, that is."

"We're single and you know it," said Stilton. "Spit it out. What's the angle?"

"Single gals? Well, that's just aces. How would you ladies like to spend a little time with some very rich guys, cream of the crop, as they say, and make a little lettuce for your trouble?"

"Yes!" said Myrtle.

"Wait a minute," said the Cheese. "With our clothes on?"

"I swear on the Virgin, just be social and look pretty," said Sal. "Dance a little, smile a little—think of it like you're being USO volunteers for rich guys."

"Yes," said Myrtle.

"Not so fast," said the Cheese. "What kind of money are we talking."

"Fifty bucks," said Sal.

"Yes," said Myrtle. Fifty bucks was more than a week's pay at the five-and-dime.

"Each," said Stilton.

"Each," said Sal.

"Yes," said Myrtle. "Let's go. There will be food, right?"

"I can't," said Stilton. "I have something to do tonight."

"I don't," said Myrtle. "Don't worry about the food. I've eaten before. It ain't strictly necessary."

Sal took his hat off, revealing his stripy comb-over. "No, no, you misunderstand me. I'm just setting this up for the end of the week. You ladies can take all the time you need. In fact, let me get your dinners for you."

"Seventy-five bucks," said Stilton.

"Wait. What?"

"Each," said Stilton.

Myrtle grabbed her arm like she was digging for a vein.

"Wait a minute—"

"Look, you want us to block out our calendar a week in advance, we need to know it's worth our time."

"Look, this is a very generous offer, sister. Most single girls would pay that much just to get in the same room with these guys."

"A hundred bucks," said Stilton.

"Holy shit, lady," said Sal. "Who do you think you are?"

"Yeah, lady, who do you think you are?" said Myrtle. She downed her cheap red in a gulp and proceeded to glare at Stilton as if she could weld her insane lips together with a gaze.

"Seventy-five," said Sal.

"What?" said Myrtle. "I thought you liked dancing?"

"C-note or nothing," Stilton said.

"Fine," said Sal, "but you gotta bring eight, maybe ten friends with you. All lookers, too, if you can manage."

"That's a tall order," said the Cheese.

"She don't have ten friends," whispered Myrtle.

"Well, do what you can," said Sal. "I got a backup angle. Let me get your number. I'll call you with the when and where. In the meantime, except for the girls you recruit, keep this on the Q.T. These are some very important guys. They like their privacy."

"Give him your number, Myrtle," said the Cheese. Then to Sal, "I got no phone. Disturbs my beauty sleep." Then to Vinnie, "Vinnie, can we get a couple of more glasses of red? The gentleman is buying."

5

DAMES, THEY COME AND GO

Two hours before closing Stilton showed up again, looking somewhat more wobbly than when she'd left. Her red hat was a little cockeyed and she'd turned the veil back on itself so it looked like a big red eyebrow across her forehead.

Sammy mixed a bourbon and ginger and placed it in front of her. "You bugged out of here pretty fast earlier. Something scare you off?"

"Nah, the colored fella was okay, but that cop gave me the creeps, like he was suspicious of me or something."

Sammy looked at her, just looked at her. Raised an eyebrow. "Punani Toons?"

"People always think that Stilton is weird."

"Yeah, smart to avoid that."

"Well, he's as dim as a three-watt bulb, ain't he? If you're planning a caper, that's the flatfoot you want flapping after you. That mug couldn't catch a cough in a tire fire. Almost makes you want to go commit some crimes just 'cause you know you could get away with it. What about you, Hopalong? You wanna go perpetrate some crimes with me?"

"Gotta finish my shift, but I'll take a rain check on that, Toots."

"Don't call me Toots."

"Hopalong?" The eyebrow.

"Fair enough. Toots it is. Let's drink to our future crimes." She took a pull on her drink until it made a delicate slurping noise—the straw at the bottom of the glass like a tiny parched elephant. She slid the empty glass to him.

As Sammy refreshed the drink he realized he really liked this broad. *Really, really* liked her. It wasn't love yet, so he might still escape, but he didn't remember ever liking anyone quite as much as he found himself liking this broad, and with that he smiled like a dog at a barbecue for the blind. He set the drink down in front of her.

She picked up the glass, then paused. "You're not going to make a girl drink alone, are you, soldier?"

He liked her enough to feel like he should really tell her that he wasn't a soldier, had never been, but he liked her enough to not want her to go away. Not right now.

"I guess not." He poured himself a double and checked his watch. Two hours until closing. "To our crimes," he said, raising his glass to toast.

"Crimes," said the Cheese, having a little trouble aiming her glass at his until the third try, when she managed to clink glasses. "Holy moly, I might need you to walk me home."

"I might be able to do that," said Sammy. "But I don't like to talk about the war."

"Don't worry, pal," said the Cheese. "That's not going to be a problem."

A cop was softly burbling the cleavage of a big blonde in the corner, holding his hat in his hand behind his back out of respect.

The gentlemen scattered about the parlor were distracted from their own comely diversions, all draped in lingerie and painted just so.

"Bess, take him in the back," said Mabel, the madam. "The uniform makes the guests nervous."

Bess cracked her gum in salute and pulled the cop by his tie through velvet curtains.

"You run a tight ship," said Sally Gab. He was a head shorter than the madam.

Mabel, packed into a green satin evening gown with her crimson hair spraying high and then splashing down over her shoulders, looked like a tube of red paint someone had squeezed hard in the middle. Standing next to her, Sal Gabelli, in his ill-fitting suit, looked like a black-and-white character that had stumbled into a Technicolor movie—like there was just not enough color and life in the joint for the both of them. He was carrying a camera, one of those small German jobs, down by his side like he was sneaking a pistol into a bank.

"Pictures are gonna cost you extra, Sally," Mabel said. "You hand me the film and I give you back what I see fit. No faces. I got a guy does the developing and printing."

"Nah, that's not my game, Mabes. I need a dame."

"Color me surprised," said Mabel. She fitted a cigarette into a long ivory holder and waited for him to light it for her. "No luck at the hardware store and the barbershop, then? Thought you'd take a shot in the dark and stop in to my joint?" She smiled—a little lipstick there on a front tooth—and blew smoke over his head.

"Why you bustin' my balls, Mabes? I'm trying to do business here. I need a specific kind of dame."

"Once again, you have come to the right place, Sal. I happen to *have* specific kinds of dames. What specifics were you looking for, *specifically?*"

"I need a looker, but she can't look too much like a floozie, no offense."

The madam clamped her back teeth down on her cigarette holder like a mug chomping a cigar. "Go on."

"She needs to be able to pull off the girl-next-door thing. Give up the goods in the end, but not make it too easy—you know, act interested in a guy, even if she thinks he's a toad. Like a real dame."

"Pretend to be a real dame. Check."

"And she's got to be smart, and a little sneaky. She's going to be the one working the camera, but she has to do it on the Q.T. These guys can't know she's doing it."

"So, you are not just looking to get your ashes hauled, am I right?"

"No, not for me. I'm working an angle."

"Not with one of my girls you aren't. *My* girls, *my* angle."

Mabel turned and walked over to the bar, forcing Sal to follow or stand in the middle of the room holding his camera like a goof. He hurried after her.

"I'm putting together a bevy of broads for the Bohemian Club, for their annual cookout or whatever up in that redwood grove they have in Sonoma County."

"Scotch and soda," Mabel said to the bartender. "Vinegar and water for Sal, here."

"Hey," said Sal, waving off the bartender. "Don't be like that. This could be worth some serious cabbage."

Mabel took the drink from the bartender, sipped a bit through a straw, then wheeled on Sal, causing him to lean back like he was about to be snakebit. "Look, Sal, I got a good business here, but it only runs at the pleasure of the powers that be, from the mayor to the cops. Some of the city supervisors are my best customers, so I got connections. Connections I use and connections I need. But the Bohemians, that's a whole different level of juice. Those guys got power that runs countries. They eat mugs like Pookie O'Hara and the mayor for breakfast. Presidents, princes, scientists, artists, Nobel Prize mugs, the whole kit and caboodle. They say they hatched the atom bomb up at their little cookout—you do not fuck with guys like that. And from time to time, they throw a little business my way, and they pay extra for discretion, which they don't have to, because if I don't have discretion, my business caves like an accordion. So tell me, Sal, why would I want or need you to pimp one of my girls to them? And before you answer, Pookie O'Hara came by yesterday to pick up his fee, and he made it clear that if you showed up looking to do anything but get laid, I was to let him know, so I got your discretion dangling, buster."

She handed her cigarette holder to the bartender, who removed the butt, stubbed it out in the ashtray, and returned the holder to her, reloaded. She waited while Sal fidgeted.

"Can I get a seltzer, rocks?" Sal said to the bartender. Then to Mabel: "This ain't about peddling tail, and you know it. I got a guy wants into the Bohemians. Wants in bad, but he can't find an angle. So he wants normal Bettys, shopgirls and secretaries and whatnot, which I can find. I think I can find. Anyway, he's paying a pretty penny over what the girls get, but I'd be willing to give all that lettuce to you, and you're in the wind, clean as a whistle. I'll work my angle from there."

"Which is blackmail?" Mabel smiled.

"Have you heard what they get up to? Guys dressing up like broads? Secret rituals, naked dancing, singing show tunes, and that's before they get rolling with the booze and the broads. I ran booze for those mugs during Prohibition, and they can put some away. I figure the right shot of the president of Lisbon dressed like Garbo while a dame yanks his crank could be worth some serious cabbage."

"Lisbon is a city, you dope, not a country." She teed up her cigarette holder and waited while Sal dug his Zippo out of his pants and lit it for her. Mabel leaned back, elbows against the bar as she blew smoke out into the room. "I will not be a player in blackmail, Sal."

"Aw, c'mon, Mabel—"

"But . . ." She didn't look at him, just scanned the room as she spoke, looking out for business. "I have been known to make recommendations, arrange talent for someone who is perpetrating such a heinous crime."

"That's all I'm looking for."

"Then what kind of talent fee are we talking about?"

"Two G's."

Mabel let the ash fall off her cigarette into the carpet, but did not look at Sal. "For one girl? For one night? Two grand?"

"Less a few expenses. I might need a few more dames, for fill-in, in case my guy doesn't come through. Nothing special."

"That's a lot of folding money for one night."

"And their thing goes on for a week. If the girls work out, stay longer, there's more."

"And you'll give all that up?"

"I figure I'll get a fair stack myself, you know, for taking the risk."

"This blows back, Sal, those guys will have you put in a sack and dropped in the bay and be halfway around the world when it happens. They won't even know the guy who knows the guy who ties the sack."

"That's why I'll have the pictures. Insurance."

"This blows back on *me,* Sal, *I'll* have you put in a sack, and I don't give a good goddamn about the pictures. Are we clear?"

"So you got the right broad?"

"Two G's. One girl. One night. We never talked. I don't know you. And if anyone asks, you're a stranger and a douche bag, got it?"

"Got it. She's got to be fresh-faced. Like Judy Garland in *The Wizard of Oz*."

"Call me tomorrow. Lunchtime. Give me a time and the place for the girl to be."

"And if I need a few more dames, all scrubbed-up Bettys from down on the farm, you can do that?"

"Give me a time, a place, and how many farm girls you need."

"Thanks, Mabel. You're the best."

"Get out of my place, before I change my mind and have you put in a sack on principle. And leave the camera."

There were six boxwood bushes neatly trimmed into bullet-shaped pillars lining the walkway into the Victorian mansion that housed Mabel's, so when a seventh shrub, taller than the others but bullet-shaped as well, stepped out of the dark to accost Sal as he exited, he was more than somewhat startled.

"Christ on a crutch, Pookie," Sal exclaimed, stepping back and gathering his wits, which had scattered like a handful of loose pearls when the big cop materialized. "What the hell you doing lurking out here in the yard like a goon? I coulda had a heart attack."

"Taxman," said Pookie O'Hara. He snatched Sal up by the front of his coat and lifted him until he stood on tiptoes. "Nobody peddles tail in my town what they don't pay the tax, Sal. Time to pay up." Pookie pulled a leather sap out of his back pocket and pushed it up under Sal's nose.

"You got it all wrong, Pookie. What am I, stupid? I wouldn't think of stepping on your action."

"That's not what I hear from a little bird down to the Bohemian Club. I hear you're setting up something for some military mucky-muck for their campout." He dug the leather-wrapped lead sap into Sal's cheekbone. Sal busted his lip trying to squirm away. Pookie shook him like he was a dishrag and popped him lightly on the forehead with the sap. The blackjack had barely moved, but Sal could feel the blow all the way in his back teeth. A full swat with that thing would put him in the drooling ward for good.

"Ow! Fuck! Yeah! Yeah, I was talking about it, but it wasn't me. I got nothing to do with it. I was just delivering a message."

"For who?" Again the shake.

"Two-Toes! Sammy Two-Toes," Sal squealed. "That guy's bad news, Pookie. Doesn't know his place. Doesn't understand the order of things."

"You're running errands for your gimpy bartender?"

"Yeah. He ain't what he seems, Pookie. That guy has me over a barrel. I been covering for him because he knows my old lady—threatened to tell her about my visits here to Mabel's for services." Sal stifled a little grin, he was so pleased with himself for explaining his presence at Mabel's at the same time he was throwing the heat on Sammy.

"You let a skinny gimp like that get the drop on you? That's pathetic." Pookie loosened his grip on Sal's coat, allowing the douche bag to settle to his heels on the sidewalk.

"Yeah, he's more of an operator than he looks like. When he first came to me he told me he coldcocked a cop and walked away from a work detail at the jail. For all I know, his name ain't even Tiffin. Check the records, two years ago or so. Try Tuffelo. He was in on a drunk-and-disorderly, but he knocked out a cop and ran."

Pookie let go of Sal's coat and stepped away. Sal watched the big cop's anger shifting, scanning for a place to settle, like a street mutt looking for a fight.

"You go after Two-Toes, who knows, you collect your due and you teach him a lesson about clocking cops," Sal said, gilding the lily.

Pookie pocketed the blackjack, shot the lapels of his overcoat. "He at your place tonight?"

Sal checked his watch. "Not anymore. Closed. But I got his home address in my book." Sal patted his coat over the breast pocket.

"Give it," Pookie said. "And Sal, I find out you're lying to me, I'll write my name on the street with your brains."

Sal shuddered, pulled the black address book from his coat pocket. "Well, don't let the kid fast-talk you, Pookie, and don't let him get the drop on you. He's quick for a cripple."

"Yeah, don't you worry about it."

6

A SWEET DISASTER

It was two in the morning and they were the only ones left in the joint. She was up on her knees on the barstool, elbows on the bar, her face about two inches from Sammy's, who was leaning over from his side of the bar. They'd been like that for a half an hour and hadn't noticed the place clearing out.

"You like dogs?" he asked.

"Yeah. You?"

"Yeah. You got swell nostrils."

"Thanks. I like yours, too."

"Your eyelashes are first-rate."

"Can you even see 'em?"

"Kind of. I memorized them from before."

"You'd better walk me home now."

"I'll pack a lunch."

Sammy took a bottle of gin that was three-quarters full from the well and filled it to the top with Rose's lime juice, and the Cheese packed it in her pocketbook for the walk home. She stumbled on a turned heel as he was locking the door and he caught her by the waist. That's when the first kiss happened. It was the kind of kiss that he wanted to wake up to and keep refreshing periodically until he got one long last one, salty with tears, in his casket.

They both came out of it a little lightheaded, but safe, as there was no open flame to ignite their breaths.

"How far?" asked Sammy.

"Not far," said the Cheese.

She led him in a somewhat wobbly way down Grant Avenue a few blocks, then, arms around each other, up Greenwich Street, where the stairs began.

"How far?"

"Not far."

Up the stairs of Telegraph Hill, switchback, another set of stairs, a few steps on a path, more stairs. At a hundred and fifty steps or so, Sammy leaned against a wooden rail and tried to catch his breath.

"You said not far."

The Cheese thought it was cute that he believed her.

"Not far from *here*," she said. She booped his nose and started up another flight of stairs, pulling him behind by one hand. Another hundred steps and they were almost at the top. He sat down on the wooden stairs. Moonlight filtered through pine trees. He threw up a little. Just a little.

"Almost there," she said.

"I should tell you," he said. "I'm in pretty good shape. I work out every day. Nearly every day. It's just, well, I've been drinking."

"You can use my toothbrush when we get to my place."

"Aw, you don't have to do that," he said. She was nice.

She pulled him to his feet, then up another hundred and a quarter steps until they walked out into the clearing of Pioneer Park, overlooking the entire city. On a clear night you could see Oakland, Alameda, and Berkeley across the bay, and since the war the Bay Bridge even had lights on it. Coit Tower stood like an enormous concrete phallus above them.

"You live there?" Sammy asked. "I've never been up here."

"Just a little farther."

Down the other side of the hill wooden stairs zigged and zagged back and forth, joined by paths between gardens maintained by the people who lived in houses perched on the hillside, cozy cottages and modern Deco apartment buildings, none very tall, all wound up in trees and flowers and gravity, looking out on the bay. She led him down a path, through a gate, and to a low door leading into the very bottom floor of a triplex—what looked like the entrance to a storage area.

"Here we go," she said.

He had to duck to get through the door. She flipped on a light and presented her digs. The whole place was painted bright sunshine yellow, even the floor, which was plywood. It was one room, basically, with a single window in the front that looked out onto one of the hill's gardens. A bed by the wall, a sink and counter with a two-burner cooker, and a small refrigerator, the motor on the top buzzing away like it might give out any second. At the end of the bed, a door was open to a bathroom—a toilet and shower pan in a plywood closet. On the wall opposite the bed was an old couch, an end table with a lamp on a doily, a coffee table with some movie magazines—and a radio with a record player in it. The floor extended only as far back as the end of the couch, then the plywood stopped and bedrock and hard-packed dirt, painted yellow, started to slope up with the hill. Sammy spotted something green sprouting near the couch.

"The landlord gave me a great deal," said the Cheese.

"It's nice," said Sammy. "Cozy."

"Have a seat," she said, waving to the couch. "I'll light the burners and it will get toasty in here in no time."

Sammy took off his coat and sat on the couch. She set the bottle full of gimlets on the coffee table and pulled a couple of glasses out of her pocketbook as well.

"Are those from the bar?"

"Nope," she said. "Pour us a couple, will ya?"

"That back part? That dirt?"

"Yeah, this was a crawl space. Landlord put a window in for me, so it's not bad during the day, but it was a little spooky at night, so I painted the dirt yellow."

"Yeah, really brightens it up."

"The landlord said I could dig out a sunroom back there if I want to. I thought I was going to have to tunnel out a nursery once when my period was late."

As she was heading back to the couch, he grabbed her by the arm and pulled her down next to him. "You're not so tough," he said.

She pushed him back. "You'll find out how tough I am if you try to kiss me before brushing your teeth, buster. There's a toothbrush and a can of Pepsodent by the sink."

He stumbled to the sink, pasted and brushed, and midway through looked over at her with an insane toothpaste-foam grin. She laughed into her drink, spilling a little down her front.

"I'll get that," he said. He spit, rinsed, spit again, then executed a controlled fall across the room with a giant step over the coffee table that ended with him more or less lying in her lap, faceup. The Cheese managed to keep her drink intact.

"How's it going, Toots?" he said.

She kissed him lightly to test the taste. "Minty," she said. "And don't call me Toots."

He took her drink from her, set it on the table, and then pulled a slick wrestling reverse that put her on her back on the couch, him on top, smooching the ever-loving daylights out of her. She held her own, though, reversing on him, and slickly kicking off her shoes in the process.

They commenced making an "mmmmmm" sound as they kissed, as if they each had discovered something delicious and needed to hum about it to the other, all the while trying to remove each other's clothing without coming up for air—until Sammy was stalled in a struggle with her bra and she pushed him back to give him a hand.

"It doesn't look like it should be that tough," he explained, noting with a kiss that most of her was already spilling out the top when he'd started.

"It's French," she said. "They designed it like a zoo—you know, keep 'em in, but give everyone a good look at 'em. Ah, I can't get it, help."

She rolled onto her face to give him a good shot at the hooks in the back. "Free my people!"

"I will. I am the Harriet Tubman of your breasts."

She rolled back over, her people now free of their bonds. "Well, now let me show you the underground railroad." And she pushed him down until he was backing partway onto the floor, pushing the coffee table back as he went. He resurfaced under her nearly removed dress.

"Hey, this doesn't look like Churchill at all. More like Rasputin."

"That's not the birthmark. To the left."

"Oh yeah. Would you look at that!"

She wove her fingers into his hair and directed his attention to the proper historical figure, and so it went. Crazy, desperate, drunken lovemaking—wanting and having each other all at once, building a world together—to get close enough, deep enough, fast enough, slow enough, hard enough, soft and tender and strong and sweet—and only the two of them in it. They made their way from the couch to the rug to her little bed, where they fell away from each other, breathless for a bit, glistening with sweat, both naked now, except for Sammy's one sock on his bad foot.

They listened to each other breathe for a while, staring at the ceiling—the look on both their faces of having been suddenly hit by a truck, but with fewer broken bones. She rolled out of bed and padded to her pocketbook on the floor by the couch, and he watched her go, thinking she was the most beautiful thing he'd ever seen, ever *would* see.

She took a packet of cigarettes from her purse. "You want one?"

He nodded. He didn't smoke a lot, but he smoked. Everybody smoked.

She lit two on the burner of her little cooker, snatched a candle from behind the sink and lit it, then set the candle on the drain rack and shut down the burners. "We probably won't need these."

He agreed with a nod. "Warm," he said.

She turned out the light and he could just see the contours of her body lit orange by the candle. *Aw, shit,* he thought. Okay, *that* was the most beautiful thing he had ever seen.

She fit a cigarette into his mouth, sat down on the bed, and leaned back against him.

"There's an ashtray under the bed."

He felt around and retrieved a cheap aluminum ashtray that advertised a hardware store.

She nodded toward his single sock. "You really only got two toes?"

"Nah, I have the normal number, but I only have feeling in two of them. I made the mistake of telling Sal that when he rolled a beer keg over my foot. That's when he started calling me Sammy Two-Toes."

"What a jerk."

"It was by accident. He *is* a jerk, but the keg was an accident."

"Lotta guys would be sore about the nickname. You're a pretty good guy, aren't you?"

"Ah, he gave me a job after the war. What good's staying sore gonna do?"

"You can take your sock off, you know. I'm okay."

"Maybe next time."

"Next time?"

His face collapsed like a little kid who just dropped his ice cream in the dirt.

She laughed, took his cigarette from him, and butted it along with hers in the ashtray, then slid the ashtray back under the bed, climbed up on him, and rode him back onto the only pillow.

"So there's going to be a next time?" he asked.

"Oh yeah," she said.

And they were off again. Oh yes, there were trains and tunnels, rockets blasting off, torpedoes clearing their tubes, pistons and cylinders, oil rigs pumping, bridges collapsing, stars exploding, galaxies expanding, and a squeaky part that sounded like angry mice. He was Romeo and she was Juliet, he was Heathcliff and she was Cathy, he was Tristan and she was Isolde, he was Ahab and she was Moby-Dick, she was the *Titanic* and he was the Iceberg, and they liked that so much that he was the Iceberg for a while and she was the *Titanic*. She was Snow White and he was the Seven Dwarfs, he was the Scarecrow and she was the Flying Monkeys—it was an epic and divine disaster they acted out in that little crawl-space apartment, taking breaks to breathe, and drink gin and smoke, and they even dozed off together toward dawn.

As the sun was coming up, he pulled on his pants and wrapped a blanket around his shoulders, and she slipped into a robe and led him out her front door to the little garden on Telegraph Hill. They sat on a railroad tie that terraced the garden and looked out over the bay—watched the silver of the Oakland Bay Bridge turn bright pink with the dawn. A silver seaplane, a Pan Am Clipper, slid out of the sky and onto the bay like a great pelican and settled into its taxi to Treasure Island. Even though it was still chilly out, and a low fog hung on the water, the rising sun was warm on their faces, although the brightness was less than welcome to their oncoming hangovers. They tented their heads together as the sun broke the horizon, and, sore and exhausted, they began to laugh, and they laughed until they collapsed into each other's arms, each holding so tight they lost their breath, holding back sobs of joy, for they had found it: safe harbor.

A guy can say some pretty stupid shit on a morning like that, and Sammy started to say it, but she put her finger on his lips to shush him.

"Shhh," she said. "Sammy, you know those people in the movies who can just stop their lives to fall in love, chase after being in love like they don't have anything else to do?"

"Yeah."

"We're not those people. I have to get to work."

"Okay," he said. "But—"

"I know," she said. "Me too."

"Okay," he said.

"Do I smell like gin?" she asked.

He sniffed her shoulder. "I think you smell like fresh-baked cookies."

"I'll have to shower and put on a lot of perfume."

"Okay. I'll call you."

"I don't have a phone. Go home. I'll see you."

"Okay."

He went inside, put on the rest of his clothes, then stood in her doorway getting languidly smooched before she shoved him on his way.

He limped down the hill and found the kid sitting in the doorway of his building, smoking a cigarette.

"You shouldn't smoke, kid. What are you, seven?"

"What business is it of yours? It ain't a whole one. Some mug walkin' by dropped it. Ya dirty solenoid."

"That's not a thing, kid. A solenoid is a car part."

"No it ain't. Whadda you know?"

Sammy was feeling kindly disposed toward the kid, toward everything. "Yeah, what do I know? Look, kid, what I said about not taking messages, maybe you can do that today. From now on, someone comes by, take a message. I'll owe you for the last one." Sammy fished six bits out of his pocket and handed them to the kid, who snatched the coins out of his hand and squirreled them away in his ratty overalls, then gave Sammy the hairy eyeball.

"What's your angle? You going soft on me? Turning into some kind of pushover?"

"Probably. Go to the pictures, kid. Wake me at three, okay?"

"I might and I might not. I might have business."

"Do your best."

Sammy went up the stairs to his apartment, where he crawled into bed. As he fell asleep he could smell her on his arms and he smiled.

7

THE TENDERLOIN AIN'T JUST A PIECE OF MEAT

The kid knocked me awake and was waiting in the hallway when I went out to fetch the newspaper.

The kid handed it to me. "Two bits."

"That's not part of your job."

"Two bits for waking you up. I'm throwin' in the paper for nothin' because I read it already."

The paper wasn't folded into normal sections, but rather looked like it had been spread out for puppies to poop on, then gathered in a rush to cover the tracks.

"Crash ain't in that rag, anyways," said the kid. "That Herb Caen guy at the *Chronicle* is probably covering it up. Commie bastard."

"What crash?"

"One of them flying saucers crashed. I heard it on the radio."

"I told you to keep your crummy ears off my radio, kid."

"Not *your* stinkin' radio. We got our own now. Uncle Clement give it to us."

"Clement? What line of work he in, pope?"

"He does a little popin', but mainly he plays the ponies. Jack-of-all-trades, that's what he is. Anyway, they said on the radio that a flying saucer crashed in New Mexico. Roswell."

"That's a place," I told the kid. "I know a guy from there."

"No you don't," said the kid. "So, half an hour later, this air force guy comes on the radio and says that it was a weather balloon."

"It was probably a weather balloon," I said. I went to the counter, where I throw my change when I come in, and grabbed a quarter. "Here. Now scram, kid, I got a date."

"At this time a day? You ain't even gonna put your time in on the heavy bag? You're gonna go soft, ya cream puff. Go ahead, give it a shot. I'll bet you can't even put in a good ten minutes, with me coachin' you. When the Martians get here you'll fold like a furlong."

"That's a unit of measure. Eighth of a mile."

"No it ain't, and you're a dirty lyin' furlong for sayin' it is. The Martians are going to burn you down, just like on that radio program where they finally died from germs they got from touching their willies."

"You're not old enough to remember *War of the Worlds*."

"I remember stuff."

"Look, kid, you eat?"

"I had some breakfast. What's it to ya?"

"Make some coffee, and have yourself some cornflakes, and you can coach me for twenty minutes on the heavy bag."

"What's your angle?"

"I figure I might need to stay in shape for this Martian invasion."

"All right, but I'm watchin' you."

◇◇◇◇◇

The night at work moved like honey poured over an iceberg. Mugs, thugs, and lugs, sitting in the smoke, nothing more to me than a drink order and a "here you go." Every time the door opened, the hope rising in me like a hallelujah shattered like a gut-shot crystal goblet when it wasn't the Cheese. All night like that, until around nine, when the phone rang.

"Sal's," I answered, like I do.

"I have General Remy calling for Sal Gabelli," said a young guy, kind of shouting like he's long-distance. Didn't need to, I could hear him fine. "May I speak to Mr. Gabelli?"

"Mr. Gabelli is gone for the evening," I said. "You want to leave a message."

"It's important that the general speak to Mr. Gabelli," said the guy. "Regarding a business arrangement."

"Oh, why didn't you say?" I said. "Let me look around." I didn't look around. "No, turns out he's still not here."

Then the guy on the phone, probably some air force clerk, I figured, started to get huffy with me. "Sir," he said, "what is your name?"

"Struffoli," I told him. "Pauley Struffoli."

"Well, Mr. St—Mr. Stru— What kind of name is that?"

"It's an Italian name. A proud Italian name, from a proud Italian dessert. Made of little balls of dough. It's proud and delicious. My people went to war over struffoli, you ignorant fuck." That was partially true. Struffoli is delicious.

"Never heard of it," he said.

"Yeah," I said. "Then I don't want to talk to you. Tell the general, he wants to talk to his nookie bookie, he can call himself."

And I hung up.

I was in no mood. Insulting my heritage. The mook.

I mixed a couple of Manhattans and put them in front of a couple of drunks, then the phone rang again.

"Sal's," I said, like I do.

"This is General Remy," said the general.

"Hey, General," I said, bright as a sack of sunshine. "Sal isn't here. What can I do for you?"

"About the, uh, entertainment he was arranging, you're aware of that?"

"The farm-scrubbed, pure-as-the-driven-snow entertainment? Yeah, he mentioned it."

"Well, tell him to never mind. Events have provided me with another way to achieve my purpose. I won't be needing his services."

I was a little relieved, as I had no idea how, nor intention of, coming up with a bale of Bettys for his charming pleasure. I said, "I'll tell him. But he's going to want to be compensated for expenses." Knowing Sal, if he lost a payday over this it was somehow going to turn out to be my fault.

"He has some working capital," said the general. "I'll see that he's compensated for his time."

"He'll be happy. Say, General, I hear on the radio you had a crash in your neighborhood? What's the skinny?"

"Nothing. Weather balloon."

"You are lying like a rug, flyguy." Maybe I wouldn't have done that well in the military. What the hell. Sal's got no more business with this mug.

"Tell Mr. Gabelli that I'll be in touch," said the general, all huffy. And he hung up.

The front door swung open, but it wasn't the Cheese. The whole night it was never the Cheese. A sap, I figured, that's what I am.

NOIR

◇◇◇◇◇

When I limped up to Cookie's at 2:30 in the A.M., Milo was leaning against his hack, as he is most of the time.

"Who shit in your tuba?" asked the cabbie. Milo was a slight fellow of about thirty, barely five and a half feet tall, with a perpetual five o'clock shadow and a slope to his shoulders from too much time sitting behind the wheel. He always wore his cabbie hat with the checkered hatband. Always.

"Dame," I explained. "I'll tell you over pie."

"I gotta stay put. This is my busy time."

"Gotcha," I said, and I joined Milo, leaning on the fender of his cab. Together we watched the goings-on through the windows of Cookie's.

See, the legend goes that Milo Andreas had found a parking spot outside of Cookie's Coffee shortly after the war ended, and, parking being what it is in the Tenderloin (which is basically mythical), decided to never give it up. Truth is, during the war, Milo drove a Sherman tank that took a glancing hit from a German Panzer's 75 mm cannon, and Milo escaped being burned alive only because he was dragged out of the wreckage by a buddy, so since then he really did not care much for driving, as it often gave him a case of the jittering willies, but he persevered in his profession, since he had already paid for the hack license and driving is the only job he knows.

"New waitress," Milo informed me. And indeed, through the window, I noted an unfamiliar doll in waitress togs, who approximated the shape of a mailbox, dealing burgers and fries off her arm like she'd been at it her whole fifty years.

"Yeah? She seen Lonius?"

"This, I do not know, but if she has not, I suppose she is in for a tall, dark, and terrifying surprise in the not-too-distant future."

"I don't know, she looks like she can hold her own."

"Happy New Year," cried a drunk as he came out the door of Cookie's, toasting Milo with a coffee cup held high.

"Excuse me, Sammy," said Milo. Then to the drunk, "And happy New Year to you, too."

The drunk guy, who had the look of a banker who has been packed into a jack-in-the-box like a surprise springy puppet, but failed to fully deploy upon the weasel declaring pop, stumbled across the sidewalk holding out a coffee cup like it was dragging him along behind it. He pulled his feet under him and held his cup out to Milo like he was collecting alms for the poor.

"Courage," said the drunk.

"Two bits," said Milo.

The drunk dug into his pocket, spilling most of his coffee in the process, then came up with a quarter, which he handed to Milo. Milo took the guy's coffee cup, pulled open his canvas car coat, and poured a shot from a bottle he kept in the inside pocket, all very much on the Q.T., then handed the spiked coffee back.

"Happy New Year," said the drunk.

"Happy New Year," said Milo, and this is the way Milo Andreas, the cabbie who hates to drive, made rent on his single-residency hotel room in the Tenderloin. See, Cookie's had a tradition, started years ago by theater people, who work on holidays, of celebrating New Year's Eve every night of the year to make up for the good times they missed on the real New Year's. So not only was there counting down, cheering, and the odd smooch, but diners had come to expect to imbibe spirits as well, and Cookie had been denied a liquor license after a rather blatant violation during Prohibition, when four city councilmen and a supervisor managed to crash an Oldsmobile into the city fireboat docked at Pier 22, and only three of them had the courtesy to drown, leaving the other two to rat out Cookie for spiking their coffees with hooch; thus the noble fry cook got blamed for the whole mess. So now, by the laws of supply and demand and showing up, the provision of spirits fell to Milo, who leaned on his cab and poured Old Tennessee (known locally as Old Tennis Shoes) out of his coat for two bits a shot, which he did from 11 P.M. until 4 A.M. every night.

So Milo poured a few shots to grateful citizens, and turned down just as many for cab fare, and I retrieved a cup of joe from the new waitress, who seemed stand-up to me, as she did not give me grief for taking my coffee with cream and sugar, and Milo spiked it gratis, as we are pals.

"So, dame trouble?" asked Milo.

And here I was glad to spot Eddie Moo Shoes coming up Taylor Street, his Holstein-flavored stompers flashing under the streetlamps like patent leather penguins, because, as it turned out, I did not have dame trouble in the traditional sense of the word, only in the sense that I was troubled by a dame who was not, at the moment, with me. All night I waited for the Cheese to come into the bar, and by evening's end I was a portrait in disappointment, as the Cheese neither darkened my door nor provided the light of my life, as she was a ghost, a dream, a memory, a regret, and I was nothing but a sap.

"What's buzzin', cousin?" said Moo Shoes, chipper as a squirrel munching coffee beans.

"New waitress," said Milo. "Sammy has dame trouble."

Moo Shoes leaned on the cab on the other side of Milo, scoped the action in the diner.

"Trouble with the Cheese?" asked Moo. "Already?"

"The Cheese?" asked Milo.

"Dame's name is Stilton," I said. "Like the cheese."

"Oh, I know her," said Milo. "Flapjack flinger at the five-and-dime, right? Blonde? Stacked? Kind of daffy?"

"Nah, not daffy," I said, defending Stilton's honor and so forth. "I mean kinda sad-daffy."

"Well, yeah," I said, caving like a wedding cake in a hurricane. "This is Moo's fault."

"What?" said Moo. "Has the new waitress seen Lone, yet?" Changing the subject, weasel-like.

"Since when are you leaving messages for me at my building?" I was not letting Moo off that easy.

"That kid tried to make me say 'squirrel' for fifteen minutes."

"He wanted to make sure you weren't a spy."

"He's a horrible little kid."

"Yes, he is."

"And I left you the message because I knew you wanted to know."

"That's no excuse."

"Wait," said Milo. "I just saw you guys on Tuesday. When was this?"

"Night before last," said Moo Shoes. "Broad came into Sal's and Sammy lost his mind. You could see it happening."

"You could not," I said. He could not.

"So you met this broad two nights ago and already you're heartbroken? That's got to be some kind of record."

"I'm not heartbroken," I said. "I'm just, you know—I think I got the flu."

"So you saw her?" asked Moo.

"Yeah. Spent the night at her place last night."

"She changed your oil *and* put the chill on you all in one night?"

"Nah. It was swell. Just, you know, she didn't come into the saloon tonight."

"Well, call her, ya goof."

"She doesn't have a phone."

"So go to her house, or were you too soused to remember where she lives?"

"Top of Telegraph Hill, nearly," said Milo. "Can't even drive there."

"How do you know?" I said. How did he know?

"Cabbie," said Milo, pointing to his hat.

"But you don't—" I was starting to say, *but you don't drive,* when I heard the tip-tap of Lone Jones's tap shoes and the formaldressed tower of ebony rounded the corner, top hat and all. I don't know why Lonius wears taps on his shoes, because I have never seen him dance, but no one is going to challenge him about them.

"Gentlemen," said Lone, the professional greeting of a professional greeter. "How y'all doing this evening?"

"There's a new waitress and Sammy's got dame trouble," said Eddie Moo Shoes.

"I am sure sorry to hear that, Sammy. You oughta-should come back to the gym. Make you feel better."

Lone and the guys on my welding crew had a boxing gym set up at Hunters Point, where they endeavored to teach me the gentlemanly art of self-defense. Lone's strategy, which was to be fucking enormous, didn't work for me, but a fellow called Jackson Two had actually done some boxing in the South. "You ain't never gonna be a boxer 'cause you all gimpy and shit, but I can teach you to kick a man in the nuts and you'll get a few licks in. Might keep you alive."

I've been working the heavy bag ever since.

"I'm fine, Lone. These guys are just busting my chops."

"New waitress," said Milo, caution in his voice, pushing back the bill of his hat so we could see he was raising his eyebrows, as if to say, *You know what that means.*

"Good," said Lone. " 'Cause I'm gonna need her to bring me a meat loaf. C'mon, y'all can watch me eat."

Lone headed into the diner. Me, Milo, and Moo Shoes all looked at each other like someone had tossed a hand grenade in front of us and one of us ought to get to heroically diving on that rascal. I broke the standoff and scampered after Lonius, got around in front of him so I went in the door first, like I was a blocking back busting through the line to make way for my extra-large funeral director halfback. Doris—that was the new waitress's name, it said so on her name tag—was standing just inside the door holding a coffeepot and she looked right over my head at Lonius, who is quite a sight when you're seeing him for the first time.

"Doris," I said. "I know what you're thinking, but it's not what you are thinking. Lonius here is a friend of Cookie's and he's a stand-up guy, and comes in here all the time—ask any of these mugs."

And she said, "What I'm thinking is he's gonna knock that hat off on the doorframe, he don't take it off. You guys want a booth or the counter?"

Then Lonius took his hat off, held it to his chest, and, with a half bow, said, "Excuse me, miss, but I am in disguise. You see, aspite what you think, I am not black. I am gonna be on the Secret Service for President Roosevelt, and they don't allow that, so I'm trickin' people. That's the *secret* part."

Well, he didn't have to say that. She was getting ready to seat us, but Lonius had a mission, and none of us had the heart to stop him. See, around June 1941, six months before the Japs bombed the blue bloody bejeezus out of Pearl Harbor, Franklin Roosevelt saw the writing on the wall, and that Uncle Sam was going to need to gear up for war, so he issued Executive Order 8802, which banned discrimination based on race at all defense plants. Well, for Lonius, and a lot of other blacks in the South, this was like the second chapter of the Emancipation Proclamation, and thousands left the South, where their life was little better than when there was slavery, and came to the West Coast, where they got good jobs building bombs and planes and ships and whatnot. They not only got good jobs at good wages, but Uncle Sam made sure they had a place to live while they were doing it. So Lonius came from Alabama, where he and his mama were working on the edge of starvation, and moved to San Francisco, where they spent the war years housed in the family barracks at Hunters Point, and now shared a little house in the Fillmore, where Lonius's mama could even grow flowers in the window boxes. So, to Thelonius Jones, the sun rose and set on President Roosevelt. Even when they were at Hunters Point, Lonius had Executive Order 8802 written out on a typewriter, framed, and hung on the wall in the little apartment he shared with his mother. It was only after the war, after I had talked the owner of the Moonlight, a jazz club in North Beach, into hiring Lone as a doorman, for the novelty of it, and he and his mama moved to the Fillmore, that we found out about his Secret Service angle. It went like this:

I stopped by to pick Lone up after work, and we walked down to Cookie's in the Tenderloin. By this time the Tenderloin had a pretty big black population, what with the war and the city mandating single-residency hotels there for defense workers. (It was lily-white before the war.) Anyway, I figured if Cookie had a beef with Lone, I'd just grab a couple of burgers to go and we'd eat them sitting on the curb. But when Cookie stopped Lone at the door, saying that they didn't serve Negroes, I heard the story for the first time.

"Well, that's okay, 'cause I ain't no Negro," Lone said. "I'm gonna be a Secret Service and they don't take Negroes."

Cookie was a guy caught out of time, the changes to his

neighborhood coming fast and painful through the last couple of decades, but he crossed his big arms and said, "Do tell?"

"Yes, sir. I see'd it down to the colored theater in a newsreel. They stand by the door to make sure the wrong element don't wander into the White House. I picked the spot at the White House right where I'ma stand. I don't care he don't walk. No sweat to me to carry a little ol' fella around while he run the world."

"When was the last time you saw a newsreel, son?" Cookie asked.

"Been some time," Lone told him.

"And you work the door at the Moonlight? In North Beach?"

"Yes, sir, I do."

"I been wanting to go down there and listen to some jazz. You suppose you could get me a good seat?"

"You know I could," said Lone.

Cookie just shook his head, a man who couldn't remember why he'd met us at the door in the first place. "Well, why don't you two take that booth there in the back, and if anyone gives you any trouble, you tell them about the Secret Service."

"I sho' will," said Lone.

That was two years ago, and none of us has had the heart to tell Lone that President Roosevelt was dead.

Now I said to Doris, "Oh. You're okay that he's, uh—"

"No, about that I do not give a shit," she said. "I spent the war welding Liberty ships at the Kaiser yard in Richmond. More than half the people I worked with were colored. We got along fine. Sit where you want."

"I'ma need me a meat loaf, miss," Lone said.

"A whole one," I added.

"And mashed potatoes, you got 'em," said Lone.

"I'll put your order in. You find a seat and when it comes up

I'll see if I can find you." And off she went to yell at the night cook.

But before I got another step, a mug stood up at the counter and turned and I felt my stomach drop, because grabbing his hat off the counter and fitting it onto his big coconut was no other than Pookie O'Hara. "Two-Toes," he slurred, coming at me. "I been looking for you."

And calm as you please, Lone Jones took my shoulder and pulled me around behind him like a mother bear shielding her cub.

"Stop right there, nigger," Pookie said, and he rolled right up to Lone, put his hand on Lone's white shirtfront, and pushed the big man back out the door. Lone let him, and I tumbled out onto the sidewalk behind them both.

"Your kind ain't welcome in there, boy," Pookie said.

The change in the neighborhood, the integration, was why the department had to transfer Pookie off the street. For twenty years he single-handedly tried to beat the Tenderloin white—to the point that one judge even admonished him to try to bring a suspect in *occasionally not wearing a turban,* which was to say, without bandages on his noggin, and some suspects of the dark-skinned persuasion did not live to make it to the courtroom. When the war sent the black population from five thousand to more than thirty-five thousand, the department couldn't take the bad public relations anymore, and Pookie was too connected and knew too much about everyone for them to fire him, so he became the head of vice. I'd never seen him in Cookie's before this.

"But, sir," Lone said, backing up past me, almost to Milo's cab. "I ain't black."

"Are you talking back to me, nigger?"

Pookie was drunk. Mad drunk. Drunk enough to forget he was there for me and fall into old hatred, and still moving well enough to be dangerous. He started to reach in his back pocket, where I know he keeps a lead-weighted sap, but then Lone stopped backing up.

"Sir, I'ma be a Secret Service man for President Roosevelt, and they don't allow colored men to do that job, so I'm in disguise."

"Are you sassin' me, boy?" And then Pookie stopped reaching for his sap and started to reach into his coat, where I know he has a .45 auto slung in a shoulder holster. "I will end you, nigger, and no one will do a goddamn thing about it."

So I hit him. I brought my cane around in a full arc, both hands, like I was DiMaggio swinging for the fences, and clocked him right across the back of his hat. The impact made a crack like a home run, too, but in that second I realized it was the sound of my cane breaking, not his melon caving in.

Pookie stumbled, one step, then continued to draw his .45 as he turned to address me, no little displeasure on his mug. But the gun didn't even clear his jacket before Lone hit him—the sound of slapping a baby with a pork chop—and Pookie dropped to the sidewalk like a fucking rock. Out. His face bounced on the concrete. The .45 clattered into the gutter.

"We sho' in trouble now," said Lone, shaking his head.

I hopped past my pals, who were staring down at the unconscious cop, and pulled open the back door of the cab. "Lone, throw him in the back."

Lone didn't question, he just took the big cop by the collar and the belt and slung him into the back of the cab. There was a distinct, squishy *thud* as Pookie's face hit the window on the opposite side. I scooped up the .45 and shoved it in my belt. Only then did I look around. Miraculously, no one was looking. Some famous actress from the theaters on Market had gone into Cookie's behind us and everyone's attention was turned to her.

"Milo, get him out of here before anyone notices." I was already climbing into the passenger side.

"I don't know, Sammy," Milo said. "This is my busy time. I don't like driving—"

"Give me the fucking keys, Milo, before I shoot you and take them," I said, somewhat emphatically.

"Hey, there's no need for that kind of—"

Milo held out his keys. I snatched them out of his hand and slid across the seat. "Moo, come on. If he comes to, clock him again with this." I handed my cracked cane to Moo Shoes as he climbed in beside me.

"There's a sap under the dash if you need it," Milo said, helpfully.

"Lone, go home. Now. Milo—uh, carry on."

"I was gonna have me a meat loaf," said Lone.

"Home!" I yelled as we pulled away, Moo still trying to get the door on his side closed.

8

A RECEIPT FOR POOKIE

I cut the corner way too tight turning off of Sutter onto Hyde, the tires screeched, the cab hit the curb, and we went up on two wheels for a bit. Not circus stuff, but enough so Moo Shoes slid across the seat into my lap, knocking my hands off the wheel. We almost hit a parked car before I got control again, and there was some more tire squealing and lurching.

"Do you even know how to drive?" asked Moo.

"It's been a while." I whipped the wheel for another right but missed the curb, and there was much more tire squealing, but Moo held on to the door handle, so this turn went much smoother.

"Why are you going so fast?"

"To get away."

"From who?"

"From Pookie."

"Pookie is in the backseat. You are not escaping."

I backed off the gas somewhat. The big cop moaned.

"Hit him."

Moo tried to swing my cane over the back of the seat and only managed a few rattling blows that wouldn't damage a banana cream pie, let alone a hard-hearted cop. "I can't get any leverage."

Pookie moaned again.

"Well, climb over and give him a good swat or two."

Horns blared, headlights flared, and I barely missed colliding with an oncoming car.

"Holy shit, Sammy," said Moo, as he fell into the backseat on top of Pookie. "Washington Street is one-way here."

"It is not. I go this way down Washington all the time."

"Walking."

"Oh," I said. I made some navigational adjustments, which threw Moo against a back window and caused Pookie to groan further.

"Hit him."

"I'm hitting him. This cane is broken. I can't get a good lick in."

"Well then, choke him."

"I'm not choking him."

"You told me the Chinese have hundreds of deadly techniques of hand-to-hand combat."

"We do, but I don't know any of them. Give me his gun."

"What, you're going to shoot him? What will we do with the body?"

"Well, what are we going to do with him alive?"

Despite our street-savvy appearance, it turns out that Eddie Moo Shoes and I are less than first-rate when it comes to perpetrating crimes.

Pookie groaned. Moo banged on the cop's coconut with my broken cane to no effect except to make a *ha-wang* noise like a sprung screen door with every blow.

"Give me his gun," said Eddie.

"No, we're not shooting him."

"I'm not going to shoot him. I'm going to hit him with it. It's heavy, right?"

"That won't work."

"Well, you train on the heavy bag. Why don't I drive and you hit him?"

"Fine. But see if he has handcuffs on him."

"Got 'em," said Moo, holding the cuffs above the seat.

"Put them on him. He may be cross when he wakes up."

"Yeah," said Moo. "Cross."

So I pulled up at the curb and set the parking brake. Moo and I did a Chinese fire drill changing places. When I was kneeling astride Pookie's body, I tried to figure if I actually wanted to hit him in the back of his noggin with my fist, or if I preferred to smack him a couple of times with the butt of his .45. The gun, I decided, because I needed my hands for my work and for touching the Cheese and whatnot.

"Where we going?" said Moo, putting the car in gear.

"I don't know. You're driving."

"Where were you going when you were driving?"

"I didn't know then, either. I was gonna ask you."

"I got a place. My Uncle Mao has a place."

"I thought you were an outcast from the family."

"I am, but Uncle Mao is more of an outcast than I am."

Moo took off and headed down Jackson Street toward Chinatown. Pookie groaned and started to move around. I wound up to hit him with the gun, but then I figured maybe the hammer would poke a hole in his noggin and his brains would leak all over Milo's cab, so I took his hat, which was a pretty nice heavy-felt fedora, and fit it on his melon nicely, then wound up and smacked him a good one with the flat of the pistol, to which he responded with a groggy but loud "Ow! Fuck!"

"Choke him with your belt," said Moo.

"Do I tell you how to drive?"

"Okay, but if he wakes up, he's probably going to kill us."

Which was a good point, so, since I was warmed up, I drew back and smacked Pookie just behind the ear twice hard with the flat of the Colt, which did the trick.

"Piece of cake," I said.

"This is it," said Moo, as he turned down an alley so narrow I was thinking the fenders were going to scrape the brick walls. "You might have to get out, move some garbage cans and crates."

I was lost. See, Chinatown is a mystery wrapped in an enigma, wrapped in a wonton, and fried. Which is to say, I never even knew any of these alleys existed until Moo led me down them. This one smelled like piss, diesel fuel, and rotting cabbage. The headlights picked up tiny red pinpoints in the shadows, rat eyes, like dancing embers, blinked out as the vermin scurried. Moo Shoes stopped the taxi in a spot where the alley widened. There was a naked lightbulb over a red steel door with a hatch in it—speakeasy-style.

We were parked in a pullout in front of the door where a couple of cars were parked but there was no room to open the door on the driver's side, so Moo Shoes slid across the seat and got out on the passenger side.

"Wait here."

He went to the door, knocked, waited, knocked again. The little hatch opened and I could see the top of a silk cap. Moo fired off something in Cantonese and then stepped out of the way. A pair of narrowed eyes peeped over the edge of the hatch. I waved—making friends. Next the sound of heavy bolts being thrown and a tiny man appeared in a strip of yellow light. He was dressed in traditional Chinese garb—maroon silk pillbox cap and the long silk caftan thing with the peg-and-loop buttons. He was old, like one of the scrotum-built guys from the noodle joint.

Moo Shoes and the old guy went back and forth in Cantonese for a minute, the little guy seeming somewhat furious. Moo broke off and came back to the car. I opened the car door and swung my feet out. Pookie's feet dropped out, too.

"That your uncle Mao?"

"Uncle Ho. Don't say 'Mao' in front of him. In fact, you should call him 'venerated elder.'"

"He helps us with this lug, I'll slap him on the ass and call him Debbie, he wants."

Uncle Ho appeared by the car, started twanging orders at Moo Shoes, who translated. "He says to get him inside."

I tried to pick Pookie up by the collar, but I couldn't get a good grip and he was a giant sack of staying put, so Moo grabbed one foot and I grabbed the other and we dragged the big cop out of the car backward—his forehead bounced on the rocker panel, then on pavement.

"Oops," said Moo Shoes.

Pookie groaned. I pulled the .45 out of my belt and wound up to make Pookie go night-night again, but Uncle Ho barked something to Moo in Cantonese.

"He says wait," Moo translated.

So I waited. We waited. The old guy ambled back through the door, was gone a few seconds, then came back out holding a long, stainless-steel hypodermic needle. He brushed me away and jammed it into Pookie's neck, pushed the plunger halfway.

"Shit. In the neck?"

"You were going to smack him with a pistol," said Moo, which was true, but a needle in the neck just looked worse.

Uncle Ho said something in Cantonese. Moo translated. "You want him dead?"

"No," I said.

Uncle Ho pulled out the needle, capped it, squirreled it away in one of the big pockets of his caftan. More exchanges with Moo Shoes, who looked like he was not taking Uncle Ho's news in stride.

"He says we need to get Pookie inside. He can keep him knocked out, but it's going to cost us for the drugs and to pay his people to clean him up and keep him from dying."

"How much?"

Moo asked. Ho answered. "A lot. Depends on how long."

I didn't know. This was my first kidnapping. "How long before he won't remember anything?"

Moo asked. Ho answered. "He says it would be cheaper to just kill him."

"Let's say a week," I said. Like in a week I would all of a sudden know what to do with a racist killer cop.

Moo translated. Ho named a price.

"We don't have enough money," Moo said. "He wants two hundred bucks."

That's a month's pay for me. "Tell him in a week I can get him some top-of-the-line snake whiz for his noodles. All he wants."

"Where you going to get that?"

"I got an angle. It was going to be a surprise. Tell him it'll give him the dick of death."

"The snake whiz isn't a good idea. Uncle Ho isn't interested in that sort of thing."

Before I could think of something, the old guy gently pried Pookie's gun out of my hand and said something to Moo Shoes.

"He says this will buy you two days. He says after that, you bring more money or he dumps Pookie on the street."

"This how he treats family?"

"He's charging for the risk."

I couldn't really argue with that. I did the quick arithmetic of how my own dear Pa, Northwest regional paper salesman, would negotiate for the service of stashing a dangerous, knocked-out cop for a week, and I figured this was what he'd described as a *seller's market.*

"Fine," I said.

Mao did a lot of waving and twanging and it was clear we were to bring Pookie inside, so Moo took the handcuffs off the cop and each of us took an arm. We hoisted Pookie up enough so we could drag him through the big steel doorway. Inside, the place smelled like incense, but sickly sweet, with a note of rotting fruit underneath. The place was barely lit, and after Uncle Ho led us down a hallway, we came into a room that was set up with low cots all around the walls. Each was like a little curtained booth, with a guy lying on it, some zonked out, lying on their side, others lying back, like they were waiting. Beside each bunk was a copper basin the size of a mixing bowl. Some beds had a little teapot beside them, others not. There was soft Chinese music playing somewhere, just random notes, like they were being plucked on a harp or something, not that Chinese stick-fiddle stuff you hear from the musicians working Grant Street that sounds like cats fucking. Amid the bunks old women moved like ghosts, lighting a long pipe and holding it for each guy until he got a good puff, then he'd lie back, glazed. Other old ladies came in pairs, turned the guys on their sides, held the copper bowls under their heads while they vomited, then scurried away with the results. Made me feel a lot better about my bartending job.

Mao directed us to shove Pookie into one of the bunks and turn him on his side.

"If you don't turn them on their sides they will throw up and choke on their own vomit," said Moo.

"Pookie is no way going to let some old lady light up an opium pipe for him," I said.

"No, Uncle Ho will use heroin on him. He's very good at dosages. Pookie won't wake up unless Ho wants him to."

"Let's put the handcuffs back on him, just in case. He does wake up, I don't think these grannies will be much of a match for him."

I helped Moo Shoes cuff the cop to the bunk. Uncle Mao pulled the curtains closed over Pookie and turned to us. The old man took a pad out of his pocket, scribbled something on it with a pencil, tore off a sheet, then held it out to me. "Two day," he said in English.

"What's this?"

"Your receipt," said Moo.

Uncle Mao said something, Moo translated. "He says you don't have your receipt, he can't guarantee you get your cop back."

"I don't want him back."

"Just keep the receipt," said Moo Shoes. "He started with the family laundry business. He's very big on receipts."

"Two days," Moo said. He took the receipt.

He bowed. Uncle Mao bowed. I bowed.

Uncle Mao gave me the hairy eyeball.

"What? Everyone was bowing," I said. "Two fucking days, then."

Then? I didn't know.

I drove. We needed to get the cab back to Milo. I parked it a block away from Cookie's, left the keys under the floor mat. Moo called the diner from a pay phone, left a message telling Milo where to find it. We headed back toward Chinatown together, walking down Geary Street.

So I asked, "You think Uncle Mao is really serious about

dumping Pookie after two days if we don't come up with two hundred bucks?"

"Yeah, and don't call him Mao, call him Ho. Get in the habit. Mao is a nickname. Not a flattering one."

"Why, what's it mean?"

"It means 'cat,' but the full nickname is *Gao Mao Yow.*"

"So what does *that* mean?"

" 'Cat fucker.' "

"You're kidding."

"No. It's why he's shunned by the family."

"Someone caught him—"

"My father. Yes."

"And that's not allowed?"

"No! They were going to eat that cat."

"Oh, well that makes sense then." I thought it through. "So that's why he wouldn't be interested in the snake whiz? I mean—"

"Yeah. He's sensitive about his appetites," said Moo Shoes. "So don't call him Mao."

"Got it."

"Pair of cluckberries, staring at ya!" Stilton called. "Burn some whisky and smear it with cow paste!" She slapped the ticket into the window, stabbed her pencil into her hair, and left it there. Phil, the fry cook, a rangy, scruffy mug who looked like he'd flunked out of sad clown school, slid the ticket over and peeked at it like it was his hole card in blackjack, frowned, and turned back to his grill.

"Really?" asked the guy at the counter; forties, dark hair, and going round around the middle, wearing a suit that was too heavy for summer, even in San Francisco. "Is that what I ordered?"

"You wanted two eggs, sunny-side up, and buttered rye toast, right?"

"Yeah, but it didn't sound like that."

"We have our own professional language here, mister. Like lawyers and scientists."

"Crusty cow and frog sticks!" called Myrtle from down the counter. "Drag it through Wisconsin!"

"What's that?" asked the guy in front of Stilton.

"Cheeseburger, well done, with fries."

"Why doesn't she just say, 'cheeseburger, well done, with fries,' then?"

"Look, mister, do I look like I can explain science? Look at me. Go ahead, read the name tag another hundred times." (Guys spent a lot of time reading her name tag. Pretending to read her name tag. It read *Tilly*, because she got tired of explaining the Stilton story.) "No. I take orders, I sling hash, and I pour coffee. You want a refill?"

The guy shook his head and she stepped down to the next guy, who had stumbled in on a crooked cane wrapped with electrical tape. He was wearing a white shirt that had once been crisp but now was smeared with what looked like blood. He looked like he hadn't slept or shaved in days.

"How 'bout you, sunshine?"

"Just coffee."

"Sure. How do you take it?"

He grinned into his top button. "I like my coffee like I like my women—"

"Drunk and naked?" she guessed.

Now he brought his grin up and his eyes crinkled at the corners. "No, blonde and sweet."

"Aw," Stilton said. She turned to Myrtle. "Did you hear that? Did you?"

She'd heard. "He's got charm. He might clean up nice, too."

"Where were you last night?" Sammy said. "I was outta my mind."

The guy on the stool next to Sammy started to get up and Stilton reached over and pushed him back down. She signaled Sammy to meet her at the stool at the end of the counter, by the window, and led him down there with the coffeepot in hand.

Myrtle slid down the counter to take the position in front of the eggs and rye toast guy, who had had about enough. "It's so sweet," Myrtle said. "Guys never come into the diner to see her. He's not rich, but she don't care."

"Where *were* you?" Sammy whispered.

"Where was I? Where was I? I was sleeping, you lunkhead. Remember, I spent the whole night drinking and doing the razzmatazz with you? I had to go to work when you went home to sleep."

"She was a mess," said Myrtle, who was now only a couple of stools down from them, not even pretending she wasn't interested. "It was adorable."

"Say," said the Cheese, "speaking of last night, where were *you*?" She poured his coffee, then doctored it for him with cream and sugar, two spoonfuls, because he held up two fingers.

He sipped it, closed his eyes, and smiled like it was nectar of the gods. "Perfect."

"Well," she said, "a little tip: Just like your women, a little liquor in that will smooth it out."

He laughed. Myrtle laughed, then scampered off to take an order when a guy in a booth at her end of the diner coughed like he didn't really mean to cough.

"I had a rough night," Sammy said.

"Who woulda guessed? Tell me."

"Well, I started out heartbroken and it got worse from there."

"Heartbroken? Really?" She bent down, leaned on the counter, looked into his eyes. "Tell me more."

"You could have called," he said.

"No I couldn't, I don't have a phone. And I was asleep. You could have come over."

"Could I have?"

"Sure. I might have let you in."

"Bow-wows and whistle berries!" Myrtle called into the window. "Two fat dagos in the straw! Bun pup, take a shit on it and make it cry!"

Sammy raised a questioning eyebrow to the Cheese.

"Franks and beans, two spaghetti and meatballs, and a chili dog with onions," Stilton translated. "I think she just made that last one up to show off for you."

"Then how did you know what it was?"

"I'm a professional."

"Of course. You want to do something tonight?"

"I could come to the bar."

"It's my night off. I thought we could get out of North Beach."

"Will you be sleeping and showering between now and then?"

"You betcha."

"Then I'm in. So, after the heartbreak, then what happened?"

"I'm not sure."

"I hate blackouts. Did you have your panties on backwards when you woke up? Only one shoe?"

"No, I mean, yes. I mean, I didn't black out. I'm just not sure I can explain."

"Tonight, then," she said. "I gotta work. Phil is giving me the hairy eyeball. Watch this." She went to the window, waving the coffeepot over her customers' cups as she moved down the counter. "Hot baby puke, Phil! Squeeze a bunny over it!" She turned and grinned at Sammy.

The beleaguered Phil stopped and put both hands on his side of the counter pass-through. "What in hell is that?"

"Oatmeal with raisins," she said coyly. "Everyone knows that."

Phil nodded as if he should have known that and turned toward his grill.

"Never mind!" said Stilton. "Cancel that, Phil. Instead, ax-murder a monkey and hump it three times!"

Phil wheeled back to the window, a man who was just about reaching the end of his spatula.

"Just messing with you, Philly," said the Cheese. "But that's a banana split, in case we get in the weeds."

"You girls do the ice cream," said Phil.

"I know, that's why I was just messing with you."

She quick-stepped back down the counter to Sammy. "So, I'm buying you a banana split, so I don't get fired."

"Aw, I never had a dame buy me ice cream before."

"You know I don't actually have to pay for it, right? I just said 'buy' so you didn't think I was easy."

"Right," said Sammy. "I wouldn't think that."

"Yeah, she's no floozie," said Myrtle, who had made her way back to their side of the diner and into the conversation. "So, you got some tape on your cane? Accident? I mean another accident. Not the one where you got the cane."

"Yeah," said Sammy. "You could call it an accident."

9

LAFF IN THE DARK

Stilton agreed to meet Sammy that evening at the corner of Columbus and Broadway, which he thought was swell of her, because it saved him from walking up 387 stairs to pick her up at her place, but also because it gave him a chance to check in with Thelonius Jones, who was already at his station as doorman at the Moonlight Club.

"You get home all right, Lone?"

"Sho' did. I been a little jumpy ever since last night, though."

"Yeah, well, I think that's taken care of. If anyone asks, you weren't at Cookie's last night."

"What 'bout that new waitress? Someone ask, she gone remember."

"Good point." Sammy pushed his hat back, scratched his head. "And she saw Pookie come after you. But I don't think she saw what happened after. Just say Pookie told you to scram and that's what you did."

"I sho' will, Sammy. Hey, ain't that your new lady friend?"

Sammy wheeled to see Stilton coming down Columbus Avenue, her hair down but pinned away from her face, a long, tan raincoat open over a white and red polka-dot dress, flat shoes she could walk in.

"Yes, it is," said Sammy. "Yes, it is."

"Hey, Lonius!" She waved at Lone, kissed Sammy on the cheek. "How are you tonight?"

Lone tipped his top hat. "I'm just fine, miss. Y'all going to have you an evening out?"

"Yes, we are." Stilton hooked on to Sammy's arm. "Our first date."

"You know better than to feed him, don't you, miss?"

"Oh no, is that bad? I gave him a banana split for breakfast."

"Well he yours, now. You won't never get rid of him."

"I wish someone would have told me."

"This is not true," Sammy said to Lone. "That's not true," he whispered to the Cheese.

"Whatever you say, snowflake," Lone said. "You go on now, show yo' lady a good time."

Stilton looked from Sammy, to Lone, to Sammy. "Snowflake?"

"That's what I called him, on account he my first white boy."

"Oh, snowflake, I'm so excited to hear the story," Stilton said.

Sammy pointed his cane at Lone. "I will remember you ratted me out."

"Y'all have a nice evening."

"Anyone asks, you know nothing, Lone."

"Whatever you say, snowflake." Lone's smile shone like the grille of an Oldsmobile fresh out of the factory.

Sammy led Stilton across Broadway and up Grant Avenue into Chinatown. Grant was steaming with the smell of five spices, garlic, dead fish, and incense. The vegetable and fish stands had been pulled in for the night, the fortune-tellers, calligraphers, and souvenir stands pushed out. The restaurants, massage parlors, nightclubs, and bars were still hopping, and a younger bunch streamed up and down the sidewalk: men, women, Chinese,

Anglo, Hispanic; sailors, longshoremen, hustlers, hounds, and hobos—Chinatown had gone from a place for making a living to a place for having fun. A young man in possession of a ten-spot could get his future told, his belly filled, his back rubbed, his crank yanked, and leave with a jade Buddha on his key chain, all within a twenty-foot stretch of sidewalk.

"Can we stop here a minute?" Sammy asked when they reached the big golden foo dogs that guarded either side of Club Shanghai's doorway.

"Sure. Always wondered what this place looked like inside."

"My friend Eddie works here. Told him I'd rattle his chain if we passed by."

A sharp-dressed kid opened the door for them. Down the red carpet, Eddie Moo Shoes looked up from the host's station. He met them halfway down the hall.

Sammy said, "Stilton, my friend Eddie Shu. Eddie, Stilton."

"Pleasure," said Eddie, taking Stilton's hand and bowing over it, gallant as you please.

"So, how is your houseguest?" Sammy asked.

"Resting comfortably," said Eddie. "Still recovering from his trip."

"Eddie has a cousin in from out of town," Sammy explained.

"Recovering from the trip?" Stilton asked.

"Something like that," Eddie said, then he signaled for Sammy to lean in close. "Excuse me, ungentlemanly talk, Stilton." Sammy leaned in and Eddie whispered. "Some drunk thought he saw Pookie get clocked by a guy with a cane. Guy was shitfaced, so no one's looking hard, *yet,* but you should know . . ."

"Got it, thanks," Sammy said, stepping back. "Well, tell your uncle I hope he feels better."

As they exited the Shanghai Club, Stilton asked, "Hey, you okay?"

"Right as rain, just gotta do something I been meaning to do."

He walked over to the curb, carrying his cane under his arm like a newspaper, determined not to limp or favor his good foot, then bent over and chucked the cane down a storm drain port. They could hear it clatter and splash below.

"There," he said, dusting his hands, *good riddance to bad rubbish.* He held his arm out to her. "Shall we go?"

"Wow. Just like that?"

"Been a long time coming. Tell the truth, I should have chucked that thing a long time ago. I didn't really need it."

"No?"

"Nah, I was just using it as a crutch."

She took his arm and snuggled up to him as they continued down the avenue.

"That's what you're supposed to use a friggin' cane for, snowflake," she said.

"Oh yeah," he said. "Well, I don't need it."

"If you say so. But you need someone to lean on, I'm here."

"Yeah?"

"Yeah."

They got on the B-car at Geary Street and rode it for nearly an hour, laughing and smooching and commenting between them on everyone who got on or off at every stop, making up outrageous, silly stories about street pirates and bus stop witches, mentioning neither the war nor what had come before. They got off at Ocean Beach, between the Great Highway and Playland, where, as usual, a freezing wind whipped off the Pacific at about seven hundred miles per hour, whistling through the Ferris wheel and the roller coaster, and surprising more than somewhat those tourists who had come here for a balmy midsummer night's dream, but discomfiting Sammy and the Cheese not a whit. They were locals, and knew what the author Jack London had said about Ocean Beach in 1902: "Holy fuck, you couldn't get a match lit here to save your life." Stilton wore her raincoat to protect her from the wind and Sammy wore a wool overcoat with a pint of Old Tennis Shoes in the pocket to protect against the cold.

"So, what's your pleasure?" Sammy asked as the streetcar clanged away.

"I could put on the feedbag, if you don't mind," she said.

"Sounds good. There's a diner down by the merry-go-round, if you can stand diner food."

"I built up a tolerance. Let's go."

They walked arm in arm to the Sea Lion Café, where they ordered burgers and Cokes from a counter guy in a paper hat. Sammy splashed a jigger or two of Old Tennis Shoes from the pint into their Cokes under the table.

"More," said the Cheese.

Sammy slurped some cola off the top and splashed in more liquor—a bartender used to juggling glasses.

"Okay?"

She nodded as she blew the paper wrapper off her straw at him, then drank off a quarter of her Coke in one pull. "Ah, perfect."

"Glad you liked it. Old Tennis Shoes is aged in oak barrels for several days."

"You can taste it." She put her glass down. "Sammy, I need to ask you something, and don't say no just to be nice. Be honest."

"Promise. Shoot."

"Do you think I'm an alcoholic?"

"How would I know? I'm a bartender. Everyone I know is a drunk except the kid who hangs out on the steps of my building, and I'm not even sure about him."

"What would you guess, then?"

"Nah. Considering what you been through, you're as sober as a church mouse."

"Isn't that '*quiet* as a church mouse'?"

"You'd think, but once you get a few drinks in those little guys, you can't stop them singing."

"Thanks," she said, smiling at him around her straw before she took another long pull on her drink.

"Just the truth," he said. "Now me."

"You're definitely a drunk," she said.

"No, now *I* get to ask a question."

"Oh, okay. Forget I said that. Shoot."

"What were you looking for when you came into my bar that day?"

"I was looking for you. Just you."

"But we'd never met."

"I didn't know you were what I was looking for, but there you were . . ."

"What if I hadn't been there? Would anyone have done?"

"Nope. I wasn't looking for just anyone. I wasn't looking for you until I found you. I thought, That's the guy I've been looking for, that guy, right there."

"It was because I was pouring drinks, wasn't it?"

"That did not hurt. It wasn't everything, but it was something."

"You could have lied about that."

She sucked on her straw until it made a thirsty slurping noise at the bottom of the glass, then said, "I'm not lying."

"Yeah, but you could have. I would have been okay."

"Okay, here's the truth, Sammy. I'm trouble. I'm not right. I do reckless things. Selfish things. I'm a wreck waiting to happen. You should steer clear of me."

"You want another Coke?" Like he hadn't even heard her.

"Yeah. Please." She had warned him. You can't blame her. "You like onion rings?"

"Nah."

"Me either."

Their burgers arrived and they dove in, the Cheese eating hers in four bites, cheeks puffed out like a lipsticked chipmunk. Sammy was impressed. For a slim broad, she could eat.

She was munching away at a bouquet of ketchup-tipped fries when he said, "You know, for a slim broad, you eat like a champ."

"Yeah, thanks," she said. "Been eating since I was a kid. You know, practice."

"I mean, a lot of girls on a first date would be dainty and pretend they weren't really hungry. Push the food around on their plate. But not you."

"Yeah, but what you don't know is then they go home, climb into the icebox with a spoon, and think bad stuff about you. I won't be doing that. I got plans for you, later, buster, which is why I gotta keep my strength up."

"Plans?"

"Yeah. You gonna eat the rest of your fries?"

Sammy grinned and pushed his fries to her side of the table and was about to negotiate for a hint of her plans when two cops came in the café and took seats near a window looking down the walk toward the merry-go-round. Sammy watched their reflections in the paper napkin dispenser. They were young, not particularly tough-looking, and seemed more interested in watching girls than fighting crime—like they were celebrating drawing sweet duty where the worst thing they might encounter was a rowdy sailor or a kid lifting wallets in the funhouse.

Sammy snatched the last handful of fries from his plate and crammed them in his mouth.

"Too slow," he said around the mouthful of distressed spuds. "Let's go."

Stilton laughed and the cops looked over. Sammy put on his

hat and stood, dropped some money on the table, and said, "Keep the change," to the guy at the counter.

"Thanks, folks," the counter guy said, but they were already out the door—Sammy, with a hand on her hip, was steering Stilton toward a ride called the Ship of Joy.

"You're not even limping," Stilton said. "Guess you were right about the cane."

"I'm right about most stuff," Sammy said. "It's a curse." He gave her hip a little squeeze to mark the nonsense he was talking.

The Ship of Joy was two ship-shaped gondolas, each seating twelve people, that swung on long pendulums and approximated the experience of being on a big playground swing with a bunch of strangers. They swung and they laughed, mostly at some kids who whooped like they were going over a cliff with every swing, but also at a dad who had lost his hat on the first swing, then stared forlornly for the rest of the ride at the spot over the shooting gallery where it had drifted.

As they were stumbling off the Ship of Joy, arm in arm, Stilton said, "I was expecting more joy."

"Kind of a *phonus bolognus* in the ship department as well," Sammy said.

"Ooh, I love it when you speak Latin. You been to sea?"

Sammy hoped she didn't see panic on his face. "Just transport," he lied.

"My husband was on a ship. Heavy cruiser. Went down with all hands near Savo Island, August '42. They never found him. Uncle Sam sent me a flag."

Casual as you please, like that first day in the saloon when she'd mentioned her husband. And, like then, he didn't know what to say. He said, "Sorry, kid." He pulled her close.

She pushed him away, took his hand, and pulled him toward the games of chance. "Come on, win me something."

NOIR

Sammy threw some baseballs at milk bottles filled with concrete and threatened them not at all, although Stilton cheered him on and cursed the bottles' stubborn ways. At a shooting gallery he downed a few metal ducks with a .22, because his father had given him and his brothers BB guns as boys and he was not a bad shot, although not good enough to win a prize.

"C'mon, let's kill some clowns," she suggested, pointing toward a booth where you could throw darts to pop the balloon bodies of painted-on clowns.

"How 'bout you, little lady?" called a barker as they passed. "Guess your weight for a nickel! I get it wrong and you win a teddy bear."

"And you get it right and I'll rip your lips off and stomp them like slugs," replied the Cheese. Sammy nodded earnestly to the barker to confirm her conviction. Stilton's weight went unguessed.

Sammy finally won her a prize when a ping-pong ball he tossed settled into one of a hundred baseball-size goldfish bowls, startling the fish inside somewhat, but which it soon forgot.

Stilton held the bowl aloft and looked at the perky orange occupant against the lights of the Ferris wheel. "He looks so lonely, Sammy. Win me another one so they can both be in the same bowl and have a little goldfish razzmatazz."

"I don't think goldfish have razzmatazz," said Sammy.

"Well, then how do they have little goldfish?"

"Far as I know, the female lays her eggs on the bottom, then later on the male comes along and fertilizes them."

"Really?"

"Not exactly sure with goldfish, but that's how it works for trout. We had trout in Idaho. I read a book on them when I was a kid."

"Yeah," said the scruffy guy working the goldfish booth. (You could have sanded the varnish off a coffee table on his five o'clock shadow.) "He's got it right."

Stilton handed the fish back to Five O'Clock Shadow. "Take this sad fish. Give him to a kid. Come, Sammy, I need fun." She took his arm and led him toward the funhouse with the great yellow letters painted across the red façade reading LAFF IN THE DARK. Sammy bought two tickets and they entered through a giant clown's mouth, stepping through baffles of black fabric until they were stumbling inside a ten-foot-high, rotating drum. It wasn't dark yet, but they were laughing and stumbling until they stepped out onto a very mushy field of what must have been black foam rubber.

"It's like walking on meat loaf," said the Cheese, giggling, as a skeleton dropped from above them and was caught by a red spotlight. Stilton yipped and jumped into Sammy's arms. He carried her through another set of black fabric draperies and into complete darkness.

"Should be called Pee in the Dark," said Stilton.

"Really?"

"Nah. Close, though."

"C'mere, 'fraidy cat," said Sammy. He smooched her perhaps a little too zealously for someone who was laughing and they banged their teeth. Then they separated and felt for chipped teeth with their tongues.

People, mostly teenagers, pushed past them in the dark, giggling, groping, and shrieking like joyful heretics at a clown inquisition. Someone pinched Sammy's bottom and he jumped.

"Was that you?"

"What?" said Stilton, her voice sounding about ten feet away.

"Nothing," Sammy said. "I think I mighta just made a friend. Stay there, I'll come to you."

He found her in the dark and they kissed like they'd been separated for months, clinging to each other as revelers bumped into them, shrieked and laughed and stumbled on. They blundered together through another set of baffles, these made of some kind of black gauze, which felt like spiderwebs against their faces, onto a dimly lit floor that shifted and tilted, sending them staggering one way, then stumbling another.

"I don't think I'm drunk enough to walk this way," said the Cheese.

"Relax, ma'am, you're in good hands," Sammy said. "I'm a bartender."

He pulled her through the next door and ducked under the outstretched hand of a moaning mummy that pivoted on an axis at his waist and swung his arm back, just missing delivering a backhand to the Cheese. Sammy pulled her down just in time and they crouched beneath the bandaged automaton. The mummy moaned again.

"This mug's got a moo box in him," said the Cheese.

Sammy pulled the pint from his overcoat and unscrewed the cap. "Pardon?" he said.

"A moo box," said the Cheese, taking the pint from him. "We sell them at the five-and-dime. It's like a little can and when you turn it over, it moos like a cow."

The mummy waved over their heads again and moaned.

"That does sound like a cow," Sammy said.

"Moo box," the Cheese explained. She pointed at the pint of Old Tennis Shoes. "No chaser?"

"Rehearsal's over," Sammy said.

She went a little cross-eyed as she took a swig, scrunched up her face like a kid eating a lemon, then shook her head until the burn settled down. There were tears in her eyes when she held the pint out to Sammy as if it contained a cocktail of nitro-glycerine and monkey spit, which is to say, with careful disgust. "Smooth," she gasped.

"Good for cleaning engine parts, too," Sammy said, braving a swallow himself and capping the bottle. "Let's get out of here."

They raced away from the mooing mummy and made their way across the ceiling of an upside-down room and through a mirror maze to stumble, arm in arm, out onto the midway. The smell of sea air, popcorn, cotton candy, and cigarette smoke washed over them. Sammy bought them snow cones, red for her and blue for him, and, at Stilton's suggestion, doctored the chilly treats with the last of the Old Tennis Shoes.

"Not bad," said the Cheese.

"Could use some more blue," Sammy said.

They walked by the rides and souvenir stands, and tried to find takers for bets on the merry-go-round.

"I'm giving six-to-five odds on the funny-lookin' kid on the camel!" Stilton called, waving a fan of Skee-Ball tickets in the air to show she was legit.

"I think that's a giraffe," Sammy said.

"Five-to-six on the funny-lookin' kid to win, then," said Stilton.

Sammy pulled her away before she could find any takers and they ended up in front of a caricature artist, who sat on a stool, wearing an artist's smock and a beret.

"Pinup of the little lady, sir. Only a buck."

"I don't know . . ." Stilton tried to walk away.

"I think she's worth giving a second look," said the artist. "Don't you?"

"Absolutely," said Sammy. He swung Stilton around by the arm. "Come on, Toots, I think you're worth it, don't you?"

"Don't call me—" She caught herself falling for the bait. "Aw, hell." She slurped the last of her snow cone, handed the soggy paper wrapper to Sammy, then sat down on the stool opposite the artist and let her trench coat fall off her shoulders.

"Color me pretty," she said.

A look passed between Stilton and the artist that made Sammy think she might slug the guy.

"No work for me, ma'am," said the artist, and he commenced drawing, holding his drawing board out of Sammy's sight.

"Fine," Sammy said. He walked away and fought with a half a book of matches to get a cigarette lit, noticing that the breeze had changed directions and was blowing offshore—it was warm, a rare condition on a summer night at the San Francisco beach.

"How 'bout you undo a button or three in the front there, Toots?" said the artist, when he thought Sammy was out of earshot.

"How 'bout I bop you in the beezer so hard it spins your beret around?" said the Cheese.

"Jeez," said the artist. "No need to get tough."

"And don't call me Toots," said the Cheese.

The artist finished his sketch about the time that Sammy was grinding out the butt of his smoke on the gravel of the midway.

"*Voilà!*" said the artist, in perfect fucking French. He flipped the drawing around.

Sammy took a look, then took a step back and whistled. "Holy moly."

"You're a lucky guy," said the artist.

"Yes I am," said Sammy.

The caricature portrayed Stilton in the pose of the classic Rosie the Riveter SHE CAN DO IT poster from the war—a blonde flexing a bicep, her hair tied up in a polka-dot bandana, the classic chambray shirt—except this Rosie was facing the artist, not looking over her shoulder, and the shirt was unbuttoned to the point that exaggerated bits of the Cheese were about to burst out for the world to see. It was Stilton all right, but rounder in the places where she was round, and sharper in the places where she was sharp: drop-dead sexy.

"That should be on the side of a bomber or something," Sammy said.

"That'll be a buck," said the artist.

"You got it." Sammy handed the guy a dollar. The artist tore the drawing from his sketchbook and started to roll it up.

"No, not yet," Sammy said. He took the drawing, held it up, and compared details with the model, his eyes darting from Stilton to the drawing and back. "I need to look at this Rosie."

"You two have a good evening, sir," said the artist with a wink to the Cheese.

"Wendy," Stilton said as she stood and joined Sammy in admiring the drawing, turning her back on the artist. "Rosie the Riveter was for girls who worked in airplane factories. In the shipyards we were Wendy the Welders."

"What a dame," Sammy said. Then he turned from the drawing and kissed her.

"You like it?" She pouted with anticipation.

"I like the model," Sammy said. "I like the model a lot."

"Let's go for a walk," Stilton said.

"It got warm out," Sammy said. "You notice?"

"Oh yeah," she said.

Sammy rolled the drawing up and fixed it with a rubber band the artist had given him and tucked it in his pocket. They walked arm in arm around Playland at the Beach, then out of the park and up into the dunes. They found a sheltered hollow where all they could see was the stars and sand, and calliope music from the merry-go-round sailed over them on a warm offshore wind. They lay down between her trench coat and his overcoat, wrapped the stars around them like a blanket, and made love until time disappeared.

Time returned, just before dawn, dressed in a chill fog, and Sammy awoke to the caricaturist's drawing poking him in the ribs. "Hey," he said. "How did that guy know you worked at a shipyard during the war?"

10

SURPRISE

When Sal Gabelli came through the back door of the saloon, he found a wooden crate, about three feet square, with the words *DANGER! LIVE REPTILE!* stenciled on the side in big, black letters.

"What wacky shit is this?" Sal said to himself and the four mutts who were waiting behind him outside the door. Sal had been experimenting with his dog pizza idea, and dogs of various sizes and colors had been attracted to his experiments. Now they met him at the door every morning when he opened the joint and waited for the next incarnation of dog pizza cooked up by Sal's wife the night before. "No pizza today, ya mooches," said Sal, and he slammed the door in their faces.

Folle donnola! (crazy weasel), the dogs barked in chorus, before they kicked Sal from their hind paws like shit-stained grass and wandered off to find better fare. (It is well known that all North Beach dogs bark in Italian.)

There was an envelope stapled to the crate, addressed to Sam Tiffin, care of Sal's, with PRIVATE stamped upon it in red. Sal considered, for three full seconds, not opening the envelope, before constructing a five-pronged rationale for doing so, which was as follows:

1. It is addressed to *my* saloon.
2. *Sammy* took the night off.

3. The relief bartender, Bennie, does not do my side work, and is, therefore, a bum.
4. The gimp has a lot of goddamn nerve receiving packages here.
5. Fuck him. Pookie O'Hara is probably going to put him in a sack anyway.

Sal ripped the envelope from the crate and paused an additional two seconds while he considered carefully steaming it open, then ran through his five rationales, settling quickly upon No. 5, and tore it open. The letter inside read:

Sammy Boy:

Let someone who knows what he's doing open this.
These buggers are quick as lightning and twice as deadly.
Hope your business venture works out.
Headed to China. Be back in September. See you then.
Cheers,

Bokker

Sal read the letter again, looked at the crate, then read the letter again, then set it on the crate. He could always say he found it that way. No harm, no foul. *It was open when I came in,* Sal practiced in his head. *Must have been Bennie. You ask me, that guy is a bum. Never changes out the keg at the end of his shift.* That figured out, Sal made his way over to the tap, put a pilsner glass under it, gave it a pull, and sure enough, the tap sputtered and spit foam into the glass, then hissed, empty. *A bum, I tell ya!*

Now Sal was faced with the dilemma of switching out the keg, which he did not want to do, or opening the crate, which he very much did. What kind of scam was Two-Toes running, anyway? Who did he think that *DANGER! LIVE REPTILE!* rigmarole was going to fool? And why not have it sent to his house instead of the bar? Unless Two-Toes had counted on it arriving when he was working, and it had arrived when Bennie was filling in, so the relief bum had accepted the crate. That had to be it.

Had Two-Toes found a business angle and not cut Sal in? Would he dare? Were the warnings on the crate just to keep the law from checking the package? Did he owe the gimp the privacy? Hmmm . . . Had Sammy come through putting the Dorothys together for the Bohemians? He had not. That task had fallen one hundred percent on Sally Gab. Two-Toes might have made a nice cache of cabbage if he'd done his part, but he hadn't. See No. 5. Fuck him. He didn't deserve discretion.

Sal returned to the back room and eyed the crate. It had to be illegal, or at least shady, either one of which put it in Sal's domain, because he was the implied boss of all things shady and/or illegal that took place in the saloon. Whatever game Two-Toes was running, Sal was taking a piece.

He gave the crate a little bump with the heel of his hand and it tipped up an inch, then thumped to the tile. It wasn't heavy. So it wasn't booze. Wrong-size crate, and besides, the only kind of booze you had to smuggle anymore was absinthe, and nobody wanted it anyway because it tasted like ass and cost too much for something that might poison you dead. He gave the crate another tip and let it thump down. Nope, nothing heavy. He'd be surprised if it was even full. Sal grabbed the crate by two corners and gave it a good shaking—a sliding, really. There was definitely something in there. It sounded like straw.

They kept a short crowbar on a hook above the sink that they used to pry open the crates of the few liquors that still shipped in wooden boxes, mostly Scotch and a few dago reds that they stocked for the neighborhood old guys. That would do. Sal snatched the crowbar from its hook and returned to the crate. He worked the crowbar under one corner of the lid, popped it with his palm to give it some bite, then put his weight on it. The nails screeched and the corner of the crate came up an inch. *Once a bootlegger, always a bootlegger,* Sal thought. How many crates had he had to pry open fast during Prohibition? Canadian whisky sailed into the bay on pleasure craft and was quickly repackaged in fruit and vegetable crates, under real fruit and vegetables, before it was rowed to shore.

Sal attacked the next corner with the crowbar and levered it down hard. Nails creaked. The lid lifted two more inches. He worked the short end of the crowbar around the edge of the lid like he was opening a big can, and the lid came loose. Sal leaned the lid against the side of the crate, then peered in. Nothing. Half-full with those curled wood turnings they used to pack dishes and teacups. Nothing was nesting in it. Just a box full of straw, really. But it had been heavier than that.

Sal grabbed a handful of straw and held it aloft. Nothing. He poked at the rest of the straw, stirred it around, hooked the crowbar into it, and turned some of it over. Nothing. But there, in the corner, something brown. He leaned into the crate and caught it with the tips of his fingers. A canvas bag.

"Two-Toes, you fuckstick," he said aloud, his voice a prelude in disappointment. The canvas bag was tied at the top, and while it may have once held fifty pounds of flour or rice, now it held nothing at all. In fact, one corner of it was torn, tattered, as if it had been chewed by rats. There was a noxious smell coming off it, too. Sal tossed the sack toward the trash can by the back door. It missed, by more than a little, and he angrily hooked it with the crowbar and slung it into the can. Then he saw something move out of the corner of his eye.

"The fuck?"

He turned to the crate and the snake was standing there, like a black iron rod, protruding from the crate, its head at Sal's eye level, looking at him, flicking its tongue. Sal felt something like cold electricity run through his body. Adrenaline. He had the crowbar in his hand, ready to swing. He was pointed toward the door. The snake was less than an arm's length away. Sal knew he should do something—run, fight, dodge, scream—but what he did was nothing at all.

The mamba struck, its fangs hooking into the side of Sal's neck, its lower teeth fastening around his Adam's apple while it pumped venom, a long voyage's worth of stored-up venom, into Sal's bloodstream, at which point Sal did all the things he had thought of doing an instant before. He swung the crowbar, he ducked, he dashed for the door, he screamed a high-pitched terror-yodel, and he pulled the door open into his face, then he bounced and fell back, hitting his head on the edge of the sink as he went down.

The snake whipped away and found a spot in the opposite corner of the stockroom, where it coiled and watched Sal twitch on the floor.

Born and raised in the city, Sal had never met a snake in person before. So far, he did not care for them.

The Cheese said to me, she said, "You're gonna put me through the third degree after giving me the razzmatazz all night on the sand like a hobo?"

It was maybe six in the morning and we were on the streetcar headed back to North Beach. I woulda sprung for a cab, but *you* try to catch a cab by the beach at six in the morning. The Cheese had her hair pinned up in that fountain of curls way I like, but otherwise she looked like maybe someone had given her the razzmatazz on the sand like a hobo. Her dress looked like it had been wadded up and stored in a cat box, with the cat, and there was a little half-moon of lipstick on one of her nostrils. I don't know how it got there, but I was loath to apprise her of it, as she was already somewhat peeved with me.

"First, it was swell. And second, I was the gentleman and let you be on top, so perhaps it is *you* who were giving *me* the razzmatazz in the sand."

"Swell, was it? Then why the interrogation?"

"I just was wondering how that artist knew you worked in the shipyard. He drew you without hardly looking. Like he'd done it before."

"So you want me to say I been to Playland with another guy, yeah, I have. And maybe they wanted a keepsake before going off to war, so maybe I sat for that guy before."

"They?" I said. I didn't want to know, but I asked. I thought about some mug in a foxhole on some godforsaken island in the Pacific, bleeding to death all over a pinup of the Cheese. Still, I couldn't stop myself. "More than one?" I asked.

There was an old couple leaning on each other at the other end of the car, like they could be sleeping, or maybe someone had loaded them dead onto the streetcar for a ride to the cemetery, because they had not moved since we boarded. The old guy's hat was pulled down over his eyes. The old broad wore a scarf around her head that made her look like one of those French peasants you see in paintings. Yeah, they coulda been dead.

"What if there was more than one?" said the Cheese. "It was a long war, and I was lonely. Guys shipping out were scared they might never see home again. So yeah, I gave 'em something nice to remember. If that makes me some kind of floozie in your mind, then maybe you need to rethink how *you* got that picture."

Stilton nodded toward the lapel of my overcoat. I noticed the old broad at the other end of the streetcar opened an eye when the word *floozie* was used, then closed it real fast when I looked at her, so not dead. I was not relieved. Not at all. I was standing over the Cheese, hanging on to a pole, and I felt like I was gonna be sick.

"So that's it?" I said. "You felt sorry for me?"

"Nah, that ain't it at all," said the Cheese. "I like you, Sammy. I like you a lot. But you know how it was." She took a breath, like it was my turn to say something, but I didn't, so she jumped in, like she was rescuing me. "I don't know how horrible it was for you over there, and I ain't going to ask, but at least you came home. At least you can laugh. And you make me laugh. But some of those guys probably had the last laugh they were ever gonna have the night before they shipped out. You can't be mad about that . . ."

But I could, I guess. I had no right to be, but I *was* mad. Maybe not so much mad, but empty, like my chest was caving in on me. See, for a little bit there, the whole world was me and the Cheese, and I was just fine with that. But suddenly there were all these other guys in it, haunting it like ghosts. I had nothing to say.

So I sat down. Not on the seat with her, but across the aisle. I was feeling like a bootful of shit, hold the boot. I just sat there, my legs across a couple of seats, my feet out in the aisle, looking at my shoes. I said nothing. The Cheese said nothing.

People got on the streetcar. People got off. People shuffled and muttered and read the paper. The dead couple ambled off, the woman looked back, gave me a scowl as she stepped down to the street. *Save the stink-eye, grandma, I got a whole lifetime of it waiting in the mirror when I get home.*

NOIR

After Van Ness Avenue, Stilton pulled the cord, rang the bell. The driver stopped at the next block at the intersection of Market and Polk. "I'll just get off here," Stilton said. "My uniform's at work. I'll just get ready there."

"Yeah, I get off at Grant," I said. That was all.

She tapped my foot with her finger as she went by. "See ya around sometime," she said.

"Yeah," said I.

"Watch your step," called the driver.

I watched the Cheese step off the streetcar and look back over her shoulder, eyes hooded, like she was ashamed, and I felt as if I just threw a rock and busted out the streetlight that was the only light in my miserable life.

When I got home, the kid was curled up in front of my door like a sleeping squirrel, his butt in the air, his newsboy cap on the floor in front of him. I didn't know why the kid's mom hadn't let him in last night, or why he didn't let himself into my place with his key, but I was tired enough to drop off right there in the hall beside him, so I unlocked the door, picked the kid up by the back of his overalls, and set him inside my apartment. I kicked his cap inside and locked the door behind us.

If I left the kid outside, he was likely as not to get eaten by rats, and as beat as I was, there was no way I would make it to work in time without the kid's wake-up services. I left him there on the floor, sawing logs in one of those soft kid snores, like you hear from a puppy or maybe a baby pig, because every minute or so he let out a little snort. Point is, he didn't miss a beat, and I was a little jealous that he slept the sleep of the innocent, as they say, despite the fact that he is a horrible little kid.

Oh, I slept, all right, but it was the jangled sleep of a mug who had just ruined the best thing that ever happened to him, and it seemed like as soon as I closed my eyes the kid was pounding on my door and yelling like the place was on fire. Kid must have gone out while I slept. My watch said I'd been asleep for seven hours, but it felt like seven minutes, and four of those hours were acid stomach and regret.

"I'm up, kid," I said, throwing open the door. "Why didn't you use your key?"

The kid rolled by me like I was a shadow and headed for the icebox.

"I mighta lost it," he said. "I ain't sayin'." He was already pulling out the milk and a loaf of bread I keep in the icebox to discourage the weevils and whatnot. "You're outta cornflakes. Leave me a little extra cabbage and I'll pick some up for you, no extra charge."

"There's sugar. Make some milk toast," I told him, but he already had two slices under the broiler and was about to turn on the gas.

"Look, kid, I gotta get in the shower." I grabbed my pants off the chair, pulled a buck out of my wallet, and put it on the enamel drainboard. "Get some cornflakes, some butter, and go to the hardware store and get a key made." I put my key on the drainboard next to the dollar. "You can handle that, right?"

"What am I, some kind of slave? I ain't your errand boy. I ain't some kind of dirty mascarpone."

"That's a cheese, kid."

"No it ain't."

A pain hit me in the temples like someone was shooting hot rivets into my coconut, and it wasn't from the Old Tennis Shoes. "Look, kid, the key is for you, that stuff is for you. Why'd you sleep in the hall last night?"

"None a' your business. My ma might be on a mission with Uncle Clement."

"The pope?"

"Very hush-hush." The kid was watching his toast like it was a science experiment—leaning so close to the broiler, the brim of his cap gave off a little puff of smoke. "Had to leave fast. Locked me out on accident. Whadda ya going to do? Dames can get daffy when the chips are down."

I was about to say "Tell me about it." I was about to say that maybe it wasn't his fault he was a horrible little kid, because his mother was a horrible mother.

But, "Yeah. Whadda ya gonna do?" I said as I headed for the shower. When I came out the kid was on his second round of milk toast. He slurped while I dressed.

"Where's your cane?"

"Left it at work. Get that key made, kid, and leave mine under the mat."

"I gotta listen to your radio tonight. See if the flying saucers are attacking. You can't see 'em coming from here on account of the city lights. That's how they get you."

I started to tell him to keep his dirty ears off my radio, as is my policy, but then I said, "Yeah, you keep an ear out, kid. Just turn it off when you're done. You burn out a tube, it comes out of your pay."

"Try and get it, ya dirty manchego."

"Also a cheese."

"No it ain't, you lousy—"

I closed the door on the kid's rant. Two steps into the street I was feeling like I should head over to the five-and-dime on Polk Street and throw myself on Stilton's mercy, beg her to forgive me, tell her I made the mistake of my life and I was not a war veteran and I was a liar and bum. Broads love that.

Probably.

But I couldn't dump a load of trouble on her like a bucket of chum. It would stink. It ain't right.

So I headed on to Sal's, and as I walked, I waved to the guys I know on the street.

"Hey, Vinnie! How's your mother? . . . Tony! How's it hangin'? . . . Hey, Enzo, *ba fangul,* you fucking dago fuck!" (I can say this because when Sal hired me I told him that my family name was originally Tuffelo, not Tiffin, so he welcomed me into goomba society and everyone in the neighborhood thinks I am Italian. I do not disabuse them of this ruse.)

So as I went, waving, speaking pidgin Italian, I realized I usually tipped my cane, and all of a sudden I wished I had my cane, because I was limping and my foot hurt. I thought of Stilton at the lunch counter, dealing plates off her arm all day while I was sleeping, having to deal with various mooks, mugs, and unsavory citizens, while hurt. And I knew she was hurt, and worse than my stupid foot, because she was a good kid, maybe a little daffy, sad daffy, like Milo said, but sweet daffy. I'm no good for her, and I know it.

When I got to Sal's, the front door was closed, locked, the CLOSED sign still hanging there in the window. I figured maybe Sal had stepped out for a minute, but usually he just locked the cash register and had one of the day drunks keep an eye on things until he got back. Around the back, the door was not locked. It wasn't even completely closed; something was propping it open about four inches. A shoe. It was a shoe that Sal Gabelli was wearing, and from the off-blue color of his skin, I could tell right away that Sal was more than somewhat dead.

So here I found the aforementioned snake crate sans black mamba and determined that the snake might, indeed, still be in the saloon, and indulged in two burly man-screams in quick succession, one upon finding Sal, and the other upon running into the two tall goons in black standing in my way as I headed out to find Moo Shoes and inform him that our business venture had croaked my boss, and also that we had a business venture.

The goons were nonplussed by my manly scream, but they recovered before I did, and while I tried to pull the door shut behind me, one stepped in my way.

"Are you Sal Gabelli?"

"Nope," I said. "Sal took a day off."

"Who are you?" asked the other tall guy. The only way I could tell them apart is that this one had thick eyebrows above his sunglasses, the other had eyebrows like a dame draws on with a pencil.

"I'm the janitor," I said, despite that I was wearing my bartender black-and-whites, including a vest, bow tie, and garters on my sleeves (although I had not donned my apron, due to the interruption of the corpse and so forth).

"When will Sal be back?" asked thin brows.

"I don't know, maybe Monday. I'm just the janitor."

Thick brows took a notebook out of his jacket pocket and wrote something down with a short pencil.

"Did you just write down that I am the janitor?"

"And the date and time," said thick brows.

They did not ask my name. They did not question that I was the janitor, when I was not wearing proper janitor togs, nor did they identify themselves, but they were writing down the time and, I guess, that they talked to the janitor. They didn't notice that I was sweating like a whore in church, despite the cool weather, and they didn't ask. So they weren't cops, unless they were really bad at it, and they were wound entirely too tightly for wiseguys, but the suits, the hats, the sunglasses were matched, like uniforms, right down to the spit-shined Florsheims. Maybe, I thought, they are from one of those loopy churches that send guys in ties out into the jungle to convert cannibals and so forth. Maybe Sal was running a game on them.

"Can I give Sal a message for you?" I said. "Tell him you stopped by?"

"No, don't do that," said thin brows.

"We'll be back," said thick brows.

"Okey-dokey," I said. "I gotta scram, guys," I said. "Another job. Go with God or whatever," and I pushed my way past them and headed up to Broadway, my heart still beating like Gene Krupa in my chest. Definitely loopy church guys.

11

HOW TO ICE A GUY

Turns out I can scamper like a champ without my cane after I've had a scare, so I made quick time to Club Shanghai, where the doorman gave me the hairy eyeball as I blew past him. Eddie wasn't at the host's podium, but the young guy was. I didn't remember his name.

"Hey, Skippy, Eddie around?"

"Name's Lou," said the kid. Now I remembered.

"I thought it was Low."

"Not anymore," he said. "Eddie's in the lounge." He tossed his head toward the door to the side. The cocktail lounge was all red velvet and gold dragons, less sparkly than the main room. Eddie was standing at a dark oak bar next to Lois Fong, who was not yet in her evening clothes, but who looked very well put together indeed, even in her day outfit, which involved a sage-green linen dress and a pair of dark green platform Mary Janes, the heels of which were high enough to give vertigo to a mountain goat. She sat at the bar with her heels hooked into the brass rungs of her stool.

"Kid, would you get Eddie for me? Tell him I need to talk to him a second."

"You can go on in."

"Nah, I don't think Lois likes me, and he looks like he's making time. Tell him it will just be a second."

I took a few steps back toward the door, the carpet so soft and thick it reminded me of the floor in the funhouse last night, "like meat loaf," the Cheese had said, and I felt a stab in my heart.

"What's shakin', bacon?" said Moo Shoes. Red silk jacket, gold lamé bow tie, black-and-white wingtips, of course.

"Trouble," I said.

"That other thing? Because we shouldn't mention that other thing. My uncle."

"No, not that," I said.

"Dame trouble again?"

"Yes. But no. Different trouble."

"Confess, sinner."

"Where'd you get that?"

"Bing Crosby movie. Maybe. I don't know. What's the song, Armstrong? I gotta get back to Lois. She's telling me her woes. Things are looking up."

Lou came back to the podium and Eddie waved him off. "Take five, Lou," Eddie said. "I got this." Lou took a powder. To me, Moo Shoes said, "So . . . ?"

"Sal Gabelli might be dead."

This was clearly not what Moo Shoes expected and he did a double take. "Might be dead in that he is missing? Or might be dead in that someone has put him in a sack, and dropped him in the bay? Which is understandable. Or might be dead like he is in the hospital with a bum ticker and he has only hours left?"

"Might be dead in that he is definitely dead, in the back room of Sal's."

"Whoa!" Moo Shoes looked around, peeked back into the lounge, gave Lois a wave and a wink—he'll be right back—then, "What the hell, Sammy? Did you kill him?"

"No!"

"Good."

"Well, yes. Well, kind of—"

"How did you *kind of* kill him? Because if it was an accident—"

"Well, *we* killed him."

"*We?* You and that Cheese dame?"

"No, *we* like you and me."

"Look, pal, you know I'd stand up for you, but you kill a guy—"

"It was our snake," I interrupted. "Our snake killed Sal."

Moo Shoes was a little stunned. I saw this and I gave him a second to collect his thoughts, but then Lois Fong peeked her head around the corner.

"Ed-deee, I need to talk to you."

I realized I'd have to throw a block for a pal or Moo Shoes was going to lose ground with the object of his infection. "Lois," I said, leaving Eddie standing and moving up to Lois, using my best condolences voice, "if you could just give us a minute. I got a personal situation and Eddie is giving me advice like he does so well. Okay?"

She stepped back into the lounge. "Okay, I guess. But Eddie, I gotta get ready for work, soon."

Moo Shoes nodded, smiled, put a finger in the air, *be there in a minute.*

"*Our* snake?" he said.

"Yeah, we have a snake. Deadly poisonous black mamba."

"A snake?"

"Yeah, remember that South African merchant marine who was at Sal's the other night, the one with all the animals? Well—"

"So you bought a snake?"

"It was your idea," I said.

"How in the hell could it be my idea if I'm just now hearing about it?"

"Because you took me to the noodle place with all the snake whiz at twenty bucks a scoop. So I figure it was an investment."

"Wait, this was the angle you were talking about when you wanted to pay Uncle Mao in snake whiz? So you bought a snake?"

"That is what I'm saying."

"And it killed Sal?"

"In my defense," I said, "the snake was addressed to me. There was even a note saying to be careful. Sal completely ignored the note and opened the crate."

"You had it delivered to Sal's?"

"Yeah, I figured it was safer than my place. My place they would just leave it outside on the stoop. You can't just leave a valuable snake lying around. Someone will—"

"So the snake bit Sal, and now he's dead?"

"That is true. Back room of the saloon."

"And where is the snake?"

"Dunno. Maybe still in Sal's."

"With Sal's dead body?"

"So you see the problem?"

"Yes," Eddie said. "I see the problem. The cops are going to be looking all over for you."

"Not necessarily," I say. "I mean, there's no way to prove it was our snake."

"Except it was addressed to you."

"That's it. I'll make like someone was trying to kill me, but Sal opened the box and saved me."

"No one will believe that," said Moo Shoes.

"Ed-deeee!" Lois whined from the doorway.

I went over and took her hand gently, like I was leading her onto the dance floor. "C'mere, doll, just a little bit more. You know what a sharp operator Eddie is, right? Well I really need

136

just another minute with him and he'll help me out and then he's all yours."

"Well, all right." Lois pouted and took little pouty steps back to the bar.

I turned back to Moo Shoes. "So, I need you to help me get rid of the body."

"What? No! I don't know how to get rid of a body."

"Yeah, but you know a guy, right?"

"Why would I know about that? I grew up in the laundry business."

"But you're an operator, Eddie."

"No I'm not."

"Well, you would have been if this snake deal had worked out. What about your uncle?"

"Yes. Maybe." Moo Shoes was cogitating. "No. He specializes."

"What? He specializes in drugging a kidnapped cop and keeping him gacked on smack until we can figure out what to do with him, but he can't handle one lousy dead guy?"

"Not a dead *white* guy."

"What, he's good enough to take my money for drugs but he can't soil his delicate hands on a corpse? The nerve."

"No, you Anglo mugs are too big."

"Nonsense, Sal doesn't go a buck-fifty soaking wet. And he's already down a couple of quarts. I'd say one-forty, maximum."

"Ho says it takes too long for the pigs to eat a white devil."

"Maybe since we're regular customers, he bends policy?"

"He won't do it. In fact, he wants more money if he's going to keep Pookie a few more days. Says he has to bring him around enough to pour some water into him or else he'll dry up and die."

"Well we're fucked then," I said. "Because then we've got two bodies, and Pookie is huge."

"Ed-deeee," Lois whined.

"You are going to need to fuck right off, Lois!" I barked. "Right *now*. Just give us one fucking minute!"

I may have been somewhat less delicate than I had intended in answering Lois's concerns.

"*Gwai lo,*" Lois muttered as she hurried away.

"I heard that! I know what that means! I am not a white devil!"

"Oh shit, now you've done it," Eddie said.

"Sorry, pal."

"The money," Eddie said.

"I don't have any," I said.

"I lent you a hundred bucks the other night."

"I know. Why did you make me buy noodles?"

"I told you. I needed to look broke. That's not the point."

"I spent it on the snake. Along with a C-note of my own."

"You spent two hundred bucks on a snake?"

"It is a first-rate snake, as I think we can see now."

"Ed-deeee!"

Moo Shoes wheeled on the dancer. "Scram, Lois! This is business. I'll be there in a second."

She sniffled and started to cry as she ran away. Moo Shoes turned on me then and I had to take a step back, because I was not entirely sure he was not going to sock me in the choppers for wrecking his woo. But he tightened down all of a sudden and got very scary and whispery with me, which I had not seen before, and which unsettled me more than somewhat.

"You have got to get back to work. If Sal's isn't open people will get wise. You already got them looking for a guy with a cane. Hey, where's your cane?"

"Don't need it."

"Good. Hide Sal's body, open the saloon, work your shift, and we'll figure out what to do tonight after work."

"What if the snake is still in there?"

"Then catch it."

"I don't know how to catch a snake. It's probably a big snake. Bokker said he'd get a big one. And it's probably angry because it's still got Sal's taste in its mouth."

"Use a broom or something."

"A broom?"

"Yeah. I'll call you later."

"What about the scrotum guys?"

"Who are the scrotum guys?"

"The old guys at the noodle joint. The ones who look like they are made out of scrotum skin."

"That's disrespectful, Sammy. Those are my venerated elders."

"They drink snake piss, Eddie, how venerated is that? This is mostly their fault."

"How is this their fault?"

"Supply and demand. Don't they teach basic economics in Chinatown?"

"Go to work. Don't get killed. I'll see what I can do. I'll call you."

"Tell Lois I'm sorry. I have been a little edgy lately."

"I'll tell her I'm going to have your arms broken."

"Sure, that's a good angle."

"I just need to find the money to pay a guy."

So just like that, Moo Shoes went after Lois and left me to find my way back to Sal's with no help at all.

When you hear guys say that a guy got put in a sack, it sounds much more simple than it actually is, or so it occurred to me as the evening passed.

I was completely calmed down by the time I got back to Sal's, and there was no sign of the two guys in the sunglasses, just a few sad dogs sitting vigil, or maybe waiting for dog pizza. Anyway, I let myself in the back, looking around a little bit to make sure that the black mamba was not waiting behind the door to scrag me like it did Sal, but the coast was clear. I stepped over the afore-mentioned Sal, who, to my surprise, seemed less than concerned with my bad manners, then I grabbed the mop by the big laundry sink by his head. There was a little hair and blood there on the corner of the sink, so with the keen Sherlockish detective powers that I have honed over several years of forklift driving, ship weld-ing, and bartending, I deduced that Sal had banged his melon on the way down, thus making for the small, serviette-size puddle of gore on the floor by his face.

I figured I had an hour to get the saloon ready and open before the after-work regulars started to think something was up, and—with all due respect for the dead—I did not mop up around Sal right away, because I did not care to be surprised during cleanup by the black mamba, so I brandished the mop as my weapon of choice in battling the deadliest snake known to man, as evidenced by the deceased douche bag under the sink. I thought maybe if I found it, maybe it would bite the mop head instead of me, and meanwhile I would run outside and come up with a different plan. The South African said they can outrun a man, but how are they with doorknobs, huh?

I grabbed a leather jacket out of the lost-and-found and put that on for protection, then I commenced to look around every corner, under every table, behind every stool, in every cabinet—opening the doors and leaping back, mop in hand, ready to run. Half an hour later and there was no snake, although I did surprise a small gray mouse in a cabinet under the back bar and introduced him to my aforementioned *giant-dick-in-the-door* man-scream, which sent us both scurrying off. So, the coast being relatively clear, it was time to deal with Sal.

Sal was never the best-smelling mug under normal circumstances, but now he had gone quite overripe indeed. There was a drain in the floor under the sink, so I commenced to dash buckets of warm soapy water over him until he was quite refreshed, although somewhat damp.

He would not remain so fresh, I guessed, until closing time, and besides, a customer at the end of the bar would be able to spot Sal lying in repose under the sink and curiosity would ensue, so I needed to move him. As I may have mentioned, I have limited experience in the hiding of stiffs, so a good hiding spot did not immediately come to mind. Then, there it was, like the Holy Grail, or the magic words, or free nookie (which, I suppose, could also be the magic words).

Shortly after the war ended, when Sal first hired me, there came on the market many surplus machines no longer required to defeat the Axis powers. Among these were battleships, bombers, tanks, flamethrowers, atom bombs, and ice machines. And it was the last that Sal decided he needed for his saloon, as the price was so low as to make it almost free, especially considering the savings of not having to have ice delivered every day. And there it stood. Too big to fit under the bar. Too big, even, to get through the door into the front room. Originally designed to make life somewhat less hellish for mugs in the Pacific campaign, it stood in the corner of the stockroom, opposite the sink, chugging and hissing and making various crashing noises all day, all night, every day. Roughly three times the size of a normal fridge, it had a bin that was supposed to hold five hundred pounds of ice, and now, I hoped, would also accommodate its owner.

There was no way I was going to get dead, wet Sal in there by myself and still be presentable for work in a half an hour, so

I stripped to my skivvies, folding my bartender togs and leaving them out on the bar, then I returned to the back room, hoisted Sal from under the armpits, and dragged him over to the machine. It turns out that the term *stiff* is not entirely a metaphor, which is to say, in the intervening time since he last drew breath, Sal had become quite rigid. The ice machine's hatchway was about three feet off the floor and covered by a heavy door that clunked shut when dropped into place. While quite serviceable for passing a small bucket or steam tray through, it was not the ideal portal through which to pass a rigorously morted douche bag, and I let loose with a couple of Technicolor roars into the sink during the process. Thus I was enlightened as to how difficult indeed it would be to put a guy in a sack, when I couldn't even get a well-lubricated welterweight into an ice machine. And it was occurring to me that perhaps I did not have the stomach for cutting parts off of Sal to get him in the ice machine, even if the paring knife we used for cutting lemons was sharpened up considerably, when the phone rang. I left Sal hanging mostly out of the machine while I went to answer it.

"Sal's," I said.

"May I speak to Mr. Gabelli, please?" said a woman, very official and serious.

"Mr. Gabelli just stepped out," I told her. "May I take a message?"

"Please have him call this number as soon as possible," she said, then she gave me the number, which I wrote down on a notepad we keep by the phone for just such things.

"Who should he ask for?"

"Just have him say who is calling and I will direct his call."

"Sure thing," I told her. She hung up, and I held down the phone cradle for a five-count before I dialed the number she gave me.

"Stoddard, Whittaker and Crock," answered the same dame who just hung up on me. So, without a word, I returned the favor.

What is Sal doing mixed up with a law firm? A law firm who doesn't want to give me their name? I figured I'd ponder it later and went back to the task at hand.

When I returned to Sal, I saw the solution. Right there in front of me was a perfectly serviceable snake crate, and no snake, and I would only have to bend Sal in one place to get him in there, which was easily achieved by laying him flat across the top of the crate and then jumping on him.

Before you can say Jack Robinson, Sal was sitting peacefully in the crate, which I moved over by the drain for meltage, and I was pouring buckets of ice over him. By the time it was time to flip the OPEN sign, Sal's bald spot was the only thing showing above the ice, so I put the lid on the snake crate and tapped it down with a crowbar to give him his privacy.

I mopped the sweat off me with a bar towel. Then, as I was pulling on my trousers, the phone rang again.

"Sammy," said Moo Shoes, "I got good news." Moo sounded like he had a hot tip on a fast horse.

"Swell," I said.

"Well, they found a guy dead in an alley off Kearny Street. Chinese guy."

So not a tip on a horse. "That's terrific, Moo. But I'm a little busy—"

"That's it, you still looking for your snake?"

"Kind of. I looked everywhere, but I don't know how good they hide. I'm about to open up. I want to get some people in here so if he decides to bite someone, there's less chance it will be me."

"Well, don't worry about it. He's not there. The dead guy they found died of snakebite. He wasn't dead when they found him, but soon after, so they know it's a really deadly snake. All the old guys in Chinatown are buzzing about it."

"I feel bad." I did feel bad. A little relieved, but bad.

"No, that's the good news. They all want in."

"Who all want in?"

"The old guys at the jook place."

"The nut-sack skin guys?"

"Don't call them that. But yeah, those guys."

"What about the cops? The papers?"

"This is Chinatown. Nothing gets out those guys don't want it to. They aren't going to risk losing a snake like that."

"But we don't have the snake."

"I know. We have to catch it. So I talked to Uncle Mao, he wants to help us."

"I thought he specialized."

"Yeah. This is one of his specialties."

"Oh good," I said, although I was not feeling as if this was good news. "Will he throw in getting rid of a body?"

"Don't know. What about Sal?"

"Still dead. I iced him down."

"I had an idea," Moo said. "What if we take him out and drop him in the woods somewhere? In Marin or the East Bay, up by Piedmont or something. By the time someone finds him, they'll just think that he was bitten by a snake in the wild."

"Won't work. Sal has never been out of the city in his life. Everyone will know it's a setup."

Suddenly there was a clicking on the line, loud, like Moo hung up.

"Sammy?" Moo said.

"Yeah, I'm here. You hear that?"

"Yeah, it's probably one of the Chinatown operators, they listen in sometimes."

"Maybe we better not talk about this on the phone anymore, huh?"

"Right, I'll see you after work."

"Right, see you then. Can you come here? Bring a car?"

"Nah, you come here. Besides, I don't drive."

"You drove the other night when we snatched Pookie."

"Well, yeah, but that was just to keep you from killing us. I really don't know how."

"Oh," I said. "Right."

"Did you call Sal's wife?" Moo asked. "She'll be wondering where he is."

"Oh balls, I didn't think about that," I said. "I'd better do that. See you tonight."

I saw silhouettes through the stained glass of the door, customers waiting for me to open, and despite it all, all the panic and scurrying, my heart jumped at the thought that one of them might belong to the Cheese.

PAYING MAO

Poor Sammy. His boss was dead, his snake was missing, he had no money to pay Ho the Cat-Fucking Uncle for the upkeep of his kidnapped cop, and there was no Cheese outside his door. When he opened the bar he was greeted by normal thirsty citizens, many of whom were annoyed that Sal's did not open up earlier, so Sammy appeased them with free spirits and a serviceable story about how Sal had had a loss in the family, which story had the added value of being partially true, that loss being Sal.

Also, Sammy's bad foot hurt and he had thrown his only cane in the sewer, so he was limping to the point of looking like he was skipping up and down behind the bar. Still, he was getting into the rhythm of the job, pouring drinks, washing glasses, talking small, when two uniformed cops darkened the door like a thunderstorm fat with doom. All the patrons piped down to a whisper—even guys not discussing something illegal put on the hush so more industrious criminals didn't take them for rats.

"What can I get you, Officers?" said Sammy, beaming smiles of innocence and goodwill.

"We're on duty," said the junior cop, gangly and barely old enough to shave.

"Just beer then?" Sammy grinned. Young cop cracked a smile.

"You seen Pookie O'Hara?" asked the older cop, tough-looking bullet-head, little to no neck.

NOIR

Sammy searched the ceiling as if that was where he kept his memory. "Big as a house, nose like a road map, suit looks like he's been sleeping in it since before the war?"

"That's the one," said the young cop.

"Never heard of him," Sammy said.

Bullet-head hitched up his gun belt. "Listen, wise guy—"

Sammy grinned, held up his hands, big smile. "Just kidding. Yeah, he was in here, I don't know, four–five days ago. Had a short one and was in the wind."

"He say anything?"

"Yeah, he gives me a nice tip and says to tell Sal he stopped by."

"That's it?"

"I bought breakfast and a paper with the tip."

"Did he say anything else?"

"Nope."

"Is this Sal around?"

And here Sammy suddenly had an idea that flashed in his head like flickering, dying neon, and also made that annoying buzzing noise, but he pushed through and said, "Nah. Ya know, Sal said he was going to take off somewhere—up north I think, and I think Pookie was going with him. That's why Pookie was looking for him, I think."

"Up north, where?"

"Don't know, but Sal had me open late today, didn't work his shift—he usually opens in the morning. Maybe they're fishing or something."

The two cops looked at each other, looked at Sammy like he had just farted. "Fishing?" said bullet-head.

"I don't know," Sammy said. "I'm just the night bartender. I'm just trying to help."

Bullet-head nodded. "We'll look into it."

They started to go and then the younger cop stopped at the door. "Hey," he said. "You know a thin guy, walks with a cane?"

Sammy stopped breathing. All the regulars in the place, who were concentrating on minding their own business, stopped breathing. Sammy shook his head. "Lot of thin guys walking with canes since the war. You got anything else? Age? Hair color?"

"Nah," said the young cop. "Witness thought they saw a guy clocking Pookie with a cane couple of nights ago."

Sammy stared into the bin of bottle caps by the opener, like he was thinking hard. "Check down on Third Street, by the soup kitchen." Sammy was thinking: *This witness must have been corned-up to the gills if he sees a skinny guy with a cane but misses completely the enormous black guy in a penguin suit who actually rings Pookie's good-night bell.* Sammy said: "You can't flick a butt down on Third without hittin' a guy on a cane or crutches."

"Yeah, thanks for nothin'," said the young cop. Bullet-head pushed through the door, disgusted. They were gone.

Sammy turned to check on his customers and everyone was looking at him. "What? It wasn't me." A couple of dozen eyebrows went up. "It wasn't. I don't even walk with a cane anymore."

Bunch of guys coughed politely, lit smokes, waited.

"A round on the house!" Sammy exclaimed, and everyone started talking and calling out drinks and telling lies and a good time was had by one and all.

A half an hour after the flatfoots left, I followed through with my plan by calling Sal's wife, who I met exactly one time, when she came into the bar one day to get cash from Sal for groceries. She seemed okay.

"Hello," she said. She sounded peeved.

"Mrs. Gabelli, this is Sammy down at the bar. Sorry to bother you, but Sal asks me to give you a call."

"Yeah, why?"

"Well, he was running out to go fishing with some friends and he's going to be gone"—I tried to figure how long I could push this, how much time I could buy—"at least until Monday." Gave me two more days.

"Yeah, I know," said Mrs. Gabelli.

"You do?"

"Yeah, but he told me it was camping. Yeah, right, the douche bag wouldn't know a sleeping bag from a soda bottle. So he told you to tell me it was fishing? Good for you, kid."

"Could have been camping," I said. "You know Sal . . ." Sal's wife even called him a douche bag? I'm thinking maybe the snake did everyone a favor.

"If I need him I'll just call down to Mabel's, they'll pretend he's not there, and he'll be home in a hour."

"Okay, Mrs. Gabelli, he just asked me to call you."

"Yeah, if you see him, tell him I said to piss up a rope."

"Yes, ma'am," I said.

So compared to getting Sal into the ice machine, consoling his widow seemed like a piece of cake.

So, my career in crime away alertly, as they say in horse racing, it was around midnight when I decided that I would perpetrate my first robbery. Moo Shoes and I needed to raise numerous ducats with which to pay upkeep on our kidnapped flatfoot. Since it seemed unlikely that Sal would be requiring operating cash, I decided that he was going to donate the contents of the cash register to Pookie's upkeep, but as I counted down the drawer a couple of hours before closing, and eyed the few drunks still in the bar, I realized that we were going to come up short by several sawbucks, and I guessed that Uncle Mao would not float us the difference.

After I booted everyone out, I proceeded to look for the remaining funds. As any experienced robber will tell you, if you are going to lift a guy's wallet, it is wise to do so before you pack him under numerous buckets of ice in a snake crate, because when you return several hours later, you will find that the ice has melted into a somewhat solid block, which requires quite a bit of attention with an ice pick before the wallet is liberated. Although more or less blue, Sal appeared as fresh as when he was first packaged, discounting minor blemishes caused by a few less-than-precise plunges of the ice pick. And boom, I had enough money to pay Uncle Mao and pocket a few ducats for myself, a soggy driver's license, and a lifetime membership card to the Knights of Columbus, which will come in handy if I ever need to sit around and smoke cigars with a bunch of ancient goombas.

The clock was creeping up on three. I was supposed to catch up with Moo Shoes at Club Shanghai, but I couldn't do it. Not without checking on her.

Fast as I could, I packed Sal back in ice to his crown, and before I put the lid back on the snake crate, I admitted to Sal that he was right about buying a military-grade ice machine, because without it, none of this would be possible.

I left my other side work undone, stepped into the alley, and locked the door. The bakery down the street was proofing their bread and you could smell the yeast in the air along with a hint of cinnamon, which must have come from something else they were fixing up for the morning. It was clear out, but cool, which I was grateful for, because before I got halfway up the stairs to the top of Telegraph Hill, I had my overcoat over my shoulder and my shirt was steaming with sweat.

The whole climb and half the way down I was practicing groveling in my head. The closer I got to the top of the hill, the more desperate and panicky I felt. What if she said no? No second chance? Would I beg? Maybe I wouldn't start with begging, but I'd get there quick. Or maybe she'd give me a break and it would start with a big backbreaking smooch and we'd be off to the races again. Or maybe I'd get there and she'd be doing the razzmatazz with some other mug, and I'd stand outside the window as pieces of my heart broke and fell on the little stepping-stones in the garden. No, even thinking that made me want to collapse and roll down the hill and just fucking die like a dog in the dirt.

When I got to her place there were no lights on at all. No sound from inside. I listened at the door for a second, caught my breath, then knocked, softly-like.

"Stilton?" A whisper. Another light tap. "C'mon, Toots?" Couldn't help it, I smiled, thinking she might be smiling inside. But she wasn't. Five or six more tries, tapping with apologies, then I tried the knob. Unlocked.

Without her in there, her little dug-out apartment felt like a grave. The bed was made. It looked like a kid's bed, small and neat and unruffled, a white chenille bedspread looking like it was fresh off the line, like it would be undisturbed forever—like the bed of a kid who drowned that was being kept just like it always was, like a bed for a kid who would never come home.

Holy shit, I had to get out of there.

There was a book of order tickets on her little kitchen table, and a pencil in a cup. I left her a note. *I'm sorry and I'm sorry and I'm sorry, and I want to see you,* and I signed it *I love you, Sammy.* And I was out of there and down her side of the hill to Kearny Street as fast as I could go without tumbling ass-over-teakettle and breaking my neck, although right then I was thinking maybe it wouldn't be such a bad move, given my situation.

◇◇◇◇◇

By the time I got to Club Shanghai the doorman had gone home and I just waltzed in like I was dragon of the walk. Eddie Moo Shoes was at the host station alone. He looked up, gave me the *just a minute* finger in the air, then called something into the cocktail lounge. Suddenly Lois Fong was on him like a gold lamé anaconda, wrapped around him like the long golden evening gown was wrapped around her, which is to say, quite snugly. Lois smooched him mercilessly, causing Moo Shoes to have to steady himself against the host station. Just as I was thinking, *Well, she's going to do it, she's going to give him the old razzmatazz right up against the wall,* Eddie twisted out of her clutches, kissed her quick on the temple, and patted her bottom to steer her back into the cocktail lounge, where she wiggled in a most disappointed and unsatisfied manner, very much on the pout.

Eddie looked up at me and grinned like a complete idiot, then quick-stepped down the hall to join me.

"What's the haps, paps?" he said, still grinning.

"Don't act like that didn't just happen. And you got lipstick over your goofy mug." I handed him a handkerchief I kept in my overcoat and he wiped away as we headed out.

"I know," he said. "Can you believe it? Ever since you told her to buzz off she's been on me like white on rice."

"In my defense," I said, "*you* also told her to buzz off."

"Like I said the magic words," said Eddie. "Guys always tell me that dames love that, but I don't believe them, but now . . ."

"I am not an expert, but I do not think it works with all dames. Still, I do not want to stand between you and your good fortune. I can handle this if you want to go tend to Lois's wants and/or needs."

"Nah, you can't handle this. And I don't want to press my luck. Besides, if she puts the chill on me again, I'll just tell her to buzz off again."

I nodded. "You are an operator, Moo Shoes, that is what you are." As we made our way down Grant and swung a left onto Pine, I said, "I got the money for Uncle Mao."

"Uncle Ho," Moo Shoes corrected. "And good, because that's where we're going."

"Oh," I said. "Yeah, I know that." I did not know that.

Soon we were in an alley with less than adequate lighting but with more than its share of garbage odor and creatures scampering in the dark. "How's your foot?" Eddie asked.

"It's fine. Hurts a little, but I am distracted by other matters."

"You okay without a cane?"

"It would appear so," said I.

Before I could elaborate, we were knocking on the steel door and Uncle Mao let us in. Eddie said some nonsense to him in Cantonese and then said to me, "Give him the money." I did and the old guy counted it, then led us through the dimly lit opium den to the bunk where we stashed Pookie. He pulled back the curtain and there lay Pookie O'Hara, curled up like a little piggy on his side, naked except for a pink silk kimono that was too small for him in all dimensions. There was more of Pookie than I ever cared to see, and if I had not spent my whole day strengthening my resolve by packing and unpacking a stiff, I would probably have blown lunch at the sight of the cop.

Uncle Mao said something and Moo translated. "It's easier to take care of him and clean him up this way."

"Fine," I said. "But we'll have to take his clothes for my plan to work." Then I told them both the plan. I talked and paused, talked and paused, to give Moo Shoes a chance to translate for Uncle Mao.

We would get Pookie right to the edge of never waking up, then we would drive him and Sal's body out into the country somewhere, where there are woods, but we would make a note of where we put them. We would lay it out so it looked like Pookie offed Sal, then we'd give Pookie one last dose, pour some liquor on him so if anyone found him they'd think he was drunk, then we'd call the cops, anonymous-like, say we saw two guys fighting by the side of the road and we think one of them is hurt. When the cops showed up, there would be Pookie, out drunk, and Sal, still dead, but it would appear at the hands of Pookie O'Hara.

When I finished, and Moo finished just behind me in Chinese, they both looked at me.

"So it looks like Pookie killed him?" Moo asked.

"Yeah."

"With a snake?"

Uncle Mao said something. Moo said something back. I realized I might not have thought the plan through as completely as I should have.

"So we gotta make it look like Sal is killed in a way that Pookie would kill him."

"How would that be? Beat to death?"

"I don't know. Wake Pookie up and ask him." So I smacked Pookie lightly on the cheeks to wake him, the way you bring a drunk to who has dropped his head on the bar, but it didn't work. So I pushed the cop over on his back and his head lolled to the side, then I gave him a good slap.

"Pookie! How would you croak a guy?" I said. To Moo I said, "What about Pookie's gun? We can blast Sal thoroughly, covering up the snake clue."

Uncle Mao said something. Moo translated. "He says he sold the gun. You're going to have to kill Pookie."

I resumed trying to get Pookie's attention with the flat of my hand.

SMACK! "Give it up, Pookie. Do you hear me? How would you off a guy?" SMACK!

Moo said, "Maybe we can just find a way to destroy his mind, make him forget everything so when he wakes up he just drools and has to eat strained peas and stuff that you don't have to chew?"

"Yeah, that would be the humane thing," I said.

"Good point," Moo said. He stepped in, gave Pookie a smack. "C'mon, Pookie. You're going to ice a guy, how do you do it?"

"Don't say 'ice,'" I said. "I have unpleasant memories."

"Sorry," said Moo.

Uncle Mao made a throat-cutting motion behind Moo's back, pointed to Pookie.

SMACK! My turn. "Give it up, Pookie. How do you do it?" SMACK! "What's your angle, flatfoot?" SMACK! But Pookie just gave a little smile, and even in the dim light of the opium den I could see his cheeks were burning red from being slapped, but he was not feeling it.

Mao made the gesture of putting a gun to his head and pulling the trigger.

SMACK! "How would you kill a guy, Pookie?" SMACK! Apparently I had some residual anger at Pookie for attempting to ventilate Lone Jones with his .45 for the crime of being black, so I wasn't as concerned with getting him to talk as I was with smacking him around.

Mao tied an imaginary noose, hanged himself to show his opinion.

SMACK! I hit him again. Then Pookie's big paw came up off the little mattress and caught my hand. "No," he said, his voice sounding like he was gargling marbles. "I wouldn't hurt nobody never," he said. Then his hand fell limp, his eyes rolled back, and he was off to dreamland.

"Well, you ruined him," Moo Shoes said. "Now we're going to have to kill him."

Big grin on Uncle Mao, who gestured a dozen arrows hitting in the chest, made the *zzzt-zzzt* noise as each one hit, then mimed croaking, his tongue hanging out.

"We're not going to kill him," I said. SMACK!

"He's not going to tell you anything."

"I know," I said. "But I'm probably not going to get the chance to do this again."

"Good point," said Moo, who took that opportunity to give Pookie a couple of good swats for luck.

"Tell your uncle to knock him out. We'll need some time to figure it out. Let's go get Milo's cab and pick up Sal."

As we walked to the door, Moo Shoes said some stuff to his uncle, and as the old guy gave his answer it did not take an abacus for me to figure out he gave us two more days. Then there was a long exchange in Chinese and I got the feeling that the meter was running as the old guy talked.

Moo Shoes turned to me. "He says he can help us catch the mamba."

"I don't have any more money."

"He knows that. He says he'll do it, but he gets to keep the snake."

"We paid a lot of folding fodder for that snake."

Moo Shoes gave me the inscrutable eyebrow that only Chinese guys can give you. I whispered, "You think he can do it?"

Moo nodded. "You know he's only asking because I'm family. He doesn't really need our permission."

"Fine," I said.

Uncle Ho said something.

"He'll need some rats."

"There's a whole goddamn alley full of rats on the other side of this door."

Uncle Ho shook his head, babbled some bullshit.

"Fresh rats," Moo translated.

"Fine!"

Then Uncle Ho let us out and as we walked away shouted something at Moo Shoes through the little hatch.

"What'd he say?" I asked.

"He says we should kill Pookie."

"Of course he says that," I said. "Then we'd have two white devil bodies and Uncle Cat-Fucker would figure a way to extort us over it."

"That's probably true," said Moo Shoes. "Let's deal with Sal first."

We got the cab from Milo, prying it away from him with a sawbuck and a promise, but when Moo Shoes and I got back to Sal's and I opened the back door, Sal's body was not there. The crate, the ice, all of it, gone.

"You locked the door?" Eddie asked.

"Yep."

"Anyone else got keys?"

"Just me and Sal. He gives Bennie, the fill-in guy, his keys on my nights off. And I had both pairs."

I looked around the joint, took a peek into the front room, which looked like a dark, empty bar—smelled of sour beer and cigarettes.

"So you think someone broke in, moved the body to another part of the bar, then relocked the door on the way out?" said Moo. "Seems fishy."

He had a point. "You have a point," I said.

Moo Shoes shrugged. "Well, that was easy. Can you take the taxi back to Milo, drop me at the club? Lois will probably still be there."

I wanted to say no, that I needed more time to be flummoxed by the situation, that I would like to maybe panic and yell and scream a little, but Eddie has been a good pal and Lois Fong is a dish indeed, so I said, "Sure."

By the time I got Milo's cab back to him and endured the lecture on the hardship I had caused him, the sun was busting up pink over the East Bay. Even the Tenderloin looked like a dream town in that light, like one of those Max Parrish paintings they have behind the bar at the Palace Hotel, where skinny blond kids lounge around in towels like they're any second going to take a swim. I could have used forty to a hundred winks in dream town myself, but instead of heading home I limped over to the five-and-dime on Polk Street.

The place smelled like comic books and coffee and cedar chips from the cages back in the pet section, which reminded me I needed to buy some rats. A bored, round redhead in cat glasses at the register said good morning as I passed by the sundries counter and I nodded good morning right back at her. I felt a smile coming on as I was rounding the corner into the diner section, anticipating feasting my eyes on the beauteous Cheese, but instead there was only Phil, the skinny, scruffy fry cook, standing at the counter with a coffeepot in hand, lording over two guys at the counter with their hats pulled down like they were hiding from an angry preacher.

No Stilton. I took a seat down from the browbeaten guys.

"We got two things today," said Phil. "Coffee, scrambled eggs, with bacon and white toast, and just coffee."

"Can I get my bacon crispy?" I asked, trying to maybe open up the conversation a little, but—

"You can get it the way it comes out, and the toast might be cold."

"Coffee, please," I said. Phil spun a cup, no saucer, onto the counter and sloshed some coffee mostly into it.

"Stilton around?"

"Tilly? Nah, didn't show up today and didn't call, neither."

"What about the other one, Myrtle?"

"Also AWOL. It's just me. So it's scrambled and bacon, you don't like it, take a hike. None of that, run a cow through a windmill on a mattress, extra go juice, crap."

"That a dish?"

"How the hell should I know? Sometimes I think those dizzy broads were just making stuff up to make life hard for me. Not anymore. Today I'm running this place the way it should be. You'll get breakfast the way I cook it and you'll like it or you can starve."

"You remind me of my ma."

He started to walk away.

"Hey, just coffee is fine," I said. He stopped. "So, you know where they might be? Your waitresses?"

"They were going on some big ta-do this weekend. Moonlighting. Make some extra money. Like they need it. It gets busy in here, they make extra tips, you know what I get?"

I shook my head.

"I get squat! And then they take a powder on me? Well, I hope they made enough lettuce to hold them over, because when they get back they're both fired."

"What if something happened to them?" I said, thinking, *WHAT IF SOMETHING HAPPENED TO THEM?!*

"Nothing happened except they had too much fun. They're probably just home sleeping it off."

"Stilton hasn't been home."

For the first time since I came in the anger ran out of his eyes.

"That's right. You were in here to see her the other day . . ."

"Yeah," I said, and the scruff must have seen something in my mug, because he put the coffeepot down on the burner and came back.

"Maybe she stayed over at Myrtle's? Slumber party. You know dames. Myrtle ain't answering her phone, but that don't mean—"

"You got an address?"

"In the back. I'll get it for you."

I'd go see her. In a while. I needed to eat, shower, and sleep first. When Phil got back I ordered some scrambled eggs and cold toast. I wolfed them down. Phil didn't charge me. I went to the retail side of the five-and-dime and bought some rats.

13

RATS

When I finally limped up the stairs to my building, dog tired and ready to collapse, the kid was sitting on the landing.

"What's in the bag?" the kid asked.

"Rats."

"No it ain't."

I opened the bag, a normal paper grocery bag, doubled. I showed him. Inside, six white rats, looking confused, scurried around in some cedar chips.

"Got any brown ones?"

"Nope. Just white."

The kid shrugged. "I guess they're okay. Can I have one?"

"I need you to watch 'em." I set the rat bag on the stoop by him. "Put them in a box or something they can't chew out of easy. Can you do that? It's a paying job."

"I s'pose." He gave me the skeptical squint, like he smelled a rat. "You in some kind of jam? You on the lam, like some kind of stinkin' drifter?"

"Nah, I'm fine."

"You sure? A couple of goons was here looking for you."

"Yeah?" I said. "Tell me."

"Yeah," said the kid. "Couple of mugs in black suits, looked like their moms dressed them alike for church. Sunglasses, like they was blind."

"So what did you tell 'em?"

"What am I, a squealer? Told 'em you didn't live here and I never heard of you. Told 'em I been sittin' here since '38 and if there was a guy called Sammy around I'd know him, and I don't. I didn't tell them nothin', the dirty marimbas."

"A marimba is a musical instrument, kid. Like a xylophone."

"No it ain't. You're a stinkin' liar."

"Kid, when you learn a new word, you can run it by me, see if it's legit. You know, the usage. My ma was an English teacher, so I got the skinny on vocabulary and so on."

"Ah, I don't need to know that. I only say other stuff 'cause you get jumpy when I call 'em cocksuckers."

"Oh, well, yeah, that's true. Thanks, I guess."

"Right, so I tells these xylophone cocksuckers that I ain't never heard of you, and if they don't scram I'm gonna go get my uncle Bert from upstairs and he'll blast them with his forty-five, 'cause he doesn't go for strangers asking me stuff, 'cause he's a cop."

"And is he?" I perked up a little, not in a good way—*a cop in the building*?

"Nah, I ain't got a Uncle Bert, I was just yankin' their chains."

"Didn't they see my name on the mailbox?" My building has six brass mailboxes in the hall.

"They were headed that way, so that's when I made like I'm going to go get Uncle Bert to blast 'em, so they took off."

"Good job, kid." I reached into my folding money and peeled off a buck. "Here, I need you to keep a lookout today. You see these guys coming, don't wait for them to get here, run up and wake me up. Watch my rats."

"A whole buck?" The kid's eyes got as big as coffee cups. "What's your angle?"

"These are bad guys is all. And stay here, don't go wandering off to the pictures or to get ice cream. You get hungry, come up to my place and grab something. But be quiet. Wake me up when the church rings noon. Got it?" The bell at St. Peter and Paul's down on Washington Square was the kid's watch. I figured these mooks had already been here today, they weren't coming back before lunchtime, and I had nothing left.

The kid squinted at me from under his cap. "You in some kind of a pickle? You need a gat?"

"*You* can get me a gun?"

"I might know a guy."

"I'll let you know." I was really hoping I didn't need a gun. I'm not afraid of guns, I'd just rather not have to have one. I can shoot. When my foot was on the mend, I passed some time at the shooting range learning various heaters, but I was in no rush to get into a shoot-out.

I limped up the stairs to my place and fell face-first into bed, still in my bartending clothes, and I was out like I was hit with a lead sap.

There were no English words on the sign on the shop at Stockton and Pacific, but the Chinese characters translated to "Upright House of Harmonious Cabbage." Vegetables were their trade and they traded a ton of vegetables every day. Mrs. Wong was the matriarch of Harmonious Cabbage, and she did accounts, haggled with farmers and truckers, set up displays along the sidewalk, and barked prices and tales of freshness and flavor at customers from dawn to dusk every day. She was not above sweeping the floor herself when her worthless husband, worthless daughters, and mostly absent sons were too lazy to do it, and that was what she was doing today. Her metal dustpan, most of the black paint worn off, the metal polished by dust, the edge knife-sharp after years of scraping the concrete floor, was as wide as a man's shoulders (just narrow enough to fit down the aisles of Harmonious Cabbage) and held two quarts of dirt knocked from root vegetables, fallen leaves, the odd carrot top or tomato stem, peels from sampled oranges, and other detritus of the trade.

The pan was full now, so she bumped through the back door to the alley to empty it into one of the trash cans back there, and what did she see but a large gray rat standing up in the top of the can like he owned the joint. Mrs. Wong was accustomed to rats, she was not afraid of rats, and she was, in fact, taking secret joy that this rat was standing so still and not skulking away, because she planned to dump her dustpan and deliver a devastating backhand with its razor edge before the rat had a chance to duck. She made her plan, and wound up slowly, letting the dirt trail out of the dustpan in an arch on the bricks. Then she saw it.

She was not the only one hunting this casual rat. Beyond the trash can was another predator. A shiny-smooth serpent the color of asphalt rose, as steady as running liquid, until it stood like a dark and elegant dingus of death, taller than her, the rat between them. Fear flowed to action and she and the mamba struck at once.

The phone woke me up. It was Eddie Moo Shoes.

"Where are my rats?" asked Moo.

"I got 'em, I had to sleep."

"Well I gotta get to work. Can you take them directly to Uncle Ho?"

"You have to work? Wait, what time is it?"

"Almost five."

"Damn kid was supposed to wake me up."

"I don't have time to get there and back before I have to start setting up. Can you do it?"

"Yeah, maybe. Sure. Look, I got some things to do. I will if I can."

"Do that. It's the alley off Pacific."

"I know."

"Between Powell and—"

"I know! I've been there twice."

"Fine. Gotta go." Moo hung up.

I had no idea where to find Ho the Cat-Fucking Uncle, so I figured I'd just wander around the back alleys of Chinatown with my sack of rats until I found him. I wasn't going to give Moo Shoes the satisfaction of giving me directions, though.

I threw open my door, expecting to see the kid there so I could give him a good ass-chewing, but there at my feet was the bag of rats. Except the kid had put a little cardboard box inside the double bags. There were air holes in it, and it was tied with a string. When I opened the box it contained six white rats, who were lounging in some shredded newspaper along with a jar lid full of water and a few cornflakes.

Oh, and a note. *You owe me two bits for fixing up your rats.*

I gotta give the kid credit, he had fixed up my rats in the equivalent of the Rat Ritz, but he also had taken a powder on waking me up, which reminded me that he was still a horrible little kid. I could deal with rats later. For now I had to get Sal's open so nothing looked suspicious.

I had Bennie the fill-in guy's number, and I call him and tell him that Sal was off camping and I had business so I needed him to open the bar and work until closing time. Bennie is what we call a *high-level day drunk,* which means that he is able to go about pulling off a pretty normal life while always being about half in the bag, except for those times when he goes off on a full bender, at which point he can usually be salvaged from the county jail. He is a pretty young guy, maybe twenty-five, to be so disposed, but he saw some action in Europe during the war, which set him to shaking and screaming sometimes, so he was generally given a pass. Anyway, he was happy to have the work, but didn't have bar keys, so I arranged to meet him at Sal's in half an hour.

I was happy to be out of my bartender togs from the previous night, as they were somewhat less than fresh from the evening's goings-on, so after a shower and a shave I put on the double-breasted gray pinstripe suit I bought for job hunting right after the shipyard closed. I put on a gray linen shirt that I had let steam while I showered and a black silk tie. I topped it all with a wide-brimmed Stetson fedora I won from a guy on a bar bet and I was in the wind. A player. An operator. With my sack of rats.

I wished the Cheese could see me, looking sharp and smelling only slightly of mothballs. The thought of her was a punch under my heart. I tried to shake it off. I just needed to drop off the keys and get back on the trail, a little behind the game, though, because the kid didn't wake me earlier.

Bennie, the big, blond goof, was waiting for me at the back door of Sal's. I gave him my keys (I kept Sal's set) and wished him luck, told him that he was low on change in the register, but nothing he couldn't work through. Sal walked with most of the cash a lot of the time anyway.

The address Phil the fry cook gave me for Myrtle was over near Fourth and Mission. It's maybe a thirty-minute hoof, but I caught the cable car at Powell and rode it over the hill, so I got off at Market Street only a block away in ten, and I hadn't even shaken up my rats.

The building was built in the twenties and had good times and denial written all over it—ten stories with a pink granite façade and bronze Art Deco inlays of streamlined Greek gods dancing across the cornice like the market crash, the Great Depression, and World War II could never happen. It might have started life thinking it was going to be a nice hotel, but now it was cut up into tiny apartments that looked down on a skid row full of broken veterans and low-rent hustlers. Olympus had fallen on tough times.

I rang the bell of apartment number 403. The doorbell was one of those twist jobs in the middle of the door under the peephole, confirming this place was a hotel at one time. It sounded like the bell on a bicycle, and after a minute with no answer or footfalls I rang it again. I was getting a bad feeling and I leaned against the wall, took a breath, and tried not to let my worry over the Cheese get to me. This was my only lead, and if Myrtle was missing, too—ah, maybe Phil the fry cook was right, maybe they were just two girls having too much fun out on the town.

I was failing to console myself and I could even feel my rats getting anxious, when I saw movement in the peephole across the hall—light, then dark—someone looking, then looking away. The sliver of light coming under the door showed a pair of feet there that weren't moving.

I decided to place my bet, take a chance that what I was seeing was a habit.

I gave the bell another twist, then I gave Myrtle's door a good pound. "Ah, come on, sis, don't be like that. Ma needs you. She wants you to come home. She ain't got that much time." Another ring. "For the love of God, Myrt, she's dying." I let my voice break on the last bit—it was very fucking sad. My rats wept.

And then there was the beautiful click of the nosy neighbor's door behind me.

"She is not there," said an older broad, housedress of dying flowers, support stockings, and slippers, built like she could play linebacker on the tiny European grandma football team. "She is not come home two days now," said Granny Nagurski. "You are brother?"

"Yeah, yeah. But we been out of contact. Estranged, you know. Some hard feelings. But our ma is sick."

"She tell me mother is die three years ago."

"So you can see how it is? Myrt told us we were dead to her. You know how that is . . ."

"Oh I know. Do I know? Oh, I know. Many are dead to me. Many, many." She started to count on her fingers. "No-good brother. Dead! No-good nephew . . ."

"You don't know where she went, do you?" Sorry, granny, I don't have time for inventory. "She leave you a number? Anything? Honest, Ma just wants to make amends before she passes."

"No. She not say. We are not good friends. Just neighbor. She is bit of floozie, you ask me."

"Anyone been by? Besides me?"

"Yes. Is one, young man. Thin. Dark hair. He have key. Go in her apartment, come out with things. Clothes, maybe."

I felt a chill. Thin? Dark hair? "Just one?"

"Yes, one."

"Tall guy? Black suit, white shirt? Black fedora? Maybe glasses?"

"No, is not suit. Is suit with, how you say? Like bird." She made a gesture down below her bottom.

"Tails? A tailcoat? Like a tux and tails?"

"Yes, that is it. Tails. Very shiny. Very shiny shoes. Hair slick back."

"A little guy in a tux?" I took a breath. At least it wasn't the two guys who were shadowing me.

"I think is actor, maybe."

"Why do you say that?"

"Lips is very red, eyes dark, like for stage, maybe."

"Oh." Well, we weren't far from the theater district, maybe five or six blocks. "Have you seen this guy in the tux before?"

"No. Myrtle is not have men visitors before this. Just skinny man and you."

"Then why do you think she's a floozie?"

"Your sister is dress like whore. Sorry. But she go out showing the this and the that." She gestured at the this and that on herself and I started to feel a little brotherly protection for my slutty sister. I hadn't seen my real little sister in years and maybe I missed the feeling of wanting to pound someone on her behalf, but this Russian or Polish grandma was probably not the best target for my protective wrath. I shrugged it off.

"Well, thank you. If Myrtle comes in, will you have her call this number and leave a message for Sammy?" I wrote down the number for Sal's. I figured Bennie would answer and take the message, but better than if I left my own number and trusted the kid to answer. Bronko Nagurski in a housedress took the cable car ticket I wrote it on and looked at it like I had rubbed cholera on it.

"Okay," she said. "I will."

Outside, on the steps of Myrtle's building, I was lighting a coffin nail and trying to figure out what to do next when I spotted a black Chrysler rounding the corner at Fourth Street carrying the two mugs in the black suits from outside Sal's. I knew it was them right away because I spotted the sunglasses on the one in the passenger seat, and while there was still some daylight left, it being summer, the fog was coming in and a guy in shades now had better be playing piano in a smoky club or selling pencils on the street or he would stand out more than somewhat. I didn't know who these mugs were, or if they were following me to Myrtle's building, but I knew where they were going now, and I was suddenly regretting giving my name and number to the Russian granny. Maybe the old broad would mind her own business. I would give six-to-five against.

I pulled my hat down and hustled my bag of rats down the sidewalk and I was into an alley before they could get out of the car. I waited, listened, there's still a lot of hustle and flow on Mission Street that time of night—citizens heading home from work late or out to dinner early, winos shuffling to their next drink or a doorway to bed down in—but Myrtle's building had twin revolving doors that sounded like brush cymbals when they turned, so when I heard the sizzle, I risked a peek around the corner. Yeah, they were inside. And yeah, the trunk of that Chrysler was plenty big enough to hold a crate full of dead Sal on ice. The trickle of water running out below the bumper gave me the idea that Sal might still be relaxing inside.

I couldn't figure it. They weren't wiseguys, and they definitely weren't cops, not unless the cops were suddenly snatching stiffs out of locked rooms and neglecting to mention it to the papers. But then, I hadn't seen the papers today. Maybe I should check, I thought. Nothing worse than to think you figured an angle on something, then have someone tell you they read it last week in "Hints from Herb." I figured I'd grab a *Chronicle* once I was out of back alleys, see what I could find out. Not that I expected to open the paper looking for Stilton and have a page-two headline say, "The Cheese Sleeping Off a Bender in a Rattrap Hotel off Van Ness Avenue." No, if I found her in the paper she'd either be getting married or she'd have gotten dead. The thought gave me a chill. I pulled my collar up—wished I'd worn my overcoat.

I broke out of the alley in the middle of the block on Third

Street—the fog off the bay was streaming between the buildings like a scarf through a stripper's legs, leaving everything damp and smelling of sailors' broken dreams. Some rough-looking guys huddled in a doorway nearby, sharing a no-label green glass jug of something, probably something sweet and strong, fortified wine—four guys guaranteed drunk for a buck. There was a sax man sitting on the sidewalk across the street, his sax case laid out before him, playing a blues riff, mournful and wailing. A lull in the traffic, no streetcar ringing for blocks, just the sax, the low growls of the winos, and the hum of wires overhead. The sax man's notes hooked me in a spot right under my jaw where I was all knotted up with fear and heartbreak and hope, so I limped on over.

The sax man stopped playing, adjusted his reed, smiled out of the corner of his eye.

"Leg hurt when it's damp, huh?"

"Foot," I said. "Yeah."

The sax man pulled up a pant leg and revealed a dark wooden shin. He knocked on it. "Aches like a bad tooth when the fog's in, and it ain't even there. Land mine."

I could see a lone nickel resting in the dirty red velvet of his sax case. I pulled out what cash I had, thirty-six bucks and some change. I threw in the coins, then looked at the money in my hand and threw in the ten and the twenty. Six bucks to last me the rest of my life. It would have to do. Small price.

He looked in the case, then up at me.

"You crazy?"

"Probably. That'll get you a room, hot meal or three."

"I could use a drink. You wanna share a drink?"

"Early for me. Miles to go," I told him. "But you get out of the cold and have one for me."

"Yeah." The sax man tipped his horn. "What you wanna hear?"

"Whatever you were playing before is fine."

"Sad."

"Yeah."

As he played, I walked my rats up to Market Street, back into the flow of the unbroken. I bought a paper at a news kiosk and tried to wrestle it into the *ferryboat fold,* tucking my rats under one arm like a banker with flowers for the wife, and reading from streetlight to streetlight as I made my way into Chinatown.

"Need more rat," said Uncle Ho.

It only took me about thirty blocks of backtracks and zigzags before I found the opium den's red door. A big Chinese guy in traditional silk jacket and hat let me in and led me through the sickly sweet smoke to a back room where Uncle Ho sat drinking tea at a carved mahogany table under a red paper lantern over a bare bulb. I guess the fire marshal doesn't include opium dens on his rounds.

I put my sack of rats on the table by Ho's tea. He opened the sack, untied the box, peeked in.

That's when he said, "Need more rat."

"You use those up, then I'll get more."

Uncle Ho scrunched up his mug in disapproval until he looked like one of those dried-up faces you carve out of an apple in third grade to teach you that time is cruel and we are all just going to shrivel up and die, so there's no point in getting out of bed. (Third grade was my broken-heart year, so I may have absorbed a different lesson from the dried apple face than other kids did.) That was the face Ho put on.

"Need many rat to bring snake."

"There are many rats in the alley out back. Have your gorilla go catch some."

"Only white rat work."

"That's malarkey," I said. "How do you know this, anyway? You sure you're gonna use these rats to catch a snake? Maybe you get a cat or two by accident? Huh?"

As soon as the word *cat* left my yap I was aware that I had stepped deeply into dog shit, as far as Uncle Ho went. He gave me the dried-apple face of scrutiny.

"Brother lie! I only play with cat."

"Right, our animal pals. Who doesn't have a special animal friend as a kid?" I was shrugging so hard I looked like I was trying to sprout wings.

"Bring more rat in morning," said Ho.

"Okey-dokey," I said. "Will do." I saluted, which I'm not sure is absolutely kosher in Chinese circles, so I bowed a couple of times, too, just in case.

"And take fat cop away in morning."

"Uncle Ho." I was pleading. "I don't—Eddie doesn't—" I was stumbling. I got nothing.

What the hell were we going to do with Pookie O'Hara in the morning? Ever? I mean, Eddie and I had discussed that we had no solution to the Pookie problem, but we hoped that something would occur to us before our rent on the opium bunk ran out. "Hey, Ho, we are paid up for two days. You said—"

"Morning," said Ho. He waved a hand to dismiss me, and the palooka in the silk jacket took my arm to make the point.

"Those are first-rate fucking rats," I added as I was escorted out the door.

14

JUKIN' TO JIMMY'S

I did the climb, 387 steps up and half that down the other side, back to Stilton's place, just to check, maybe she came in. Nothing was moved except the note I'd left her. The note I signed. With my own name. What a dope. Someone had been there, but there was no sign it was the Cheese. No clothes thrown around; the shower pan and sink were dry.

I ran all over the triangle around City Hall from Van Ness Avenue to Market Street to Golden Gate Avenue that we call the theater district. Actually, no one calls it that, and if someone does it's because they are from out of town, because it is the Tenderloin, but it also happens to contain most of the grand theaters in the city, and I peeked my head into every one, looking for a tux-and-top-hat revue, even asked around about a period play that might involve an actor dressed just so, but no dice. No one had seen such a thing since Gene Kelly was last in town, kicking high and tapping toes and whatnot. The *Chronicle* revealed no such revue going on in the various clubs, either, so I was left without direction for finding the Cheese.

I headed to Cookie's in search of some tea and sympathy, or maybe a grilled cheese and scuttlebutt. Milo was manning his station, pouring shots and wishing happy New Year to one and all. I joined him at the side of his cab.

"Happy New Year," said Milo. "That is a very sharp suit, Sammy. Very sharp indeed, but it does not disguise the sadness that leaks out of you at the various corners."

"Yeah?" I asked.

"Yeah," Milo replied. "May I buy you a cup of New Year's cheer to help bolster your spirits?"

"That would be nice, Milo. Thanks."

Milo caught the eye of the new waitress, Doris, who was no longer new, and signaled to her with an upraised digit, to which she inquired by pointing to me, to which Milo nodded, and lickety-split Doris delivered a coffee with cream and two spoons of sugar to me at the curb. Which was new.

"That's new."

Milo said, "Yeah, she is a swell broad, Doris. We have an arrangement."

"An arrangement as in dividing the pie, or an arrangement as in hiding the banana?"

"Alas," said Milo, "Doris has a few more years on her than I usually prefer in a broad and reminds me a little of my mother, and besides, she is stubbornly married to a longshoreman who I hear is easily sored up."

"Alas," I sighed. "But her java is top-shelf and just a snort short of perfect." And she does not bust my chops for not taking it black, which makes Doris a stand-up broad.

Milo perfected my cup with a short pour from the pint under his jacket.

"So?" Milo inquired.

"So," I said, and here I considered my position before launching into the whole megillah. Milo knew about Pookie, of course, because we had commandeered his cab for the kidnapping, and he knew we had him stashed somewhere, but he did not know about the snake, about my dead boss, or the strange guys in the black suits who were, apparently, shadowing me. So, rather than endanger a pal with needless details, I quickly rehashed the Pookie situation and filled him in on my short and heart-breaking history with the Cheese, wrapping up that I was distraught that I did not know where to find her.

"Ah, dames," Milo said. "I told you that one was daffy."

And suddenly I was miffed that Milo would disparage the Cheese. "Milo, you don't know a thing about dames. I've never even seen you with a dame."

Milo did not detect my ire, and replied in an academic manner. "Sammy," he said, "you'd be surprised at the number of dames who wouldn't turn a trick in a million years, but will bargain themselves into giving it up for cab fare when it's late and they want to get home."

He was right. I was surprised. The circumstances of Milo's personal life had never occurred to me before. I always viewed him as a solo act, despite much talk of trim and making time that was passed among the gents leaning on the cab. I was suddenly struck with a horrifying suspicion.

So I asked, "Milo, I know you said you know her. Did Stilton ever give it up for cab fare?"

"Nah, she was a hard case. I offered to take her home from the Fillmore for a five-count peep at her fun bags, once, and she told me to jump up a monkey's ass."

That's my girl. I was so relieved I nearly poured out my coffee by accident. I said, "Guess she bargained you down some—"

"Are you kidding, it woulda been worth it, that broad had a great set of cans."

Has, I was thinking. *Has* a great set of cans. "Has," I said.

Right then I would have given a year's pay to run my lips down the luscious canyon of her cleavage, and drift to sweet oblivion in her arms . . .

The Cheese does indeed have a great set of cans on her, but Milo can't talk about her that way.

"You are spinning yarns like a Stiltskin, Milo. No dame ever offers you so much as a smooch on the cheek before you'd run her off the meter."

"No, they would, they do, there are often offers of hand jobs and so forth"—and here Milo removed his hat for the first time since I knew him, and I was surprised that he had quite a respectable head of dark hair—"but it always involves driving, so then I'm nervous and in no mood for romance."

"Romance?"

"Yeah, romance."

"Having a dame yank you off for cab fare is romance?"

"I'm a poet at heart, Sammy."

"Yeah? Me too." I would have given a year's pay to know she was safe, whoever's arms she was in.

We both leaned back against the cab and stared wistfully into the diner, which was jumping with late-night merriment, but by the cab, there was none.

Milo finally said, "So, you track her to her friend's place?"

"Right. Maybe. And the neighbor sees this skinny guy in tux and tails. But I been to every show in town, and no one features a guy in tux and tails with stage makeup and red lips."

"Whoa, whoa, whoa," said Milo. "Tux and tails and red lips?"

"Yeah, like I said. No one sees him."

"But you do not mention the red lips before, Sammy. The reason you can't find this guy is that he is not a guy. What you describe is an entertainer, but the show is at Jimmy's Joynt."

"Jimmy's Joynt? On the Embarcadero?" I'd heard of it, but I did not know it.

"Yeah, it's a drag joint."

"Like Paper Dolls? Like Finocchio's?" Both were well-known drag show clubs that had been knocking it down in North Beach since the thirties. I'd been to Paper Dolls, they did it up large, guys made up like Mae West and Sophie Tucker, not lipstick in a suit.

"No, not like that," Milo said. "Broads in drag. Dressed like Sinatra, Fred Astaire. Lady lovers."

"That's it! Milo, how do I not know this?"

"As a poet, perhaps, a lot of practical knowledge gets by you."

"I gotta borrow your cab. I can't hoof it all the way over Telegraph Hill again."

"Nah, I need it to sleep in it. Kind of forgot to pay my rent this week. I'll drive you."

"But it's your busy time."

"Yeah," said Milo. "I can drop you off, be back in two ticks."

"I'm not giving you a hand job."

"That's okay," said Milo. "I'm a poet."

Jimmy Vasco liked vodka martinis, rare steaks, and leggy redheads. Jimmy had slicked-back black hair, wore a tux and tails, a diamond stickpin the size of a puppy's eye, and spats over patent-leather tap shoes. Jimmy smoked Pall Malls in a long black holder, drove a '36 pearl-black Ford coupe with a rumble seat, and, when the occasion required, carried a German .380 automatic pistol. Jimmy could shoot pool like a shark, tap a toe like Bojangles, and croon a tune as smooth as Mel Tormé. Jimmy was the owner and master of ceremonies at Jimmy's Joynt, just off the Embarcadero, and she was quite the dame.

Milo told Sammy all of this while driving him through a chowder-thick fog to Jimmy's Joynt, a onetime warehouse on Pier 29, so Sammy was prepared and showed no surprise at all when he was greeted at the door by a broad in a double-breasted men's pinstripe suit, not unlike his own, but two sizes *bigger* and somewhat less rumpled.

"Good evening, sir," said the host. "Welcome to Jimmy's Joynt. You on your own, or will friends be joining you?"

"Just me. Nice threads," Sammy said, eyeing the dame's suit.

"Thanks," she said. "Right back at you. Can I find you a table, or maybe you want to find a spot at the bar. I'm afraid you've missed the last show."

"Well, actually . . ." He paused, thinking *ma'am,* thinking *miss,* thinking maybe *buddy.* His experience of the lesbian community was somewhat limited, which is to say, limited to what he had read in certain novels, such as *Gunslinger Gym Teachers of Lesbo Gulch, Jailhouse Sex Kittens in Heat, Little Women,* and so forth.

"Butch," provided the door dame—big grin, more friendly than challenging. This was her turf and she tended to it with delight.

"Butch," Sammy said, returning the grin. "I'm Sammy." He offered his hand to shake and she gave it enough of a squeeze to strangle a beagle, in case he wondered how she came by her moniker, which he did not. "I tend bar over at Sal's in North Beach. Not a classy joint like this. The liquor is watered and the clientele is mostly scum, but the long hours and bad tips make up for it."

Now Butch gave him a nod and a genuine smile—he was in the business. "What can I do for you, Sammy?"

"I'm lookin' for a friend of mine. Friend of a friend, really. Someone saw her with a skinny guy with slicked-back black hair—tailcoat, tux, and lipstick. Sound familiar?"

"This friend of a friend of yours got a name?"

"Myrtle. I don't know her last name. Tallish redhead. She works with a dame I might be somewhat smitten with, who's gone missing. I just need to find out if she's okay."

Butch considered him for a moment—sussed out Sammy's vibe. "Take a seat at the end of the bar. Anyone comes in, flag down the bartender. Her name's Mel."

Butch moved through the club like a shark patrolling a reef, which is to say, with the smooth grace of knowing no one dares fuck with you. Sammy thought that Jimmy must be good at spotting talent and he doubled down on the thought when Mel, the bartender, came over. She was a stunner—tall, angular, and androgynous. Short blonde hair brushed up into a pompadour. She'd be a knockout in an evening dress at a cocktail party and look just as good in a tux escorting a Nob Hill broad to the opera. Tonight she was in the same togs Sammy wore to work, black-and-whites, vest, garters on the sleeves, except she wore a pearl choker with an onyx teardrop under her open collar instead of a tie.

"Butch says to set you up," she said. "On the house. What can I get you?"

"Gimlet," Sammy said, then cringed a little, like he was ordering up a memory—that first night at Stilton's when they drank gimlets mixed right in the bottle . . . "Beefeater's if you got it, but well gin's fine, too."

"Got it," said Mel. As she made his drink, Sammy looked around. The place was dark now, smoky, but it was a big room with a runway stage—lots of tinsel and shine on it. When the show was on, probably all you could see were the entertainers and the stage lights, but now he could see through the crepuscular haze where this was still a seaside warehouse—ductwork and wiring painted black to disappear, heavy pulleys and hooks hiding in the rafters. The carpet was dark red, matted with years of traffic and a thousand sloshed drinks. At the tables were mostly couples, talking soft, heads close together, dressed in suits and dresses, some wound up in each other's arms, others smoking and listening and staring into each other's eyes over dying candles and half-finished cocktails. All women.

One dame at a table by the stage, dressed like a guy, looked up from her girly partner to Sammy and gave him an *are you lookin' for trouble?* glare. Sammy looked away. Not only was he not looking for trouble, but he did not know how to proceed with a dame if he found it, as his pop taught him that you must never hit a girl, especially your sister, even if she was being a pest.

Butch returned from the back at the same time Sammy's drink arrived.

"Come with me," Butch said. "You can bring your drink."

Sammy flipped a tip on the bar with a toast to Mel over his shoulder as he followed Butch through the club to a discreet door behind a screen, down a short hallway made of rough lumber painted blood-red, to a black lacquered door marked PRIVATE. Butch held the door for Sammy. He entered, found himself standing before an aircraft carrier desk made of some dark wood, walnut maybe—streamlined and trimmed out with bits of brass set into the wood—the finish around the rounded corners showing wear from countless thighs brushing past. Sammy figured the desk was about as old as he was, the dame behind it, somewhat older.

Jimmy Vasco stood up as Sammy entered. She was exactly as described by Milo and the Russian granny, except she was not wearing lipstick or a tailcoat—but the tux shirt was there, with French cuffs held closed with diamond-studded initials: J.V. She was shorter and older than Sammy expected—five two, maybe forty years old—but she could pass for a younger guy.

"Jimmy, Jimmy Vasco," she said, offering her hand.

"Sammy Tiffin," Sammy said, shaking, looking her in the eye the way his dad taught him, man-to-man. She smiled, a crooked smile, like she had something up her sleeve.

She gestured for him to sit. He sat. She sat. She said, "So how do you know Myrtle?" Down to business right away.

"I don't, really, Mr.—" He caught himself.

Jimmy threw her head back and laughed, a full guffaw, then snorted and dismissed his discomfort with a wave. "It's okay. Just Jimmy. Go on."

Sammy liked her on the spot. Since he had come to the city he had become used to being the odd one out, but never was he put at ease so quickly. The thing Milo didn't tell him? Jimmy Vasco was a stand-up guy—kind of. He could see her sharing lies over spiked coffee and meat loaf with the guys at Cookie's.

"I barely know Myrtle," Sammy said. "Met her once. She works at the five-and-dime with a gal I've kind of been seeing, and they're both missing. As far as anyone can tell, anyway. I figure maybe they're together. I'm worried sick."

"And what brings you here?"

"Myrtle's neighbor lady sees someone looks a lot like you through the peephole, picking up clothes and whatnot. I asked around."

Jimmy nodded, fit a Pall Mall into a holder, and offered one to Sammy. He shook it off. She lit hers.

She said, "You know, Sammy, most of the time a guy shows up here looking for his girl, he's in store for a big surprise. Sometimes the girls go away with the guy, claim it was all a big mistake, they was just here for the show. Sometimes they stay, and sometimes it gets unpleasant and the gentleman is persuaded to leave."

"That's not me," Sammy said.

"So you got it bad for Stilton, do you?"

"You could say," he said.

Jimmy nodded, smoked thoughtfully—blew a stream of smoke to the corner.

"Myrt, you wanna come in here, help this poor mope out?"

A louvered door over by some file cabinets opened and out stepped the gangly redhead that was Myrtle, gray slacks and a white silk blouse—heels. She kept her eyes to the floor and moved in tiny sidesteps over behind the desk, next to Jimmy. Jimmy put a protective hand on her waist.

"Hi, Sammy," Myrtle said, still not looking up.

Sammy looked from the door, which he hadn't noticed before, to Myrtle, to the door.

"Hi, Myrtle." Then, to Jimmy, "Is that a closet?"

Jimmy burst out laughing, blasting a cloud of smoke and spittle over the desk—the laugh broke down into a cough. She gasped. After a second she regained her composure, butted her cigarette in a marble ashtray, wiped a tear from her eye, and pulled Myrtle close, hugged her hip.

"Why yes, Sammy, in a manner of speaking, I guess it is, but it is also my dressing room, and there's a bed and a shower back there. You know, club hours—you bunk where you can. But for Myrt, right now, that would be what we call *the* closet." She gave Myrtle an affectionate squeeze at the waist. Myrtle looked down at the desk, mortified.

"You gotta promise not to tell Tilly," Myrtle said to Sammy. "She'd just shit."

"She's not here, then?" Sammy said. When he saw Myrtle he'd really hoped he'd found them both.

"No," said Myrtle. "I'm not sure where she is."

"But you've seen her?" The tone of her voice gave him a chill.

"Tell him," Jimmy said.

Myrtle came around the desk like she was pleading a case to Sammy. "Tilly ain't no floozie, you shouldn't oughta think that. We was just trying to pick up a little folding money. And that douche bag guy, Sal, offered us a hundred bucks for one night. Actually fifty bucks, but Tilly talked him up."

"Sal Gabelli?"

"Yeah, guy that owns that bar you work in. He comes on to me and Tilly last week at Vanessi's, says if we go on this campout up in Sonoma, he'll give us a hundred bucks apiece. All we have to do is be nice to some rich guys, maybe a little dancing. Nothing else. So we think, why not?"

"This is the Bohemian Club thing?" Sammy asked. It was all falling into place. Fucking Sal. He had thought the campout was another of Sal's goofball plans, like the dog pizza.

"Yeah, that's them. So Sal calls me, tells me he'll pick us up at my place. We're expecting a car, but what shows up is a bus, like a little bus, and there's a bunch of other girls on it—I don't know, eighteen–twenty, all of them are scrubbed up like farm girls. No makeup or lipstick. Me and Tilly were just in our on-the-town duds and I'll tell you, when we saw this bunch, we both felt like tramps. A lot of them were dressed like Dorothy from *The Wizard of Oz,* I don't know why. But then, on the drive up, which takes an hour and a half, we find out that they aren't farm girls at all— they are all working girls, from Mabel's."

Sammy raised a hand to stop her. "Myrtle, where is Stilton?"

"I'm getting to that. Give me a second. So we get to this camp, and I gotta tell you, these guys have got to have some serious cheddar, because they have some of the biggest trees I ever seen."

"Doll face," Jimmy interjected. "Strictly speaking, I don't think the size of their trees has anything to do with their income." Jimmy gave Sammy a roll of the eyes: *Dames, whadda ya gonna do?*

"Stilton?" Sammy said, bringing Myrtle back to the point.

"So the bus driver gets stopped at the gate, and the guys at the gate get very stern about no dames in the camp. But the driver says, 'Alton Stoddard the Third,' and I remember the name because it is like magic words, and the guys at the gate waved us through. Then the driver just dumps us off in this dirt parking lot in the woods. Don't get me wrong, they're nice woods, but all of a sudden we're just a bunch of girls standing around waiting to get raped and murdered and whatnot."

Sammy cringed and Myrtle dismissed his concern with a wave.

"But it's fine. Pretty soon some guys in ranger shirts or something come down and they go on about it being strictly 'no dames.' Then one of the working girls, a tall, skinny gal like me, only blonde, called Pearl, says 'Alton Stoddard the Third.' Again with the magic words. Suddenly the ranger guys lead us up this little road to a dining hall with a kitchen and there's chili cooking and other snacks and guys bartending in white coats and so forth. The bartenders and the guys serving are from the city. The guys in the ranger shirts are country guys that live in those little towns up there in the redwoods. But these local guys skedaddle and the bartenders are very nervous about breaking the no-dames policy, even when Pearl says 'Alton Stoddard the Third,' they hustle us into a room behind the kitchen which is their dining room. Suddenly Tilly and I are happy we took our hundred bucks up front, which sets off the working girls when we mention it because they are not paid up front or anywhere near a hundred bucks.

"So we are peeking through the crack in the door when the Bohemians start coming in, and most of them are older guys, like banker types, but you can't tell, because they are wearing work pants and stuff, although none of them looks like he has done a day of work in his life.

"Pretty soon they have all split up and taken off into camp-sites, and the bartenders tell us we should just relax until they consult with whoever brings us here. Well, none of them have ever heard of Sal, but they have heard of *Alton Stoddard the Third,* and Tilly says that it's a good thing because she thinks if they don't we might all be buried in a trench somewhere. She's a hoot. What a joker that girl is." Here Myrtle leaned over the desk, so her face was even with Sammy's, and she said, "At least that is what I think at the time!"

"Oh hell," said Sammy, hopeless.

"Baby, don't do that," said Jimmy.

"What?"

"The drama, doll. Don't add the drama."

"It's how I tell a story."

"But Sammy here does not need the extra drama. Look at the poor guy, he's dramatized already. Also, he has probably already figured out that you do not end up buried in a trench in this story."

"Sorry, Sammy," Myrtle said, demurely. She came around the desk, sat in the chair next to him, patted his arm. "There, there, sweetheart, Tilly is probably not dead in a trench."

"But you never know," said Jimmy, like a little ray of sunshine.

15

LET'S SAY, TAX GUYS

Because he was a higher rank, Bailey got to take the feet and Hatch had to take the shoulders. When you're loading a cold, wet, dead Italian onto an airplane, the guy with the shoulders is going to get a lot wetter. Rank has its privileges. The only thing Bailey knew about Hatch, other than that they were roughly the same size physically, was that Hatch held a lower rank. He didn't know his real name, where he was from, or even if he was married, and he wasn't supposed to know. They belonged to an agency that was so new, and so secret, that it had failed its basic mission the day the second guy joined, so, except for the immediate instructions for the mission, which they received from a monotone voice at the other end of a long-distance phone number, they knew nothing about each other. Until tonight, when they were instructed to meet two other agents and drop off the Italian, Bailey and Hatch thought they were the only members of the agency.

Bailey was nervous about it. He didn't trust these other agents. He wasn't supposed to.

The Chrysler was parked at the end of a deserted runway that was the Santa Rosa airport, about twenty yards from a DC-10 with air force markings, which was where they were taking the dead Italian. Sal Gabelli was frozen in a sitting position and had little chunks of ice clinging to his clothing. He streamed meltage on the runway as they carried him.

"I can't wait until this is over and we can go back to hunting Nazis," Hatch said.

"Commies," said Bailey.

"Yeah. That's what I meant. Commies. Sorry. Old habits."

"Down," Bailey said, when they were under the left wing. They lowered the corpsicle to the ground.

Hatch rubbed his hands together for warmth and tried to look through the passenger windows of the airplane. "I can't see anything. Are they in there?"

Bailey looked over the top of his sunglasses. They had been issued the glasses and told to wear them at all times. Evidently, the *subject* might be capable of producing some kind of radiation that would burn the retina and the glasses would protect them. Bailey sometimes took them off to sleep, which made him feel quite the rebel. Over the sunglasses he could see the beam of a flashlight playing around the inside of the airplane. They were in there.

They had to have heard the Chrysler pull up, the trunk open, Hatch yammering on like an auctioneer on truth serum about Nazis and sunglasses. Why didn't they come out? He fished a quarter out of his pocket and tapped it on the wing. The latch on the small door behind the wing turned and the door swung open. A man in a black fedora knelt in the doorway and lowered a small set of stairs, then came down them and joined them beside the melting Italian.

"Clarence," said the new agent. He didn't offer his hand. He wore a black suit, a white shirt, a thin black tie, and sunglasses.

"Bailey," Bailey said. "Hatch," he said, pointing to Hatch.

Hatch touched the brim of his hat. Vestigial salute instinct. Bailey frowned at him.

"Everything in order?" Bailey asked Clarence.

"Two on board."

"Dead?"

"Soon. Ether and Pentothal. Enough fuel to get it to altitude. Just need to get this one aboard."

"Just two?"

"The others are yours," said Clarence.

"Nothing else. They give you anything?"

"Nothing. The general denied it all. He was indignant. The woman knew nothing."

Bailey was at an impasse. Clarence hadn't mentioned the *subject*. Did he not know that was what he was looking for—why they were there? He could ask him what he knew, but then that would be tipping his hand that he knew more. Of course, he could lie, but was he supposed to? He didn't even know if Clarence outranked him.

"You have any leads on the others?" Clarence asked.

"They may be holed up with a club owner named Jimmy Vasco," Bailey said. "We were on our way there when we called for orders at zero-zero hours."

"What about the *subject*?" Hatch asked. Bailey wanted to draw his .45 and shoot his partner on the spot. Blabbermouth!

"No word," said Clarence. "The general claims he was knocked out. When he came to, the *subject* was gone."

"Taken?" said Bailey.

"Well, presumably," said Clarence, with much more sarcasm than Bailey cared for.

"After?"

"Pick up my partner, then back to the Grove," said Clarence. "Mop up and stand down until orders at zero eight hundred."

There were footsteps from the plane and Bailey turned to see another agent coming down the stairs. "Potter," said the new man. "Let's get this one on board so I can get in the air." Potter wore sunglasses, a black fedora, and a parachute pack. Over a blue suit.

A blue suit.

Bailey felt the order in his world spin into chaos.

It was getting late, and Sammy needed to call Bennie at the saloon before the place shut down, but first he had to keep from strangling Myrtle for not getting to the point on the whereabouts of the Cheese.

Myrtle said, "Anyway, all us girls are in the room behind the kitchen enjoying cocktails and filing our nails and talking about the pictures and stuff, and after it gets dark, we start to hear music coming from farther back in the woods. And Tilly says she's going to go see what's shakin', even though the bartender told us to stay put. Well, the rest of the girls could care less, they just want to do what they were brought up for and go back to the city and get paid, but Tilly is not having it. We have had a few cocktails, and I don't know if you've been around her when she gets a little hooted, but she can be a firecracker. You tell her the sky is blue and she will fight you about it. So Tilly and I excuse ourselves to go to the little girls' room, which there aren't any, and Pearl wants to tag along, so she does. Anyway, Tilly finds a back door through the kitchen and out we go. Up into the woods.

"There is a path, with gravel and everything, but I am a city girl, and it is the woods, at night, so naturally I am thinking, Lions and tigers and bears, oh my! Right? I want to head back out to the gate, but there is a Benny Goodman song playing in the distance, and Tilly says lions and tigers and bears do not go for swing music in the least, so I go along with her and Pearl, who is turning out to be a pretty savvy broad, because as we come up on this big clearing with a lot of torches and chairs arranged like a theater, she pulls a camera out of her pocketbook. One of those little German jobs, like you see in the pictures.

"So we creep up on this clearing that is a little lake with about a thousand guys sitting around it in folding chairs, and in the middle of this lake is a big giant owl. Like five stories tall, which is large, in my book, for an owl. But this one is made of stone or cement or something, and they've got it lit up all spooky with torches and whatnot. And the band starts playing this spooky music, just drums and tubas and so forth, and these guys come out from behind the owl in red robes, with hoods covering their faces.

"So we are crouched behind one of these giant trees, and Pearl starts snapping pictures with her little camera and starts to creep up so she can get a better look, but Tilly holds me back, whispering that this looks sorta screwy. Which it is. But Pearl is hunkered down almost right behind the guys in the last row, clicking away with her camera.

"All of a sudden, a bunch of old guys dressed like dames come out from behind the owl. But not like day-to-day dames, but like with the Roman robes and stuff, and little crowns in their wigs, vestigial virgins."

"My favorite kind," said Jimmy.

Myrtle shot Jimmy a tough, *shut-up* look, which Sammy seconded.

"So the guys in drag—and I don't mean to be unkind, but they make for some very ugly broads—march out this little casket they are holding in the air, with like a little kid in it. And the head robe guy, who you know is the head guy because he has a stick, starts saying this long speech about the *cremation of care*.

"And Tilly says like, 'They are going to burn that little kid.'

"And I get ready to scream, because I am against the burning of anyone, especially little kids, but Tilly puts her hand over my mouth and says like, 'Hush, the kid is already dead and they are just giving him a sendoff.'

"So then the drums get real loud and the vestigial virgins put the kid on this big pile of sticks and two of the robe guys put torches to the sticks and that's just about it—I'm going to scream either way, and that's when Tilly gets yanked back, someone's hand over her mouth, and I got another hand over my mouth, then two guys in ranger shirts run by me and grab Pearl, and before we know it, we are being dragged away from the ceremony and stashed in this little cabin nearby.

"Then as soon as they let go of Pearl, she yells 'Alton Stoddard the Third!' at them. And I gotta tell you, what scares me the most is, the ranger guys seem more scared at that point than us. And these poor mugs tell us to stay put, and then they lock the door and leave us there. And we hear one say to the other, 'Run up to Dragons Camp, ask them what to do.' Then they are gone.

"So I asks Pearl, 'Who is this Alton Stoddard the Third?'

"And she says, 'Fuck if I know, but the way his name makes these mooks jump, I'd think he's someone we should get to know.'

"She is a very cool customer, is this Pearl broad, even for a hustler. I hope she makes it out of there."

"You don't know where she is, either?" Sammy said.

"No, that's what I'm getting to. See, we're looking around this little cabin for ways to get out, and it is very ooky, no kitchen or icebox, just a little bar counter, bunks for sleeping, with only a couple of windows that don't open, and a metal latch on the door. And the ranger guys take the latch handle from our side with them. So we can't figure. But then Tilly starts digging around in the bar and comes up with a knife. So I tells her right then, 'You got to stab them in the throat, otherwise they scream.' And she looks at me like I'm daffy or something, and she goes over and starts to work the knife through the crack on the door by the latch, which is a relief, because the ranger guys don't seem like bad guys at all, you know, just doing their jobs. So she just about has it, and we hear voices outside the door, and quick-like, Tilly chucks the knife under one of the bunks as this guy comes through the door in full military uniform. Like a general's uniform. With lots of medals and stuff. And he says 'dismissed' to the ranger guys who bring him, like they are soldiers and not a bunch of Sonoma County rubes. And they say, 'Yes, sir, General,' and start to leave. But he gets the handle of the door latch from one of them before he sends them off.

"So Pearl tries the Alton Stoddard the Third angle on him, but the general ain't biting. He says like, 'Yes, I am acquainted with Mr. Stoddard.'"

Here Myrtle put on a big-man voice. "'Ladies, I'm afraid a mistake has been made. You are not allowed to be here.'

"And it turns out this guy is some kind of muckety-muck general in the air force, and he arranges for us to come up to their campout, which is a surprise to me, because all the time I think Sal Gabelli set this all up. Anyway, this general guy, Ramsey or something."

"Remy?" Sammy said.

"Yeah, that's it. Anyway, he don't seem like he belongs here with those other guys. For one, he's in uniform, and the other guys are casual. And second, he's stumbling around the cabin like he's trying to figure out what to do. Sweating and mumbling and stuff."

Big-man voice again: "'I had no idea when they said no women, they really meant *no* women. I thought that was a ruse for their wives. Well, you'll all have to stay here until we determine what to do with you. I need to discuss it with the members.

I'm just a guest. But I don't believe that will be the case after tonight. Perhaps we'll keep you here until I've made my presentation.' He's thinking-like, pacing and mumbling. Me and the girls are looking at each other like we are at the mercy of a loony.

"So Tilly says, 'What you do need to determine is where our hundred bucks apiece is.'

"And the general says of course and he'll get right on it and so forth. He even checks his wallet, and he only has like a hundred and fifty bucks, so he gives us each fifty and promises the rest, we just have to hold tight. Then he asks, did we see anything of the ritual?

"And we are all shaking our heads and acting like we just woke up five minutes ago and found ourselves in the woods. See, Pearl managed to stash her little camera up under her Dorothy dress somewhere, so even she was acting like she fell off the turnip truck earlier in the evening.

"So Tilly says, 'Oh no, buster, a hundred bucks each, *right now,* or I'm gonna start screaming, and my pals here are gonna scream right along with me.'

"But the general makes like he don't have it on him. Says he already pays a guy, so Tilly tells him okay and puffs up to scream, at which point the general tells her wait, he is staying at Dragons, which is another camp, and has to go get it. And Tilly says fine, but she is going with him, and quick as you please she is on his arm, saying, 'Just you and me, General, you know, we'll go get that money together' and 'We might be a while.' She gives me a wink.

"Well, the general is like he has never been spoken to by a dame before, because he goes all red-faced and shy and goofy, and says 'of course' a lot, and Tilly has him. She can have that effect on a guy."

"Yeah, I know," said Sammy, feeling another stab in the heart at the thought of the Cheese making time with the general.

"So," Myrtle went on, "Tilly goes to give me a little kiss on the cheek, toodles, and says in my ear, 'Get the knife, open the door, you guys run,' and then loud she says, 'Don't wait up.' Then she's out the door on the general's arm, and of course, that jerk takes the door handle with him. So I'm feeling horrible about Tilly, but in a jiffy Pearl is under the bunk and back working the door latch with the paring knife, and before you can say 'Open, Sesame,' it's open. The ranger guys are long gone.

"So I start to run back to where we left the other girls, but when I turn around, Pearl has pulled out her little camera and is headed the other way. She says to me, 'Go on, I got a little side job I gotta do.' And I try to talk her out of it, but she won't listen, so I run down to the dining hall. I tell you, I feel awful about Tilly, but I figure maybe with all the other girls we got safety in numbers; we can make them bring her out and we can all go home. Just a big misunderstanding. I'm thinking this as I'm dodging from each one of these little camps to the next in the dark. They're like fenced off, and some got cabins, some just got a fire ring and some benches, some big tents, but all of them are full of older guys that are three sheets to the wind and going on four.

"And when I get to the dining hall, all the other girls are gone, the bartenders and kitchen staff are even gone. So now I don't know what to do. And there's no telephone anywhere. So I run back down the road, and up in the woods, around the gate, until I get to the little town, which is just a gas station with a general store at the end of the drive. And there I find a pay phone and I call Jimmy, and then I hide behind the gas station in the dark untils he comes to get me."

Jimmy said, "Normally an hour and a half to Monte Rio, but I got there in under an hour."

"Jimmy's a swell driver," said Myrtle. Then: "Oh, Sammy, I'm so sorry. I feel like a yellow-bellied coward leavin' Tilly like that, but what could I do?"

"She's a good kid," said Jimmy. "She was just scared. Don't be too hard on her."

Sammy dismissed the notion with a wave. "Myrtle, can you draw me a map of this place?"

"I don't know, Sammy, it was dark. I was just following Tilly and Pearl."

"I can give you directions there," said Jimmy.

Sammy thought about it for a second, but only a second. "Look, I'm going to go after Stilton, but you two need to know, there are some guys about two steps behind me looking for Myrtle. They were at her place right after I was, so if I found her, I'm guessing they'll find her, and these are not good guys."

"That lousy Sal," said Myrtle.

"It was probably Phil at the five-and-dime told them, Myrtle. Sal's dead."

Jimmy stood up. "These guys that are after Myrtle scragged Sally Gab?"

Sammy considered his answer, the whole snake-and-noodle angle, and said, "They are carrying his body around in the trunk of their car."

"Well that's it, then," said Jimmy. "If these guys are two steps behind finding Myrt, you got to take a step they don't know. You got to hide her, Sammy, in a place where she's never been, and where I won't know where she is."

"I could do that, Jimmy, but I don't even have a car."

"How were you going to get up to Monte Rio?"

"I hadn't figured that far."

Jimmy reached into her pocket, pulled out some keys. "Take mine. It's the black Ford coupe in the back." To Myrtle, Jimmy said, "Pack a bag, doll. Quick-like. Grab the stuff I brought from your place and a toothbrush. Couple of my dresses. They'll be short on you, but no one will complain."

Sammy raised his eyebrows at the mention of dresses.

"What?" said Jimmy. "Sometimes I enjoy being a girl, and sometimes I just enjoy a girl, and sometimes both. You gonna bust my balls about it?"

"Wouldn't dream of it."

Jimmy led him out the office door and down the hall, toward a steel fire door at the back of the hallway. She stopped by the door and said, "North on Highway 101. Get off on the River Road past Santa Rosa. Twenty miles and you're in Monte Rio. That's where the Bohemian camp is." Then she drew a small Walther automatic out of the pocket of her trousers. She pulled back the slide and let it snap shut, lowered the hammer, then presented it to Sammy. "Take this. Loaded and ready to go." He thought about turning her down, telling her it was okay, he had a guy, but then he realized that his guy was only nine. He took the gun.

"Safety there, clip release there." Jimmy pointed to the spots on the gun, pulled an extra clip from her other pants pocket, gave it to him. "Any of those nobs gets near Myrtle or gets in the way of you finding Stilton, you blast the cocksuckers."

Sammy smiled. "You ever think about adopting? I know a kid I think you'd hit it off with."

"Nah, I think the mother train has left the station for me."

"Don't sell yourself short," Sammy said. He nodded to Myrtle, who now stood behind Jimmy, holding an overnight bag.

"Wiseass," said Jimmy. "I ain't that much older than her. C'mere, doll." With that the petite emcee laid a backbreaking Argentine tongue tango on Myrtle that left the redhead still gasping as Sammy pulled her out the door.

16

THIS AND THAT, NOW AND THEN, HERE AND THERE

Bennie the backup bartender might not have been the sharp-est spoon in the drawer, but he could take a message like a champ. He was sweeping up when I swung by in Jimmy Vasco's Ford, around 2 A.M., Myrtle in tow. I didn't introduce them. Myrtle waited in the doorway, shifting from foot to foot like she had to pee.

Bennie said, "So a guy called Eddie Shu calls and says you need to call him or go by his work as soon as you can."

Fucking Moo Shoes. What now? More rats?

"Anything else?"

"Not for you. Couple of calls for Sal."

"Sal asks me to take those messages for him," I lied.

Bennie parked his broom and went to a pad by the phone. "A guy named General Remy calls, doesn't leave a number, and a dame called Mabel, also no number. She says to tell Sal she wants her money and she wants her pearls back or she is going to have his nuts cut off. She sounds kind of steamed. She calls back a couple more times, says Sal knows how to get hold of her." Bennie looked up from the paper. "Sal knows a general?"

Bennie had been an infantry grunt who humped a BAR all over Europe during the war and he never even saw a general, so that is what stuck with him.

"Air force," I said. "Not a real general."

"Oh, okay."

"Bennie, Sal is going to need you to cover tomorrow night, too. Can you handle that?"

"That'd be great." Bennie grinned like a fat kid in a bakery. He was usually over the moon if he just made it through a shift without blowing a fuse, and this being a night shift, with more pressure and cheddar, he was so far over the moon the cow was airsick. A couple of times Sal called me in when Bennie went around the bend in the middle of a day shift—it was a sad and distressing sight. Sal kept Bennie on because the poor mope would work for tips only, and Bennie stayed on because otherwise he would be living in a doorway down on Third Street with the other broken soldiers.

I made a sign to put on the door to alert the day drunks of the later hours, then went to the register and opened it. There was maybe a hundred bucks and change in there. "You had a good night," I told Bennie.

I planned to take the cash and pay Milo's rent so I could borrow his taxi, but now I took sixty for operating expenses, left ten in the drawer for change, and gave the rest to Bennie, who lit up like the Fourth of July when the cash hit his paw.

"You sure?"

"Yeah. Emergency bonus. Sal's orders. Don't drink it."

"Oh, I won't. I know better."

I hoped so. I needed Sal's delicate condition to remain secret until I figured out where his stiff was. Although, strictly speaking, Sal was no longer my problem, and the snake crate was gone, too, so the last anyone heard, Sal was going camping with Pookie O'Hara. No matter what, the saloon needed to stay open, at least at night.

"Look, kid," I said to Bennie, who was maybe two years younger than me, "I need you to take any messages, and if anyone comes in looking for me, you tell 'em Sal is away camping, I was here, and I took the cash out of the drawer. Tell 'em all that." I figured the bad guys already knew anything else Bennie could tell them, like where my apartment was, so no reason to make them feel like there was more to learn. "But you don't mention that dame over there and you didn't take any messages, you got that?"

"I got it," Bennie said, shaking his big blond head like a lion with a flea in its ear.

I bid Bennie adieu and asked Myrtle if she had to pee.

"Nah, I'm just nervous. Where we going next?"

"I have no idea, doll," I told her, because I didn't.

I was starting to get a feel for driving the Ford coupe and it was decidedly easier driving over here from Jimmy's Joynt than it would have been climbing over Telegraph Hill on foot, although it was the first time I had to drive in Bay City fog, and it was like trying to find your way in a bruised martini full of lightning bugs. I headed up Grant Avenue into Chinatown because I knew it wasn't a one-way street and the way I needed to go was to Club Shanghai.

Even at two in the morning there's no parking on Grant, so I double-parked the Ford out front and left the engine running. I told Myrtle, "Anyone comes by, tell 'em I'll be right back and if they don't like it I'll blast 'em."

"What if it's a cop?"

"Leave out the blastin' part."

The doorman had gone home for the night so the first person I saw inside Club Shanghai was Eddie Moo Shoes, leaning on the host's podium, wearing a red-sequined dinner jacket, smoking a cigarette.

"What's the riff, Biff?" he said, by way of greeting.

"You look like you should be hangin' on a friggin' Christmas tree," I said, by way of reply.

"Master of ceremonies went home early with the trots, so I been filling in. You go by Uncle Ho's?"

"Earlier. Dropped the rats. Just got your message. I been busy." So I explained about being shadowed by the guys in the black suits, about them being the ones taking Sal's stiff, about finding Myrtle, et cetera. I summed up with a quick overview of the business with the Bohemians and my urgent need to find the Cheese.

"So Jimmy gives you her car?" said Moo.

"And her dame, both of which are double-parked out front."

"You do not seem enough of an operator to be on the run, Sammy."

"That would explain why I am not particularly good at it, Moo. So, keep an eye out for these goons in the black suits."

"As it happens, those goons have already been here and left. I spotted those *phonus bolognus* tax men outta the gate."

"Tax men?"

"Yeah, they say they are investigating for the IRS. In the middle of the night. Wearing sunglasses. Evidently, to them, I appear to have just fallen out of the stupid tree."

"Did they ask about me?"

"They did."

"What did you tell them?"

"I pretended I didn't speak English."

"I should have thought of that."

"Well, you *are* just learning. Also you are not Chinese and do not speak Cantonese."

"I know eight to ten words."

"*Chop* and *suey* are not Cantonese words."

"Eight words."

"So they keep asking me stuff even though I can't understand them, and I am saying various colorful things about their mothers in Cantonese, but they won't scram. Finally Lois comes out and offers to translate if they buy her a drink and they leave posthaste, as Lois can be frightening when she wants something."

"Lois is turning out to be a stand-up dame. How goes that?"

Eddie bounced his eyebrows in the manner of a guy who has wang-dang-doodled the dragon and can park in the Forbidden Palace anytime he likes, but as a gentleman, he changed the subject. "Why do you think the tax men take Sally Gab's stiff?"

"Courtesy?" I ventured.

"I did not get the sense that courtesy was their strong suit."

"It has something to do with this general that Sal sets up dames for."

"The one you were supposed to pimp for?"

"Yeah. Maybe military secrets or something. Maybe the general is going over to the commies or something. There's not a lot to do in New Mexico."

"Yeah, maybe they have great communism weather," said Moo. "Look, I need you to take some stuff to Uncle Ho's."

"Can't you do it? Your uncle does not care for me."

"You mentioned the cat, didn't you?"

"I did not."

"These," said Moo. From behind the podium he pulled an umbrella and a CO_2 fire extinguisher.

"Why can't you take them?"

"He insists *you* bring them. He said, 'Have the wiseass *gwai lo* bring them.'"

"I may have *mentioned* a cat. There may have been a passing cat reference."

"He said bring a car," said Moo. "So it's good you have a car."

"An umbrella and a fire extinguisher?"

Behind Moo I noticed Lois Fong slithering her way up the runway from the club. Her silver cheongsam was slit up the side past the curve of her hip. She was easy to notice.

"Edd-ieeee!"

"Go," said Moo, holding out the extinguisher and the umbrella. "Take them. Call me when you can. Don't get put in a sack."

"I won't," I said, and I was down the hall and out the door to find Myrtle, sitting in the running car, chatting with a cop.

"Oh, good," said Myrtle, matter-of-fact, "you got them. I was just telling Officer Bill here that we were here borrowing some stuff for Jimmy."

I noticed then that she was waving the car registration around, which she had unhooked from the spring that normally held it on the steering column.

"I told the nice officer that you would never double-park, but it's an emergency and that's why you left me here to explain."

I climbed into my side of the car. Myrtle took the fire extinguisher from me like she'd been waiting for it and braced it on the floor between her knees. I threw the umbrella behind the seat, nodded to the cop.

"Thanks for giving me a break, Officer," I said.

"A fire extinguisher?" asked the cop.

"I said it was an emergency," said Myrtle.

"Well you better get going, then," said the cop. "And don't

double-park in this neighborhood again, I don't care what time it is."

"Sure thing," I said. "Thanks." I started the Ford, ground the gearshift a little getting it into first, and we were off. Then I took a breath.

"Pretty smart," I told Myrtle. Bars and restaurants are always lending stuff to each other, glasses, booze, chairs, whatever you're short of, the guy across the street or even across town will lend it to you because he never knows when he might be in the same boat. It's an unwritten law, and until a place welshes and doesn't pay you back, you live by it. Myrtle knew this and so did Officer Bill, evidently. As Myrtle hooked the cellophane envelope back around the steering column I could see the car was registered to Jimmy's Joynt. "Really smart," I said.

"A single girl in the city, you learn to improvise," said Myrtle. "Besides, I didn't want you blastin' anybody until I'm at the hideout."

"Which will be soon," I said, even though I had only just now considered that I did not know of any hideouts that were not also known to the phony tax men. "One more stop."

Myrtle played Miss Perky Pollyanna until we got about half a block down the alley to Uncle Ho's House of Opium and Snake Catching. The Ford's tires made a sound like we were rolling over shrimp and the fenders brushed wooden crates on either side, rocking them as we went by. A cat darted ahead of the headlights and disappeared into the dark. *Run, kitty! Uncle Ho will have his way with you!*

"This is spooky," said Myrtle. She hugged herself and shivered.

"We won't be long. I just need to drop off the stuff we picked up."

There was a turnout off the alley in front of the red door—enough room to park maybe three cars. As I pulled in, the headlights raked a pile of pink, gelatinous debris that leaned against the wall by a trash can. Pookie O'Hara.

"Stay here, doll," I said, climbing out of the Ford. I left the engine running and the headlights on. I could smell Pookie from ten feet away—rotting meat and ammonia—and I thought, *dead*. I held my breath and moved closer where I could see that he was still breathing. So, not dead. Unconscious and rancid and naked except for an undersize pink kimono, but definitely not dead.

Myrtle rolled the window down. "I'm not sure an umbrella and a fire extinguisher is going to be enough, Sammy."

"It's not for him," I said, but the stench hit Myrtle and she cranked up the car window like she was reeling in a flounder.

Dead or alive, there was nothing I could do for Pookie short of seasoning him for the rats, so I pounded on the red door and Uncle Ho himself opened the hatch—he had to be standing on his tiptoes to see through the little window.

"I brought your umbrella and your fire extinguisher."

"Leave by door. You take cop."

"Fine," I said. "I'll take the fire extinguisher and the umbrella with me."

"Fine! Take cop." Ho snapped the little hatch shut.

And then I knew I had been beaten by the tiny cat molester. I couldn't leave Pookie lying in the alley, and even if I did and the rats didn't eat him, when he woke up he was going to be sored up more than somewhat. I knocked again. The hatch slid open—Ho, on tiptoes, peeked out.

"Okay, but I need help getting him in the car."

Ho made a satisfied sighing sound, like he had vanquished a lifelong enemy or was taking a satisfying whiz. The bolts were thrown and two big Chinese guys came out, followed by Uncle Ho, who barked orders to them in Cantonese. Myrtle watched in horror as they carried Pookie O'Hara to the Ford. I opened the rumble seat and they poured Pookie in, headfirst, then, after I did some yelling, pulled him out and put him back in, feetfirst. The big cop nearly filled the whole space, and his arms hung out over the fender like he was lounging on an inner tube in a pool.

"I need his clothes," I told Ho, who sent one of his goons to fetch Pookie's effects. Meanwhile I got the fire extinguisher and umbrella out of Myrtle's side of the car.

"That dead guy is coming with us?" she inquired.

"He's not dead. Just resting. And yes."

"What is this place?"

I gave it a thought. "Bathhouse. This guy had a little too much steam."

"What are they bathing in, sewage?"

So maybe bathhouse wasn't the best angle to play. "Stay here," I explained, and shut the car door.

I handed over Ho's snake-catching supplies; he handed them off to his guys and turned back to me. "More rat?"

"No more rats. Look, Ho, how long will Pookie be out?"

"Three, maybe four hour." Ho wobbled a wizened hand in a *three, maybe four hour* way.

"That might not be enough. Can you give me something to keep him out?"

Ho made the gestures of shooting himself in the head, cutting his throat, catching arrows in the heart . . .

"Come on, Ho. Just give me a few more hours." What I was going to do with a few more hours, I did not know, but I'd take them if I could get them. "I'll come back with more rats, how about that? It's for Eddie. He's family."

I must have hit a soft spot in the geezer, because he said, "You wait," and tottered back into the opium den. One of Ho's thugs set Pookie's clothes on the hood of the car and followed the old man in.

Myrtle rolled down the window and held up a folded-up wool blanket. "Hey, Sammy, Jimmy keeps this behind the seat. You want to wrap your friend up? It gets chilly at night in just your nightie."

"Thanks, doll." I took the blanket and gathered it around Pookie, tucking his arms inside the rumble seat. Among Pookie's clothes was a set of suspenders, so I clipped them around the blanket and Pookie was all wrapped up, snug as a mug in a rug. I pulled his hat down hard on his big coconut and stepped back. *Voilà!* To the untrained eye, he looked like nothing more suspicious than a dead-drunk palooka trussed up in a blanket in the rumble seat of a Ford.

Just as I was starting to get nervous, Ho came back with a small leather box, such as you might keep a nice fountain pen in, if that is your fancy. He opened it to show me a loaded glass syringe and needle.

"You wait four hour, give cop here." He touched the vein in my neck. It was like being touched by a crêpe-paper ghost, and suddenly I was feeling kinship with all the cats in Chinatown, past and present, as the heebie-jeebies had their way with me.

"Thanks, Ho." I took the box from him.

"Wait, two, three hours. He may no sleep, but will no move."

"Sure thing." I dropped the leather box in my jacket pocket and jumped in the Ford.

Myrtle said, "What was that?"

"Medicine," I said. "For him." I nodded to the back, fired up the Ford, and made a slow crawl out of the alley to Jackson Street, where this time I turned the way the arrows pointed. I did a left and a right and we were on California Street, heading up Nob Hill as sweet as you please.

"There's the Mark Hopkins," said Myrtle, as we passed the Mark Hopkins Hotel. It, and the Fairmont across the street, put us in a canyon of light in the fog. "I used to go up to the Top of the Mark during the war. Bunch of us girls would get all dolled up, go up there—say good-bye to the guys shipping out. They'd always go up to the Top of the Mark to say good-bye to the good ol' USA. You can see all the way from the Golden Gate to the Oakland Hills from up there. We'd dance all night and never have to buy a drink. Of course it's too swanky for me now, but during the war they let us in outta patriotism and stuff."

"Yeah?" I said. "That where you met Stilton?"

"Nah, I didn't meet her until after the war, when I got the job at the five-and-dime. After her old man got killed, she worked up at the Kaiser yard in Richmond. I was over across the bay in Sausalito, working on Liberty ships. She had it tougher than me. I didn't lose nobody close. Bet I said good-bye and danced with dozens that didn't make it home, though. You don't like to think about it, but the odds . . ."

"That was good of you," I said. "Going up there to dance with those guys. A day in the shipyard is no cakewalk. You had to be beat." And as far as I knew, she didn't even *like* guys.

"Yeah, but you get a couple of free cocktails in you, the piano is playing—you got a guy thinks you're the last good thing he's ever gonna see, tells you you're beautiful. It wasn't shoveling shit."

I couldn't help but laugh, then I caught myself, thinking of the last time I saw the Cheese and how I treated her. Myrtle sensed something was up, patted my hand on the shifter.

"Don't you worry, Sammy. Tilly is a tough broad. She'll be okay. You'll take care of her. Look how you're taking care of me. She told me you were a swell guy, but now I can see that for myself."

I just threw a smile at her. Yeah, I was taking care of her. I had no idea where to take her. I had no family here, no job to speak of, anymore—nothing—just a bunch of guys who would watch my back. A bunch of guys who were all a couple of onions short of a Gibson, but, you know, pals.

"Why, you must be a hell of a friend," Myrtle went on, "to go get your buddy when he's been tossed out in the alley behind a joint like that, not even hesitate. Nah, Sammy, you're a swell guy. Tilly is lucky she found you." Again with patting my hand.

I wanted to puke.

"Tilly'll understand, don't you think?" Now Myrtle squeezed my hand like she wanted to juice an answer out of it. "About me? I mean, about me and Jimmy? I mean, she's just about the best pal I ever had—I just love her—and not in that way. It would just about kill me to disappoint her."

"You and me both, kid. That's why we have to get you somewhere safe. Somewhere the tax men will never think to look for you."

"Tax men?"

"Bad guys," I said. I downshifted and headed through the light at Van Ness into the Western Addition, the Fillmore, what used to be Japantown, what the cops now called Dark Town.

17

THE ROAD TO
LONE'S

Every guy can basically be boiled down to what he wants and what he's afraid of. What Sammy wanted, right then, was to find Stilton. And what he was afraid of was that something had happened to her and he might never see her again. What he wanted, if he found her, *when* he found her, was to bring her home, safe and sound, and to let her know just how swell he thought she was. But what he was afraid of was that she would find out that he had not hurt his foot in battle, had not, in fact, even gone to battle, and that she would be in the wind when she found out. He was afraid because it had happened to him before, like this:

Sammy grew up in Boise, Idaho, the second son of a paper salesman and a schoolteacher, two brothers and a sister, pot roast on Sundays, church on Christmas and Easter, Little League, picture show on Saturday, the Great Depression, occasional bum in the yard, kid crush on Shirley Temple, the whole can of American soup.

So, Sammy was about to turn sixteen and his pop said to him, "Sam, you want to drive when you turn sixteen?" And Sammy admitted that he would very much like that. And Pop said, "You're going to need to get a job." And before the kid could protest, Pop saw to it that he was hired at the warehouse at the paper company Dad worked for, and Sammy was moving, stacking, and counting all manner of pressed wood pulp after school and on weekends, which Pops reminded him was a privilege, as there were grown men who would love to have that job so shut up, kid.

Sammy's older brother, Judges, also worked for the paper company, so Sammy figured he had also answered the "you want to drive?" question a year earlier. Judges was named after one of the books of the Bible, as was Sammy—Samuel—as Sammy's mother found great comfort in her faith during labor, when she swore to God that if Sammy's dad ever got that thing near her again she would murder him in his sleep. Sammy's sister Ruth only missed being called Deuteronomy because by the time she arrived, Pops has learned to slip the doctor a double sawbuck to have Mom sedated when it came time to fill out the birth certificates. Unfortunately, this was not before Sammy's younger brother got the moniker of Second Samuel, which caused no little confusion around the house until he turned two and they decided to call him Skip.

By age seventeen Sammy had an old Chevrolet sedan and a girlfriend called Shirley, a sweet Catholic girl whom he was pretty sure he was going to marry, if for no other reason than she would not let him use condoms because the pope said they were a sin (although she was less concerned about how the pope felt about doing the backseat bonk with Sammy in the first place).

So Sammy got through high school, and was just about to turn nineteen when one day at work he was directing the loading of some enormous rolls of newsprint onto a truck, and as Sammy looked down at his clipboard, the guy driving the forklift lost his grip on the steering wheel, sending a loaded pallet into the edge of a trailer, scissoring Sammy's right foot against the trailer, crushing it into a pulp of bones and toes and skin. When he woke up the Japs had bombed Pearl Harbor and his mother was about to sign consent for the removal of Sammy's foot, which the doctors said could go gangrenous any second, but Sammy said no.

"Patch it up, Doc, and get me back on my feet. I got to do my part."

The docs did the best they could, stitching and splinting and binding the foot, and after a couple of months, Sammy was walking with crutches. Meanwhile, his brothers and just about every guy he went to school with had signed up and shipped out to fight the Japs and the Jerrys. Shirley tried for a while to stick by Sammy, visiting him every day at first, but after a month she showed up less and less, always having an excuse that she was doing something to support the war effort instead of coming by. Three months in, she showed up at the house with tears in her eyes.

"I can't do it anymore. I just can't. People are saying things. Awful things about you."

"Things like what?"

"Like you're yellow. Like you got hurt at work so you wouldn't have to go off to war. Like those guys that shoot their own toes off so they can come home."

"But I got hurt before we entered the war."

"People don't believe that."

"What people?"

"You know, people who are going off to war."

"Like guys who are trying to make time with you?"

"No. Brave guys who are serving their country."

"Like Johnny McElhenny?" Johnny had been sniffing around Shirley since before she and Sammy had started going out.

"We're getting married before he ships out."

It was years before Sammy realized that he had dodged a

Shirley-shaped bullet, and that the next soldier in line took the hit, but even then, even when he knew better, the heartbreak stayed with him. The next soldier, which was Johnny McElhenny, indeed shipped off to the Pacific and eighteen months later was significantly blown up on some godforsaken lump of birdshit-capped coral. Sammy didn't know how Shirley took this, because by that time he had left town, over the protests of his folks and his sister, who had helped him learn to walk again and had given him much rah-rah support and *it is not your fault* talk. With his life and shame packed in a leather suitcase, Sammy headed for the West Coast, where no one knew him, no one knew about the accident, no one thought that he was a dirty coward, and no recruiter was going to call his old employer to find out why he'd left work in the winter of '41, but was only getting around to signing up for service in the spring of '43.

His foot healed. There was no arch to speak of, and Franken-stein scars ran back and forth across it like a railroad map, but it healed. He had to buy shoes a size bigger than he'd worn before, but dammit, it would pass. His head, on the other hand, hadn't healed quite as well, and he got himself into a number of fights and spent a number of nights in jail while trying to prove that he wasn't a coward, when, in fact, nobody in San Francisco but him really cared.

"Son," said the navy doc, "there's no way I can send you off with your foot like that. What are you going to do the first time there's a twenty-mile hike?"

"That's why I signed up for the navy," Sammy said. "How much marching can there be? Across the boat?"

"That's not how it works, son. You want to get yourself killed, that's your own business, but once you're in the service, you got the lives of other sailors in your hands. There are minimum standards, son, and you don't meet them."

"Why? I can put in a full day's work, and I can run five miles if I need to. I've done it."

He *had* done it, and the next day he had spent in bed with a quart of Old Tennis Shoes, trying to put out the fire in his foot, but the navy didn't need to know that.

"Look, there are plenty of ways to serve your country without shipping out. They need workers in the shipyards. Smart kid like you should be able to nail down a great job, maybe something where you won't have to be on your feet all day. Drive a forklift or something."

"Yeah," said Sammy. "Or something." He snatched his 4-F papers out of the doctor's hand and stormed out of the examining room.

Two days later, his savings running low, Sammy took the bus out to the Hunters Point Naval Shipyard, filled out some papers, and found himself standing in front of a mug who looked like he was born wearing suspenders and never grew out of his baby-shaped body, although now he was fifty-something, needed a shave, and chewed a cigar. His office door read MAX UTLEY, HIRING FOREMAN.

"So, do you know how to do anything?" asked the foreman, looking over Sammy's application.

"It's all there," said Sammy, nodding at the paper.

"I can see what's here. What I can't see is anything I need. You got a 4-F deferment. What's the deal?"

"Forklift crushed my foot."

"So you're not fit for service. What *do* you think you're fit for?"

"I suppose I'd do all right sittin' on my fat ass in an office, chewing on a cigar and giving guys shit for wanting to work for a living."

Of the many skills the foreman was looking for, knowing

when to keep your yap shut was not among them, so he said, "I may have just the spot for you, kid. When can you start?"

Sammy was somewhat nonplussed, expecting to be thrown out rather than offered a job, but he managed to recover enough to say, "Anytime. Right now, if you can use me."

"Oh, I can use you, kid. I'm going to put you on the crew with the *presidents*. Come with me."

Sammy followed Max Utley, who set him up with some goggles and a leather apron and gloves. As Sammy followed the portly foreman down a very long concrete walk past what looked like warehouses, he thought perhaps he should have mentioned that he did not know how to do anything that required heavy leather gloves, except perhaps building a snowman.

They climbed up a series of scaffolding ten stories tall, until they were at the deck of a ship that was being built in dry dock. Another ten stories of the hull rested in a deep cradle below the water level of the bay. Fountains of sparks cascaded down the hull. Air hammers and drills, grinders and torches, clanged and sizzled and whirred, while great diesel-powered cranes lifted and shifted sheets of steel as thick as a layer cake and as wide as a handball court. From the ship's deck—steel plate waiting to be bound with hardwood—Sammy could see the loading cranes across the bay in Oakland, and railroad cars loaded with raw materials lined into the distance to the south until they disappeared in the mist.

The foreman led him down narrow staircases for several decks, then down ladders until daylight disappeared and the only light came from bare bulbs in cages. Sammy had some trouble wrestling the leather apron down the ladders and was thinking that maybe he had judged the fat fuck of a foreman too harshly, since these ladders were no easy going.

"Put on your goggles," said the foreman. "Don't ever look directly into the arc of a welder. You'll burn your retinas and end up going through life blind *and* stupid."

"Huh?" said Sammy. But he fitted the goggles on his eyes just like the foreman did his own pair and nearly missed the next ladder because he couldn't see shit until they entered a room that was alive with the hiss and zap of arc welders—the smell of burnt rust and ozone, and men doing dirty, sweaty work. He looked around and saw five guys: four working in teams, one operating the welding torch, another feeding him cord and hose and supplies, the extra man running a grinder on the edges to be welded. They were like flashing ghosts through the dark goggles. Sammy felt like the whole chamber was closing in on him, even though he had no idea how big the room was—the artificial darkness obscured the edges.

"Take a break!" barked Utley. Arc welders made a few last pops, sparks settled, the men all stood and turned. When the welding ceased, the grinder spooled down, and the men were just shadows through Sammy's goggles. "I call this crew the dead presidents!" shouted the foreman. He called off their names and each man nodded. "Jefferson, Jackson, Washington, Lincoln, and Jackson Two, no relation. Men, this useless piece of shit is Tiffin."

"Pleased to meet you all," said Sammy.

"Take off your goddamn goggles, Tiffin," said the foreman.

Sammy pulled his goggles up on his head and noticed at once that all of the men were black, and none of them looked pleased to see him.

"And Jones," came a voice from a hatch below.

"Jones wasn't a president, dummy," said one of the men, a tall, dark-skinned man of about forty, muscles in his arms like ropes, gray shadow of a beard peppering his cheeks.

"Was too," said the voice from below. A big voice. "President John Paul Jones."

"John Paul Jones wasn't no president, dummy!"

"That's Jones," explained Jackson Two—forty to forty-five, shortest of them, powerful shoulders and arms, slick with sweat, a pink scar dividing one eyebrow. "He a dummy. His mama drop him on his head when he a baby. Landlord throw'd them out for denting the floor."

They all laughed.

"Don't talk about my mama," said the big voice. "I will whip yo' ass."

They all laughed together, slapping each other on the arms and snickering until they sounded like they were sharing an asthma attack, but they didn't say anything more to Jones below.

"Washington," said the foreman. "Tiffin doesn't know his ass from a hot rock. Teach him enough to keep him from killing himself or somebody else."

Washington, thirties, maybe forties, wore a leather apron but no shirt, as lean as a greyhound, a face as angular as flaked obsidian. "Uh-huh, so y'all gonna give us another dummy? Jones already like having two dummies, now we got a white boy don't know nothin' too? Shee-it." Two sadly sung syllables of disappointment in that one word.

"Teach him," said Utley. To Sammy he said, "Do what Washington tells you to do, and don't give him any guff. He's crew chief. Come by after the shift and finish your paperwork."

"Uh, thanks," said Sammy, watching Utley drag his fat ass back up the ladder.

Washington said, "Well, you must have fucked up extra good to end up down here in the dark with the black folks."

"You sho'-nuff fucked up big-time, white boy," said Jackson Two.

"I have a brother named Second Samuel," said Sammy, thinking Jackson Two might see some common ground.

Jackson Two rolled his eyes. "Well yo' mama must be a dummy too, then."

"Don't talk about a man's mama," warned the big Jones voice.

"Shut up, dummy," said Washington. "Work yo' grinder."

"So we got a white boy on the crew?" said Jones. "I hope he stay. He be good."

"You ain't even seen him?"

"But he can be the dummy so I don't have to."

"Shut the fuck up, Lone. You always gonna be the dummy." To Sammy, Washington said, "You the *white* dummy. Put yo' goggles down and come over here. Don't need you to be the blind, white dummy, too."

"Don't let him talk about yo' mama, white dummy," said Jones from below. "Whup his ass."

Sammy had never been in the company of black guys before, as Boise had a distinctly unblack population, so he was only guessing when he figured that these guys were probably going to murder him.

At mid-shift, the whistle blew and the crew made their way up the ladders and out onto the deck of the unfinished ship to sit in the sun while they ate and Sammy got his first look at Thelonius Jones, the guy who was previously working with a grinder on the deck below. Jones crawled into the daylight like a bear coming out of hibernation, squinting against the sunlight, rolling his shoulders like he needed the whole open sky to stretch in. The dead presidents sat together, eating, drinking coffee from thermos bottles, laughing, smoking, talking jive. Jones sat a few yards away and dug into a .30-caliber-ammo box that he was using as a lunch bucket. Sammy sat on his own where he could watch them all. Jones was digging in the box for his third sandwich, the first two having disappeared into the dark giant as slick as cards up a crooked dealer's sleeve, when he gave Sammy the once-over.

"Where yo' lunchbox?"

"Don't have one," said Sammy. "Didn't know I was going to have a job when I came out here."

"You gots to have a lunchbox. They's a cafeteria, but you can't get there and back before the whistle."

"Tomorrow."

Jones looked at his third sandwich, wrapped lovingly in wax paper by hands more delicate than the big man's paws. Sad, like he was surrendering a friend, he held the sandwich out to Sammy. "Here you go."

"Don't do it, Lone," called Washington.

"You can't feed 'em," said Jefferson. "You feed him you won't never get rid of him."

"Egg salad," said Lone. "My mama put pickles in it. I likes pickles in my egg salad."

"I'll get by." Sammy waved it off.

"My mama made it," said Lone, which Sammy saw was the end of the issue.

Sammy got up, went to the big man, took the sandwich, sat down across from Lone, and leaned back against a great metal flange that would someday anchor a cannon. "Thanks."

"You welcome," said Lone.

"You done did it now, dummy," said Washington. "Didn't yo' mama teach you never feed a stray? He won't never go away now. He yours."

"Don't talk about my mama, Wash. I'll whup yo' ass." Statement of fact.

"Whatever you say, dummy," said Washington, but he and the others calmed their laughter and started to turn attention to other, less dangerous pursuits.

Sammy unwrapped the sandwich and took a bite. It was good. He smiled.

"You like?" asked the big man. He waited for an answer and Sammy thought that it was in his best interest for it to be the right answer.

"Best I ever ate," said Sammy around some egg salad.

Lone let loose with a grin that broke his face like a toothy crescent moon. "I ain't got 'nother cool drink, but they's water coolers on every deck. They got to give us water 'cause some of them boys dried up and died back when."

"Good to know," said Sammy. "Thanks."

"I ain't never had my own white boy before," said Lone Jones.

Sammy took three buses back to his hotel in the Mission in the evening, and three more back to Hunters Point in the morning, a sandwich in one coat pocket, a bottle of Coca-Cola in the other. He limped past the employment office, the only way he knew into the shipyard, fifteen minutes after the shift whistle blew. Foreman Utley was standing on the steps, actually twirling a cigar under a wooden match. Up till now, Sammy thought Utley was one of those mugs who had a cigar stub installed in their kisser at birth and nursed the same charcoal-tipped turd their entire stinking life, but no, he was actually starting a new one.

"You're late, Tiffin."

"Yeah, the first two buses were full."

"You're living in a hotel, right?"

"Yes, sir." Sammy knew he was in the doghouse, and with his

savings about down to pocket lint, he couldn't afford to lose the job, even if his crew would probably murder him.

Utley nodded, admired the coal on his stogie, waved out the match. "We got housing for our workers. Come by after shift, I'll set you up with a place. Five-minute walk to work."

"That would be great!"

Sammy was feeling pretty chipper. A whole day's work and not murdered by his welding crew, a job without much walking, and the prospect for a place to hang his hat. It wasn't going over the top for God, Freedom, and Uncle Sam, but it beat waking up bruised and hungover in jail, which had sort of been his pattern since arriving in San Francisco. He didn't notice Utley's snicker as the foreman headed back into the cinder-block employment building; otherwise he would have put his guard up when he came back at the end of shift.

It was December and the sun had already bubbled into the sea on the far side of the Golden Gate. Utley met him on the steps of the employment building with a key and a half a brown-toothed grin trailing off his cigar like the tail of a rotting comet.

"Look at this, kid." Utley dangled the key like it was a neck-lace pulled out of a pirate treasure. "Your very own place."

Sammy took the key. There was a number stamped in the brass like a hotel key: FF-27.

"Go past those cranes, head right toward the hills beyond, you'll see barracks. You'll have your own room, but you share a bathroom and shower with eight other men. Rent comes out of your pay, but it's just enough to keep the heat and water on, since you men are performing a vital service for the war effort. It's a lot less than you're paying for that fleabag in the Mission.

"There's a cafeteria open first and second shift, and three can-teens where you can buy food and razor blades and stuff. Show them your key. They'll give you credit until you get paid. There's even a pool hall and a couple of gin joints at the edge of the yard. The guys in your crew will show you. Got it?"

"I guess."

"Good. God bless America. Get the hell out of here."

Sammy looked at Utley like he was trying to pull a fast one—raised that eyebrow like he did, which was a gesture that never won him friends, he would soon realize.

"Head toward the goddamn hill, nitwit," said Utley. "It works by alphabet and numbers. You can say your ABCs and count to a hundred, can't you?"

A hundred smart-ass replies rocketed through Sammy's head but he pushed them down and said, "Thanks, boss," and looked at his feet because he needed the job and punching this jamoke in the beezer was not going to get him anywhere but the gray-bar hotel.

"Get out of here." Utley snickered and ambled back to his office.

All the lights were shaded, windows in the fabrication buildings were blacked out, there were even tarpaulins stretched over where guys were welding topside, to keep the Japs from spotting them from the sky. Sammy navigated by moonlight, by the pop and sizzle of arc welders echoing off the corrugated steel buildings, the screech of grinders, machines of industry pounding out machines of war. It was a longer walk than he figured, but as he got to the rows of barracks a half-mile away he was glad. The noise had faded to where he thought he might actually be able to catch forty winks. Once he found his room he could take the late bus into town, grab his suitcase, settle up with the hotel, and get back to his new digs, maybe get some supper.

He saw figures moving in the moonlight, heard people talking, a woman's voice, a kid's laugh. A kid? People brought their kids here? Go figure. On the ends of the clapboard barracks he saw big white letters stenciled: A, B, C, D. He walked an alphabet of buildings, some with a single entrance on the end, others with little porches, each barracks building divided into eight homes. Kids on the porches. Men outside, smoking, talking to their neighbors, sharing a beer. Cooking smells.

He just moved in the dark and no one gave him a second look. This was a small city, and no one here knew him or knew why he wasn't fighting overseas. Felt like the shame should fall away. AA, BB, CC, he moved on, noticing something now as he turned down the lane that ran between buildings EE and FF. Everyone he passed since the letters doubled had Southern accents. All of them were black. Building FF, marked 1 through 10. Building FF, 20 through 40.

Outside of his new home a group of men were playing dice by candlelight—laughing, cursing, invoking Jesus and the devil to bring up the right number. Sammy moved across the lane, thinking he'd slip by and double back to the entrance of building FF 20-40.

"I think you in the wrong place, snowflake," came a deep voice from across the lane.

"Wrong place, wrong time," said another voice.

The smart thing to do would have been to turn and run, but Sammy was not known for doing the smart thing. There were mugs dying in the mud in Europe, fighting all over the Pacific, and that's what he'd be doing, too, if they'd let him. No, Sammy Snowflake Tiffin would not run, dammit. He was not a coward.

"I got a key," he said, coming at the craps players, holding his key up like a badge.

"Let's see," said a tall, thin guy, still in his work clothes, stained with soot and sweat. Sammy could smell the booze coming off of him.

A couple of the other dice players slipped pints and half-pints of booze into their pockets as they gathered around Sammy. The tall fellow snatched Sammy's key out of his hand.

"FF-27. Well, this key do go to this building, but you don't go to this key. This strictly a *no-snowflake* building."

"No damn snowflakes," said another player.

"Give me my key," Sammy said, made a grab for it. The tall man pulled it away, pushed Sammy backward.

Sammy smacked the tall man's hand away from his chest and threw a roundhouse punch like he was trying to knock out Hitler himself. The tall man dodged the punch easily and laughed, surprised.

"Ah, snowflake," he said. Before Sammy could wind up again, the tall man hit him in the mouth, twice, two quick jabs that sent him reeling back, to be caught by one of the other players.

"You done did it now, snowflake," said the player holding Sammy's right arm, and he pushed him toward the tall man. Sammy tasted blood in his mouth, tried to uppercut the tall man, and ended up off balance again. A fist crashed into his temple and a bright light went on behind his left eye. Before he could shake it off he was hit from the other side so hard it nearly spun him around. He righted himself, his fists up, and saw he was facing the wrong guy. One of the players who caught him shook his head, sadly, and pointed in the direction where the tall man was standing, waiting, his dukes up, bobbing in the moonlight as light as a dream. Grinning.

The next punch sent Sammy to his hands and knees. He blinked and could just make out dark drops on his hands, blood running out of his nose in a steady stream. A clattering ring to his left—the Coca-Cola bottle from his coat pocket skittering on the tarmac.

"What this?"

"That's mine," Sammy said. He looked up at the tall man,

who held the seven-ounce Coke bottle by the neck. "I'm gonna turn it in for the deposit."

"Here your deposit," said the tall man.

Sammy tried to get his hands up before the bottle crashed across his head—dodged back hard enough to send him back on his ass—but the blow never came. Instead he saw the tall man yanked back like he'd caught a cannonball and he just kept going, backpedaling until he crashed into the clapboard siding of the barracks. As the tall man bounced off the wall he was caught by the throat by an even taller, bigger figure, who lifted him against the wall and held him there in a way that was in fashion long ago in a galaxy far away.

"Don't mess with a man's Co-cola bottle," said Thelonius Jones. "They's a deposit."

The tall man tried to nod, handed the Coke bottle down to Lone.

"This here white boy mine. I appreciate you don't mess with him."

The choking man again tried to nod. Lone looked around and all the other dice players nodded with deep sincerity.

"All right." Lone pulled the man off the wall and threw him to the ground. The formerly tall man threw Sammy's key at Lone's feet, then scrambled across the concrete to his companions, who lifted him up.

"Go home!" Lone said, and they all limped away, having strained their pride ligaments to a man.

Sammy sat splay-legged on the tarmac, blowing threads of blood and mucus down the front of his coat and shirt as he tried to breathe. Lone threw the key on the pavement between Sammy's legs.

"Snowflake, you gonna have to learn to fight before you take a swing on a fella like Louis."

"I'm not afraid of him."

"I didn't say you was."

Sammy blew a blob of gore at the big man. "Give me my god-damn Coke bottle before I whip your ass."

By the time Lone was done laughing he was sitting on the pavement beside Sammy, holding his sides, rocking, and squeezing back tears.

18

DARK TOWN

Someone had rolled a piano out onto the sidewalk outside Jackson's Nook, a jazz club, and a piano player was trading riffs with a sax man while scores of people were dancing and bopping halfway out into the street. Sammy drove slowly around them. There wasn't a white face in the crowd.

"We could leave Pookie here for safekeeping," Sammy said, throwing a thumb out the back window at the drooling cop. He grinned. Myrtle didn't know why.

"I don't think he's dressed right for dancing," said Myrtle. She slid away from the window a little until her left leg was nearly against the shifter.

They drove on.

Much of the Fillmore had been destroyed in the earthquake and fire of '06, although a few of the grand Victorian homes had survived. After the quake, most of the neighborhood was rebuilt with little wooden box houses, the bare minimum to get a family through until more permanent housing could be built: earthquake shacks. The permanent houses were never built, and over the years the Fillmore had become a slum, where the poorest people outside of Chinatown lived. For a while it was Japantown, until the Japanese were shipped off to internment camps during the war; then, for a short while, it became a ghost town, until housing was needed by defense workers faster than it could be built at Hunters Point, Richmond, and Marin City. And so around '43, the Fillmore filled up with black families moving from the South for work. That's when the cops started calling it Dark Town.

It was still a poor neighborhood—a lot of broken-down earthquake shacks—but it was still a neighborhood: home for a lot of people who couldn't move away even if they could afford to, because zoning laws wouldn't allow black people to live 'in most other neighborhoods in the city. Some people treated those rented earthquake shacks as if they owned them, and turned them into little jewel boxes, with fresh paint, manicured postage-stamp lawns, and window boxes filled with flowers.

Around 3 A.M., Sammy pulled up in front of just such a home. The two windows on either side of the front door shone yellow in the fog, just frosting the tops of some red geraniums in the windows with light.

"We're here," Sammy said. He jumped out of the Ford and headed toward the cottage. When he was halfway down the walk he looked back to see Myrtle, sitting motionless in the passenger seat. (And Pookie, equally motionless, but for different reasons, in the rumble seat.) Sammy went back to get her. She'd locked the door.

"We're here," Sammy said, knocking on the window. "Come on. This is it."

"Where are we?"

"Friend's house. Guy I bailed out in a fight once."

"It doesn't feel safe."

"Really? You're going to *love* Lone."

Sammy coaxed her out of the car and escorted her up the walk, Myrtle clutching her little overnight bag against her chest like a schoolgirl carrying books. Sammy knocked on the door.

"It's kind of late," Myrtle said.

"It's fine. Lights are on. Lone is just off work."

The lock clicked, the door swung open, and Lone Jones stepped into the doorway, still in his tux shirt and trousers, eclipsing the light from inside the house. Myrtle yipped and jumped back.

"Hey, Sammy," Lone said around a mouthful of something substantial he was chewing. He had a dish towel tucked in his collar as a napkin. "Come on in." Lone stepped out of the doorway and held the door with a slight bow, which still left his head above the doorframe.

"Evening, miss," Lone said to Myrtle, reaching for the brim of his top hat, which he was not wearing. Habit.

Myrtle tried to take a wide path through the door, which wasn't possible because it was a narrow door, and ended up tripping over her own feet and into the tiny parlor. Sammy caught her by the elbow and steadied her.

"Myrtle, this is Thelonius Jones. Lone, this is Myrtle. She's in a spot and I need you to look out for her—keep it on the Q.T."

"A pleasure, miss," said Lone Jones.

"Charmed," said Myrtle, her eyes going wide enough to admit a pair of ghosts.

"Sorry to show up so late," Sammy said.

"Ain't no thing," said Lone. "We was up."

Lone looked out to the street before closing the door. "You get a new car, snowflake?"

"Borrowed it from a friend."

"You get a new friend?"

"In a manner of speaking, I guess so," Sammy said.

"That the po-lice I bust upside the head in the rumble seat?"

"That it is," said Sammy, looking past Lone to see if Pookie was moving. He wasn't.

A woman's voice from down the hall. "Is that Sammy?" Myrtle jumped.

"Hey, Mrs. Jones!" Sammy called.

"Mama got up and made me a meat loaf," said Lone. "Since I can't go to Cookie's after work no more."

"For a while," said Sammy.

"Y'all want to come in the kitchen and watch me eat a meat loaf?"

"Sure," said Sammy. Lone bowed again, ever the professional, and presented the narrow hall with a flourish. "After y'all."

Sammy pushed Myrtle, who moved in tiny, resistant steps down the hallway and into a small kitchen where a petite black woman in a housecoat and hairnet was tending to a teakettle at the stove. There was a drop-leaf table under a little window, with enough room for a chair on either side. One side was set with a dinner plate, where half a fork-worried meat loaf stood amid a mound of mashed potatoes that looked like a meaty ship that had crashed into an iceberg of steaming spuds.

Mrs. Jones shuffled over to Sammy. She wore fuzzy slippers and walked as if they would slip off her feet if she dared to lift them from the floor. She fluffed Sammy's shoulders, then stepped back and took a look at him.

"That's a sharp suit, Sammy, but you skinny. Thelonius takin' good care of you?"

"He sure is, Mrs. Jones. Don't know how I'd get by without him."

"Well, that's good. You know I told that boy, he don't take care of you, he ain't never gonna get him a wife. When he was little, he got a little catfish out the crick—little itty-bitty thing. Lived in a bowl by his bed. Well, it done died."

"Wasn't my fault," said Lone, now looming over the meat loaf.

"So you say," snapped Mrs. Jones at her son. "I didn't allow him no pets after that until he come home with you. Boy was so excited, and you was so beat-up and sad, I didn't have the heart to say no to neither one of you."

"I'm glad you didn't, ma'am," Sammy said.

"Now who this?" Mrs. Jones looked Myrtle up and down.

Myrtle curtsied, nearly dropped her overnight bag. "I'm Myrtle, ma'am."

"You Sammy's girl?"

"No, Mrs. Jones," Sammy said. "Myrtle's a friend. She's in some trouble. Nothing she did, but some bad guys are looking for her. I was hoping she could stay with you and Thelonius until the trouble blows over."

"I suppose so," said Mrs. Jones. "Nobody will look for her here in Dark Town."

"That's what I'm hoping," Sammy said.

"Well, let's get her situated. I got church in the morning."

"She can sleep on the couch, Mama," said Lone.

"*You* can sleep on the davenport. She a guest."

"I don't fit on the davenport, Mama."

"You will sleep on the davenport and give this young lady your bed or I will whup your ass, Thelonius W. Jones."

Sammy nudged Myrtle and whispered, "See, you'll be fine. Everybody's looking out for you."

"It's okay," Myrtle said, seeming to relax for the first time. "I like the couch. I'll be fine on the couch."

"Thelonius *W.* Jones?" Sammy said. "That's new. What's the *W* stand for, Lone?"

"You don't need to know. Mama, don't you tell him."

"Wedgewood," said Mrs. Jones. "Thelonius *Wedgewood* Jones."

"It's a nice name," said Myrtle. "Sounds British. Fancy."

"The Wedgewood his daddy's idea."

"Ah Mama, you don't got to tell that story." Lone dropped his fork into his mashed potatoes.

"'Cause Lonius conceived on top a Wedgewood stove," said Mrs. Jones. "Right there in the kitchen where I was workin'. Lonius's daddy, may he rest in peace, just come up on me, talkin' sweet like he did—"

"Don't tell that, Mama." Lone unfolded from his chair, was across the kitchen in two strides, and back up the hall toward his bedroom. "Come this way, miss. I'll show you my room."

Mrs. Jones leaned into Myrtle conspiratorially. "That man had a dick like a dinosaur."

"Oh Mama!"

"You seen pictures of 'em dinosaurs? Just like that. I mean, they don't show they dicks in the pictures, but you know they big. Man like to split me in two. Don't get me wrong, I got used to it, but them first few times—well—it was a surprise."

"You like one pillow or two?" Lone called from the little room off the hall. "I got two. You can have 'em both, you want."

"I'm sure that's why I couldn't have no children after Lonius. That man ruined me. He wasn't tall as Lonius, but that man dick a menace."

"Mama, please," Lone called.

"Don't get me wrong, Lonius got a respectable dick on him, too—take him half an hour to wash it sometime—but not like his daddy's."

"Well, I better be going," Sammy said. "I have a drive ahead of me."

"You want me make you a cup of coffee, Sammy? Look like Lonius ain't gonna finish his meat loaf. If you hungry, I can fix you a sandwich to take."

"That would be great, Mrs. Jones."

"Mama, he said he got to go."

"Myrtle, you hungry?"

"A sandwich would be nice," Myrtle said, more at ease now than was Lonius in his own home.

"I think that why he died so young," said Mrs. Jones. "Just thirty-two. Man's heart just gave out from having to pump up that big ol' dino dick."

"Mama, Sammy have to go save his lady."

"I'm fine, Wedgewood," Sammy said.

"I will whup your ass, snowflake."

"Don't talk to your white boy like that, Thelonius. They'll never let you on the Secret Service."

"Secret Service?" Myrtle said.

"Lone will explain," said Sammy. "Don't tell him about President Roosevelt."

"What about President Roosevelt?"

"You'll see," said Sammy. "Lone has a phone. I'll call you, let you know when it's okay to go home. Let Mrs. Jones answer."

"Call me when you find Tilly. So I won't worry," Myrtle said.

"I will. And I'll check in with Jimmy for you. Don't you call him. I think these guys might have a line on the phone."

"And what was the name of that camp, the one the guards said to check with when you were locked up in the cabin?"

"Dragons. I remember because it fit with all their other spooky stuff."

Sammy took her hand and gave it a squeeze. "Thanks."

Lone Jones reappeared behind them, filling the hall. "I got Executive Order 8802 from President Roosevelt in a frame in the parlor," Lone said. "You wanna see it?"

"That would be swell," Myrtle said.

"You want catchup on your meat loaf sandwich, Sammy?" Mrs. Jones asked.

"Yes, ma'am," Sammy said. To Lone he said, in a whisper, "Lone, you see two white guys in black suits coming to the door, you take Myrtle out the back. If you don't have time, don't hesitate. Do what you have to do."

"Always do, snowflake," said Lone.

Ten minutes later Sammy was checking Pookie's pulse: faint. He was cold but alive. He climbed into the Ford, put the paper sack with the thermos of coffee (cream and sugar), a cup, and a meat loaf sandwich wrapped in wax paper on the seat beside him, then headed across town to Mabel's on Post Street to play the one outside chance that Stilton might have made it back to the city before he charged north into the redwood forest.

19

SAMPLING SOCIAL CLUBS OF SAN FRANCISCO

Maybe it speaks to my lack of sophistication, or maybe it speaks to my lack of desperation, but I had never been inside a whorehouse before. I was not apprised of the etiquette, and I was not in the market to purchase some tail, yet I sensed it would not be kosher to stroll in and announce that I was just browsing, and could I speak to any girls who had recently been on a small bus. I figured I'd come in on the level and hope that would work.

After I parked the Ford at the curb on Post outside of Mabel's and smacked Pookie a couple of times to make sure he was breathing but not awake, I sauntered up the stairs of the big Victorian and through beveled glass doors into a grand foyer, where I was greeted by an extra-large gent in a suit who wished me a good morning and inquired if the weight in my jacket pocket was a heater, which I admitted it was.

"Hand it over," said the palooka, gesturing *gimme* with his hand. He said this with no malice or threat implied. "No guns in the house. You'll get it back on the way out."

"Of course," I said, and I handed him the Walther, which he took with two fingers like he was handling a dead bird.

"Walther is a dame's gun," he said.

"That is true," I confirmed. "A dame gives it to me. There's one in the chamber, there, sport, so you might want to avoid dropping it."

He shrugged like that would never happen in a million years, then locked the gun in the top drawer of a credenza made of some dark wood, with a couple of silver candleholders on top composed of figures of couples entwined in some serpentine razzmatazz.

"Enjoy yourself," said the mug, waving me through to an expansive parlor, where an abundance of Bettys of various shapes and sizes were strewn about, reclining upon furniture while smoking, looking bored, and discussing the current shortage of gents in need of company, of which there were presently none. My entrance drew an eye from here and there, but only a substantial dame in a green-sequined evening dress and enough face paint to refinish a carload of clowns approached: Mabel. I knew her by reputation and description, and she was the only one in the room besides me and the bartender wearing more than her underwear.

"Well look what luck has brought to our door," said Mabel, tossing a lock of strawberry hair off her shoulder. "What can I do for you, handsome?"

I felt myself flinch a little, as Mabel said "handsome" to me with the same inflection as the Cheese, not so much a nickname as a promise. It wasn't that she was older than my mother, which she was; it was the fact that the Cheese was wound up in me like a fork in a plate of spaghetti.

"I'm Sammy," I said. "Sammy Tiffin. I work at Sal Gabelli's place. You got a minute?"

A sneer played across Mabel's painted-on smile. "Step into my office." She spun on a heel and moved in a hula of green sparkles to the bar, where the bartender handed her a cigarette in a long ivory holder and lit it while she gave me the once-over like I had all the charm of a wet sneeze. She said, "You can tell fucking Sal that he owes me—"

"Sal's dead," I said, which stopped her mid-threat. "He was—"

"Shhh." She had her hand up, eyes down, and took a slow drag on her cigarette that she let trail out her nose and the corners of her mouth.

"But he—"

"Shhh," she said. "Moment of silence."

"Sorry," I said. I let her have her moment. Kind of. "Do you want to say a few words?" I asked.

She nodded, not looking up, paying her respects to Sal as if he were the pattern in the Oriental rug.

Deep breath. "He was a douche bag."

"Amen," said the bartender.

"Amen," I repeated.

"Amen," said Mabel. She dismissed Sal's service with a wave of her cigarette holder. "So, Sammy Tiffin, where the fuck is Pearl? Where the fuck is my money? What the fuck happened at the Bohemians? And who the fuck were those guys in the black suits who came by here asking questions but giving no answers?"

"And unwilling to relinquish their firearms," said the bartender.

"Don't you want to know what happened to Sal?" I asked.

"Does it answer any of my other questions?"

"Well, his stiff was last seen in the trunk of those guys in the black suits, and I don't know who they are, but they seem very persistent but not particularly sharp. I don't know where your money is. And I don't know where Pearl is, but last time anyone sees her, she is up at the Bohemian Grove with a dame called Stilton, who I am very fond of, and who has not returned, either, which is why I am here."

"Sorry, kid," Mabel said. "Your girl isn't here." She let that sink in. The bartender slid a note to her, which she looked at quickly, then handed back. "The guys in the black suits wanted to talk to all of my girls who went to the Grove. Wanted to know who and what they saw. I told them that it is their business to see nothing and not remember anyone, but in matter of fact, my girls never got out of the dining room up there and didn't talk to anyone but a couple of bartenders. When they inquired further, Mr. Powers, who you met in the foyer, asked them to leave."

The bartender leaned in. "At the point of a twelve-gauge pump he keeps behind the credenza for just such occasions."

I was suddenly glad I did not give Mr. Powers any trouble when he asked for my heater. "So you haven't heard from your girl Pearl, either?"

"I'm afraid not," said Mabel. "And I'm worried about her. She had a very particular trick she was going to perform. The kid's got moxie for miles—I think it might have gotten her in trouble."

Mabel must have seen something in the way I reacted to that, because she butted her cigarette and put her hand on my shoulder. "I'd love to help you, kid, but I wasn't lying to those guys. None of my girls saw nothing. I put them through the third degree when they showed up a day early and a dollar short without Pearl."

I nodded. "I'm going up there to find Stilton. If I find your Pearl, I'll bring her home, too."

"You're just going to rush into the Bohemian Grove and de-mand they give up your girl?"

"Nah. I think I know the camp where the guy is that Sal set this whole thing up with. An air force general. And some nob called Alton Stoddard the Third."

"Lawyer," Mabel said. "Financial District. Money goes back to before the earthquake. One of those guys who never go to court or anything, just sit behind a big desk in a big office and pull strings. You going to just run up to him and demand he tell you where your girl is?"

"I'm new to this kind of thing, but I thought I'd just start shooting parts off him until he tells me."

"Couldn't happen to a nicer guy. Maybe you put one in him for me, even if he tells you right away."

"Happy to. None of your girls could help me with a layout of the Grove, could they? Know where the Dragon Camp is?"

"Afraid not, but the Bohemians got a map of the camp on the wall down at the clubhouse on Taylor."

"How do you know that? I thought dames weren't allowed."

"Do I look like the kind of broad lets rules like that get in her way?" She grinned, like a boomerang of lipstick and teeth, then she bopped my shoulder with the side of her fist, careful not to snag a knuckle-duster full of gems on my jacket. "Pullin' your chain, kid. Herb Caen did a spot on that place in the *Chronicle*. Described the whole caboodle. He said there was a map of the camp on the wall in the front bar."

"Got it. Thanks." I started to go, she called me back.

"And oh, kid, if during your adventures you happen to lose Pookie O'Hara in a permanent way, your money will never be any good here."

I shook my head. "You know about Pookie?"

"Mr. Powers sent word about your passenger right after you came in."

"Long story," I explained.

"Don't care," said Mabel.

"You won't say anything?"

"Discretion is my business."

"Then why'd you tell me about Stoddard, the map?"

"You know what you learn from thirty years of selling sex?"

I shook my head.

"You learn what a guy in love looks like. You're not my business. You watch your back, kid. Have a word with Mr. Powers as you leave."

I did what she asked and after Mr. Powers handed the Walther back to me, he said thus: "Cinch up your belt and tuck it in the small of your back. I'd have never known you had a gat if you carried it that way. I don't frisk guys, just ask if it's obvious. Besides, you'll never clear that rod from your jacket pocket in time if you need to use it, so best case, you got one shot before the slide jams on the cloth and you've already ruined your jacket. Get a waistband holster for back there if you're gonna make a habit of it. You still got Pookie's badge?"

"Yeah, I think so. Another guy took his money and his gun, but I think the badge is with his clothes."

"Good, you can use that," said Mr. Powers.

I came through the door to the Bohemian Club with Pookie's badge out in front of me. I didn't announce anything, and there was no doorman, just a very tired bartender who was close to nodding off. The place was empty. A big oak bar with a cut-glass mirror, lots of empty captain's chairs, a wide, arched doorway that led into other arched doorways. From what I could see it was a lot of wingback leather chairs and expensive rugs, crystal ashtrays and newspapers hung on sticks in a rack. Not a soul in the joint.

"Inspector," said the bartender, "the club has an arrangement with the police. A number of our members are policemen."

"Yeah?" I said, letting the badge sag. "Where is everyone?" I had really been expecting a lot of resistance. A lot of guys with big white mustaches saying, "*Now see here, my good man, how dare you*" and so forth. What I got is an exhausted guy of about sixty years in a white waiter's jacket who just wanted to go home, eat breakfast, and hit the hay.

The bartender checked his watch. "It's four thirty in the morning, and even if it wasn't, everyone is up at the Grove. You know that."

How would I know that? Was everybody supposed to know that? "Is Alton Stoddard the Third here?"

"I can't tell you that, Officer. This is the Bohemian Club—" He said it like that explained everything, but I cut him off.

I was tired, jangled from coffee, and out of my mind worried about the Cheese, so I pulled the Walther from the small of my back, pointed it at his forehead, and cocked the hammer. Strictly speaking, I didn't have to do this to shoot him, but it clarified my intentions somewhat.

"Why don't you tell me more about club policy and I'll stop you when your brains are sprayed all over that mirror." As soon as I said this I knew he would be horrified, because as a bartender myself, I have had to clean a big beveled-glass mirror like that, and the idea of having to get it gleaming again after a brain spray—well, it's a nightmare. Also, they were his brains.

"He's at the Grove," said the bartender. "I don't know which camp he's staying at. He belongs to Mandalay, though."

This was information that meant nothing whatsoever to me, but since he answered my question, I didn't shoot him.

"Where's the map of the camp?" I waved the Walther around a little as I had seen done in various films.

The bartender pointed. It was right there, on the wall before the big arched doorway. A long rectangle, maybe one by three feet, with a very detailed hand-lettered map. THE GROVE was printed above the legend. Each of the camps was marked off and I spotted the Dragon Camp right away. I tried to pull the map off the wall, frame and all, but it was screwed on.

"Give me your ice hammer," I said to the bartender. He started to shrug like he didn't know what I was talking about, and I shrugged right back in the direction of the Walther. *What do you want to do, buddy?*

He reached into the well and came back with a silver-plated ice hammer, brought it to the end of the bar, and presented it to me, rosewood handle first.

"Silver? Really?" We use a meat-tenderizing hammer at Sal's. He shrugged. *The club.*

I put the gun in my waistband and turned my head as I made quick shards of the glass in the frame. A few touch-up taps to take out some sharp parts around the edges and I put the ice hammer back on the bar.

"Knife?" I said. The bartender started to reach for a wine knife. "Garnish knife," I said. He grabbed a paring knife from a cutting board by the well and placed it gingerly on the bar. "Thanks," I told him.

In four quick zips the map was out of the frame and I had it rolled up and stuffed in the inside pocket of my jacket. I pulled a buck from my pocket and threw it on the bar along with the paring knife. "Sorry about the glass."

"We aren't permitted to accept tips, sir."

"Well then they ain't paying you enough." I left the buck on the bar and went outside.

On the corner, a guy was throwing a bundle of newspapers off a truck. A kid cut the strings on the bundle with a pocketknife.

"Paper, mister?" said the kid, holding up a morning edition of the *Examiner*. I waved him off, but when I looked, a two-column story, above the fold, announced: AIR FORCE GENERAL'S PLANE CRASHES OUTSIDE NAPA, THREE DEAD.

"Yeah, give me one, kid." He handed me the paper, I threw him a nickel.

"How 'bout one for your buddy?" asked the kid, nodding at Pookie.

"Nah, he's resting. Thanks."

Two quick pinches of Pookie's cheeks to make sure he was still among the quick, but not too quick. I took his hat so it didn't blow off on the highway and threw it and the newspaper on the seat beside me with my thermos and my meat loaf sandwich, then I was in the wind.

20

THE NAME OF
THE SNAKE

The name of the snake is Petey. No need to make a big deal about it. And I am the one who has been telling you this tale when Sammy falls down on the job or doesn't know what's what. See, like I said, I know things. My people know things, but I had to hold out until now to clue you in on my part, because really, what kind of credibility is a story going to have that starts with a talking snake? Am I right? Of course I am. I'm always right. It's a curse.

So, before I go any further, since I am giving you the inside line on this story, Chinatown rats are fucking delicious. You're sliding along, minding your own business, and suddenly your tongue picks up the taste of five spices, fear, garlic, and chili paste? To die for, is all I'm saying. Granted, it is much chillier here in San Francisco than I care for, as I am generally a desert and savanna kind of guy, but I'm comfortable when I can find a spot under a steam pipe or curl up by a boiler chimney on the roof. They never look for you on the roof.

I settled down one night in a pigeon coop a guy keeps on the roof. It was lovely. Warm, a little nook to warm up in, all night the gentle cooing, *and* a delicious breakfast in bed. Although the pigeon guy did overreact somewhat when he reached in the coop to calm his girls to find me there, smiling, just wanting to wish him "top of the morning, and thanks for the scrumptious squab." But no, he had to run around making with the shouting and the disturbing grabbing of a broom and I had no choice but to bite him. BITE, BITE, BITE. Pump venom. Well, I gotta tell you, he nearly dragged me over the edge when he ran off the roof, and I was barely able to get my fangs out of him before he took the big dive to splattersville in the alley below. Six stories. Not my fault. I reared up, gave him the tongue flick and the little head wave that is the universal signal for "Buddy, I am going to bite the shit out of you." But did he back off? He did not. Rest in peace, pigeon guy.

Let me make it clear, lest I give you the impression I am just some murderous thug: I do not like biting people. In fact, like it says in the books, unless I am hunting, I will bite only when threatened. Although, I am easily threatened. What are you looking at?

Humans are a waste of venom. You can't even eat them. A rat, you bite him, ten–twenty seconds, tops, he's a twitching delicious snack; a human, sometimes takes six hours, and even then, you can't eat them. I've tried. You get one hand down, maybe up to the elbow, then you have to barf them up and go find a rodent or bird or something decent to eat. Just for the record, I am not the villain here, I am just the narrator.

I gave that old Chinese broad behind the cabbage place fair warning. Fair. Friggin'. Warning. She was eyeing my rat, and then she takes a swing at me with a dustpan? Grandma, what am I, some squiggly kid fresh out of the egg? You swing on me, you get the fang. That second guy in the alley tried to grab me as I slid by, which is about six kinds of stupid, so I was forced to give him a little something I'm coming to think of as *the San Francisco Treat. BITE! BITE! BITE!*

And Sal, well, it is well known to one and all that Sal Gabelli was a douche bag and had it coming. See, what Sal doesn't know is that when they put me in the cotton bag, in Cape Town, they also throw in a couple of rats, you know, to sustain me through the voyage. But I don't eat them right away, because gnawing out of a sack is not among my assorted talents, but it turns out that rats are quite good at that. So, for a couple of days on the ship, we lounge in the sack, tell some tales, have a few laughs, and the rats, to help pass the time, gnaw a hole in the sack. Only then do I bid them a fond farewell and send them off to hors d'oeuvre Valhalla. So yeah, both Sal and I are surprised when he pries the top off the crate. To be fair, probably him more than me.

Which brings me to Ho the Cat-Fucking Uncle. Among the many things I know is that Ho got a bum rap all those years ago. He was only ten years old, and he was actually petting the cat. True, he had no pants on at the time, but if that is a crime, we would all be doing time. I myself often go about sans trou. No, Ho is a little kid, who is just being friendly to the kitty, but his brother, who is Eddie Moo Shoes's grandfather, is a rat, and not in the tasty sense of the word, and he makes up a tale of Ho molesting the cat and tells it far and wide in the streets of Chinatown, so Ho has a hard path growing up, and consequently ends up quite a bit more squirrelly than he might have from a childishly misguided session of kitty-fuck. Thus I was willing to give Ho a pass if he did not perpetrate these current hijinks.

See, I am having a pleasant early-morning slide down the very alley where I find it necessary to croak the cabbage broad, minding my own business, when suddenly I pick up a tongueful of rat panic. It comes from above, so I take a gander over the top of some trash barrels, five or six of them arranged in a bunch, and each barrel full to the top with various paper and vegetable trimmings and other detritus of the restaurant trade, which rats find attractive indeed, although I would not give a forked squirt of snake spit for all six barrelsful. But what do I spy above the bok choy and carrot tops but six white rats, thrashing about on tethers, emanating many smells of distress and other delicious flavors, and I assume squeaking to beat the band, but I cannot say for sure, as I am more than somewhat deaf, myself, although the vibrations I pick up across the trash seem to be saying, "Eat me, please, as I am deeply delicious."

So, cautiously I make my move, coming in from the side for the closest rat, for although these morsels are tethered in a star pattern, I do not care to get bitten because I am careless. So close, closer, and BOOM! BITE. BITE. BITE. And the first guy is off to never-never land. I will move on to his pals and allow him to twitch and tenderize for a bit, which is an added benefit of venom. But as I am going for the second rat, he rises up, as do all of his pals, and at the center of the star pattern there is a big bell-shaped straw gardener's hat, such as Japanese guys sometimes wear, with eyeholes cut in it. In a twitch, I see that the rats are tied to the ends of the long, bare ribs of what used to be an umbrella, and the ribs of the umbrella are attached to the crown of the hat, and under the hat is a guy, who is none other than Ho the Cat-Fucking Uncle, who has been crouching in the middle barrel.

Oh Ho, you have been unjustly maligned, you have been an outcast from your family over a falsehood, but I will give you absolution, cat fucker. I will give you a seat by your ancestors.

Where to bite? Where to bite? That straw hat will catch my fangs before they make purchase.

Out of his barrel Ho brings something round, points it at me—a mouth as wide as a blunderbuss. Not a gun, a fire extinguisher. Time to bolt. But it's cold. Colder than I've ever been.

Colder than I knew it could be. Something's slipped over my head, holding me, choking me. BITE! BITE! BITE! I hit nothing. So cold. Can barely move. Ho, you dirty son of a bitch, you got me.

I shoulda seen it coming. The CO_2 fire extinguisher slowing me down. So cold! I should have known. Because I know things. My people know things.

Hatch drove, while Bailey, in the passenger seat, transcribed his notes by dome light from his pocket notebook onto a legal pad in disappearing ink. After each sheet of his pocket notebook was transcribed, he tore it out, lit it with a Zippo, and held it at the edges as long as he could without burning his fingers, then dropped it in the ashtray. (Sometimes he let it burn the tips of his fingers.) The ink on the legal pad would remain visible for only five minutes, so there was no second draft. The completed report would be put in a waterproof envelope and left in a dead drop specified by the voice on the phone. Later it would be retrieved and couriered to Washington, where an agent with clearance would develop the invisible ink, and read every other word to a blindfolded typist. Later another typist typed every other, other word, after which the original would be burned and the ashes flushed down the can, then the entire assembled typescript would be marked TOP SECRET, every word redacted except for conjunctions, and the whole thing filed in a locked cabinet in a locked room to which someone, presumably, had a key.

Bailey was most nervous when writing the actual report, because it was then that Hatch might see something that he hadn't previously known about and start asking questions.

Bailey wrote: *Body was packed in ice, in a crate, but upon exam-*

ination showed signs of having been injected with some kind of poison. Agent determined that examination of the body by a coroner might present a security risk to the project—

"Why did we need to send the Italian up in the plane with the general?" asked Hatch. "Clearly someone else killed him and was going to dispose of the body."

Bailey snapped off the dome light, annoyed. He hadn't mentioned the marks on Sal Gabelli's neck and Hatch hadn't noticed them. "Containment," Bailey said. "Gabelli was one of the general's connections here. We don't know how much he knew. Orders were to tie up the connection by putting them together. A murder would be investigated. A plane crash is just an accident."

It was the longest speech Bailey had ever shared with Hatch, and he felt something. Was it shame? Still, he wasn't clear, himself, why they had transported the body, and he knew more about this operation than Hatch.

"But why the woman? Clarence and Potter said she didn't know anything. Why put her on the plane?"

"Orders," Bailey said. He didn't know why. The general, well, had opened a ridiculous hole in security that had to be closed, but some good-time girl? Now Hatch had him questioning orders, which you don't do.

A minute passed. Hatch said, "Won't whoever really killed Sal Gabelli know he didn't die in a plane crash?"

Bailey thought. "That is a hole that will need to be filled." He checked his watch. "We call in for orders in three hours. Best not to ask questions."

Two minutes passed. Bailey flipped the dome light back on, resumed work on his report. The previous text had disappeared. He couldn't remember where he had left off. What had he written? He flipped the dome light off.

Hatch said, "Done with the report?"

"Yes," Bailey said.

Hatch had noticed that Bailey had written less than half a page. A lot more than half a page had happened.

"I'm having trouble seeing the road for some reason," Hatch said.

"You're wearing your sunglasses," said Bailey. "It's night. Take them off."

"What about radiation?"

"It's only a theory."

Hatch removed his sunglasses, sighed in relief.

Five minutes ticked away. Cars passed, just moving lights and a *whoosh* as they went by. Fingerlings of fog were leaking into the valleys from the bay, still forty minutes away. They washed over the car like flights of ghosts.

Hatch said, "Hey, you ever feel like you might just be the construct of an unyielding, all-seeing bureaucracy beyond our perception that is molding humanity to its own will and pleasure?"

All the time, Bailey thought. *Sometimes when you're sleeping, Hatch, I sneak away and call my wife, look at a picture of us together while she says my real name, over and over, just to confirm that I really exist.*

"No," Bailey said.

Hatch nodded, drove in silence for a while, then said, "Ever think we might be just pieces in a self-building, evolving machine, forming itself to crush the human spirit?"

Every goddamn day, Bailey thought. "Pie," he said. "When you start to thinking that way, think about pie. Your favorite kind. Pie is real; everything else is your mind trying to trick you."

"What's your favorite kind of pie?" Hatch asked.

"I can't tell you that," said Bailey.

They drove in silence for ten minutes. A sign said "City of Novato" but there was no town there, just a road.

Hatch said, "I've never met a lesbian before."

"Shut up, Hatch," Bailey said. "Just shut the fuck up."

Hatch drove.

Blueberry, Bailey thought.

The entire town of Monte Rio consisted of a gas station and a tire-flattened raccoon. At a quarter to six in the morning, the raccoon was the liveliest thing about it. First thing I saw was a sign carved in wood, school bus yellow against outhouse brown, with an arrow: BOHEMIAN GROVE. So my top-notch detective work of getting directions from Jimmy Vasco was paying off. From the River Road, so called because it runs along the Russian River, I could see the little gatehouse with a guy dozing behind the glass, so just driving in was not an option. Even if I could bluff my way past the guard, explaining the unconscious cop in the rumble seat might get sticky.

I parked the Ford by a bin of old tires behind the two-pump gas station, unwrapped the blanket around Pookie, then gave him a couple of slaps to make sure he wasn't waking up. I still had an hour or so, I figured, based on Uncle Ho's instructions, before I had to jab him with the rest of the heroin, so I pushed him as far down in the rumble seat as I could manage and covered his head with the blanket so he didn't attract attention and also so the blanket would soak up most of his drool so there wouldn't be a stream running down the side of the car.

A quick check of the map. Looked like this Dragon camp was maybe three or four hundred yards up the road into the Grove. If the Cheese was there, I figured, I should be able to get in, get her, and get out—a half hour, tops. If she wasn't there, well, I didn't know. Maybe I'd start blasting guys until someone told me where she was and save one for myself in case I found out the worst about the plane crash I read about in the *Examiner*. It couldn't be her. (Yeah, I read the story by the dome light on my way up. That guy I ran off the road outside Petaluma had no business driving at that hour of the morning and *needed* a roadside rest. Probably.)

I crossed the River Road in a crouch, sneaky-like, and made my way into the woods about fifty yards parallel to the camp road. Myrtle was right, these were some heavyweight trees indeed. The bonus of which was, unlike the woods in Idaho where I grew up, there was almost no undergrowth, so even in street shoes and a suit, and with a bum foot, making my way through this forest was a piece of cake. All due respect to Mr. Powers, the doorman at Mabel's, though, you can't tramp through the woods with a gun in your waistband, unless you got a boiler like Pookie's and a seat cushion to match to hold it up, but on a lean guy like me, it slid down my leg, so I put it in my jacket pocket until further notice. In the city, on smooth ground, yeah, he had a point.

I skated along the camps, most of them fenced off with split rails, to mark territory only, as split-rail fences are less than useless in keeping out skunks, bears, weasels, and even the random guy sneaking in from the city. There were big army wall tents in some camps, others had permanent cabins, but none of these nobs was sleeping outside on the ground like real campers. Real campsites, I am told, seldom come with waiters, bartenders, and a staff of private park rangers, but then, I do not hob among the nobs. What campfires might have raged the night before were only smoldering now. The only stirring was the occasional fat guy stumbling out of a tent to have a sleepy whiz against a giant redwood.

I passed a big log building that the map said was the dining hall—trash cans out back and a couple of surplus ice machines chugging away under an awning. I crouched behind a tree that was as big around as a small house and checked my map again. The camps had names like Claimjumpers, and Rough Riders, and other unlikely monikers as were probably bestowed by a banker from Nob Hill imagining he was on an adventure. Dragons was only four camps up. Through the trees I could see a couple of little log cabins, a light on in one of the windows, which was small enough to be considered a gunport. There was also a mug in a ranger-type shirt standing by the front door of that cabin. Why would the Bohemians have a guy guarding a cabin unless there was something in there of value? I hoped that thing was the Cheese.

I dodged from tree to tree until I was just outside the camp. With the cabin between me and the guard, I slid between the rails and got up against the wall by the window. A quick peek and my heart went drum solo—the Cheese—sitting in the corner, party dress, surprise hair—looking like she was about to doze off. I didn't see the Pearl dame. In fact, I couldn't see anyone else in there, so I assumed the Bohemians were just using this as their dame stockade and they were doing their sleeping in the other cabins. I just had to take care of the guy by the door.

I could pull the Walther on him, but if he yelled, I'd have to shoot a lot of guys, which I did not wish to do, so I figured I would sap him into nap-land. He was not a big guy—about my size, which is to say average—so I figured I could maybe knock him out, but for all the trees and campfires, there was not one piece of firewood suitable for bludgeoning anywhere in sight. Now, during my boxing training, Lone Jones admonished me on many occasions to never hit a guy in the head with my fists if I could help it, as fingers break easier than a guy's coconut, but in this case I had nothing but the Walther, and while it would do fine to ventilate a mug most dead, I was not sure about its sap potential. It is not a large pistol and given how many times I had to hit Pookie with the .45, which was much more substantial, I figured I would have to put this guy's lights out with my own dukes.

"But I have seen you hit a guy with your fists, Lone," I told him back then.

"Sho', me, but you can't hit nobody with them little ol' bunny hands," Lone said. "You need to find you a brick or somethin'."

To appease my teacher, I slipped my belt out of the loops and wrapped it around my knuckles to protect and serve.

I slid under the window and along the wall, and I got a good bead on the guard, as I could just see the tip of his nose around the corner. I took a deep breath and came around the corner in a full haymaker swing, my whole body in it, and the poor ranger guy must have heard my breath, because he turned into the punch. I caught him right between the eyes and he completely changed direction, his head snapping back and hitting the doorjamb. He went down like his bones had liquefied.

Before I even got a chance to try the door, it opened, and there stood another medium-sized guy in a ranger shirt, freckled face with a red brush cut. "What did you do to Jeff?" he said, looking at his downed buddy.

Where this guy came from, I did not know, because he was not visible from the window. I didn't know whether to clock him or go for the gun in my jacket pocket. I started to go for the gun, since I was sort of bunched up with the knocked-out Jeff at my feet. But I forgot I still had my belt around my right hand, so I couldn't get my hand in my pocket. I started to panic, thinking the new guy was going to knock my block off, when the Cheese pulled him back.

"I'll handle this, Rusty," said the Cheese. "I know this bum." Then, to me, she said, "Sammy, what are you doing to Jeff?"

"I'm not doing anything," I said, and only then did I realize that without my belt, my pants had fallen down to my knees, and I was standing there in my boxers and a suit coat, with my belt uncoiling from my right hand. So, yes, I was doing something. I was panicking.

"What do you mean, nothing? It looks like if we didn't open the door you'd be giving Jeff here the razzmatazz." She looked over her shoulder at the ranger guy called Rusty. "And believe me, tomorrow poor Jeff would be crying in his coffee and this bum would be down the road."

"I would not. I did not. I don't even know Jeff."

"That's just like you, Sammy. Have your way with poor Jeff and don't even get his name."

I finally threw my belt over my shoulder and pulled up my trousers. "I'm here to rescue you." I pulled the gun. Pointed it at Rusty.

"Why do you have a gun?" asked the Cheese.

"Because I'm here to rescue you."

"I do not need to be rescued," she said.

"Yes you do. These guys are holding you prisoner."

"No, they aren't." She turned to Rusty. "Are you?"

He looked embarrassed. The ginger's skin was nearly transparent except for the freckles, so he couldn't hide that he was blushing. "Sort of," he said.

"You said we were just waiting for some guys."

"Yeah," said Rusty, talking to his shoes now, completely forgetting I had a heater trained on him. "But those government guys who went away with the general told us if we found you we were supposed to keep you here until they got back. Mr. Stoddard told us to do whatever they said."

The Cheese looked at me, shrugged. "Well, thanks, tiger, I guess I do need to be rescued. Keep the gun on Rusty, he's shiftier than he looks." Then she stepped over knocked-out Jeff, threw her arms around my neck, and gave me a very big-league smooch, as one might expect as thanks for having pulled off a rescue. She smelled of gin and cupcakes, and while that was mysterious in itself, I figured I would ask her about it later. I kept one eye on Rusty while trying to return the Cheese's smooch with similar enthusiasm, despite the distraction.

"Is Jeff going to be all right?" Rusty asked.

"Yeah, if I don't shoot you both. Now get in there. Over against the wall." He did. I handed the Walther to Stilton. "Here, doll, hold this on Rusty. If he moves, shoot him. The safety is off. Just squeeze the trigger."

"I don't know . . ." The Cheese was reluctant.

"You don't have to kill him. Just shoot his dick off or something."

With that, I had Rusty's full attention, and he stood against the wall so hard he started to merge with the logs. I put on my belt, then grabbed Jeff under the armpits and dragged him inside. He groaned a little, which was a good sign, because killing a guy in a ranger shirt would have consequences, even if it was by accident.

I took the gun from the Cheese and backed away. "Rusty, you got any rope?"

"Nope," said Rusty.

"That's too bad. I was going to just tie you guys up, but since you don't have any rope, I'm going to have to shoot you."

"There's a box around the side of the cabin with tent stakes and rope," said Rusty. "You can use my flashlight."

He nodded to the flashlight on a hall tree by the door. (Who brings a hall tree to a campout? In fact, this whole cabin was somewhat nicer than my apartment, which I consider more civilized than a campout.)

"Got it," said the Cheese. She grabbed the flashlight and was out the door in a blink. I could hear her rummaging around in a box outside, and before I could get any more of the skinny out of Rusty, she was back with a coil of cotton rope such as one might use to secure a tent or tie up a couple of ranger guys.

"Can I tie them up?" asked the Cheese, bouncing on her toes. She was pretty perky for a dame who had been up all night, but then, so had I, and I was feeling pretty awake myself.

I was conflicted, but I figured less could go wrong than if I let her hold the gun, and I really didn't want to touch Jeff now that she had made it weird. "Yeah, tie up Jeff and we'll see how you do. Then I'll just shoot Rusty."

"Hey," said Rusty.

"But see how much better you're gonna feel about getting tied up, huh?" I said, from the sunny side of the street. "So, Rusty, these guys that went away with the general? Black suits? Black hats?"

"Yeah. And sunglasses. And it was dark. I don't think they could see very well."

"They say when they'd be back?"

"Just before morning. They just said that if we found this dame we were to hold on to her until they got back."

It was no longer *before* morning, and I was not feeling good about our timing. "Rusty, they have another dame with them?"

"I ain't supposed to say. Mr. Stoddard—"

"I can ask you again after I shoot your dick off."

"Yeah. A skinny blonde," he said so fast he stumbled over the words. "She had a little camera, but they took it away from her."

"That's Jeff," said Stilton, pulling the last knot tight on Jeff's hands behind his back like a calf roper. (I'm from Idaho. It's the

West. We have rodeos. Yes, also spuds.) It was a pretty good tying job.

"That's a pretty good tying job," I told the Cheese.

She just winked at me, which meant "thanks." Pretty sure.

"Now you, Rusty," I told him. "Have a seat."

The ginger sat in the chair I had seen Stilton sitting in, a basic oak kind of thing, and Stilton had him trussed up in a couple of minutes. "Gag 'em?" asked the Cheese.

"Why not," I told her.

She went to a little bar cart on wagon wheels I hadn't noticed until now. Wagon wheels? Fuck these guys. She found a couple of bar towels, which she fashioned into gags. "Now, Rusty," said the Cheese, very gentle and kindergarten-teacher-like, "open up. I'm not going to make it hard for you to breathe or anything, but if you yell, Sammy will come back and shoot your dick off." She grinned at me like a kid in the school play who just hit his mark for the first time.

"That's it," she said when they were both gagged. "Let's blow this dump."

"We gotta go through the woods, doll, you can't go in those heels." She was wearing some tall Mary Janes that matched the polka dots on her dress but did not look suited for running through the forest.

"You watch me," she said.

Once we were out the door, she closed and latched it, then threw her arms around my neck again and squeezed the breath out of me. "I was so scared," she whispered wet into my ear.

"Really?"

"I saw them take the general and that blonde girl away."

"What was all the bit with Jeff?"

"I was improvising. Give you a chance to get the drop on Rusty."

I smooched her lightly, gave her a squeeze. "I like a dame can think on her feet."

"And off," she said. "It was creepy. The general—"

"We gotta go," I said, letting her go. "Tell me while we run." I took her hand and led her to the back of the camp, where she side-saddled over the split-rail fence. We followed the same route out that I took in, but now it was completely light and there were a lot more fat guys wandering around peeing on trees. Some ranger guys were building fires for them, I guess to give them something to stand around while they drank their coffee.

As we went the Cheese whispered, pausing her story when we dashed to the next tree.

"The general likes me, I guess," she whispered. "So I play up to him, so Myrtle and that other girl can get away."

"Pearl," I provided.

"How do you know?" she said.

"Myrtle got away. I helped her hide in the city. She's okay."

"Aw, ain't you just the ant's pants?"

She pinched my butt, which was not something I was accustomed to, but apparently it was a sign that I was out of the doghouse. We crouched behind the same tree I had paused at on the way in, or one that was very similar, and I started to make the final dash for the River Road, but she yanked me back. "No, we gotta get something."

"Doll, those guys that took the general away are very bad guys. We do not want to be here when they get back."

"The general is no choirboy himself," said the Cheese, somewhat urgently. "Look, when he gets me alone at that cabin, he gets very creepy—like he's never talked to a dame before. And I'm not having it. So he starts telling me how important he is, and how arranging to have us girls come up here was a mistake, he realizes now, but after the Bohemians see what he brought them, he's going to be one of the club. And on, and on. About which I do not give a warm squirt of pee. So then he says he'll show me, and he opens this metal box he has stashed in the cabin, like a big beer cooler, and shows me his special thing. And I think, Uh-oh, this is trouble. So I bashed him over the head with this big crock they have under the bunks, thing must weigh a ton, and knock him out, and I take his prize and run. But it's too big for me to get it back to the city, so I stashed it. I figured I'd come back tomorrow and get it, but Jeff and Rusty caught me, so now we gotta go get it."

And before I could say anything, she grabbed my hand and pulled me right into the camp, instead of away, where it was sane—right to the big dining hall, right up to one of the big surplus ice machines, where she threw open the lid and said "Ta-da!" in the spirit of a magician who has just presented as whole a broad previously sawed in half.

"Ice," I observed.

The Cheese looked into the machine, where there was, as I have pointed out, ice.

She started digging like a dog at the beach, and ice was going every which way, and I was looking around very nervously, because it was not a quiet process, but she was determined and apparently in charge, so I kept trying to peek around her, because there was not enough room in the ice machine for me to help. Then she seemed to have found something, tossed a few more handfuls of ice behind her, and stepped back, once again with the "Ta-da!"

I looked in. I didn't know what I was looking at. Maybe a rubber puppet. "What—?"

"It's a moonman!" said the Cheese.

21

THE MOONMAN

As much as I would have loved to stand there making surprised noises and give in to going completely wacky over the Cheese's moonman, I instead snatched that rascal up and commenced to repeating, "Holy shit, a friggin' moonman!" over and over as we ran. The Cheese assured me she had had a similar reaction when she first swiped him, and repeated, "I know, a friggin' moonman!" in response to my refrain. When we finally got the moonman back to the car, Pookie O'Hara, the naked, heroin-addled vice cop, was gone.

I looked around, but there was no sign of Pookie. His clothes were gone, too, along with the little leather box with the loaded syringe I had left in the rumble seat with him, and half of my meat loaf sandwich, which I had been saving for the Cheese in case she needed sustenance after her ordeal. At least Uncle Ho had the big cop's gun, or I might really have had something to worry about. Pookie's hat was still on the seat, so there was a good chance he was not firing on all cylinders when he scrammed.

"It's okay," I told the Cheese. "I still have my receipt." I slung the moonman over one shoulder and pulled the receipt from my jacket pocket. The moonman weighed no more than a small kid, maybe forty pounds, I'd guess, but I'd been carrying him for a couple of hundred yards through the woods and he was starting to get heavy.

The Cheese snatched the receipt out of my hand. "Well this is no good," she said. "It's in Chinese. Why'd you bring a knocked-out cop along, anyway?"

"Look, doll, you are on very thin ice judging the company I keep," I said, tossing my head in the direction of the rubbery gray passenger I had over my shoulder. "I'll explain on the way."

"On the way to where?"

"Not here," I said. I put the moonman in the rumble seat and started to pack him down. He'd fit fine. I just might not be able to get it closed, unless I mashed his melon a little. The dead moonman's body was skinny-kid size, and only four foot or so tall, but his noggin was large economy size—shaped a little like a lightbulb, with big almond eyes that were glossy black; in fact, they kind of matched the lacquered pearl-black finish on Jimmy Vasco's Ford, only more lifeless.

"Prop him up in the corner," said the Cheese. She grabbed the kimono that Pookie had left behind and tied it around the moonman's head like a scarf, then wrapped him up in the blanket, so he looked like someone's granny who might be sleeping. Stilton does not mess around when it comes to getting stuff done. "There. Let's go." She climbed in the passenger side and I got behind the wheel and after a last quick look around for Pookie, we pulled out of the gas station to the River Road just as a big black Chrysler went by and turned into the driveway to the Bohemian Grove.

I turned the other way and took off nice and easy, trying to catch my breath, which had nothing to do with carrying the moonman. The Cheese saw them, too.

"Where did those guys take the general?" she asked.

"The general is dead, kid," I said. I slid the copy of the *Examiner* across the seat to her. It was ferry-folded open to the plane crash story.

She picked it up, read, "Two others were killed in the crash, San Francisco saloon owner Salvatore Gabelli and an unidentified woman." She looked up. "Pearl?"

"Yeah, and that's what they were going to do to you. I guess it's all been about hiding the moonman."

"But Pearl didn't see the moonman."

"Neither did Myrtle, but they are definitely after her, too, but it's just you three, I think. The other girls were sent back to Mabel's."

"So that's what the ranger guys were holding me for? So those guys could put me in a sack?"

"Something like that. But first they would have hurt you until you gave up the moonman."

"Never. He's mine. Hey, when did this paper come out, anyway? I saw the general and Pearl last night late."

"Trucks were throwing out the morning edition when I was leaving the city, maybe five this morning."

"It says the plane went down in the hills outside of Napa. That's an hour out of the city. Even if someone got to the crash right away, how could the *Examiner* know about the general and the other two so fast?"

"They couldn't. Those guys in the black suits had to have called it in. For one thing, Sal wasn't killed in a plane crash. He was dead long before that plane went down, and I had his body stashed in a box full of ice in the back of the saloon."

"You killed Sal? He was a douche bag, but—"

"I didn't kill him."

"Whew, you had me going—"

"My snake did."

I let that news settle a little, as I was trying to figure where to start.

The Cheese spun on the seat, leaned back against the car door, folded her arms across her chest. Gave me the cocked eyebrow of inquisition, which I am sure she learned from me.

"I'm gonna explain," I said.

"Well?"

So, as I drove I explained about the snake-whiz noodle joint, about the South African merchant marine getting me a black mamba so Moo Shoes and I could make a fortune, about Lone clocking Pookie and stashing the cop with Uncle Ho, who knocked him out with heroin, about finding Myrtle and hiding her with Lone, although I left out the bit about Myrtle and Jimmy Vasco, as that was not my tale to tell, about the rats, about searching high and low for her, about Uncle Ho dumping Pookie on me at the last minute, and I finished up with busting into the Bohemian Club in the city and taking the map. Then I took my eyes off the road for a second to see how the story went over.

She said, "So these tax men are going to be very upset that I have their moonman?"

"Looks like it."

"I don't see what the big deal is. The general said they have two others. A flying saucer crashed on the base that he is—*was*—the boss of, so they have extras."

"And he brought one here just to impress the Bohemians?"

"Yeah, I get the feeling that the general is not the flying ace of keeping secrets. Not an ace with the ladies, neither, if I do say so myself. A very awkward old guy, and I have known some awkward guys in my time."

"What are you trying to say?" I asked.

"Oh, not you, Sammy. I mean other guys."

"Then you didn't come up here because you were sore at me?"

"Nah. I agreed to come up here *before* you acted like a shit heel. I came up here to make an easy hundred bucks."

"I didn't know you were hard up for cheddar. I'd have helped you out."

"Don't make it sound desperate. I said, *easy*. Besides, Myrtle wanted to meet some rich guys. How's a girl supposed to get by now? I know a hundred girls can run a bead with an arc welder as well as any guy, but what are they doing since the war? Typing memos or answering phones, if they're lucky—folding shirts and changing diapers if they ain't. And the real unlucky ones, well, you know what they're doing. Besides, Sal said there would be dancing."

"I didn't know you liked dancing."

"I didn't want to mention it, what with your bad foot and whatnot."

"That was nice of you."

"Yeah, I got my moments. Hey, you got anything to eat in here? I could eat a horse."

"I brought you half a meat loaf sandwich, but Pookie took it, that fuck. But there's some coffee in a thermos under the seat. Cup down there, too."

"You fix it like you like your women?"

"Yep, sealed in a metal tube with a screw top."

She dug under the seat, came up with the thermos, dove again for the cup, surfaced with the cup and a big grin. "So, you get what I mean, about the general being awkward?"

"I do," I said, because I do. "So, you have this moonman—"

"Strictly speaking, I think he's probably from Mars or Jupiter or some other place, but I like the sound of *moonman*." She poured herself a cup, offered me a sip, I shook it off.

"Me too," I told her. "But now you got him, what are you going to do with him?"

She lit up like a kid on Christmas. "Are you kidding? I'm going to sell him to Ripley's Believe It or Not so they can put him in the museum down on Fisherman's Wharf. Charge tourists two bits to take a look at him. I'll be rich. I might even tunnel out a couple of extra bedrooms in my place. Heck, I might dig out a closet big enough to put a chair in so I can look at all my new outfits."

"That is an excellent angle, but I think first we have to take him to the *Chronicle* and let them take pictures of him and you, because these tax men seem quite determined to send any and all witnesses of the moonman to the bottom of the bay, so to speak, and if they will scrag an air force general, I don't think they will hesitate to ice a couple of feisty kids like us."

"So we should take him to the city?" she asked.

"Yeah, to the *Chronicle,* or the *Examiner,* or both."

"Oh, okay, then according to that sign back there, we need to go the other way."

"I knew that. I just went this way because I thought you'd want to see the ocean. Besides, if we go back to the city, there is a chance that Pookie O'Hara will be more than sored up at me and my friends and will put us all in a sack, different sacks, although he will need an extra-large sack for Lone Jones."

"Every plan has a few bugs," said the Cheese.

"I shoulda just popped one in Pookie's noodle when I had the chance."

"Ooh, tough guy. You know the safety was *on* when you handed me that heater back at the cabin, right?"

"Someone coulda got shot."

"Turn this jalopy around, you gotta buy me breakfast and make me famous."

It took Clarence most of the night to find his partner Potter wandering around the hills of Sonoma County. As it turned out, Potter was a decent pilot, a skill that Clarence was not aware he possessed until it was needed, and Potter had done a bang-up job of crashing General Remy's DC-3. What Potter was not quite as good at was skydiving, as he had only done the requisite emergency training for pilots during the war, of which calculating altitude and wind drift were not a part. He had also neglected to take a field radio with him, so consequently, when the wind took him several miles from where he and Clarence had agreed to rendezvous, he wandered the countryside for several hours before he encountered a road, which he walked on for several more hours until Potter found him and picked him up. By the time dawn broke, both were quite angry, as well as forty miles from where they needed to be.

"We should have just put a couple of slugs in their domes and buried them in the woods," said Clarence. He had not been a pilot during the war.

"Where did the plane go down?" asked Potter.

"Nowhere near where you bailed out. North of Napa. It's already in the papers. The other team called it in."

"How many other teams do you think there are?" asked Potter.

"I don't know. Don't ask me about operations," said Clarence. He hadn't eaten for twelve hours or slept for thirty, and Potter's blue suit was stupid and he hated it and he wished Potter had died in the crash with the other fucking idiots. His mood deteriorated when they returned to the Bohemian Grove and found the two local yokels, Jeff and Rusty, had been tied up by the missing blonde, and she had been rescued by a guy with a gun. The *subject* was still missing.

"We should process these two," Clarence said. "Witnesses."

"They are not witnesses," said Potter. "Those guys don't know anything."

"Security," said Clarence.

"Your ass," said Potter. He checked his watch. Almost eight. "We need to find a phone and report in."

"There's a phone at the gatehouse," said Rusty.

"See," said Potter. "You process him, we'll never find the phone."

They headed down the path, back to the Chrysler. They'd parked in the most remote corner of the parking lot. As Potter unlocked the car, someone called to them.

"Hey, you bums cops?" A large, apparently drunk guy in a very rumpled suit stumbled out of the forest toward them.

"No," said Potter. "We're just tourists. Nothing to see here, sir."

The big man kept coming toward them.

"Don't give me that shit," he said. "I saw it all. I remember it all." He was pulling something from his pocket. "Where the hell did you guys bring me?"

"That's close enough," said Clarence. "We can't help you."

The big man stumbled forward, carried by the slight slope out of the forest. He caught himself on the front of the Chrysler, then pushed himself back and squinted at Potter. "Someone sapped me and you know it."

"What's in his hand?" Clarence whispered.

"Looks like a sandwich," said Potter.

Clarence drew his gun and shot Pookie O'Hara in the chest. Pookie fell back, dead. "Things are not always what they seem," Clarence said.

Potter approached Pookie's body, poked him with his toe, then, when he got no response, crouched down and examined the remains. "No, it *was* a meat loaf sandwich."

"Witness," Clarence said. He holstered his gun, checked his watch. "Turn the car around. I'll help you get him in the trunk. We need to report in."

Bailey hung up the phone, turned to Hatch. "Washington says that Clarence and Potter lost the *subject*. When they got back to the Bohemian Grove the other girl was gone. She was rescued by a thin man with a gun. I'd guess her bartender boyfriend. Washington thinks they may have taken the *subject*."

"What are our orders?" Hatch was shaving. They were sharing a motel room in the Marina District. Businessmen. On business, they told the desk clerk.

"Same as before. Find and return the *subject*, process any witnesses."

"How do we do that?"

"First we find her friend. We try the lesbian club on the Embarcadero."

"After breakfast, right?"

"Now," said Bailey. "Washington said highest priority."

"So we're going to go to a nightclub at eight in the morning? Do you ever think Washington doesn't know what they're doing?"

"Yes," said Bailey. "Get dressed. We go now."

"I don't see why we can't have breakfast," said Hatch.

"Now," said Bailey. "I can't tell you why."

Hatch knew, because Bailey had told him, that there had been three bodies pulled from the wreckage at Roswell. Three *subjects*. The general had brought one to California, and the other two were at Wright-Patterson Air Force Base in Ohio, where medical teams were studying them. What Bailey knew, that Hatch didn't know, was that one of the two *subjects* in Ohio had woken up.

Sometimes a guy's past is like a stone around his neck that drags him so far down in the dark, he'll never see light again if he doesn't find a moment to cut it loose. My moment came on the road outside the village of Jenner on the coast, where I bought some gas at a little store and grabbed a Coke and some cheese crackers for Stilton to hold her over.

I pulled out and headed back the way we'd come. I got the Ford up to third gear and patted my shirt pocket for a smoke. No luck, lost somewhere in the woods, I guess. Maybe when I was lifting the moonman. Without a word from me, the Cheese checked the glove box and came up with half a pack of Pall Malls. She tapped out two.

"Got a light, mister?"

I fished my Zippo out of my pants pocket and handed it to her. She lit the pair and handed one to me. We smoked. This was that moment, when I needed to cut loose my past . . .

"Look, Stilton, before, I was a louse. I'm really sorry—"

"Sorry? You kidding? You ask a lot of guys to carry a dead, wet moonman through the woods they'd be barfing up their toenails." She leaned over and gave me a smoky smooch on the cheek.

I wanted to throw her across the seat and hammer her like Martin Luther on the church door, such was the power of forgiveness, but I wasn't done confessing. (It does occur to me that perhaps it was best that I never heard back from the seminary as a kid, though.)

"Look, that's sweet, but I swore to myself that if I got you back, I'd come clean. I don't want to lie to you anymore. I was never a soldier. I didn't go to war. Spent the war welding ships at Hunters Point and I slept in a warm, dry place with no one shooting at me every night. I hurt my foot in a warehouse accident the day before Pearl Harbor. I'm a phony. A coward."

"I see no evidence of that." Sip of Coke, drag on her smoke. "None. Never have."

"But I lied to you."

"No you didn't."

"I let you think I served, fought, but I didn't."

"You would have, if you could, right?"

"Yeah, I tried to sneak into the service. Left home in Idaho to come here, to see if the navy might take me. And I never even wrote my folks. I couldn't. I lost two brothers in the war. I couldn't go back after that."

"Because you thought it would be better on your folks to lose three sons?"

"That's nothing like you went through."

All of a sudden tears sort of shot down her face and I almost drove into a ditch before I looked back at the road. "Hey, don't cry, Toots. It's okay."

And she hauled off and punched me in the arm at the same time she let out a big sob and a little hint of a smile. "You jerk."

I'll take that. I deserved it.

She sniffled, wiped her nose on the back of her hand. "Look, Sammy, I don't want to lie to you, either. Thing is, the whole husband-killed-in-the-war, yeah, that happened. But I didn't turn into a grieving mess for the rest of the war. I barely knew the guy. We'd been going out a couple of weeks when he got called up. I was just out of high school, and James, that was his name, he says he can't go off to war and not have anyone to come home to, so he asks me to marry him. I said yes. It was the right thing to do, right? That's what everyone told me. He was an okay guy, but I hadn't even run him through the books to see if he'd pencil out as a husband. So I did the *right thing* and in a few days he went off to boot camp and I saw him once again before he shipped out to the Pacific. That was it. He wrote me all the time, and I wrote him, too, but I didn't even know what to say to him. He met my folks at the wedding, for Christ's sakes. Everyone acted like I was supposed to make this nice little home for us, keep the home fires burning, but it was all fake. We didn't have a life together, we didn't even have a place together. I was still living with my folks. So when I got the chance to work at the shipyard I took it, and I moved to Richmond, and nights I went home to a room in a residency hotel where I shared a bathroom with seven other girls. It was okay, I guess. The pay was good, I learned how to do something useful. Well, useful during the war, anyways. On the weekends a bunch of us girls would come into the city, have some fun. After he was killed, coming into the city, talking to the boys who were shipping out, that's what I looked forward to. I was lonely and alone and it made me feel special. I didn't love James. He was a guy I knew who didn't make it back. There were a lot of them. So much for the tragic, heartbroken war widow, huh? Pretty horrible, huh?" She wasn't crying anymore. She was kind of daring me to shoot her down. Petulant, I guess.

"I think you're pretty swell," I said.

"No you don't."

I looked up ahead, where there was a turnout, so I wouldn't hit a tree or go into the river if I pulled off, and so I did. I pulled off and I set the parking brake and I turned to her.

"Yeah, I do," I told her. "And forget about before, *all* about before. I know I've only known you a week, but it's long enough to know that I want to know you another week, and another week after that, and as many weeks as there are, that's how many weeks I want to know you. That's how swell I think you are."

"Yeah?"

"Yeah." I released the brake and put the car in gear and pulled back on River Road.

I drove for a little bit and she held her Coke in her lap like a kid holding a kitten.

"Me too," she said.

"Yeah?" I said.

"Yeah," she said.

"Okay then," I said. And I drove some more. We passed back by the Bohemian Grove driveway and I hunched down a little. I couldn't help it.

"I'm also somewhat wanted by the law for knocking out a cop and walking away from a work detail."

"The cop that was in the car before?"

"Nah, a different cop. Long time ago."

"Was he a jerk to you?"

"Made fun of my foot."

"Ah, he had it coming." And she patted my knee in sympathy.

We drove for a minute, quiet, sort of basking in the sweetness of it.

"You know," I said, "maybe if you're nice, later on I'll let you touch the stick of sorrow."

She snorted a laugh. "That is the worst come-on line I ever heard."

"I don't know, you were crying the last time."

"So were you, tough guy."

"That is not tr—"

But I didn't get to finish, because there was a noise right behind my head, like a bird hitting the windshield, except it was the back window, and when I turned, when the Cheese turned, he was there—*right there*—his big, black, almond eyes staring in the window, his little tree-frog hands against it. He was making a frantic chirping noise.

"Holy crap!" said the Cheese, diving up on the dash, and I let loose a very manly scream myself and tried not to wreck the car.

The moonman was alive.

22

NONPLUSSED

The Cheese and I were more than somewhat nonplussed. I pulled the Ford off the road and we sat there, staring straight ahead, listening to him back there.

"Maybe he'll go off into the forest," said the Cheese. "Just give him some time."

I sneaked a peek out of the corner of my eye. The moonman was looking right back at me, his little gray mug only a foot away, which was closer than I am strictly comfortable being with a creature from outer space. He made a clicking noise.

"He's not going away," I said.

"You think he's sore I put him in the ice machine?"

I sneaked another peek.

"I can't tell. He looks the same as when he was dead, except he's moving."

"Well do something," she said.

"I am doing something. I'm thinking."

"That's not doing something."

I wanted to tell her he was *her* moonman, so *she* could do something, but that was not the check I just wrote by professing unending weeks of love for her, more or less. So, while the moonman chattered, I tried to put myself in his place. If I were a moonman, and I suddenly woke up in a strange rumble seat on a strange planet, what would I want? I thought of when I have been the only one of a kind in a bunch of different guys. When I was on the welding crew with all the black guys, Lone Jones gave me a sandwich. The first time I went into Chinatown at night, Eddie Moo Shoes bought me an eggroll, and both those guys were still pals.

"Give him one of your cheese crackers," I told the Cheese.

"Yeah?" she asked, looking at the last of her Nabs, reclining in cellophane on her lap. She picked it up with two fingers, cranked the window down just enough to get her hand through, then closed her eyes and held the cracker out the window with all of the caution of sliding a cheeseburger through the bars to a bear.

I watched the whole thing from my side. The moonman stopped chattering. Reached out with his thin little tree frog fingers. Yeah, I call them that because there were little round pads on the end of his fingers. I don't know if they were sticky, because until a minute before I didn't think he would be needing them for anything, especially wrangling cheese and peanut butter crackers.

"Does he like it?" asked the Cheese, who still had her eyes scrunched shut like she was at a creature feature and Boris Karloff was about to strangle some hapless dame who had a sprained ankle.

"He's sniffing it, I think," I said. "Although he doesn't really have a nose."

The moonman looked directly at me, which gave me a case of the willies that shook me to my very scrotum, but he seemed to be saying, "What's the tune, June?" Or would have been if he were a jazzy cat like Moo Shoes.

I gestured for him to try giving it a taste, with my best mime of *give it a taste and chew like you have lips.* (If the moonman had lips, they were very minimal indeed.)

So he gave it a lick, with a very black and shiny tongue, and a second later popped the whole thing in his mouth and appeared to swallow it whole. He then reached around and tapped on the window through which the Cheese had just handed the cracker.

"What's he doing?" she asked.

"He wants another one," I told her. "And you can look. He just ate it, normal-like."

"Does he look ticked off?"

"Nah, although he has no lips, no nose, and when he blinks, a little window-washing membrane seems to go across his eye like a frog. I'd say from his expression he thinks you are swell."

"I don't have any more."

"Maybe we should get some real chow," I suggested, like it was as natural as could be to have a live moonman in the rumble seat.

"I'll bet he's thirsty," said the Cheese. "I drank my Coke."

That was it, then. I put the Ford in gear, revved her up, and threw some gravel as I popped the clutch and headed out. Just as I hoped, my takeoff threw the moonman back in the rumble seat. In fact, he looked a little worried as we went, his little froggy hands clutching on the edge of the seat, his eyes just over the edge.

"You're scaring him," said the Cheese.

"Good. We're even then."

We were going to need someplace where we could eat outside—a burger stand or something. We blew past another gas station and through a dreary forest town called Guerneville, where I took a right because a sign said it would take us back to the city. Maybe ten minutes, then, over the river, winding through the redwoods, the Cheese checking on the moonman the whole time, signaling him to hang tough and be strong, signaling everything is okay, using her best Rosie the Riveter *we can do it* mimes through the back window. We pulled into a little burg called Sebastopol, which was a metropolis by Sonoma County standards, as it had more than one stoplight and even a hardware store, which did us no good at all. I slowed down and the Cheese mimed to the moonman to stay down, which he picked up on; he ducked down so only the mound of pink kimono wrapped around his head was visible to the world.

"He gets it," said the Cheese. "He understands."

"Sure," I said. "You gotta figure he has *some* smarts. He came from outer space in a flying saucer."

"But he crashed," she said. "We could have the village idiot of moonmen here."

"Just because a guy isn't a great driver, does not make him a dim bulb. Besides, he might not even have been driving." This was my first time defending a moonman, so I was still getting my pitch down. Then it hit me. "You know, usually, when a guy comes back from the dead, we show him a little more respect."

She turned on me with a very sour face, and I could feel she was winding up to call me nine kinds of creep for flipping a Jesus card, but then I saw the sign.

"Look, burgers!" Big red letters at the top of a tall sign, in among a row of roadside shops—shiplap boxes with dirt pullouts large enough for about six cars each, a souvenir stand, a liquor store, the burger joint, and a junk shop next to a little fenced-in junkyard with piles of stoves and washing machines and hubcaps strung on wires. I pulled in between the burger joint and the junk shop so we weren't in front of the window.

"I'll go in," I said. "You stay with the moonman."

Before she could answer, the moonman vaulted out of the rumble seat and was sort of wobbling off. He walked kind of funny, or it looked funny to me, like someone was working him with strings, but then I thought maybe I should cut him a break.

"Hey, hey, hey, buster," said the Cheese as she jumped out of the car and took off after him. "You hold on." Without a word, she caught him by the shoulders and steered him back to the car. She was fearless. A few minutes ago she couldn't bear to watch him eat a cheese cracker; now she was manhandling—or, you know, dame-handling—him. "Go," she said to me, waving me in. "I want two burgers, medium, everything but onions, some fries, and a Coke. One for the moonman."

"That all?"

"I wouldn't complain if you came back with a pack of smokes and a pint of Old Tennis Shoes."

"Got it," I said. I sort of stumbled a little myself, looking back as I headed into the burger joint. She was putting Pookie O'Hara's fedora on the moonman, which fit perfectly, with enough brim to cover his big shiny eyes, and she got the pink kimono on him, belted and draped in such a way so that if you were not looking closely, you would think he was just a perfectly normal moonman in a cop's hat wearing a floor-length pink kimono.

Ten minutes later, when I came out with our sack of snacks, the moonman and the Cheese were not there. I flirted with panic a second before I spotted her bright polka-dot dress across the lot at the junk shop. She was waving me on, like everything was fine, so I shrugged and went over to the liquor store, where I picked up a pack of smokes and a pint of whisky as instructed. *If we get out of this alive, the Cheese and I should probably think about cutting back on the sauce,* I thought.

Back at the car the Cheese was holding a cardboard box full of junk and wearing a big smile.

"Look, he picked out a bunch of stuff."

The moonman stood next to her, looking excitedly at the box. It held parts of old radio parts, doorbell batteries, a screwdriver, rusted pliers, a bunch of parts from things I didn't recognize, and a tarnished cornet with one working valve.

"Hey, he likes jazz," I told her, trying to be enthusiastic.

"We got the whole box for a buck and a quarter. You should have seen him, he was running around that junkyard like he was the boss, his little kimono trailing behind him. Pointing at this and that, chirping and clicking to beat the band."

The moonman clicked and chattered to back her up. I noticed a skinny guy in overalls coming out of the junk shop to give us the hairy eyeball again. I could guess what had happened. He didn't even see the moonman. The Cheese bounced into his junk shop out here on the tapered end of the turd of Shit's Creek, and he was stunned by her radiance, his mouth watering like a squirrel licking his nuts, while the moonman ransacked his wares. Now he was coming to his senses. I understood.

"We'd better eat these down the road, doll," I said, returning the hayseed's hairy eyeball in kind.

"I'll put the junk in the rumble seat and he can ride up here with us," she said.

"Put the junk up here with us," I said.

With the junk between us, and the moonman in the back, I headed down the road a few miles to a shady spot under a huge oak tree at the edge of a pasture. I parked the car and a picnic was had. Me and the Cheese sat on the blanket munching our burgers, while the moonman sat over by the fence with his box of junk, chirping and clicking and having a grand old time. Some Holsteins stood nearby chewing grass and whatnot and doing other cow things, such as standing by the fence looking content and chewing some more.

The Cheese laid out a burger, a tray of fries, and a Coke on the torn-open sack by the moonman and backed away. "He'll figure it out," she said.

He did. For a guy with a little mouth and a scrawny frame, he could sure pack it away. The burgers and fries were memories in seconds. He poured more of the Coke out of the paper cup onto his kimono than he got in his mouth, but he got what he needed, I guess, because he flipped the cup over his shoulder and started digging in his box of junk.

"What did you tell the guy at the junk shop? About him?" I asked the Cheese.

"I said what a nice junk shop he had, and asked him could my daughter look around, as she is an enthusiastic kid when it comes to junk. Which she, he, is. He dragged me over there."

"And the guy does not think anything is fishy."

"He didn't say a word," said the Cheese. She gave me *the smile,* posed, changed angles with her shoulders to show off her charms.

"Sneaky," I said.

"Nothing sneaky about it." Now the smile slid into a grin and I was awash in her moxie.

"Your dress has a little stain from carrying wet moonman," I pointed out with a french fry.

"Yeah, he didn't notice."

"Good thing," I said.

She uncapped the Old Tennis Shoes and poured a splash over her Coke, then looked at me. "Too early?"

I shook my head.

She offered me a splash. "Driving," I said. It's too early.

"Look, he's making something," she said.

The moonman was messing with his tools, the dry-cell batteries, the cornet, twisting parts together with baling wire.

"He's so cute. You know we can't take him to the *Examiner* now?" said the Cheese.

"Why not? Those tax guys are not going to care that he is cute. They are only worried that we know about him."

"But he's ours. If we show him to the world they are going to take him away and do experiments on him and stuff."

"Doll, I don't know how else to keep them from punching our tickets as witnesses otherwise."

"We'll figure something out. I'm not selling him to Ripley's Believe It or Not, either. If he wants to get a job down at the wharf charging tourists to look at him, that's his choice. I'm not selling him. Wouldn't be right."

"Stilton, he's not a kid, he's—"

"What's he doing now?" She jumped up to her knees.

The moonman had his bundle of crap wired together, and now he was straining—his big almond eyes going narrow like he was squinting—pointing one of his little froggy fingers, which developed a bulb at the tip, then squirted black fluid.

"Yikes!" said the Cheese. "That's gotta smart."

But out of the fluid oozed a crystal, like he was growing a fingernail, but it wasn't a fingernail. It was like a blue-green crystal a couple of inches long. With his other hand he snapped the crystal off with the rusted pliers. Then he fitted the crystal into his bundle of crap.

"What do you think he's doing?" whispered the Cheese.

"I think he's fitting that crystal into a device that will contact the guys on his home planet. See, every crystal has a certain frequency it vibrates at. You can build a radio out of just a crystal and a battery. That crystal probably has the same frequency as his planet, so it will just call them up. The bell of the cornet will direct the signal."

"No kidding?" said the Cheese, giving me the wide eyes of wonder. "How do you know all that?"

"I read it in a *Popular Mechanics*."

Then there was a huge *P-PHOOM!* noise and a blinding flash of light from the moonman's direction and when we could see again, where one of the two Holsteins used to be was now a little pile of white ash and a beefy mushroom cloud rising into the sky above it.

"Holy crap!" said the Cheese.

"It was an old issue," I explained.

It was sunny in the city; the water around Pier 29 threw spectral reflections on the old warehouse walls. Bailey and Hatch crouched outside the back door of Jimmy's Joynt ready to make their move.

"Guns?" Hatch asked.

Bailey considered for a moment telling Hatch that the *subject* might be alive, and might be venomous. They had no idea what the *subject* was capable of and Washington had not been forthcoming with any details, but drawing guns in broad daylight might be noticed.

"Vasco is supposed to be a small woman. Less than a hundred pounds, and this Myrtle Simmons is also slim. The bouncer won't be here this time of day. We knock. When the woman in the tuxedo answers, we take her and leverage her to control anyone else."

"Standard operating procedure?" said Hatch.

"There is no standard operating procedure, Hatch. No one has done this before."

"So, from now on, this *will* be standard operating procedure, right?"

"Yes. *Knock on the door and grab the tiny lesbian in the tux.* That's how they'll put it in the manual." Sarcasm made Bailey feel dirty, out of uniform, but he couldn't help it. Hatch could be such a nitwit.

"Right," said Hatch. He knocked on the door.

"Come on in, it's unlocked," came a woman's voice.

The heavy wooden door grated on rusted hinges as they pushed on in. A long hallway, dark, with light spilling out of a door twenty feet down on the right.

"Come on in," came the woman's voice again. "Close the door behind you, would ya, gents?"

They moved inside, Bailey first, signaling for Hatch to close the door. He did. Through his sunglasses Bailey could barely make out the patch of light coming through the door. He took a tentative step. "Jimmy Vasco?" he said.

"Yeah, that's me," said the voice. "Step into my office."

Before he got two more steps he saw the bright V of a tux shirt on black, the bow tie at about his eye level. He tried to look over his sunglasses and saw an enormous shade coming toward them, beneath the bright white line of French cuffs, balled fists like the heads of two massive pit bulls. Bailey reached inside his jacket for his .45 and light exploded in his head as he was hit first from the right, then from the left. He heard Hatch shout, then everything went away.

They awoke sitting in the Chrysler, parked by Pier 29, their black hats in their laps, both their guns gone. Bent remnants of their sunglasses sat on the seat between them. Bailey looked at his partner, who was trying to lift his arm, but giving up and letting his hand fall into his lap, the effort too much. Hatch did manage to moan. His right eye was purple and nearly swollen shut. Bailey tasted blood in his mouth, felt for broken teeth on one side, and winced. He touched his jaw. It felt as if a painful grapefruit had grown there. He managed to get the key in the Chrysler's ignition.

"Where?" Hatch managed to ask.

"Motel," Bailey said.

After they stopped the bleeding and used most of the room towels to make ice packs, Bailey sat at the little table to write his report.

Subject *may have the ability to greatly enlarge lesbians. Extreme caution recommended in future,* he wrote.

Across town, in the Fillmore, Mrs. Jones was making tea for her guests. Thelonius said they'd just be here a while, until it was safe.

"That's a very fancy suit," said Mrs. Jones.

"Thank you, ma'am."

"My boy Lonius got one just like it."

"Yeah, we're like two peas in a pod," said Jimmy Vasco.

"Sugar?"

"Yes, please," said Myrtle.

23

THE CHEESE HOLDS SWAY

P-*PHOOM!*

The second cow went up in a flash and a mushroom cloud without so much as a moo and the moonman was drawing down on a third Holstein out in the meadow.

"Stop that!" barked the Cheese. "What's wrong with you?"

And the moonman turned and looked at her and made a sad whistling noise. I was just watching the muzzle of his cornet cow-blaster so he didn't point it our way.

"Maybe he's a little loopy from being dead for a couple of days," I offered.

"We probably ought to go," the Cheese said to me. "C'mon, Moonman." She waved him over and to my surprise he followed. The moonman walked kind of goofy, more like he was prancing than walking, and I was trying not to laugh, in case he took it the wrong way and blasted me into cinders.

We got to the car and the moonman climbed up over the bumper into the rumble seat and cradled his cornet cow-blaster in his little arms like a baby doll.

"We should probably take that from him," I said.

"You go ahead," said the Cheese. "Wait just a sec." She ran around my side of the car. "You got the keys?"

"Yeah," I said.

"Let me have them."

So I handed her the keys. "Okay," she said. Then she kissed me, patted my cheek, and said, "Go take it from him."

I looked at the moonman, who suddenly looked very tough in Pookie's hat and the pink kimono. I held my hand out. The Cheese gave me the keys. I got in my side of the car and waited for her to get in on her side.

"You're a quick study," she said. "I like that in a guy."

"Yeah," I said. "Thanks, Toots."

There were more fields and an orchard or two, and the sign said "Petaluma 18 miles," which was where I'd catch Highway 101. From there it was less than an hour to the Golden Gate and into the city. I stepped on the gas to put some miles between us and the disintegrated Holsteins. The Cheese smiled and shook her hair out in the wind. In the mirror I saw the moonman holding on to Pookie's hat with both froggy hands, which meant he was not holding his blaster. Good. It was a moment. Then the siren.

And there he was in my mirror, a flatfoot, Johnny Law, a copper on a motorcycle—so it was probably a highway patrolman. I was feeling the Walther heavy in my jacket pocket, thinking maybe this guy got a call from Pookie and was laying for us. I pulled over and handed the Walther to the Cheese. "Chuck that under the seat, doll, would ya?"

She did without a word. Fluffed her hair in the mirror. Checked her lipstick. I rolled my window all the way down. The cop flipped open his ticket book as he approached, stopped alongside of the moonman, who was slouching now in the rumble seat. About all I could see was the big hat and the tarnished brass bell of his death ray.

"Good afternoon, Officer," I threw back.

The Cheese scooched over to my side. "Hi," she said. Somehow during her quick personal reassessment she had undone the top couple of buttons of her dress, and now, with her nearly in my lap talking out the window to the cop, I felt uncomfortable in several ways I had never experienced before. The '36 Ford coupe has many attractive features, but large side windows are not one of them, and my face, and the Cheese's face, and her charms, filled up nearly the whole space. I'm guessing we looked like a comedy and tragedy mask set to the cop. Or maybe fear and lust.

"You shouldn't let your kid sit back there," said the cop.

"Kid?" I said.

"Yeah, your kid, in the rumble seat," said the cop.

"Oh yeah," I said. "Our kid."

"What's wrong with him?" asked the Cheese. "Officer," she added, with extra flooze.

"Not the kid, the rumble seat. It's not safe. That's why they don't make cars with these anymore." The cop looked over the moonman, closer than I cared for, and the moonman raised his cornet a tick.

"He's Chinese," I offered quickly.

"But you're not Chinese," said the cop.

"We adopted him. Poor kid. The missus can't have kids of her own, on account of she caught the clap from a sailor during the war."

"He died at Okinawa," said the Cheese.

"God rest his soul," I added.

"So you married her?"

"Yeah, the sailor was my brother. Only decent thing to do was to marry her, after her clap cleared up."

The cop looked back at the moonman. "Why's his head so big?"

"Shhhhh, you wanna hurt his feelings?" I said. "The kid can't help it."

"What's wrong with him?" pleaded the Cheese. "Honey, what's wrong with our Chinese big-headed son?" She slid over me until she was hanging out the window. "Hey, buster, are you saying he doesn't deserve a break just because he's a little funny-looking? His father was a goddamn war hero."

"For the Chinese?" asked the cop.

"No!" I said. "My brother wasn't Chinese, just the kid." I was losing the thread of our story. Out of the corner of my eye, I caught the moonman rising, standing up on the seat, drawing a bead on the cop.

The Cheese started wailing, "Oh my God, our son is cursed!"

With the Cheese completely filling the window frame, the cop couldn't really see me, and I was furiously shaking my head at the moonman, hoping to discourage him from reducing the cop to ashes.

"No!" barked the Cheese with a stern look past the cop at the moonman. "No, no, no, no," she kept on, then she covered her face and resumed the sobbing. I grabbed her around the hips and pulled her back into the car, then peeked around. The moonman was sitting again, hiding under his hat. The cop had backed a couple of steps out into the road, like maybe we had some kind of crazy that was catching. If there had been any traffic, he woulda been creamed, but there wasn't.

"Sorry, Officer," I said. I unsnapped the registration from the steering column, dug for my wallet. "The war was tough on a lot of folks. She's still trying to get over it."

The cop flipped his ticket pad closed and fitted it into his back pocket. "You got enough problems, buddy. I'm gonna let you off with a warning. Just slow it down and get that kid out of the rumble seat."

He backed away toward his motorcycle. The Cheese let out one big last wail of grief to seal the deal. The cop hopped the last few steps, jumped on his Harley, and kicked it to life. The moonman made a sad whistling sound that ended in a click. Which could mean good-bye or "I wish I woulda zapped that guy." Who knows?

The Cheese came out of her grief pose. "Maybe we should let him ride up here with us?"

I was suddenly wiped out. The last two days wrung out of me in the last two minutes. "How about we get a room down the road and hole up until we figure out what we're going to do?"

"I'm game," she said. She looked out the back window, then back to me. "What about him?"

"Maybe he sleeps in the car?"

"You would make our son sleep in the car?"

I winced at the sound of that. "I don't think I'll be able to sleep with him in the room, doll. He kind of gives me the willies."

"Bathtub?" she said.

"Deal." I fired up the Ford and put it into gear.

"I still have the fifty bucks the general gave me," she said. "May he rest in peace and whatnot."

We checked into a clapboard motel outside of Petaluma, and when I got back from fetching dinner I walked in on the moonman motorboating the Cheese.

"Hey!" I exclaimed, barely hanging on to my sack of sandwiches.

The Cheese was sitting on the bed, and the moonman was standing between her legs, face deep in her cleavage, making a burbling noise I didn't even figure was possible for a mug with no lips.

"Oh, it's okay," said Stilton. "I was helping him fix his kimono and he just stepped up. Kinda cute, really."

"It's wrong in multifarious fucking ways, is what it is," I exclaimed. "Back off, buddy." I pulled the moonman back by one of his little shoulders and he made his sad whistle noise. I glanced around to see where his cornet was before I scolded him further. When I spotted it across the room on a wingback chair decked out in flower fabric, I let loose. "No," I said. "Those are mine. No!"

"Aw," said the Cheese. "You're jealous. He doesn't even have a willie. And his kimono smells like dead skunk."

"C'mon, Stilton, you don't know where he's been."

"That's true. What did you get?"

"Grilled ham and cheese sandwiches, fries, Cokes."

Stilton and I ate sitting on the bed, like a little picnic indoors. The moonman ate his stuff sitting in the wingback chair, looking from me to the Cheese and back like he was watching tennis. We watched him right back, like we were munching popcorn at a moonman matinee.

"How do you suppose he poops?" whispered the Cheese around some fries.

"I don't want to think about it," I told her. But then I started to wonder. "He has no butt to speak of. Nothing but smooth, really, below the waist. We don't even know if he's a he."

"Well, keep an eye on him," she said. "There's a tub in there and I haven't had a bath since Moses was a kid."

"You need any help scrubbing stuff?" I offered.

"Not in front of the moonman," she said with a wink. "But see if you can get the kimono off him and throw it in the laundry. The stink would knock a buzzard off a shit wagon."

"Pookie," I explained. "I'll throw the blanket in, too. Lock the bathroom door." Before I headed out the door, I pointed to the moonman, who was still worrying some fries in his chair. "You stay right there, buddy."

There was an ice machine along the walk to the office where the laundry was, and I thought maybe the moonman would be more comfortable in there for the night. Maybe that's the kind of weather they have on Uranus or wherever he was from. I don't know.

I put the kimono and the blanket in the washing machine along with my shirt, which was pretty gamy, so I was in my suit jacket and undershirt, talking to the desk clerk like I was an operator, while the wash ran.

"That your coupe?" he asked. He was a kid, maybe seventeen—thin, dark hair and eyes—was gonna be a lady-killer when his skin cleared up.

"A friend's," I told him. "Borrowed."

"Don't you want it parked in front of your room?"

"Nah. In fact, if anyone comes in asking, you don't know who it belongs to."

"Fine with me. You wanna go back to your room, I'll switch your laundry over when it's time. I gotta be here anyway."

I thought I might take him up on that, but then again, I had a pretty good view of the car and the room from a chair in the little lobby. "Know what, I gotta grab something from the car. I'll be right back. You want anything from the diner? Cup of joe?"

The kid was happy that I thought he was old enough to drink coffee and got a big grin. "Please," he said. "Black."

"Yeah, I take mine with cream and sugar," I told him.

"Yeah, me too," said the kid, now that he had permission.

Looking at the Ford, I remembered that the Walther was still under the seat where the Cheese threw it when the cop stopped us, and I was getting a little of the heebie-jeebies about someone being on our tail, even though we were off the main highway, so

I pocketed the gat. I peeked into the room before I headed back to the front desk. The moonman was in his chair, tuning his death ray with a pair of pliers. I called to the Cheese that I was going to watch the laundry. I looked for the pint of Old Tennis Shoes to share with the kid behind the desk, but it appeared that the Cheese was enjoying it in her bath. Oh well, probably not a great idea saucing up the desk clerk anyway. The moonman clicked at me as I closed the door, like "not to worry." I was worried.

I grabbed a couple of coffees from the little diner next door and sat in the lobby talking baseball and movie dames with the kid until my laundry was done. The kid noticed that I was looking out.

"You want me to buzz the room anyone starts sniffing around?" he asked.

"Can you do that?"

"Yeah, until ten. After ten, I just turn on the no-vacancy sign and there's no one on the desk till morning."

"That would be swell, kid." I slid a buck on the counter for his trouble and headed back to the room with my bundle of laundry. When I let myself in, the Cheese was reclining on the bed in just her slip. The moonman was nowhere in sight.

"I built him a nest," said the Cheese. "In the bathtub."

I snuck over, eased open the bathroom door, peeked in. The moonman was relaxing among some pillows and a blanket, just the top of his gray noggin showing over the edge.

"What about his blaster?" I whispered.

"Wrapped around it like it's his teddy bear. He's asleep. Sleeps with his eyes open, but you can tell because he snores a little. Kind of creepy."

"I could use forty winks myself," I told her, stretching.

"Yeah, me too," she said. "But not quite yet." She patted the spot next to her on the bed, toasted me with the water glass she was nursing with an inch of bourbon in it. I put the gun on my nightstand and I was down to my boxers and beside her in two blinks.

"That bathroom got a lock on it?" I asked.

"From the inside," she said.

As if the moonman had heard the cue, the lock clicked.

"You think he can read our minds?"

"If he can, right now he's reading about giving you the razzmatazz," she said.

"What if he has given us superpowers, like in the comic books?"

"Could be. You *do* know your way around a clitoris."

"I read a lot when I was a kid."

"That why you furrow your brow when you're at it?"

"That might be the moonman's fault."

"He doesn't even have eyebrows," she said.

"Inspiration, then," I told her.

It was different than before. Not so hungry. Sweet. We fell asleep in each other's arms. I woke up with the barrel of a .45 jammed in my temple.

I jumped to a sitting position but the goon in the black suit and sunglasses pressed the gun to my forehead. "Easy," said Black Suit.

Stilton came awake with a start, but before she could draw a breath to scream, Black Suit said, "You make a sound, he gets it." She settled, pulled the sheet up around her neck.

"Who's in here?" said a guy in a blue suit and sunglasses, rattling the bathroom doorknob. A blue suit? These were not the guys I saw outside of Sal's. This was a different team of tax men.

"No one," I said. "I accidentally locked it when I got up to take a leak."

Blue Suit shrugged, like, *yeah, right.* He shouldered open the door and I could hear the jamb crack. I took the opportunity to look for the Walther on the nightstand. It wasn't there.

Blue Suit shook his head. "Nothing."

Did he look in the tub? He was a government agent or something. He would look in the tub, right?

"Where's the *subject*?" asked Black Suit, stepping back from me so he could cover both of us with the .45.

"What subject?" I said. "It's just us." I noticed there was no light coming in at the side of the curtains and I couldn't get a look at my watch on the nightstand, but I guessed it must be past ten o'clock and that's why the kid at the desk hadn't warned us. Or maybe they croaked the poor mug. I got kind of sored up at the thought of it.

"Maybe you should hit him," said Blue Suit.

Black Suit backhanded me across the eyebrow with the .45. There was a flash of pain, the Cheese screamed. I could feel blood running into my eye.

"Stop it, you fucks," said the Cheese. "I put it in an ice machine at the Bohemian Grove and then I hightailed it out of there. That's the last I seen of it."

I felt my heart sink. Our only chance was if we hadn't seen the moonman. Black Suit looked at Blue Suit, then at us. He said, "We can take you with us, make you show us."

"Just leave us alone," she said. "It's there."

"We don't have to take *him*," said Blue Suit.

"What's with the blue suit?" I asked. "They give you hand-me-downs? You haven't earned your black suit yet?"

"There are no rules," said Blue Suit.

"Yeah?" I said. "Then why do you mopes wear sunglasses at night?"

Then I spotted it: The Walther was on the wingback chair where the moonman had been sitting. They must have just thrown it there. A long way to go with two goons with .45s between me and it, but it was loaded and the safety was off, just like I left it.

"None of your business," said Black Suit.

"I suppose you are the ones who crashed the general's plane. What I don't get is why you put Sal in there? He was already dead."

Black looked at Blue, Blue looked back at him. They didn't even know why.

"And why did you put Pearl in there?" asked Stilton. "She didn't even see your stupid moonman."

"That was irregular," said Blue. "Orders from someone outside the organization. Not under our normal purview."

Black looked at him like he was going to shoot his partner. That's when I was sure we were not going to get out of there alive. Their .45s weren't cocked. I'd have maybe one second to dive across the room, get the Walther, and hope they missed the first shot they could get off. I took a couple of deep breaths, thinking of a distraction.

Like she read my mind the Cheese said, "Hey, fuckstick!" and threw the sheet off her in one grand swoop.

They were stunned for an instant. I tried to make it across the room in a dive, cover maybe twelve feet, over the edge of the bed to the chair, hoping my hand would land on the Walther as I fell to the floor. I leapt, eyes on nothing but the gun. Stilton screamed. Blue Suit stepped back and sighted me in as Black Suit trailed me and cocked his weapon.

Which is when the moonman came through the door and blasted the cocksuckers.

24

TWO P-PHOOMS

P-PHOOM! P-PHOOM!

Blinding flashes, then great fed-scented mushroom clouds were washing across the ceiling. There was enough heat from the flashes that I felt like most of my small hairs on the side where Blue Suit used to be were singed. Where a second ago stood federal agents now were two little piles of white ash, each with a pair of sunglasses resting in it. The tax men, guns and all, were gone.

The moonman clicked furiously in celebration, or to ask us if we were okay, or something. Who knows? He clicks when he's happy. I hoped. Maybe where he's from they just go out vaporizing stuff for fun and this was like bowling for him.

"You okay?" asked the Cheese. I was in a tangle on the floor between the bed and the chair. She got out of bed and knelt over me, brushed her thumb over my eyebrow, which smarted more than somewhat.

"Ow!"

"You might need stitches. I'll grab a washcloth, I can't see how bad it is." She got up, went to the bathroom. The moonman clicked.

"Maybe put your slip on or something, Toots. The moonman is getting an eyeful."

She came back with a warm washcloth and wiped at my eyebrow as I winced and acted brave. "Oh, it's not so bad," she said. "You might have a shiner in the morning. Hold this on it until it stops bleeding."

I did. I finally got a look at my watch. It was one in the morning, which explained why the kid at the desk hadn't warned us. I took a peek out into the parking lot. Looked like there was one other car besides Jimmy Vasco's Ford coupe and the big black Chrysler the tax men came in.

"Stilton, can you drive?"

"Absolutely," she said. She was pulling on her dress, and had definitely gotten the message that we couldn't hang around.

"I hope they left the keys in that," I told her.

I got dressed and grabbed some change off the nightstand. "Look, I need to make some calls. Can you sweep up these guys? The moonman is tracking them all over the place." The moonman was tracking fed ashes all over, leaving his little three-toed footprints on the green linoleum.

"I live to clean up your messes," said the Cheese. Turns out, she didn't have a naturally crooked smile; that was just the look she had when she was busting my chops, which it appeared was most of the time.

"He can help," I told her. "It's his mess."

Like the kid on the desk had told me, there was no one in the office after ten, so there was no one to work the switchboard. I wanted to make an outgoing call, I had to go to the phone booth out by the road. Felt a little spooky standing out there in a glass box in the dark, on a deserted road with the stars splattered out over me like a suicide's brains on the ceiling, the neon no-vacancy sign buzzing like a barber's clippers, but I was comforted by the fact that a creature from outer space was helping my girlfriend sweep up two vaporized government murderers in our room, so it was highly unlikely that things were going to get much weirder in the near future. I dropped some coins and called Jimmy's Joynt. Jimmy wasn't there, but when they asked who was calling and I told them, Butch, the host, came on the line.

"Jimmy told me to tell you that she's with your lonesome friend until further notice. That mean anything to you?"

"Yeah, Butch," I told her. "Thanks, I owe you a drink when I see you."

I jangled some change, talked to an operator, and Lone Jones's mother came on the line. "He at work, Sammy. You want to talk to this little fella?"

"Yes, ma'am. Please."

Jimmy Vasco came on the line. "Yeah," said Jimmy, "I shoulda listened to you. Myrtle forgot some of her girlie things, so she came by the club to pick them up in the morning. Luckily your pal Lone came with her. Those mugs you warned us about showed up and your pal scrambled their eggs for them good. Left them in their car with stars and birdies flying around their noggins. Thought it was a good idea to lay low here until the coast is clear."

"Good call, Jimmy. You and Myrtle okay?"

"Yeah, didn't even scuff our shoes. How about you? You find your squeeze?"

"She's with me now. Fine as frog fur."

"Myrtle will be glad to hear it. She's been worried sick."

"We're coming back to town. Hold tight until you hear from me."

"Will do, but I need to get back to work. Place ain't called Jimmy's Joynt for nothing."

"Soon," I told her. I rang off, juggled some more change, talked to an operator who connected me with Sal's. Bennie shoulda been winding down his shift. I looked up and saw the Cheese coming across the parking lot, her red-on-white polka-dot dress and blonde hair catching the moonlight, making her shine against all the gray gravel and black asphalt like the ghost of razzmatazz past. She stepped into the booth with me, crushed me against the glass, and closed the door.

On the line, Bennie the backup bartender said, "Sal's."

"Bennie, it's Sammy, you got anything for me?"

"Yeah," said Bennie. "Just a second." I heard late-night bar sounds in the background, a murmuring slur of sad. "Here you go. A guy named Lonius called when I first came in. Said to call him. And another guy called a couple of hours ago, wouldn't say who he was, but he said you'd know. He said you can reach him at your place. He said he has the kid. You got a kid, Sammy?"

"Nah, Bennie. Thanks." I hung up.

"They have the kid," I said to the Cheese.

"Oh no!" said the Cheese. "What kid?"

"You stinkin' wallabies are in hot water now," said the kid.

Hatch looked to Bailey, confused. "Small kangaroo," Bailey explained.

"No it ain't. You're a dirty liar," said the kid, who was bound to a chair with some of Sammy's ties.

"Can we gag him?" asked Hatch.

"If we gag him we can't interrogate him," said Bailey.

"I ain't telling you nothin'. I ain't a rat fink. You wait till Sammy finds out about this. He beat a mug to death once just for talkin' jazz at me. Didn't even break a sweat."

"Can we just shoot him?" asked Hatch.

"Sammy hit a guy so hard once, he pooped his kidneys out. Right out his butt."

Bailey wished for the tenth time since the morning that the giant lesbian hadn't taken their guns.

"I told my uncle Howie about you guys last time you was here and he said you guys were probably morons from Salt Lake City. Stupid black suits. Morons, that's what you are."

"No, kid, we're not," said Bailey.

"My ma had a record of that Moron Tallywacker Choir singin' Christmas music. Sounded like someone hurtin' a dog. I broke it and melted it on the radiator."

"Why don't you give it a rest, kid?" said Bailey.

"What, you think Sammy's gonna call? You don't even know how smart he is. He's way ahead a you morons. You're probably in his trap right now."

The phone rang. Bailey picked it up. "Yeah?"

"That you, Sammy?" the kid yelled. "I didn't tell these dirty bungalows nothin'!"

"So you got him," Sammy said. "What do you want?"

"You have the *subject*?"

"Your moonman? Yep."

"Shh, shh, shh," shushed Bailey. "The *subject*."

"Don't shush me, you son of a bitch. You kidnapped a kid."

"Fine. You want to see the kid alive. We want the *subject*."

"That might work," Sammy said.

"It *has* to work. Is the *subject* in the same condition it was in when you—when you first encountered it?"

"Meaning what? Dead? Yeah, it's still dead."

"It is?" *Then the report about the enlarged lesbian will need to be amended,* he thought. The venom might have been a passive ability. The *subject* didn't have to be alive to poison the saloon owner. "Right," Bailey said. "Look, you have to be careful moving the *subject*."

"Yeah, the *subject* is pretty hard to move," Sammy said. "I don't know . . ."

"We'll handle it. Just avoid contact with any venomous spines or—try not to touch it."

"Don't give 'em nothin', Sammy!" the kid yelled. "I got these cocksuckers on the ropes."

"Well, sounds like you have everything under control," Sammy said. "I'll call you later."

Bailey looked at the phone receiver, looked at Hatch, looked at the kid, looked back at Hatch.

"What?" asked Hatch. "What? What? What?"

"He hung up," said Bailey.

"He's got ya now, ya rotten backhoes," said the kid. "You goons are gonna die like dogs in the dirt. And he's gonna kill you slow and watch you suffer."

Hatch looked to Bailey. "You don't think he'd come here, do you? I mean, we don't have weapons. Maybe we should change locations."

"Then who's going to answer the phone when he calls?"

"Maybe I can procure some weapons," said Hatch.

"He's a bartender, not a gunfighter," said Bailey.

"Like dogs in the dirt," said the kid.

"What happened?" asked the Cheese.

"They need some time to think," I told her.

"But they got the kid from your building?"

"They want the moonman in exchange."

"They can't have him."

"Thing is, these guys have never seen the moonman. On the phone just now, one told me to avoid any poisonous spines."

"He doesn't have spines."

"Exactly. They don't know what he looks like. And I got the feeling they're not sure if he's dead or alive. I think they think the moonman killed Sal. The two tax men the moonman blasted didn't have any idea why they put Sal's body on the plane. *They* weren't the ones who took Sal's body. The guy on the phone was the one that saw Sal. I guess, because I had him on ice already, they must have thought I was preserving him for an autopsy or something, and when the tax men saw the snakebite, they thought the moonman did it."

"But the moonman was still in a cooler up at the Grove then."

"I don't think they know that. These guys are all working in the dark. They got some powerful friends, but whoever they're working for isn't telling them everything. They aren't even talking with their own guys."

"They're still very bad guys," said the Cheese. "They killed Pearl and the general. We need to help that kid."

"We will, but not right away. Let them get to know him."

"So they'll feel sorry for him?"

"Yeah, something like that. You ever read a story called 'The Ransom of Red Chief'?"

"Don't think so."

"We get done with all this, I'll read it to you."

"Aw, you're sweet. Nobody's read to me since I was a kid."

"Well I'm gonna read your socks off, Toots."

"I can't wait. By the way, I scraped the tax men into an ice bucket with a diner menu. Couldn't find a broom. That okay?"

"Perfect. Let's see if we can find the keys to that Chrysler. We need to get back to the city. I need to talk to Moo Shoes."

"Yeah, and that's going to be a long walk on a broken leg, you keep calling me Toots."

◇◇◇◇◇

It's me: Petey. Yeah, I'm in a sack, but being put in a sack is different for a black mamba than it is for other people. It's not permanent. It's just where I am until I get the chance to bite Ho the Cat-Fucking Uncle, who put me here. BITE! BITE! BITE! I can't believe I didn't see that mug's play with the fire extinguisher. In my defense, five-spice white rats are delicious.

Anyway, I can still tell a story, because, as I have stated before, I know things.

As it turns out, Sammy and the Cheese were less than successful at finding the ignition key to the tax men's Chrysler, but after ten minutes with the moonman's tools and the penknife from Jimmy Vasco's key chain, the Chrysler thundered to life. The Cheese emerged from under the dash with a sly grin and a pair of pliers.

"Ready?" she asked. "It's got Fluid Drive transmission. No shifting!"

"Okey-dokey," said Sammy, as he had no idea what she was talking about, and was still adding "Where did you learn to hotwire a car?" to his mental list of things he meant to ask her about when she came up with a trunk key she found in the glove box.

"Ta-da!" she said.

Before they pulled out, the Cheese opened the trunk to stash the moonman's blanket and they found Pookie O'Hara lying in repose, with various fluids leaking out of him, quite dead. "So why won't Uncle Ho get rid of the body?" asked the Cheese.

"Moo Shoes says it takes too long for the pigs to eat a white devil."

"They keep pigs in the city?"

"The Chinese are an ancient and mysterious people," Sammy told her.

"Right," said the Cheese. "Let's drag him out of here so he's not near the gas tank."

They stood twenty feet away, wearing the tax men's sunglasses, the Chrysler idling in the background, while the moonman let loose on Pookie's remains with his cow-blaster. Sammy noticed the froggy membrane cover the moonman's eyes just before he shot. *A good tell to remember.*

"Want I should scrape him up?" asked the Cheese after the flash.

"Nah, the moonman's got his hat and I got his badge to remember him by. Let him blow away."

They left the pile of fine white ash there in the motel parking lot as Sammy steered the Ford out onto the road, followed by Stilton and the moonman in the Chrysler. An hour later they were sitting in Cookie's Coffee with Moo Shoes, Milo, and Lone Jones, making a plan, leaving the moonman to relax in the trunk of the Chrysler with his hat and his blaster.

"So you're not worried about the kid?" Milo asked.

"The kid will be fine," Sammy told him.

"He's a horrible little kid," Moo Shoes added.

"I could use a change of clothes," said the Cheese. "How 'bout I run by my place real quick?"

"They know where you live, doll. How about you go with Lonius? Myrtle's probably got some fresh togs."

"I'll drive you," said Milo.

"He's only saying that because he knows you have a car," Sammy said.

"That's true," Milo said.

"And don't let the moonman drive," Sammy said.

"He did good coming here," said the Cheese. "I had to work the pedals for him, but otherwise, he drives like a champ."

"Well, I could drive like a champ, too, sittin' on your lap, doll," said Milo. The guys all gave him the hairy eyeball. Lone Jones shook his head slowly at Milo, like it might have been a crying shame he had just witnessed.

"Sorry," Milo said, trying to shrink into his coffee cup with little success. "None of you guys ever brought a dame in here before. I don't know how to act."

Stilton patted his arm across the table. "It's okay, sweetie." Then, changing the subject, "Hey, any of you guys know where I can find an arc welder in the wee hours?"

"Sure," said Milo, perked up from being newly washed of his sins. "Bert's Garage down on Hyde has one, and he opens up at five. You guys know it—the joint where I took you to look at the dames on the Snap-on tool calendar."

"You guys are creepy, you know that?" said the Cheese.

"Guys," I explained.

"Y'all are just sad," said Lone Jones.

It was so early the streetlights were still on, but Sammy and Moo Shoes were hoofing it down Stockton Street just as the fishermen were delivering their catches and the trucks were arriving from up and down the coast. You can buy a lot of things in Chinatown you don't find for sale down by Fisherman's Wharf.

"Fur Man Chu?" Sammy read from the sign on a shop that was still closed. "Really?"

"That's for Anglos," said Moo. "Chinese don't name their businesses based on English puns for themselves."

"What's that one?" Sammy asked, pointing to a sign in Chinese.

"*Place of Abounding Longevity,*" Moo translated. "Tea store."

"That one?"

"*Expanding Prosperity Drugstore,*" read Moo Shoes.

"Your people are big on promises," Sammy said.

"Nah, they're big on luck. Did I tell you about the I Ching?"

"That's the coin-and-stick thing, like dice, right?"

"It's more like a horoscope, except you're throwing the stars."

"Hogwash, then?"

"Oh, complete hogwash. How about that thing?" Eddie nodded to a truck driver dragging a skate, a speckled ray–like fish about four feet long, across the sidewalk into the fish shop.

"Yeah, that's perfect, but we're going to have to get the car. We can't drag that thing on foot."

"No problem," said Eddie. "You're sure this is the angle you want to play?"

"Yeah, as long as the women who work for Uncle Ho can do the sewing."

"They can do it, but he's not going to be happy about it."

"We'll get him a better snake. One that's smaller but just as deadly. Bokker is coming through town again next month."

"I guess that's the song, Armstrong. You go get the car."

By the time Sammy and Eddie Moo Shoes left Chinatown, they had purchased the skate ray, an enormous spiky monkfish with a mouth you could get your head in, if you wanted your head to be shredded on hundreds of needle-like teeth, and a giant octopus that had just been trucked down from Seattle and was still squirming. (Although it was not your Jules Verne pull-the-ship-under giant octopus, but your basic giant Pacific octopus, and the one they bought was maybe big enough to spread out across a sun umbrella, with arms maybe four feet long.) Much of this seafood salad was sticking out of the rumble seat of Jimmy Vasco's Ford coupe as they drove it to Uncle Ho's to be assembled.

◇◇◇◇◇

Sammy called his apartment a little before eight in the morning.

"Yeah," answered Bailey. "Took your time."

"You busy?" Sammy said. "Want me to call back later? No problem. Bye."

"No!" Bailey barked. "No, sorry. No, right now is fine."

"Sammy, that you?" yelled the kid. "You're out of milk. Cornflakes, too."

"You have the *subject*?" asked Bailey.

"Yeah, I got it. But I'm not bringing it there. Someplace public."

"It can't be public," said Bailey. "Obviously."

"Okay," said Sammy. "Then neutral ground."

"Fine. Meet us in the parking lot of Mary Vasco's place in an hour."

"Who the fuck is Mary Vasco?"

"The lesbian club owner."

"You mean Jimmy? Jimmy's Joynt?"

"Yes."

"Well, then why didn't you just say Jimmy's Joynt?"

"I don't know."

"These moron fucks ate all the cornflakes, Sammy!" yelled the kid. "I say knock their blocks off."

"Kid's a gem, ain't he?" said Sammy. He couldn't help but grin.

"One hour. Bring the *subject*. Don't try to pull anything, either. We know about you."

"Really, what do you know, tax man?"

There was a pause. Bailey shuffled through his notebook. "Well, I know that your real name is Samuel Tuffelo Jr., I know where you live, I know you don't have a service record, and I know you're working without a Social Security number."

"Oh yeah, you do know stuff. See you in an hour at Jimmy's. Bring the kid." Sammy hung up and turned to Moo Shoes, who was standing by him at the pay phone. "These mugs really think I'm Italian."

"Milo called Cookie's line while you were inside. The Cheese says that the Chrysler isn't ready."

"He didn't call her 'the Cheese' to her face, did he?"

"Probably. It's Milo."

"Well, we can't take the moonman to them in the rumble seat."

"I'll call Milo back at the garage," said Moo Shoes. "He can bring the cab. Where are we going?"

"To Uncle Ho's, then to Jimmy's Joynt at Pier 29."

"That's a lot of driving for Milo all at once."

"I think he's getting better," Sammy said. "I think the Cheese has cured him."

Across town at Sammy's place, Hatch was fieldstripping the new .45 he'd bought at the all-night gun store. Across from him, at Sammy's little breakfast counter, Bailey had the parts of his new .45 laid out in front of him.

"When you're ready," said Hatch, "say 'go.'"

25

THERE WILL BE DONUTS

Bailey and Hatch had had an hour of sleep between them over the last two days, and even when they tried to sleep in shifts at Sammy's apartment, the kid started mouthing off and waking them up. They tried gagging the kid, but he had a stuffed-up nose and proceeded to suffocate, which degraded his value as a hostage more than somewhat. And while Hatch was very large on knocking the kid out with a skillet to the melon, Bailey had no training in knocking out a kid and feared that the kid might succumb to their pent-up enthusiasm. So they settled on locking the kid in the closet, which helped not at all, since when the kid dozed, they did not see him, and just as each of them was thinking the coast was clear and started to doze off himself, the kid launched into much pounding and calling of names, as was his habit.

They arrived at Jimmy's Joynt a half hour early, only to find Sammy leaning on the back of a taxicab like he had been there all day, smoking and drinking a cup of joe. The cars in the lot were parked in such a way that there was only a narrow corridor for the Chrysler to pull into. They rolled slowly toward the bartender, who gestured for them to turn their car around and then back in.

"Is this guy messing with us?" asked Hatch.

"Sammy's gonna moytalize you mugs," said the kid.

"That's not a word, kid," said Bailey.

"Not yet it ain't," said the kid. "You just wait."

Bailey flipped the car around and backed in until Sammy signaled he was close enough. Hatch was in the backseat, holding the kid. They climbed out and positioned the kid between them.

"Stop right there," Sammy said when they were about twenty feet away.

They stopped. "You have the *subject*?" Bailey asked.

Sammy opened the trunk of Milo's cab. There was a canvas tarp with a short figure lying under it.

"Let's see it," said Hatch.

Sammy threw back one side of the tarp. The creature was laid out as if for a wake. Sammy stepped aside so they could get a good look. They saw a wide, flat gray torso, from the center of which sprouted a mass of thick, red arms lined with suction cups. Atop the torso was what must have been the head, a black, needle-toothed maw more than a foot across, surrounded by wicked spikes that jutted out in every direction.

Hatch recoiled at the sight. "Holy—"

"A Martian," gasped the kid.

"You were right about the spikes," Sammy said.

"You pansies are in for it now," said the kid.

Bailey and Hatch reached inside their jackets.

"Stop," Sammy said.

Car doors on either side of them were kicked open. On one side Eddie Moo Shoes was lying on the front seat of a Chevy, pointing a .45 Colt at them. On the other, Milo had another Colt trained on the tax men. Bailey and Hatch froze.

"Sammy brought his Nip spy friend," said the kid. "Those guys are tricky—they have a way to hit you that makes your eyeballs explode."

Sammy said, "Hands out of your jackets, slowly and empty."

"I lived through the Battle of the Bulge," said Milo. "I'm not squeamish about seeing a guy's guts blown out."

"Who is that guy, Sammy?" said the kid. "He's the tits. Hey buddy, you wanna be my new uncle? You'd have to give up the stupid cabbie hat."

"Send the kid over," Sammy said. Bailey and Hatch let the kid go and held their hands limply out to their sides like they were dripping paint and didn't want to get it on themselves. The kid's hands were tied, but he turned and started to sand the soles of his shoes across the toes of first Bailey's, then Hatch's, shiny black shoes. When both were completely scuffed up, the kid ran over and stood behind Sammy. "You fucks," said the kid.

"That will buff out," Sammy said. "You had a nice shine on those stompers. Shinola?"

"Kiwi," said Hatch. Bailey glared at his partner.

"Yeah, Kiwi is best for a spit shine," Sammy said.

"Mr. Tuffelo, that is government property behind you," said Bailey. "If you don't turn that over to us, you are committing an act of treason."

"And you mugs kidnapping a kid, murdering an air force general and a dame, that was just in the wrong place at the wrong time? Was that just being patriotic?"

"That was not standard operating procedure," said Bailey. "Special orders."

"These orders come from the same people who gave you the background on me?"

"I can't tell you that."

"Okay," Sammy said. He reached into his jacket pocket and came out with a pair of sunglasses exactly like the ones that Bailey and Hatch were wearing, except not all bent up. He held them up so the two could get a good look at them. "The guys who gave you your orders, they tell you about this?

"You guys can have this pair." Sammy threw one of the pairs of sunglasses on the tarp with the Martian. "I'm keeping this pair." He pocketed the shades.

Bailey and Hatch looked at each other.

"I give you this thing," Sammy said. "Are the guys who gave you orders going to come after me and my friends?"

"What happened to Potter and Clarence?" asked Hatch.

Sammy shrugged. "Might never be heard from again. Might have run off together. Might be hunting you two, right now."

"We haven't killed anyone," said Hatch. "Something is going on in Washington. Something out of order."

Bailey cringed, then shrugged, nodded. "That's the truth. We never saw Potter and Clarence before two nights ago."

Sammy waved to the Martian. "I'd say that's out of order, wouldn't you?" He reached into his coat pocket, pulled out the Walther. "Look, gents, I'm going to give you this thing, but you have to promise to forget everything about where it came from. Now I'm going to come take your guns. If you move, or try to get the drop on me, I'm going to shoot you, or my friend the cabdriver is going to shoot you, or my friend on the other side is going to shoot in your general direction."

"No idea what I'm doing," said Moo Shoes. "Probably will kill you all by accident."

"That's the spirit!" said the kid. "Blast the sons a' bitches!"

"Shut up, kid," Sammy said. "I'm saving you."

He gently took the .45s from each agent and threw them onto the car, where Moo Shoes was lying on the front seat. "Now, open your trunk, and go get your creature," Sammy said. "Lift it by the tarp; you don't want to touch the *subject*. That's what happened to Sal."

"Thought so," said Hatch. "How, though, if the subject was at Bohemian Grove?"

"Delayed reaction," Sammy said. "The general showed it to Sal when he first arrived. Before he even unloaded it from his plane, and like a dope, Sal touched it. Few hours later, I find him in a puddle in the back room of the saloon."

"Why did you pack him in ice?"

"Well, your guys told me to."

"Potter and Clarence?"

"I guess," Sammy said. "I never saw them. I got a phone call, lots of threats. When I saw you mugs at the saloon, I thought you were the ones on the phone; that's why I pretended to be the janitor."

Bailey nodded as if it was all falling into place. Sammy backed off, keeping the Walther trained on Bailey as he opened the trunk of the Chrysler. They carefully moved the Martian out of Milo's trunk and slid it into the Chrysler, holding only the edge of the canvas.

When Bailey slammed the trunk and turned around, Sammy said, "You know they're not telling you anything. I don't mean everything. I mean *anything*. You know that, right?"

Bailey looked at him, lifted his sunglasses, looked Sammy in the eye. "Yeah, I know."

"So," Sammy said, lowering the gun. "Are they going to leave us alone? Or are a bunch more people going to get scragged because some general in New Mexico went loopy and tried to impress some nobs?"

Bailey let his sunglasses drop. "I haven't filed a report since this started. Everything kept changing."

"Which means what?"

"You keep your mouths shut, you and your friends should be fine," said Bailey. "We don't hurt civilians."

"Yet, the evidence says you are lying like a rug."

"Like Hatch—er—the other agent said, that didn't come from our people."

"Then who did it come from?"

"Someone over our people. I can't say who, but someone high up."

"High enough that you guys can ice a general?"

Hatch nodded. "You going to give us back our guns?"

"Nope."

Again, Hatch nodded, just a twitch of a nod. "You're sure this thing hasn't moved?"

"I'd keep an eye on it, I were you," Sammy said. "Drop the seat of the Chrysler. It goes right through to the trunk, right?"

Again the nod.

"Where are you taking it?" Sammy said.

"I can't tell you that," Bailey said.

"Long drive?"

"Maybe," said Hatch.

"Look," Sammy said, "I don't know what happened to your other guys, but last anyone saw them, they were near that thing."

"Who saw them?"

"I can't tell you that," Sammy said. "Tell your bosses to leave us alone. Or better yet, don't tell them anything. Time for you to go." Sammy waved him back into the car with the Walther, waited, then watched as the big black Chrysler rumbled away.

Five minutes later, an almost identical Chrysler jumped the curb at the Embarcadero, sending a hubcap wheeling down the wharf into the bay, then squealed around and stopped where Sammy was waiting beside Jimmy Vasco's Ford coupe. The moonman, under Pookie O'Hara's big fedora, was driving.

Stilton jumped out of the passenger side. "He's a natural!" She was holding the moonman's cornet/blaster. She was wearing Myrtle's gray slacks and a white blouse.

"You let him drive?"

"Yeah, of course. I cut the pedals off, welded some half-inch stock on as extensions, then welded the pedals back on. *Fluid Drive,* automatic transmission. It's a wonder!"

The moonman hung his head out the window and chattered.

"Where's Milo and Moo Shoes?" asked the Cheese.

"Moo Shoes went home to sleep. Milo is picking up Jimmy Vasco and Myrtle to bring them here. The kid's off getting some breakfast. Why do you have that thing?" Sammy nodded to the blaster.

"Oh, I stopped by my place to see if I could blast out a rumpus room. Turns out you have to be a moonman for it to work. I can't blast a stinkin' thing." She handed it through the window to the moonman. "Be nice," she said. Then to Sammy, "Give me your jacket."

"Why, what?"

"Just get everything out of the pockets and give me your jacket. The hat is okay from a distance, but he's going to need a better outfit."

While Sammy transferred the contents of his jacket pockets into his trouser pockets, Stilton coaxed the moonman out of the Chrysler and stood him up behind the Ford, where no one from the road could see him. "Give me your jacket," she said.

Sammy took off his jacket and handed it to her, then watched as she put it on the moonman. It hung to the ground on him. She rolled up the sleeves until his froggy little hands showed again, but he was still swimming in it. "Give me your tie," she said.

Sammy took off his tie and handed it to her. She fashioned it into a sash and, in a few seconds, the moonman was standing there in Pookie's wide-brimmed fedora and Sammy's belted suit jacket, which hung to trench-coat length on him.

"Ta-da!" said the Cheese, presenting the moonman's new look. The moonman clicked, whistled, then made a la-la noise.

He looked like a very tiny spy.

"Okay," Stilton said. "That's it, you go get 'em, slugger." She lightly punched the moonman on the shoulder.

"Where's he going?" Sammy asked.

"How should I know? I don't know what the hell he's doing. I just taught him how to drive. He can't stay here. They'll come looking for him when they figure you gave them a fake."

"I'm not sure they will," Sammy said.

The Cheese opened the door of the Chrysler and waited while the moonman crawled in.

She looked over her shoulder at Sammy as the moonman fired up the engine. "I put a switch in for him so he doesn't have to mess with hot-wiring it every time."

"You know how to do that?" Sammy asked.

"Doesn't everyone?"

"Okay, off you go," Sammy said, slapping the Chrysler's front fender.

The moonman stuck his head out the window, looked at the Cheese, and made a burbling noise while shaking his head back and forth.

"No!" said the Cheese. "You go."

"Is he asking to motorboat your boobs good-bye?"

"Go now, Scooter. Go." She waved him off as if she were releasing a bird she had nursed back to health.

"You named him Scooter?"

"Shhh, shhh, shhh," said the Cheese. "It's sad. I'm sad." She buried her face in Sammy's shoulder as the moonman drove out of the parking lot and turned onto the Embarcadero. Sammy pulled her close and kissed her hair as he watched the Chrysler go out of sight on the other side of Jimmy's Joynt.

"Don't cry, Toots. Maybe someday we can have a moonman of our own."

"Yeah?" she said, pushing back to search his face for sincerity. "You don't think they're going to hunt us down and kill us?"

"No, of course not. Probably. If we're lucky. We might have to see a guy about that."

They heard scuffling behind them, looked around.

"So this the dame that put you through all the commotion?" asked the kid. He was holding a white bag and was eating a glazed donut. He came out from between two cars, stood next to Sammy, pushed his newsboy cap back on his head with the donut. He gave the Cheese the once-over, held up the bag of donuts. Sammy took out two, handed one to Stilton.

"This is her," Sammy said.

"She's a little lumpy for my tastes."

"Hey, watch it, kid!" Sammy said. "I will pop you one."

"That's okay, Sammy," said the Cheese. "A person can't help what they like."

"He's a horrible little kid," Sammy said.

"That's okay, I like that in a kid," said the Cheese. She leaned in and whispered to Sammy, "Although we don't need to rush into having a moonman of our own."

"Hey, you keep that ice bucket from the motel?" Sammy said.

"Yeah," said the Cheese. "It's at my place."

"Let's go get it. I need to find another jacket, too."

"Sorry, but he looked like a goof in just a hat."

26

THE NOB

T he law firm of Stoddard, Whittaker & Crock was in one of those bank buildings faced with granite the color and pattern of dog vomit. It was a bank. But not a bank with counters and windows and whatnot, a bank where guys in suits sat at desks and talked to nobs about their money in quiet, civilized tones. The Cheese and me walked in like we owned the joint, but the guy working the elevator looked at us like we were there to clean the drains—me in my second-best suit and the Cheese looking sunny in a blue gingham number that would look natural on a farm girl from Kansas—*if* the Cheese wasn't wearing a pair of red Mary Janes with heels high enough to give a stripper a nosebleed. "My ruby slippers," she had said when she put them on.

Right out of the elevator there was a half-moon reception desk that was all bronze and marble, with a fortyish dame sitting behind it looking tightly wound enough to spin the hands off a clock, and enough hairpins in her coif to pick every lock in Alcatraz.

"Can I help you?" she said, like she meant to say, "Did you get off on the wrong floor?"

"We're here to see Alton Stoddard the Third," I told her, and I flashed Pookie's badge. As impressed as she was, I might as well have flashed a cockroach.

"Do you have an appointment?" she said.

"He'll want to see us," said the Cheese.

"Mr. Stoddard does not see anyone without an appointment."

"Tell you what, Toots, you tell him I have pictures of him and his Bohemian pals dressed like dames and giving each other the bent-over boogie-woogie and see if he wants to talk to us." And here I threw a manila envelope I had prepared for just such an occasion on the reception desk. The Cheese set the ice bucket from the motel next to the envelope, which visibly confounded the receptionist down to her very hairpins.

Flustered, Miss Officious worked the switch on an intercom a couple of times before she decided what to do, which was to stand up and continue to be flustered.

"You might want to snap things up, Toots," I told her. "We got an appointment at the *Chronicle* in half an hour."

This unfroze her. She said, "One moment, I'll see if he is in." And she hurried off down a hallway.

"Like she doesn't know if one of the guys with his name on the window is in or not," I said to the Cheese.

"I can't believe you called her Toots," Stilton said. "You're just a hound, aren't you? You better not be a hound."

A minute went by in which the Cheese bitterly chastised me for Tootsing another, then Miss Officious returned and said, simply, "Follow me."

She led us down a walnut-paneled hallway past several mahogany doors with reeded glass windows, until we reached the end of the corridor, where we were ushered through double, reeded glass doors into a carpeted office with another hairpin dame sitting at a desk trying desperately not to scowl as Miss Officious showed us right into the inner office. The office was about four times the size of my apartment, with the Cheese's cozy dame-cave thrown in a couple of times to give it some air. The room was all Persian rugs and dark woods, law books on two walls, paintings with gondolas and golden canals on another, a gallery of windows looking out on the bay, as well as a stock ticker that was spitting out tape in the background like a mechanized chipmunk.

There was an antique desk the size of a coal barge, and behind it sat a thin, balding guy in a houndstooth suit who peered at us over some Ben Franklin spectacles. He gave the Cheese the once-over, glanced at me long enough to dismiss me, then returned his gaze to Stilton. I could see it was the blue gingham dress and not the Cheese's abundant charms that was giving him pause.

"So who are you and what is this about?" he asked.

There were a couple of leather side chairs in front of his desk. I swung a leg over one; the Cheese sat demurely in the other and held the ice bucket on her knees.

"I'm Sam Two-Toes, and this dish of loveliness is Dorothy Gale, and we are here to talk to you about what you and your Bohemian pals were getting up to at your campout last week, and more importantly, the people you killed to cover it up."

He stood up behind his desk to show his outrage. He was taller than I expected, a head taller than me, and thinner. I really expected a shorter, fatter guy. With a monocle. Maybe a top hat. Yeah, okay, I was probably expecting the guy on the Monopoly cards.

"Now see here," he says. At which point I pull out Jimmy Vasco's Walther .380.

"Shut the fuck up and sit down, Alton," I said. Wisely, he did.

"He said, 'now see here,'" said the Cheese. "See if you can get him to say, 'my good man'?"

"The police will be here in seconds," Stoddard said. "My receptionist has already called them."

I threw the envelope on his desk and pulled Pookie's badge from my jacket pocket, let him have a good look at it. "San Francisco's finest."

"I know the police commissioner," said Stoddard. "I know the mayor."

"I'll bet you do," I said. "Give them my best. I don't work for them. That's not relevant. It's not my badge. Here, you can have it." I threw the badge on his desk.

"You think this is the first time someone has tried to shake me down?" he said.

"Oh, no. But it's my first time," I told him.

"You're doing great," said the Cheese.

"Thanks, doll."

Stoddard said, "Mr. Two-Toes, I assure you, the Bohemian Club is made up of some of the most distinguished, accomplished, powerful men in the world. We do not kill people. You have no evidence of any misdeeds at all. I don't know what is in the envelope, but it's not pictures of the Bohemians."

"How do you know that?" I asked him, pushing back my hat with the barrel of the Walther.

"Because we do nothing for which we would be ashamed."

"Except dressing up like dames, worshipping a concrete owl, and killing a stand-up dame like Pearl," said Stilton.

"That's how you know, Alton, isn't it?" I said. "You know there's no pictures because you had some goons take Pearl's camera, then they hurt her until they were sure that she hadn't stashed any film. That's how you know."

Stoddard stood again. "I'll have you know—"

I passed the Walther to my left hand and popped Alton Stoddard in the chops with a quick right jab, knocking him back into his chair.

Stilton giggled.

"Baby—"

"Sorry," she said.

I said, "You probably never even met the guys who killed the general and the girl, did you, Alton?"

"I don't know what you're talking about," he said.

"Doll, introduce Alton to his hired killers, would you?"

Stilton stood, curtsied, then took the lid off the ice bucket and dumped the ashes on Stoddard's desk. A cloud of powder splashed over the desk. Stoddard rolled back to get out of the wash. I pulled the last pair of sunglasses out of my breast pocket and threw it into the pile of ashes. A light of recognition went on in Stoddard's eyes, just for an instant, but I could tell he'd seen them before.

"That's all that's left of them, Alton. And there were others, too. You may be hearing from them. General Remy showed you his special treasure, that little novelty he thought would impress you, didn't he?"

"General Remy was—he was not suitable material for the Bohemians."

"So you killed him?"

"No, we had nothing to do with that."

"But you called a friend. Maybe a friend of a friend in Washington, and he told someone who told someone, and the next thing you know, these guys in sunglasses show up and start making people disappear. Well, this is what happened to them when they saw the thing you saw."

Stoddard dabbed at his bloody lip with a handkerchief and stared at the powder on his desk, shook his head.

"You could be making all of this up," he said, but he'd lost some of his rich-guy resilience.

"You knew your friends were going to take care of Remy, so you asked them to do you a favor and get rid of the dames who saw your little party, too. Except two of them got away."

"They said there would be dancing!" Stilton said.

I looked over at her. Gave her a *what the hell?* shrug.

"Well, they did."

"You can't prove any of this," Stoddard said.

"You're not getting my drift, Alton. I just used the pictures angle to get in here. I don't *need* to prove any of this. This isn't going to court or to the papers. You guys, you movers and shakers, who tell other people what to do. The worst thing you can think of happening to you is maybe you lose some money, maybe you're embarrassed. Things are different when you live closer to the bone, Mr. Stoddard. Things go wrong where I live, real people get hurt, real people lose their friends, lose their jobs, lose their lives—end up turning tricks or rotting from the inside down at the Third Street Sherry Society. Alton, I know it's going to be hard for you to imagine anything bigger or more important than you and your nob pals, but this is real. This will make things real for you. *I* will make things real for you."

Stoddard sagged in his chair. "What do you want? We keep a limited amount of cash in the office—"

"I want you to call everyone off, Alton. Everyone you talked to about the general, about the girls at the Bohemian Grove, about everything to do with it. You call them and you tell them to drop it. Right now and forever. They don't send investigators, they don't open files, they don't read anyone's mail or listen to their phone calls—all this, and everything to do with what happened in San Francisco is finished. You threaten them, Alton. You got them to move somehow before, so you do it again, make it clear that this is over. Do you understand?"

"I have no control over—"

"*Get* control. Because I'm promoting you into the real world, Alton. I will not ruin you, I will not embarrass you, I will not see you in court. If anyone I know so much as hears an extra click on a phone call, you are going to be in an ice bucket, Alton, just like your two goons. And so will everyone in your family. Any one of my friends so much as sprains an ankle stepping off the curb, you are ashes."

"You can't get away with this," he said.

"Don't care, Alton. All I have in the world is a few friends and this dame over here. Anything happens to them, I got nothing worth living for. Now, you can doubt me. You can send someone after me, after my friends, but if you do, you'll live the rest of your short life in fear. You think you can go over my head? *Everyone* is over my head, Alton. Maybe you get me. But there's a lot of people down here with me. Maybe you don't get vaporized. Maybe it's just a fillet knife slipped under that vest of yours one day when you step into the elevator. Thin and quick, you'll barely feel it, and you'll bleed out before anyone knows what hit you. Or, you can say no, tell me that I'm being outrageous, and I'll just shoot you right now." I shrugged. "Do some research. Ask your friends in Washington what happened to their guys. Although, it's probably not the best idea to let them think you know too much, because I don't think they'll think you're quite as important as you do. Remy was a general, Alton. One of theirs."

"All you have to do is call them off," Stilton said in her *doting on the moonman* voice. "It's easy."

Stoddard looked at her like he'd just awakened to find her there. "Why are *you* here?"

"I'm saving your life, Alton," she said. "Sammy was just going to shoot you and leave. I talked him out of it." She smiled, cut an *ain't I sweet* pose. "Also to carry the ice bucket full of goons."

Alton Stoddard the Third slumped in his chair like a puppet with his strings cut. "I'll call them off, all of them."

"Promise?" Stilton said.

"He's a lawyer, doll," I reminded her.

"I promise," he said. "As soon as you leave. And if for some reason they don't stand down, if someone shows up, don't just have me killed. It will mean they haven't listened to me. Call my office. Give me time to fix it."

"Maybe," I said. I uncocked the Walther and dropped it in my jacket pocket. "Let's go, doll," I said to Stilton.

I held the door for her, but as she left Stoddard's office Stilton turned and said, "Good day to you, sir. To you, sir, I say, *good day!*" Then she stormed out.

I caught up to her at the elevator, where we had to wait and watch the floors tick up.

"Nice exit," I told her.

"Thanks. I didn't know when I was going to get the chance to say that again."

"You did swell," I said.

The elevator dinged, but before the doors opened, the Cheese looked at me and said, "We coulda asked for money?"

"Yeah, I guess I shoulda thought of that, huh?"

27

SOMETIMES

Bailey and Hatch are about thirty miles outside of Barstow in the Mojave Desert when I start feeling warm enough to move around a little. I can't lie, I'm a warm-weather serpent. The hollowed-out carcass of the skate was a comfy den, but Uncle Ho has chilled me more than somewhat with his fire extinguisher to make me lethargic, so he could get me in there, and although the Chinese broads who sew all the fish parts together leave me a nice exit right under the octopus, it's a little chilly for my tastes. So once we're in the Mojave with the summer sun beating down on the black Chrysler, I wake up a little. I peek out, and what do I see but the two guys in black fedoras sitting there in the front seat. Bailey is driving, going very fast. Too fast. If I'm going to get out of this jalopy, I need to slow them down some. So I slide up between the rear seats, across the floor, and I come up on the window side where Hatch is sitting. He's a big guy, and even in this heat is wearing his coat, so I look for a good spot. I sort of stand up on the floor of the backseat, and there it is, a nice stripe of bare neck between his fedora and his collar. I BITE! BITE! BITE!

Then I slide down under the front seat.

Oh the yelling and the waving and the drama. The Chrysler is lurching from side to side, the tires screeching. Hatch is screaming, holding his neck. Bailey is yelling, "What? What? What?"

"Something bit me!" Hatch yells.

"What?"

Bailey finally pulls the car onto the side of the road and stops, and just in time, because with all the commotion, I am about to barf up a five-spice rat. Meanwhile, Hatch starts to have convulsions, like they do when you get them in a good spot. And he goes all stiff and twitchy, stiff and twitchy. Now Bailey gets out of the car and runs around to the other side. Drags Hatch out onto the sand. Which is my chance, because Bailey leaves the passenger door open. I slide slick as snake snot out the door and onto the sand, which is hot, but not so hot I can't make a run for some shade somewhere. Bailey sees me, but he's holding his partner's head, trying to clear his airway, and what's he going to do? Sammy took his gun. I shoot him the fork-tongue raspberry a couple of times. Ya mook. Wouldn't know a Martian if it bit ya. Ha!

Some big rocks over there, some shade. I make my way over. Not a bad spot, something has hollowed out a little den. It's cooler here, and when whatever made the den comes back, I can eat it. I'll wait out the day here, but I peek my head out to watch what's going on back at the road.

Bailey looks up, sees a Chrysler, identical to the one he was driving, pull up. At first he thinks help has arrived. He sees the hat and maybe sunglasses. Maybe. The driver's door swings open, and the next thing Bailey sees is what appears to be a tiny spy in a trench coat and a wide-brimmed fedora, carrying a cornet with batteries and other bits wired to it. It's the last thing he sees.

There's a flash and a couple of mushroom clouds rise over the desert.

Waste of venom, really. Hatch would have hung on for hours. Oh well.

I watch the second Chrysler pull away. He's getting to be a

pretty good driver. Long, straight desert roads are good practice. I coil up for a nap.

I don't know what happened with the moonman. Maybe he's still out there somewhere, driving a big Chrysler, wearing my best suit jacket. Maybe he found a way home.

It's six months now, and we haven't heard from the tax men, or anyone else involved with the Bohemians, so maybe Alton Stoddard the Third got the message out to his powerful pals. Who knows? We keep an eye out for anything strange.

I'm still bartending, although I have a stake in the joint now, as Mrs. Sal asks me to stay on to run the place for a share in the profits. I tell her, "Really, Mrs. Gabelli, I don't think what they tell you happens to Sal is strictly on the level."

And she says to me, "I know that, Sammy. Sal was terrified of flying. He wouldn't go up a stepladder to change a lightbulb, let alone get on a plane in the middle of the night. He was a douche bag. His life caught up with him. End of story. You want the job or not?"

Romance.

Lone Jones is still waiting for his call from President Roosevelt, although after meeting Jimmy Vasco he is now considering becoming a lesbian, as that seems like it might be easier to get into than the Secret Service. Lone and Jimmy have become fast friends and she sometimes joins us at Cookie's for late-night coffee and conversation.

Bokker, the merchant marine, is getting a new snake for Uncle Ho, which Moo Shoes and I are paying for out of our own pockets, although we have opted for something more portable but just as deadly—called a boomslang—so Ho can rake in some respectable doubloons in the snake-whiz noodle-soup business.

Moo Shoes and Lois Fong are an item going on six months now, and have decided to go in together on a driving school for the people of Chinatown. Lois will sing the written parts, and disrobe as needed to keep the students' attention. Moo Shoes will teach the actual driving.

"But technically, you don't know how to drive," I tell Moo.

"Yeah, but in an emergency, I do fine," he says. "What could go wrong?"

He has a point. There is a need. He has an angle.

Milo is also expanding his business by serving adult beverages to his fares while driving them to work. He is driving a little more each week, in small doses, so he builds up his tolerance, and if the cops do not catch on to his game, he will be able to rent a place where he can sleep more than one night in a row.

Me and the Cheese, well, it's not what you'd call a picket fence life. She's still dealing breakfasts off her arm, and I'm still tending bar and keeping company with citizens of the night, but we see each other every night, mostly at her place, since mine is still in-fested with the kid. She agreed to stop acting like a floozie and so did I, so we go to the pictures on my night off, or out to Playland at the Beach. We have a drink from time to time, or go listen to some jazz at Lone's club; we do the razzmatazz until the wee hours, and sometimes, afterward, we sit naked together on the kitchen floor and eat cheese and crackers off the same plate and laugh until we collapse in a heap. It's just swell.

Oh yeah, sometimes, late, with the music on her record player turned down low, we dance.

AFTERWORD

The Setting—the City

Location is a place. Setting is place and time. From the beginning, I knew that San Francisco was going to be the place where this story would take place, but what was in question was the *time*. I knew I wanted a time after World War II and before cell phones, which gave me a window of about sixty years. In a sort of emergency swing during a phone call with my editor, I picked the year 1947, which ended up being both the curse and the gift of this novel. The gift was just how dynamically San Francisco was changing at the time; the curse was that 1947 was just long enough ago that anyone I could find who had been alive and in the city at the time couldn't actually remember what happened, with the exception of one very nice guy who had come to San Francisco right after the war and who remembered (fondly) guys taking girls over to Playland at the Beach on dates. Playland ran from the 1920s to the 1970s, when it was torn down, and today the only remnant remaining is one oversized windmill still visible from the Great Highway along Ocean Beach.

The saloon where Sammy works is based on a real place, still in the location described in the story, on Grant Street near Broadway, where it has stood since 1861, one of the few structures that survived the earthquake and fire of 1906. The layout and history of the saloon, however, is completely from my imagination, as is the character of Sal Gabelli.

AFTERWORD

Club Shanghai, where Eddie Shu works, was also a real place, on Grant Street in Chinatown as I described. The Chinese clubs with dancing girls and entertainers doing impressions of Anglo entertainers had become the rage in the '30s among the "nobs" of Nob Hill and Pacific Heights, and continued until the 1970s. You can learn more about the Chinese nightclubs in Arthur Dong's book and documentary film *Forbidden City USA: Chinese American Nightclubs, 1936–1970,* as well as in Lisa See's novel *China Dolls,* which tells the story of four showgirls working in the clubs in the 1940s. The Chinese community had been insulated and mostly relegated to Chinatown, the largest community of Chinese outside of China; but after the earthquake and into the twentieth century, Chinese businessmen moved to attract patronage from the surrounding city. One of the first steps was to redesign the neighborhood with Chinese architecture for an "authentic" look. Later, businesses that catered specifically to the non-Chinese community—chop suey houses and businesses with self-parodying names like Fur Man Chu (a fur shop)—opened. In fact, both chop suey and the fortune cookie were invented in San Francisco, not China, to appeal to non-Chinese. Other businesses like the jook houses catered almost exclusively to Chinese Americans, and the eight-foot-wide, four-stories-tall jook house described in *Noir* was a real place, although I have no idea if they actually served noodles with the urine from deadly snakes. That tradition is still practiced today in Shanghai, according to my good friend Google.

Like the jook house, other locations in *Noir* are based on real places that existed but are long gone now. Cookie's Coffee was a real diner in the Tenderloin called Coffee Dan's; and like Cookie's, they catered to the theater crowd, and indeed celebrated New Year's Eve 365 nights a year. There was also a cabdriver who, like Milo, served shots of liquor to Coffee Dan's patrons for two bits a shot, although Milo owes his particular history more to the character Henri in Steinbeck's *Cannery Row*—an artist who was building a boat but was afraid of the sea—than to the real-life cabbie.

Jimmy's Joynt, too, is based on a real spot, and Jimmy is based on a real woman called Tommy Vasu, who indeed dressed like a guy and had a weakness for gambling and willowy blondes (not redheads like Myrtle). She ran a club called Tommy's Joint, on Broadway (which has nothing whatever to do with the *hofbrau* Tommy's Joynt, on Van Ness Avenue, which is still open today and serves fine buffalo stew, meat loaf, and carved turkey and dressing every day of the year). Female drag clubs were popular in North Beach in the 1940s (and into the 1950s, when the city codified hostility toward gay and lesbian clubs). The most famous of the lesbian drag clubs was Mona's 440, which is portrayed in Ellen Klages's novel *Passing Strange*.

The Bohemian Club is also a real organization. The main clubhouse is located at Post and Taylor Streets in what is now the Tenderloin (or lower Nob Hill or upper Union Square to the more charitably minded). Descriptions of the interior of the club come from written accounts, and although I was invited to attend as the guest of an artist member, I ran out of time before I had to write the scene, so I never got there. The Bohemian Grove and the ritual of the Cremation of Care, complete with giant concrete owl, come from academic descriptions. I have never set foot in the Grove, although I've driven by the entrance many times, as I keep a writing hovel and squirrel ranch nearby. The nefarious goings-on beyond the well-documented ritual are all products of my imagination because nothing but rainbows and cupcakes ever comes out of secret meetings among immensely rich and power-ful white guys.

AFTERWORD

The Neighborhoods

Most of *Noir* takes place in the neighborhoods of North Beach, Chinatown, the Tenderloin, and the Fillmore. North Beach has been an Italian neighborhood since the late 1800s, populated by fishermen from Italy who migrated and brought their food and culture with them, although in the 1940s it was also the mecca for the gay community, both men and women, before it migrated to the Castro, a neighborhood at the southwest end of Market Street, which was a solidly working-class Irish neighborhood in 1947. (Which is not to say that there weren't gay people living there, but it is pretty safe to say that they weren't out at the time.)

In the 1940s, the Tenderloin, while a fairly rough neighborhood today—a spongy center of poverty and street crime surrounded by a rich crust of gentrification—was the theater district, the center of both entertainment and government, as City Hall and the Civic Center lay in its midst. Its transformation can be traced back to World War II, when the United States started gearing up for it, opening shipyards up and down the West Coast to build war and transport ships and munitions. The factories required workers, and the workers required housing, so single-room occupancy (SRO) hotels were built in the Tenderloin to house the workers. Today the Tenderloin rings of sad desperation, but in the 1940s, with three shifts of defense workers cycling in and out of the neighborhood, not to mention the entertainers and theater crowd, the Tenderloin was jumping.

Cross Van Ness Avenue from the Tenderloin and you're in the Fillmore, which was also changed radically by the war, but for different reasons. The Fillmore, known for its Fillmore theater and the landmark rock concerts of the 1960s, was little more than a slum before the war. Many of the population living there were Japanese, and the Fillmore and Japantown were barely distinguishable. In 1942 President Roosevelt signed Executive

AFTERWORD

Order 9066, ordering Japanese-Americans living on the West Coast imprisoned in internment camps. The Japanese residents were forced to sell or store their belongings and were moved to camps up and down the coast. Another executive order, number 8802, which banned discrimination based on race in defense plants, had already caused a mass westward migration of blacks fleeing the oppressive Jim Crow South. These migrants were following the promise of good jobs and guaranteed housing and benefits. The new housing being built for workers couldn't keep up with demand, so when the homes of the interned Japanese opened up in the Fillmore, African Americans moved in. Jazz clubs began to open in the neighborhood, and by the 1950s, the Fillmore was a premier jazz destination for musicians and enthusiasts. When the Japanese were released from the camps, many returned to the Fillmore, which engendered an interesting intersection of cultures that I've written about in earlier books (*A Dirty Job, Secondhand Souls*), but many also moved into the new housing being built in the Richmond and the Sunset to house the families of returning servicemen (as referenced by Sal in chapter 3 when he's trying to formulate dog pizza).

The aforementioned changes to racial demographics in San Francisco have resonated through the years to shape the Bay Area into what it is today, but in 1947 the changes were new, and the city was trying to catch its breath after a great war, and inevitably those changes affected the people.

The Characters

It was tough to find firsthand sources for what life was like in San Francisco in 1947, so I turned to the writings of Herb Caen, the intrepid columnist for the *San Francisco Chronicle* and the *San Francisco Examiner* from 1938 until 1997, whose beat was the street and people of the city. Caen's work touched on every aspect of city life and often profiled colorful characters-about-town. In one column, he wrote about a racist cop who made it his business to try to *beat* the neighborhood white. Caen also reported how the cop was pulled off the street but kept on the force because he knew where too many of the city's power elite's bodies were buried. Caen never mentioned the cop's name, but after I read that column, Pookie O'Hara was born.

During the war the African American population of San Francisco rose from just over 5,000 at the beginning of the war to more than 35,000 by the end of it—an increase of more than 600 percent. And that was just in San Francisco proper, not including Oakland, Marin City, and Richmond, where there were also shipyards. Portrayals of indigent veterans in the Third Street Sherry Society were also inspired by Herb Caen, who wrote about them frequently.

General Remy, and consequently the moonman, came out of one of my very early web searches of "San Francisco, 1947," which returned one small item in the middle of the second page, posted by a UFO aficionado, noting that in March 1947 the commander of the air force base at Roswell visited San Francisco. The crash at Roswell, whatever it was, happened in June of that year, only a week or so after the first "flying saucer" was spotted by a pilot near Mount Rainier in Washington State. There is nothing beyond that coincidence for the basis of the character of Remy; once I knew that a general was in the city in the same year as the flying-saucer sighting and the Roswell crash, well, I had to run with it. With the general came the Men in Black, and, of course, the moonman.

My portrayal of the welding crew on which Sammy works is largely drawn from accounts I found on the digital archive at www.foundsf.org, with the dialect drawn from the novel *If He Hollers Let Him Go,* by Chester Himes, an African American crime writer from the '40s and '50s, most famous for his Harlem Detective series. *If He Hollers Let Him Go* is about an all-black welding crew in a World War II–era shipyard in Los Angeles.

Lone Jones is built of equal parts of reality and fiction. When I was a kid in Ohio I took part in a summer work program for junior high football players, designed to keep us from becoming criminals. It was run by the local police department, and six mornings a week, a cop driving a paddy wagon would pick each of us up at our homes and drive us to a strawberry farm in the country, where we would work a half day in the fields, all day on Saturday. The cop would drop us off after work each afternoon. One morning when I climbed into the back of the paddy wagon, among the twenty or so adolescent boys, mostly from the inner city, was a much bigger, powerfully built, older guy of about twenty. We'll call him John Henry Johnson. (John Henry was, indeed, his name.) Later, during the drop-off, we discovered that John Henry lived with his mother in a garage, heated by a single woodstove, across from a steel mill. Even guys on the crew from rougher parts of town were shocked and humbled by the poverty.

I worked with John Henry for two summers, and came to know him as one of the strongest, most generous and good-natured people I've ever known. He usually rode up in the front of the paddy wagon with the cop, not back in the cage with the rest of us. A slow reader, John Henry would make the driver tailgate other drivers so he could sound out the writing on bumper stickers. Because he had preferred seating in the truck, the other black guys on the crew teased him that he didn't want to be black; that, in fact, he was white, and only the accident of skin color caused people to misidentify him as black. Soon John Henry owned this and insisted that no, he was not black, and the rest of us backed John Henry up when we were among strangers.

I can hear you cringing. It was fine, it was good, it was friendship, and it was all in good spirits, but seen through a lens of to-day's political correctness and horror at cultural appropriation, I suppose it is cringeworthy.

John Henry Johnson was half of the inspiration for Lone Jones. The other half was Hazel in John Steinbeck's *Cannery Row,* a good-natured giant who becomes forlorn when a fortune-teller predicts he will become president of the United States.

Sammy "Two-Toes" Tiffin comes almost entirely from my imagination, except for the improbable accident that sent him west. My own father, several years out of the navy and working at a factory in Toledo, had his left foot nearly severed when a forklift hit him, crushing his foot against a wall. He was already enrolled and scheduled to begin at the highway patrol academy, and before he passed out in the hospital, he made his mother promise that she would not let doctors remove his foot. She prevailed over the physicians, and my father went to the academy (albeit a year late) and became a highway patrolman, a job he loved and did until the end of his life. So that bit of Sammy's history, and determin-ism to serve, comes from my father's story. Mainly Sammy fit the description of what the protagonist of a noir story should be: a regular guy in a sketchy situation. Which brings me to the genre.

Noir

When I first moved to San Francisco, ten years ago, I attended a charity dinner hosted by the public library for authors and read-ers. The theme of the event was noir. During dinner, one author at my table, an accomplished writer of crime novels himself, said, "Really, I think the best noir author was Jim Thompson."

"Oh, no, no," said a nearby author of children's books, also very accomplished. "Raymond Chandler was definitely the best."

In a rare exercise of restraint, I kept my mouth shut, because for my money they were both right, and they were both wrong.

Scholars and scribes with far more knowledge than me have made careers out of creating, curating, defining, and presenting the noir genre, but I shan't let that stop me from waxing ignorant. It seems to me that the whole noir genre comes from the term *film noir,* and that encompasses a whole set of aesthetics that don't always translate to written fiction. In written fiction, you have your hard-boiled detective guys created by Dashiell Hammett, Raymond Chandler, and Mickey Spillane. Then you have your dark-streets, desperate noir that usually starts with some poor, hapless working mug who gets roped into some nefarious goings-on by a dame; in that tradition, you have James M. Cain, David Goodis, and Jim Thompson. When I started *Noir,* I envisioned it would be a work of the second type of noir, a story about the poor working mug, Sammy, and the dangerous dame who tumbles into his life, the Cheese. It was gonna be dark, it was gonna be desperate, there would be fog, and gunplay, and danger. That's what I thought. I know, I know. What I ended up with is essentially "Perky Noir," a lot closer to Damon Runyon meets Bugs Bunny than Raymond Chandler meets Jim Thompson . . . but what was I going to do? *Noir* was already typed at the top of every page.

So, here you go. Thanks for stopping by.

CHRISTOPHER MOORE
SAN FRANCISCO, CALIFORNIA
JUNE 2017

ABOUT THE AUTHOR

CHRISTOPHER MOORE is the author of fifteen previous novels, including *Lamb, The Stupidest Angel, A Dirty Job, Fool, Sacré Bleu, The Serpent of Venice,* and *Secondhand Souls.* He lives in San Francisco, California.

TOUGH-GUY TALK

(SPECIAL TO THIS B&N EDITION)

first came to this noir joint thinking I would string out tough-guy metaphors like a robot crapping out toy train cars after eating a bad springs-and-screws taco. I thought I'd be dealing dangerous dame similes like a sandwich jockey slinging salami at Subway. See, before the bums, the hustlers, the floozies, the grifters, the lowlifes, the coppers, and the crooks, there was the talk.

See, even as I was learning my first language, lo those many years ago in London, Ohio, there was this show on TV on Sunday nights, prime time, in glorious black and white, called *The Bugs Bunny Show*. There I first picked up tough-guy talk from the Looney Tunes cartoon tricksters. How's that? you say. How could Bugs and Daffy and that French skunk with the cat fetish leave an impressionable and incredibly clever kid of say, three, with anything but the odd "What's up, Doc?" or the occasional "meep, meep!"?

See, in the early days of Looney Tunes, in the 1930s and '40s, the animators and directors were working in their own little barracks on the Warner Brothers lot, where, at that same time, various gangster films such as *Little Caesar, The Public Enemy, The Petrified Forest,* and I'm not even kidding, *The Amazing Dr. Clitterhouse,*[*] were being filmed with such soon-to-be-iconic fast-talking actors as Edward G. Robinson, Jimmy Cagney, Humphrey Bogart, and George Raft—all talking tough, smacking up dames, and waving smoking gats around like they were going to ventilate the world. And those very tough guys would occasionally peek in on the Warner animation

---

*Amazingly, a real movie, starring Humphrey Bogart and Edward G. Robinson. Equally amazing, it's not about a gynecologist.

studio, where the directors, the writers, and the voice-over guys would pick up the rhythm and rhyme of tough-guy talk, put it in the mouths of Bugs, Daffy, Sylvester, and even Porky Pig, where it filtered down through the decades and into the vocabulary of an angelic and charming kid of three, sitting on the floor in front of an expansive twelve-inch black-and-white Motorola.

By the time I was four I could threaten, cajole, and hustle like the best of them. I was talking fast and tough, adding in the pausing "see"s of Edward G. Robinson and the affected lisp of Daffy Duck, and from what I'm told, the only way to shut me up was to lock me in my room where I'd shout they'd "never take me alive, see!" until I tired myself out and fell asleep. My dad was a copper, see, and my mom, well, she was running some kind of racket in fine furs in a department store in Columbus, Ohio, so you knew she couldn't be trusted.

Even my first dog got his name from some tough-guy talk I picked up on TV. Dad was at the breakfast table, see. And I was about five, I guess. We'd gotten this new boxer puppy, who might have been cute, might have been running a fuzzy con on us, I don't know. So, I see Dad sitting at the table, reading the paper, and I'm all full of moxie and Lucky Charms, vibrating with the sugar, and I roll up on Dad, who is not wearing his gun because he is still in his PJs and therefore is probably a pushover, and I challenge him to "put up your dukes, ya mug." I started doing the dance, dazzling him with my footwork, trying to rope him in, get him to drop his guard, maybe look over the paper, and he says, "That's it. Duke. We'll call the puppy Duke." So yeah, my first dog got a tough-guy name and I completely forgot I was supposed to clobber the copper at the table.

So, we called the dog Duke, and because he had a tough-guy name he soon fell in with a bad crowd, started riding the bus to school

with the Catholic kids across the street, and
during school hung out at the local Dairy
Queen, where he would knock over little
kids and eat their ice cream when it fell on
the sidewalk, then ride the bus home in the
afternoon.

Occasionally we'd have to go down
to the pound to bail him out. By the time
he was two, Duke had a rap sheet as long
as your tail, but when he cut his paw on
a broken bottle and tracked the blood on
Mom's white carpet he was doomed for
the big catnap. They said he went to live
on a farm, but I suspect there is some dame
walking around with a Duke-looking fur
coat stained in blood and chocolate swirl.
All because I picked up a tough-guy catch
phrase from Daffy Duck.

So, I go to school and learn about
violence and recess, which often were
the same thing, and Ohio weather being
what it was, during after-lunch recess,
they fired up a 16mm projector and
showed us "Little Rascals" shorts. And

I'm not talking about Spanky and Alfalfa, but Jackie Cooper and Stymie, the bunch from the early 1930s—poor street kids with their pit bull, Petey, who were talkin' tough and running scams just to get by during the Great Depression. (Full disclosure, Stymie was not a fast-talker, but more the thoughtful philosopher of the gang.)

When I got home from school there were gangster movies on the four o'clock movie, Bogey and Cagney fallin' hard for dangerous dames they called "Slim" and "Toots," getting double-crossed or gunned down in ninety minutes or less. (Except on Thursdays, which was Tarzan or Bomba, the Jungle Boy day, so my tough-guy talk became peppered with Anglicized Swahili, leading to multicultural playground taunts like, "Listen here, my *rafiki*, you put your grimy mitts in my lunch box again you're gonna need a *daktari* to put you back together.")

On Saturdays, after morning cartoons (more Bugs and Daffy) came the Bowery Boys, tough street kids who first appeared

in *Dead End* (1937), a Bogart movie
about a crook coming back to the old
neighborhood in New York. The "Dead
End Kids" would appear in movies
and TV shorts until they were all well
into middle age, so as a little kid I was
watching grown men, dressed like street
urchins, pulling scams and perpetrating
shenanigans and felt like I knew what
career I was going to choose when I
grew up, if my ambition to be Zorro
did not work out, which I figured it
wouldn't, since I didn't know a word of
Spanish.

I'm not saying I was cracking wise
and talking tough all through my
school years. There was a period after
I discovered the Marx Brothers where
I was only cracking wise, and after
some guys at school who actually lived
in tough neighborhoods pounded me
into pink paste, I reserved the tough
talk for playing cops and robbers or
army men with my buddy, Mike, across

the street, who was a year younger than
me and somewhat smaller. (Although his
sister, Murphy, a year older, would knock
my block off if I tried to push her little
brother around. Apparently, along with her
first holy communion, Murphy received a
wicked right cross, so I have always been
very respectful of dames of the Irish Catholic
persuasion and other dames as well just in
case they convert.)

So, where was I?

Oh yeah, so the Marx Brothers. Fast
talking, New York–sounding smart alecks who
were protected from harm by some magical
obliviousness—well, that's the life a kid with
an above-average vocabulary and a lot of
time on his hands should prepare himself for.
Consequently I spent A LOT of my elementary
school time sitting in the corner or standing
in the hall, and if my mother had been the
kind of broad who saved that sort of thing, she
would have had a pretty tall stack of report
cards with Cs in conduct and comments such
as "needs to control his talking" in the "could

use improvement" field.* This, because
there was no box they could check for
"please, for the love of God, make this kid
shut the hell up."

So, after being briefly sidetracked by
a James Bond phase, and several colleges
opining that I would be better suited for
self-education or sustained ignorance, I
found myself living in Southern California,
selling insurance, and watching late-night
movies so I would be too tired to go to
work in the morning, I happened onto
the Robert Mitchum version of *The Big
Sleep*, which was just swell. The next
day I went to the bookstore and bought
paperbacks of all of Raymond Chandler's
books, and after I read those, I bought all
of Dashiell Hammett's and read those. It
was a different kind of tough talk, and in
Chandler's case, even lyrical, and I was
back down the rabbit hole of fascination

---

*She did save one, which appears after this essay.

with tough-guy talk. A year or so into that, I
went to a writer's conference in Santa Barbara,
where someone steered me to Damon Runyon,
a guy who had made an entire art form of
wiseguy dialect. So, I bought all his stuff
and read those. (If you haven't, you should.
Start with *The Bloodhounds of Broadway*, a nice
sampler of Runyon's stories.)

Over the years, as I've made my way as
a writer, Runyon's influence has popped up
here and there. A scene or two in *Island of
the Sequined Love Nun*, another in *Secondhand
Souls*, but this time—this time—when I
decided to write my own version of a noir
book, I was going to go the whole magilla.
I knew there would be a plucky, down-on-
his-luck guy; a dame with moxie for miles;
a few denizens of the dark city who would
bring their own brand of street smarts to the
story; layers upon layers of bad guys; and, of
course, I knew there would be a kid—a foul-
mouthed, obnoxious little kid, because I think
we can all agree that kids are annoying. (No,
not your kids, your kids are fudging treasures,

but you know, other kids. But you say, Chris, all of your previous kid characters are charming and funny and poignant, and that is because I based them on me when I was a kid, and despite what everyone else says, I was a fudging delight. Not at all like the annoying kids.)

So, once I decided on the elements, it was time to bring my own special spice to the genre.

See, the problem with all those— Bugs Bunny, the Little Rascals, the Marx Brothers, '30s gangster movies, and even tough-guy books—is they don't have much profanity, because in those days there were standards, by which I am not constrained. I have written vampire profanity, Goth kid profanity, Native American profanity, Shakespearian profanity, French Impressionist profanity, and even Biblical profanity, and when you start forking around with Biblical profanity you're likely to smite some Philistines or razz some cities just by accident.

So that's what I brought to the genre. Also a snake.

Enjoy.

CHRISTOPHER MOORE

SAN FRANCISCO, CA 2018

The author, age 5, in his early sportscaster/
tap-dancing outfit, about to be yanked offstage by
a harsh critic, and his only surviving report card,
promoting him to first grade.
Mrs. Patterson's remarks read: *Chris is a very alert
child and full of enthusiasm. He has creative ability and
seems to enjoy school. Sometimes he wants too many turns
to talk. This kid is a forking delight!*